THE CHRONICLES O  IE

SHAHLY'S QUEST

FOR EVERYONE WHO DARES TO BELIEVE...

J. R. KNOLL

ARTWORK BY SANDI JOHNSON

Email: Vultross@aol.com

ISBN: 1450596037
ISBN-13: 9781450596039

A FEW
DEDICATIONS...

This is for everyone who dares to believe in the impossible, everyone who has dared to make a friend of an enemy, and everyone who still looks hard into the deep of the forest for that elusive unicorn they know is watching them.

To my brother Ron who got the ball rolling,
Mariah who helped along with the editing process and I'm sure still believes in unicorns,
My cousin Don Lee, whose personality was the model for the wizard
Joyce and Clifton Knoll, two parents who never let me give up,
My Grandmother Sybil Lee and my late Grandad M. M. Lee,
For everyone who stuck by me when I lost faith in myself.
For kindred spirit, good friend and mentor Peter S. Beagle,
Connor and Terri who believe simply because they do,
Lisa, Alyssa, Charlie, Lou Ann, David,
And my wife Tami, Shahly's biggest fan ever!

CHAPTER 1

Early Spring, 989 seasons

The land is forever changing. Plants and animals are born, grow and die. They are replaced by the next generation, and the next in an endless cycle. I have seen this happen many times in my long life. Change, death and birth are what drive the land. They keep the land healthy and in balance.

Some things must remain constant for the land to remain in balance. Predators must hunt lower animals, who must quickly and constantly replenish their numbers. The seasons must change from summer to autumn, to winter to spring and back to summer. This must be. It is most difficult for humans and their kin. They seem determined to make their own laws rather than live in the harmony of the world, though, hunters and hunted, they are far from immune.

Yet, through all of the balance, the change and the constant, the day would come when the perpetual law would indeed be violated. The lines between natural enemies, between prey and predator would be blurred. This would not come at the hands of dragons or humans, human kin or some out-worlder. It would be an innocent of the wild who would bring about this catastrophic shift, forever changing the destinies of those who live here, forever changing the order of things. And she would not know to rise to the defense of a law she would violate, but never knew existed.

Shahly's big brown eyes opened slowly.

The warm morning sunlight filtered through the canopy of blooming trees until it was little more than specks of dancing light on the forest floor. Lush, thick grasses grew even here, their broad blades capturing as much sunlight as they could. Smaller trees also pushed up through the thick layer of pine needles, discarded leaves and ground moss.

The sweet perfumes of the spring blossoms were heavy in the air this day as sleeping plants and trees opened themselves to the world once again. New and awakening green things filled the forest air with their different scents, carried to Shahly through the huge trees by the gentle spring breeze.

Forest animals also awakened. She heard deer wandering among the trees, stopping occasionally as a squirrel would chatter his disapproval of their presence. Occasionally, a hawk would screech somewhere overhead, an owl would answer. The songbirds carried over them all.

One was especially loud.

Shahly slowly raised her head, crossing her eyes as she looked to the end of her spiral horn which was ivory in color and even more enchanting with the ribbons of gold within the spirals.

Perched there on the end, a blue and yellow bird sang loudly, his short wings extended to show off the bright yellow and orange feathers beneath them.

Shahly shook her head and the bird responded with flapping wings and a rapid succession of clicks and shrieks, but finally hopped from her spiral and flapped to the ground where he darted into the trees on long legs and disappeared.

Blue sapling birds were common and Shahly gave him not another thought as she stood and shook her head and neck, her long, sparkling cloud white mane flailing in every direction until she was still again, then it fell evenly to the sides of her neck. Her coat shimmered as she turned and wandered down an obscure path between the huge trees and the underbrush that struggled for sunlight beneath them.

In body, she appeared very horse-like, though only pony-size and not as heavy, sharing some of the fleet form a deer would have. She trekked on shiny gold, cloven hooves which found the earth beneath them and would not falter, no matter how awkward the terrain. Her head was also horse-like, though thinner in the nose, much like a deer's. Her eyes were alert, betraying her every mood and feeling.

The breeze shifted slightly, gently caressing her face.

Shahly stopped and closed her eyes, raising her nose as she slowly took a deep breath of the sugary nectars and all of the other smells the breeze offered her. The blooms of the forest meadows that filled the air with their sweet aromas called to her.

She started forward again, faster this time, and finally emerged from the trees, stopping as she scanned the open field before her. Her eyes sparkled as the colors seemed to explode all around her, undulating like waves on water as the breeze gently swept over the top of the small lake of grass and flowers.

Shahly reared up, sharply whinnying her excitement, then leaped into a gallop and ran as fast as her hooves would propel her, racing the spring wind and greedily inhaling the fragrances of the meadow flowers. At the center of the field, she stopped abruptly and plunged her nose into the lush grass, grazing for some time, then she launched herself forward again.

Another unicorn danced into her thoughts, one who she always kept near her heart. Excitement swept through her as she saw him in her mind and she scanned the meadow and forest with her eyes and essence, searching for the unicorn who she knew in her heart was the one for her. She loved him dearly but had always been too afraid to explore his feelings.

No matter. She enjoyed every moment with him, chosen by him or not.

She plunged back into the forest on the other side of the meadow and darted nimbly around the huge trees, ignoring the warnings of the elders to move as a shadow through the forest. The undergrowth was dense here and the trees grew close together in places. Shahly knew it was not safe to run so fast where the forest did not offer much room to maneuver, but she was as agile as she was fast and bounded carelessly among ancient timbers and their young, the thick scrub brush and over the fallen trunks of those trees whose lives had ended.

She leaped over a dense bush and stopped, finding herself in the middle of a clearing.

No. Not a clearing. A path. A very wide path.

She raised her head and tested the air. Nothing upwind.

Curiously, she looked to the ground, lowered her head and sniffed there, too. Many creatures had passed this way, leaving their tracks as proof of their presence there. Goats and deer had crossed. Ahead were the scent and paw prints of a forest cat, its tracks the largest of any left. The cat had also just crossed the path, and quickly from the look of its prints.

Spying other hoofed tracks, Shahly raised her head and followed them down the path with her eyes. They were similar to the unicorns but not cloven, and these were the only animals who trekked down the path and not just across it. There were prints left by many of them and they appeared to travel in groups. With such big, deep tracks left behind and traveling in such numbers they did not seem to need the safety of the forest to elude predators.

A whistle in the distance caught her ears and she looked behind her. That was no bird. Was it? She could make out heavy hooves on the path, sharp clicking, the neigh of a horse. She turned fully, her eyes locked on a bend in the trail about thirty paces away.

Voices.

Her eyes narrowed slightly, curiously, and her ears perked.

These were not like the voices she was accustomed to, not like the animals of the forest. They spoke in a deliberate, complex language, not unlike unicorns speaking to one another.

A horse snorted.

Shahly leaned her head. Had the horses learned to communicate with each other in such detail?

No. The voices were not horse-like. They were more...

Shahly blinked and chewed some of the grass she had grazed earlier as she stared at the bend in the path. These voices made sounds that were too complex to be wolves, mountain cats or monkeys.

She raised her head. Birds! Birds could make such sounds. It must be.

Whatever they were, they were unknown and a little frightening, and were getting too close.

Before they could round the bend in the trail, Shahly turned and darted back into the forest, back the way she had come.

Only ten paces later she stopped and looked back. They were nearing the place where she had been standing half a moment ago.

She turned fully and listened, unable to see the path. Curiosity was overwhelming her. She had to know!

Like a shadow, she moved noiselessly toward the path and stopped just within view. Though her sight was obscured by brush and low tree limbs, she could finally see the horses, and the animals with the complex voices.

Upon the horses' backs they rested on their haunches, their hind legs straddling the horses. Their forelegs were much like a monkey's, ending in long digits. Hind legs, however, ended in feet that more resembled hooves, lacking the digits the monkeys had. Their heads were round and mostly had manes on top and down the back. Some had hair on their jaws. Their bodies and hind legs, and on a few of their forelegs, were covered in various kinds of fur and skin, but not their own. All of them carried various objects, including leg length straight sticks which hung on their sides.

Two of the horses also carried much longer sticks, pointed and barbed on the ends. These sticks had a feeling about them, something that felt like vibrations of light, though the power felt to be at rest.

Their minds were foreign to the forest and the strangest Shahly had ever explored, thinking complex thoughts that did not seem all that different from many of the animals of the forest.

One of the strange animals carried by the horses was different. Much smaller in body and build, this one had a much longer mane which was auburn in color and its dainty feet ended in blunt digits. It appeared to lack the long hind legs, and upon closer study, Shahly realized its bright white covering concealed them for the most part. This one also lacked the pungent aroma of the others, as if it had just swum in the river.

A mare! Shahly thought, realizing this one was female.

Another caught her attention, a male like the others, but this one was different somehow. His mane was as long as the female's, but very straight and coal black. His covering was lighter in color, more of a tan color, and different in its make than those the others wore. His face lacked hair and his features were very deeply chiseled, his dark eyes very focused.

This one stopped his horse, right in front of Shahly!

She breathed shallowly, very nervously watching the black haired one as he scanned the woods where she was standing.

His dark eyes narrowed slightly, then he kicked his horse's flanks and moved on.

Something about this one was different and Shahly reached out with her essence, touching his mind to have a little better insight into him, but quickly retreated as he turned and looked behind him, reacting directly to contact with her.

None of the others had.

Sensing the approach of another unicorn, Shahly turned her head slightly to see him.

He was a stallion, larger than Shahly and taller with a shiny silver coat and snow white mane and tail. A long white beard dangled from his chin and his ivory and silver spiraled horn sparkled in the small rays of sunlight which filtered through the trees. His dark blue eyes were locked on the procession out on the path.

Shahly also looked back to them and softly asked, "What are they?"

The silver unicorn's eyes narrowed and he spitefully answered, "Humans."

"They look strange," Shahly observed. "Why do the horses carry them?"

"The horses are slaves to them," was the old unicorn's answer.

Shahly watched a few seconds longer, then lowered her head and admitted, "I don't understand."

The old unicorn was silent for a moment, then he explained, "They are not like the creatures of the forest. To understand them is to understand evil."

"You explained evil to me once," Shahly reminded. "They do not seem evil."

"That does not matter," the silver unicorn warned. "Shun them. When you see them, hide and conceal your essence."

Shahly leaned her head as she watched the humans and horses pace by. "But they look harmless. Why shouldn't we approach them?"

"Would you approach a dragon? Or a wolf or Dread?"

"They are not dragons," Shahly insisted. "The horses don't seem to mind their company and I do not feel from them that they would cause us harm."

The old unicorn loosed a deep breath. "No, Shahly, not now. But when they see us their only thoughts will be of possessing us."

Shahly glanced at him. "Like the horses?"

The silver unicorn turned and paced back into the forest, answering, "Like the horses."

Shahly watched as the last of the humans and horses passed, then she turned and cantered to the silver unicorn's side. "Well shouldn't they be afraid of us like dragons are?"

He slowly turned his eyes on her.

She looked back at him, her ears drooping. "Aren't dragons afraid of us?"

"Hardly," the silver unicorn corrected, almost laughing. "Our essence may be deadly to them, but they do not fear us. They just have no reason to hunt us."

"But if our essence is so deadly to them—"

"Shahly, by their very nature, dragons are our deadliest enemies. They have far greater advantages over us than we have over them, and we use our essence against them only when offered no other choice."

"I understand," Shahly conceded, glancing away, then she raised her head and looked back to the old silver. "What about the humans?"

His ears twitched. "Their minds are relatively complex, but weak in the senses and are very easy to trick. It's all a matter of suggesting to them what they want or need to see or not see."

Shahly looked ahead again. "That could be useful."

"Shahly." The silver unicorn's voice was suddenly in a tone or warning.

"I'm not going to approach them," Shahly defended. "It's...well, in the event... Have you seen Vinton?"

The silver unicorn snorted a laugh and looked down to her. "Do you two speak of nothing but each other?"

Shahly raised her head and defended, "Sometimes."

"Well, it's surprising to see you without him nearby. You were barely out of smelling distance from each other for the last four or five seasons."

"Have you seen him? Please tell me."

The older unicorn grunted a laugh, then looked to Shahly and confessed, "Yes, Shahly, I've seen him." He looked ahead again, amusement in his eyes.

Shahly walked along with the silver unicorn for a moment, eyeing him impatiently, then butted him with her nose and demanded, "Where?"

"The river!" he laughed. "The last I saw of him he was grazing by the river."

"He shouldn't be grazing now!" Shahly insisted. "It's spring! It's time to play and run!" She turned and bolted away from the older unicorn, toward the river, her heart racing anew with Vinton back in her thoughts.

Shahly darted around the trees on hooves that were as nimble as a deer's, easily leaping over clumps of ferns, boulders and fallen logs.

Something touched her mind and she abruptly stopped, staring ahead of her. There was the mind of her stallion, feeling at rest but still alert and a little distracted. Impressions of Shahly were strong and his thoughts did not seem to stray far from her.

She trotted toward him, not seeing him as he was some distance away and beyond her field of vision, but she could feel his powerful mind very clearly and knew right where to find him.

As she emerged from the trees near the river she saw him there with his back to her and his snout in the tall grass as he grazed peacefully near the water.

Vinton was a big unicorn, fiery red-brown with a long, glossy black mane and tail fluttering gently on the breeze and a long black beard concealed in the grass. As his head moved slowly, the morning sun brightly sparkled off of the copper ribbons within the spirals of his long horn.

Her eyes locked on the stallion, Shahly lowered her head and paced toward him from directly behind, concealing her essence from his mind and senses as she neared. Her thoughts were not so pure at this time. They focused on Vinton, a nip on the haunch, and the amusement at watching him jump straight up for half his height, the same as he had done to her many times.

She slowed as she neared, folding her essence around herself to avoid his senses.

Nearly within touching distance, he raised his head, looking toward the river as he greeted, "Good morning, Shahly."

She stopped, her eyes locked on him as he turned toward her.

He looked very amused.

"How did you know?" she asked, feeling a little frustrated.

He paced to her, complementing, "You masked your presence very well this time."

"So how did you know?" she demanded.

He glanced down at her hooves. "I could hear you coming up on me."

She snorted and looked up. "It is always something!"

He nudged her with his nose, whickering a laugh. "Just give it time. You've mastered nearly everything else."

"I know," she sighed, looking away from him. "It just seems to take so long."

"Patience, Shahly. It never comes quickly." He looked up river. "Would you care to walk with me?"

"You needn't even ask," she said softly, turning with him.

She walked with him in silence through the knee-deep grass, listening to the singing birds and the water flowing steadily over the rocks in the river. Her thoughts remained on the stallion at her side. This was the unicorn she wanted at her side forever, but uncertainty and inexperience had always made her too afraid to peer into his thoughts, his feelings. If he did not truly feel the same way she did, if he did not want her as his mate, she knew she would be devastated. But that couldn't be it, it just couldn't! They had spent too many seasons together.

"You're very quiet," he observed.

His gentle voice startled her and she flinched, her ears perking up. "Oh, I'm just thinking."

"Oh," was his hesitant reply. "These thoughts seem to burden you."

She tried to reply, but could only manage a slight shrug.

"You slept late again," he observed. "Were you awake thinking half the night as well?"

Looking down, she smiled slightly and shook her head. "No, I was just awake late in the evening, enjoying the bright moonlight with someone."

He also smiled. "It wasn't *that* late." He glanced at her and informed, "The moon will be full tonight, and should be as bright and beautiful as it will be all season. The whole herd will probably gather at the river to see it."

"That sounds lovely," she said wistfully.

"Yes," he sighed, "that it does. I don't think I'll join the others there."

She gave him a sidelong glance. "Why not?"

He did not answer for a few paces as he seemed to be scrambling for the right words, and finally replied, "Well, there is a mare in the herd I would like to share it with alone."

Her ears drooped a little and she looked the other way. "Really." She was trying to sound interested and not a little hurt, still hoping she was the mare he spoke of, but facts were facts. He was almost her father's age, after all, and a well respected leader of the herd. She was still very young for her kind, and one of many who vied for his time and attention. Many mare unicorns of the forest spent copious time with him and really seemed to enjoy being in his presence, though Shahly could not imagine anyone enjoying his company more than she.

Lost in thought again, she did not realize that many paces were behind them in silence, and when she looked back to him, his eyes were on her.

"I've really cherished our friendship," he finally said, and her heart sank a little lower as he continued, "and I've so enjoyed the time we spend together. I feel you've learned a great deal from me."

"I have," she admitted softly, almost choking on her words, "and I've also cherished the time we spend together."

He smiled a little. "Your friendship and your company mean a great deal to me."

Shahly forced a smile back and nodded a little. She hoped that long eyelashes would conceal what she really felt and hide her eyes from his seemingly endless perception. Thankfully, he looked forward again.

Vinton seemed to struggle with his words once more. Shahly knew in her heart that he knew how she felt about him, how she loved him. Today, she sensed a shift, and found herself unable to brace for the worst.

"There is something I need to say to you, Shahly," he finally told her, "something I should have said some time ago. I realize that your senses as a young unicorn are still developing and it may be many seasons before you can easily read the emotions of others. Believe me it will become something more of instinct and it will be something you will do as easily as listening to someone speak." He drew a breath. "I can sense what you feel every time I'm near you, and your feelings toward me are very sweet."

She was not ready to hear this, not ready for rejection and whinnied, "Catch me!"

He did not seem to expect this and raised his head as she veered sharply into the forest and launched herself into a fast gallop toward the trees. She looked back to see him just turning to pursue her and smiled a little as she leapt over a fallen tree and plunged into the woods beyond, running hard on nimble hooves and dodging between the great trees, the bushes that grew beneath them, and around a few half buried boulders that spotted the forest floor. Shahly was a fast unicorn and very agile, but she knew the long strides of the stallion made him very fast as well, but not quite as maneuverable, and this chase had to last.

What he had to say to her would come in time. It was inevitable, but she still could prolong what she had enjoyed with him, and cling a little longer to the dream that he would one day be her stallion. Even if he was not to choose her, she would have one last chase with him.

Looking back once more, she realized she had lost sight of him, but could still feel his presence in the distance behind her, and she smiled. She could feel his mind and emotions racing. He did not dread catching her for that talk. Quite the contrary. He was enjoying the chase with her and seemed to have every intention of catching her, just like he almost always did. And today, she would be as elusive as she had ever been.

Deep into the forest, Shahly charged from the trees and stopped in a clearing as something touched her mind. It was strange and not of the forest, and very nearby.

There! Toward the center of the clearing.

She trotted toward it, reaching out with her essence to explore it further. It felt female and strangely familiar.

Shahly saw the girl sitting in the grass and facing away from her. She did not feel that the girl was aware of her, so she slowed her approach and moved silently so as not to startle her.

Shahly touched the girl with her essence, feeling strange sensations that fed her curiosity. She was pure of heart and unknown by her males, and a little sad.

Shahly paused, then moved closer, exploring the girl's mind and feeling with her own. Such contact with a creature so odd as a human will drive the curiosity of a young unicorn wild.

Responding to the meeting of her essence with a unicorn's, the girl leaned her head back and took a deep, soothing breath, then turned and looked to Shahly, gasping as their eyes met.

Only five paces away, Shahly stopped, staring back at the girl. Something pitiful, shameful was in the girl's eyes.

Shahly stepped forward.

No! came the impression from the girl's mind. *Run away. You are in danger! Please, run away!*

Shahly raised her head, only now feeling the presence of the other humans.

Many others!

She looked back at the human before her, knowing the girl had not betrayed her. She had been used by the others.

She was bait!

Shahly slowly backed away, glancing around as she finally felt the minds of other humans, minds which were not pure. Only gain was in their thoughts, things which Shahly did not understand. They wanted her, and ruthless thoughts of what they had planned were terrifying!

She turned to flee, stopping as she saw them emerge from their hiding places. She recognized them. These were the humans she had watched in the forest, the very humans the old silver unicorn had warned her about.

She turned to run and froze, seeing more had emerged behind her and were advancing. Still others approached on horseback. They were everywhere!

She backed away from those in front of her as they advanced on her, pivoted and backed away again, pivoted and backed away. There was nowhere to go!

Many on horseback raised lassos to snare her with.

Shahly cringed, lowering her head.

Vinton charged from the trees, running among the humans where he stopped and reared up, whinnying loudly.

Following the bay unicorn's command, all of the horses did as well, many throwing their riders.

His lashing hooves found a man on foot and knocked him to the ground. He came down and wheeled to one side, catching still another man with his neck.

The humans converged on him, lassos flying.

He warded off several with his horn, but one finally found its way over his head, pulling taut around his neck.

Vinton snorted and pulled back hard, toppling the man who tried to hold him.

Another rope dropped over his head and tightened, then a third. Somehow, a rear leg was snared.

He brought his horn down on one of the ropes. His essence would cut right through it, but light flashed from his horn and the rope. Sparks took to the air. He whinnied in pain and stumbled away.

The ropes were enchanted!

"Shahly!" he whinnied to her. "Run! Get away and warn the herd."

She started toward him, insisting, "I can't leave you!"

He was pulled hard by the ropes, stumbled, and somehow kept his footing. "Shahly, go! Get away and warn the herd!"

"Vinton!" she cried, then saw six of the humans on horseback charging her, two with lassos ready to throw. She backed away a few steps, looked to her stallion, back at the charging humans, again to her stallion. Leave him?

He fought valiantly, but could not free himself, and she knew she would have no chance against them. Apparently, Vinton knew as well.

As the humans neared, she turned and darted back into the forest, running at a full gallop.

Her mind whirled as she dodged through the trees and some distance later emerged into the field near the river, slowing her pace to catch her breath.

Her ears perked back as she heard something crashing through the woods behind her, and she fearfully looked over her shoulder.

"Surely they could not have followed me *that* fast through the trees," she tried to reassure herself. Her eyes widened as she saw them explode into the clearing, shouting and whistling as they found her again.

Shahly whinnied and fled again, across the wide, shallow river of ice-cold water, across the deep grass on the other side and into the trees. A morning of running had already left her weary and, though the horses behind her were burdened with large men and equipment, they were big animals, strong of leg and seemed not to notice the extra weight as they relentlessly pursued her.

Time passed quickly as the little unicorn sped through the forest, dodging around trees and brush, fleeing the sounds of the big horses behind her.

Through the terror she felt, she thought of Vinton. She had to get back to him. That meant losing the humans and horses behind her.

She glanced back, wondering how they stayed on her trail even when she widened the gap enough for them to lose sight of her.

The trees were becoming smaller and fewer in number and large clumps of brush grew thicker all around. A hot, dry breeze blew into her face, carrying smells Shahly was unfamiliar with, smells of plants she had never experienced, animals she had never seen or sensed before, and nectars that were sweet mixed with those that smelled like carrion.

Nearly exhausted, Shahly knew she had to stop and rest or she would be run down and taken by the humans.

She dodged around a huge thicket of dense, dark green brush and charged in, praying she would find no thorns within.

The brush was more open within but Shahly was crawling on her belly to maneuver herself out of sight. She finally managed to get in deep enough to feel safe and out of sight of the outside. She moved forward a little more so as to see out and settled gently onto the cool earth beneath her. Very little sunlight filtered through the dense leaves, giving her an added feeling of security.

Only seconds later, she heard the humans and horses approaching fast. They wheeled around both sides of the thicket and stopped.

Right in front of her!

Seeing them added to her terror and she prayed they would just move along.

"Damn!" one of the humans swore.

"Can't believe we lost it," another grumbled. "All this way with 'er in sight and just gone."

The black haired human rode into view, scanning the forest around him. "No. She's stopped running."

"You mean it's hiding?" another human asked.

"Watching," the black haired human confirmed.

"Lets split up," another advised. "If it's too tired to run we should find it without too much more trouble. Couldn't have gotten far."

The black haired human scanned the forest near where she hid and informed, "She's not far."

His mind was different from the others, much more perceptive, and his essence felt to be more of the forest. He was difficult to read as his emotions were vague.

This human she feared the most. He was not just a predator, he had insight into things only unicorns should know, things his companions were blind to.

Shahly cringed as he looked down to the thicket where she lay. She could not tell by his eyes if he had seen her nor could she sense it in his mind, and that made her that much more afraid of him. Still, she felt safer as long as she did not move.

Until she heard a low growl to one side.

Her heart slammed away harder and she turned her eyes, barely moving her head.

It was two thirds a human's mass with dark brown fur which was almost black in the shadows and specks of light beneath the thicket. Its form was something between a human and a bear; its head looked much like a wolf's, though the snout was broader and full of long, pointed teeth. Solid black eyes glistened in the speckled light of the brush, locked on Shahly in an unblinking stare.

It appeared to be ready to pounce, yet reluctant, almost as if it was waiting for something.

Shahly heard another growl behind her and felt the presence of a third on the other side. She had been so involved with the humans she did not even sense this new threat coming up on her. Looking back to the humans, she realized she was quickly running out of time.

The creature growled again and Shahly felt it and the one behind her move closer.

Only one way out of this predicament.

She slowly looked back to the creature, boring into its essence with her own. As with most forest predators, its mind was very easy to read as its simple thoughts did not stray far from its next meal and how easily it could be acquired. That was the key.

Calming herself, Shahly stared into the creature's eyes and convinced it that she could be a very dangerous adversary, that she had the power to kill dragons.

It blinked and settled back on its haunches. Like almost all creatures, it feared dragons, and something that could kill dragons made it all the more apprehensive.

The others felt uneasy.

Shahly glanced at the humans, then subtly suggested that one of them might be an easier prey, no enchanted horn or lashing hooves to contend with.

The creature turned its eyes to the humans, hissed, then grunted to the others and turned toward its new quarry.

When it and the other two launched themselves at the humans, utter chaos ensued.

"Dreads!" one of the humans shouted.

Shahly looked toward the skirmish before her as the humans drew their weapons, as the Dreads howled and pounced on three of them, as the horses reared up, whinnying loudly.

With everyone occupied, Shahly slipped out of the thicket and bolted past them, running as hard as she could toward the sun. She could not dare a look back, but she felt the eyes of the black-haired human on her. As their minds touched, she knew he would never stop coming for her.

Shahly reached with strides as long as she could manage. She had never been so afraid and just wanted as much distance between her and the humans as possible.

Thin trees, brush and cacti had blurred by before. Shahly's flight had taken no deliberate direction and she felt more distant from her forest than ever before.

For now, she paced slowly through the scrub country, oblivious to the almost pungent aromas of the blooming bushes and trees. Clumps of grass littered the sandy earth all around. Everything growing here seemed to struggle just to survive. Birds all around sang and chattered, none of them flying above the treetops as hawks screeched occasionally, clearly vigilant of any prey they might see move.

Shahly's whole body ached, yet she felt numb, somewhat thankful for that as she did not want to think or feel at all. She felt so alone. She felt lost.

She stopped and raised her head, finally looking around her.

She *was* lost.

Shahly scanned the area once more, then raised her nose and tested the air. The faint smell of water was carried on the breeze, water and many, many lush green things, some of which she was not familiar with.

She turned and followed the scent to a place where the plants grew bigger, greener and more abundantly. A well traveled path led into the thicket and she reasoned that would be the easiest way to what she sought.

Along the trail, birds and other animals were much more abundant. Rabbits munched on grass on both sides of the trail, monkeys barked at one another, birds chattered and peeped, and a few deer glanced up from their grazing just inside the trees as she passed by. The sandy soil gave way to a darker earth which felt a little damp beneath her hooves.

A short distance later she exited the brush and trees and found a small field of grass and rocks surrounding a pond.

She stopped some paces away and just stared out over the calm water. Across the pond she saw the rocky spring that fed into it. Flowers and ferns grew abundantly there and a few small animals approached without fear to drink. The trees and dense brush stopped most of the wind from getting through and an open sky allowed the sun to warm the clearing, making it feel a little steamy. This place was as enchanting as the forest, but Shahly could not enjoy its splendor.

She approached the pond slowly, wandered into the water and lowered her head to drink, doing so slowly and savoring the taste of the sweet water which eventually quenched her thirst. She raised her head and watched the ever expanding rings glide across the water's surface, the sunlight dancing on their rims as they raced away in every direction.

New rings were born as a tear struck the water, then more.

Shahly lowered her head and took a long, trembling breath, staring down at her reflection for a time as recent memories assaulted her like nightmares from which she could not awaken. She could still see Vinton in the brutal grasp of the humans as he fought gallantly to free himself, as the ropes tightened around his neck and grew ever tighter as he struggled against them. She knew he wanted her to help him. She could feel his fear. Alas, they both knew she could do nothing but escape, something which she barely did.

With a heavy heart she slowly turned and strode from the pool—and froze as she saw the humans and horses emerge from the trail. She had been so involved in her thoughts she did not even feel them coming.

They fanned out about two paces apart and, approaching slowly, attempted to back her up to the water. Four held ropes, ready to snare her.

Shahly backed away, scanning the humans back and forth. Her eyes paused on the black-haired human. Somehow, she knew he was responsible for finding her again.

She glanced behind her, pondering what to do. There was nowhere to go.

The humans on the far left and right quickened their pace, circling inward.

Shahly retreated further, stepping into the water.

They advanced, slowly closing the half circle around her.

Shahly's heart thundered as her eyes darted from one human to the next. She laid her ears back and backed further into the water. The coolness was already above her ankles and she knew she dare not retreat further.

A human directly in front of her pointed to one side and ordered, "You mates close it in. Don't let 'er bolt."

Shahly glanced that way, then looked straight ahead, noticing the horses were coming closer together.

"Ready with them loops," another human said.

Three of them held their lassos up, one poising his to throw.

Shahly lowered her head as she watched them stalk toward her from eight paces away.

Seven. Six. Five.

Her ears perked. She would have only one shot at this.

The black-haired human stopped his horse.

Four paces.

Shahly charged forward and reared up, whinnying loudly as her hooves lashed out toward the faces of the two closest horses.

One jerked away, running into the horse at his side; the other pulled her head aside and reared up, throwing her rider.

Confusion ensued as the other horses also panicked, snorting and whinnying as they attempted to retreat from the disturbance, their riders trying in vain to control them.

Shahly allowed the chaos to escalate, then easily slipped through them and darted for the trail, stopping just before the trees and brush to look back. She gasped, her eyes widening as she saw the black haired human already turning to pursue, and others gaining control of their animals to do the same.

She whinnied and fled.

Unwilling to be pursued like she had been before, Shahly glanced back as she cleared the trail out of the thicket, noticing the riders were grouping together nicely again. She slowed her pace slightly, allowing them to close the gap, then turned toward some heavy clumps of brush and a grove of thin trees.

Predictably, the humans pursued.

She veered left, glanced back to be sure they were also doing so, then cut sharply to the right, bounding over a clump of brush, darting through the trees and, once she found open range again, launched herself into a full gallop.

Behind her, she heard humans yell, horses whinny and snort and bodies pile up in the brush.

She risked a look back.

Humans and horses struggled to stand, two humans chasing their horses out into the scrub country.

Shahly almost smiled as she looked ahead again and ran faster into the sun, but she could feel the eyes of the black haired human following her. He knew the unicorns. He would never stop pursuing them. Or her. She could not allow him to find the herd. She had to lead him away.

So she ran hard toward the sun, toward a land she had never seen.

CHAPTER 2

Mountains of tan stone streaked with orange and red stood ahead of her. Snow capped only the highest peaks. No trees grew on their slopes; they were just bare stone.

Untold hours had passed when Shahly stopped and looked around her. Nearly all cover was gone; only round clumps of brush, many different cacti and boulders dotted the landscape. The ground, which was very soft beneath her hooves, was tan and red sand, speckled by red, pink, gray and black pebbles. The air was very dry and the sun was already uncomfortably hot.

Traveling on the breeze were the faint smells of nectars, some sweet and others bitterly unpleasant. Even in this desolation, Shahly could smell many animals and occasionally a bird would sing from one of the bushes or tall cacti that somehow grew in this forbidding land.

She looked behind her, unable to see her human pursuers, but knowing they were following her, feeling their presence in the distance, especially the black haired human.

Then she noticed her hoof prints in the sand.

She turned ahead again and just stared for a moment, then whinnied, "No wonder I cannot lose them!"

Another look back and she trotted forward again, angling toward the mountains. Stone would not leave tracks like sand would and finding a good place to hide would be far easier.

The mountains did not seem very far away, but she trotted for nearly an hour before reaching them. The long journey had left her weary and very thirsty.

After climbing a shallow slope of sand and various sized and shaped rocks, she stopped at the base, stepping onto the wide stone ledge and looked up it. The sun was nearly to the other side and already some of the shallow caves and ledges offered shade from the uncomfortable heat, though her throat was very dry and she would have preferred water.

Shahly turned and paced along the mountain, following the flat stone ledge at the mountain base and glancing at the cool stone frequently. The tan stone would occasionally give way to a dark gray stone, almost black. Dotted in this rock were small gemstones that sparkled brilliantly, almost like water.

Her ears perked as they caught the sound of falling water ahead. She quickened her pace, not seeing the water but finally able to smell it on the breeze which seemed to circle the mountain. Thirty more paces and the smell was stronger and joined by many plants and cacti.

A large boulder blocked her path so she hopped down from the stone ledge, back onto the slope of sand and rocks and trotted toward the sound. The sand was very loose here and her hooves sank deeply into it, making her journey more difficult, but she finally rounded the boulder and stopped as she saw the pool ahead of her.

The dark gray stone of the mountain was hollowed out twice Shahly's height, at least thirty paces wide and about ten paces deep. It was taller and narrower at the rear where a tiny waterfall cascaded down the bare gold and crystals at the back. White and crystal stalactites hung from the ceiling, mostly toward the rear, each slowly dropping its little beads of water into the pool below. Shimmers of light danced and sparkled on the walls and ceiling.

All around the hollow, ferns, small fruit bearing trees, bushes and clumps of lush grass flourished, a miniature forest in the middle of all of this desolation.

Shahly coughed, her dry throat reminding her still again to drink. As she paced toward the water, one of her hooves found something hard beneath the sand.

It moved!

Shahly jumped half her height in the air and backward, landing stiffly three paces away and facing the moving sand with her head low and her eyes very wide. She stepped back further, watching the sand part as something horrible began to emerge.

Its modular, glossy brown tail, ending in a long, hooked stinger flanked by black pincers, burst from the sand first, curling over its body which rose quickly from the sand. Black claws as long as Shahly's head thrust upward and opened wide, ready to grasp. They were slender and pointed near the tips, growing wider as they reached the arms of the beast. Like a crustacean crawling from the water, the scorpion walked from the sand on powerful black legs, propelling its dark bronze, horse-sized armored body easily from the sand.

Shahly knew scorpions were blind as she had encountered much, much smaller ones in the forest, but this one had more of a bulbous head with two huge, black-red eyes directed forward, giving it something of the features of a giant leaping spider of the forest.

It turned slightly, directing those huge eyes on Shahly, then it was still.

Unicorn and scorpion stared at one another for long seconds.

Shahly glanced at the small oasis, then looked down at the creature before her. She did not want to test her horn against it and was certain it would not hesitate to wield its deadly weapons against her, so she bored into it with her essence, looking for its mind. What she found was so alien that she had no idea how to read it, or even what it was she felt.

It thrust its claws toward her, clacking them loudly.

Shahly whinnied and jumped back.

To her horror, the scorpion pursued.

Shahly turned and fled, running as hard as she could away from it.

Some distance later she looked over her shoulder.

Though she had put some distance between herself and the scorpion, it was surprisingly fast and still in pursuit.

She turned ahead, finding a hill of piled boulders and sand before her, and headed for it. Avoiding the shaded side, she wheeled around it as fast as she could, feeling the sand shifting beneath her hooves as she ran. The few impressions she had gotten from the scorpion's mind did not lead her to believe it was very intelligent, and she reasoned out-maneuvering it would be easy.

She ran as close to the hill as she dared, veered sharply around a large boulder and locked her hooves firmly into the sand, sliding to a quick stop five paces in front of the humans she had been fleeing.

They all looked as surprised as she felt.

Shahly looked behind her and saw the scorpion still coming, then turned and fled back toward the mountains, looking back to see the humans after her again.

Ahead, she saw an opening in the mountains, a canyon or pass she could flee through and hopefully find a place to hide. Running at a full gallop between the walls of glistening gray and orange and tan stone, Shahly noticed to her dismay that they narrowed and grew taller ahead. She was exhausted and her throat burned for water, and her pace slowed.

She turned with the canyon, kicking her stride as long as she could as the walls seemed to open up and the path became very wide, then she locked her hooves into the sand again, dropping her haunches nearly to the ground as the canyon walls suddenly came together in a sheer face of gray, tan and red rippled stone.

"Oh, no!" she cried, staring up at the stone cliff before her.

She turned her eyes ahead, locking them into the blackness of a cave that opened before her.

It was over six times her height at the highest point and at least as wide.

Shahly glanced around her, noticing the stone all around was blackened and deep red in places, burnt, and countless bones were strewn all over the place. A burnt odor lingered in the air and the sulfur smell of brimstone was potent here.

She felt something humming within her essence. It was beautiful, yet menacing and unfamiliar. Even at rest as it was, the power and overwhelming presence of intricate thoughts cascading about intrigued her. Such a fantastic mind this was.

Yet, there was something about that mind, something the elders had taught her. It seemed infinite and very complex, very intelligent.

Predatory!

She gasped and backed away.

This was the mind of a dragon!

She heard something cut the air behind her and a rope dropped over her head and tightened brutally around her neck.

"Got her!" a human shouted from behind.

The rope was pulled hard and Shahly staggered, then turned fully and tried to back away from the humans who were fanned out and advancing on her.

Whinnying sharply, she reared up and pulled back against the rope, but the other end was tied to the saddle and she could not match the horse's strength. Channeling her essence into her horn, which began to glow emerald, she brought the spiral down onto the rope. Her horn should have cut right through the rope, but somehow the rope struck back, sparks exploding from it where her horn touched it. The painful sensation, like fire lancing through every part of her, nearly rendered her unconscious.

As she staggered, struggling to keep her hooves under her, another rope fell over her head, tightening around her neck.

Regaining her wits somewhat, she shook her head and fought hard against her captors, whinnying and trying to leap backward.

Even through her fear, Shahly felt the presence in the cave awaken and explode into a strength and awareness she had never even imagined before.

She stopped struggling and looked over her shoulder, her flanks still heaving as she stared fearfully into the cave. The mind of the dragon seemed to sweep through the canyon and she felt it whirl around her.

Her heart thundered. It knew all of the creatures in the canyon. It knew her! And yet, it masked itself. She knew it was dragon, but could not feel the extent of its power, nor could she peer into its emotions or thoughts.

Hoof beats approached and she tore her eyes away from the cave, seeing the black haired human sitting atop his agitated horse. He, too, stared into the blackness as if he sensed the presence, then he turned his horse and rode toward the other men, ordering, "Release the unicorn. We have to leave."

Shahly watched him ride past the other humans, and one protested, "We'll not give up our bounty on this animal!"

The black haired human stopped and looked back at him. "She will only slow us. I suggest you lower your voice and come with me." He raised his chin. "Unless you intend to face what is in that cave."

"There be nothin' in there," another sneered. "Quit actin' the coward and get a rope on 'er."

The black haired human glanced at Shahly, into the cave, then turned and continued on his way.

"You'll get no share of this bounty, then," one of the humans shouted.

Shahly looked back into the cave. Something in there moved!

Near panic, she turned back and pulled hard against the ropes, rearing up and whinnying loudly.

A horse responded, throwing his rider.

The humans pulled back hard on the ropes, tightening them around her neck.

A faint, thunderous growl rolled from the cave.

Shahly came down and stared blankly ahead.

One of the humans jerked on his rope.

"Careful!" one shouted. "We don't need her injured!"

Aware of the humans, she barely felt them now, and barely noticed one of them slowly approaching her on foot. She looked directly at him and he stopped five paces away.

He raised his chin to her and said, "She thinks there's somethin' in that cave, too."

"Nonsense," another scoffed. "Nothin's in there, mate. Maybe a toothless old bear or a hermit gnome. See if you can get another loop around 'er neck."

Shahly's ears perked as she heard movement within the cave again, and she looked over her shoulder.

"Stallion and mare they are," another human observed. "Worth their weight in gold, I'll say."

"Aye, she'll pay a pretty copper for two," another laughed.

"She'll pay more than a copper for these two, mate."

Shahly looked back to the humans. The man on foot had advanced a pace and held his rope ready. The others watched her and continued to talk among themselves, and it became clear that they really did not know what was in the cave.

"We have to flee this place!" she whinnied to them as she struggled again to free herself.

The human on foot advanced slowly.

Shahly glanced around as she felt the mind of the dragon whirl around the canyon again.

How can they not sense that? she asked herself.

A thunderous growl erupted from the cave.

The human on foot froze, and dropped his rope.

Every nerve in Shahly's body was suddenly alert. She looked to the humans, noticing they all looked very uneasy, as if they finally realized what was in the cave.

A ground shaking thump echoed from the cave, then another. Another, closer.

The dragon was coming out!

Shahly bolted forward, stopping as she reached her human captors. Somehow, she felt a little safer among them.

The thumping stopped.

Just out of the light, Shahly could see the eyes of the dragon. They glowed crimson, offering a hint of his head and the scaly brow that was held low.

Shahly still could not sense his emotions, but she knew disturbing him had not been a wise thing to do.

The dragon growled again.

"Slowly, mate," one of the humans said softly, very monotone. "Ready that spear."

Another power awakened, something she had felt in the forest that morning.

Glancing to her side, Shahly noticed one of the humans held the long, barbed stick that the horse had been carrying. It glowed violet at the tip and hummed with a bitter power that felt of death, and it felt poisonous.

She drew a quick breath, looking back to the cave.

The humans meant to turn it on the dragon!

Another growl echoed from the cave, then the sound of a gusty wind.

"Ready," the human said.

Fire exploded from the mouth of the cave, lancing out in many directions like long tentacles of flame.

Horses whinnied; humans yelled.

Shahly danced backward, turning her eyes away from the heat. Feeling it stop, she looked back to the cave, wincing as her eyes found what remained of the human who had been on foot, only a blackened skeleton within the white silhouette of ash that had been his body. She looked back, watching as the remaining four humans tried to regain control of the horses and regroup. Turning her eyes down, she noticed the ropes meant to hold her had been severed by the fire.

A shuffle and heavy drag on the stone within the cave drew her attention back there. She retreated a few steps, watching with wide eyes as the dragon emerged.

Clearly fearless of the humans, the dragon seemed to casually lope out of the cave on all fours, the sunlight reflecting many dark greens and blues from his black scales. His brilliantly glowing eyes darted from human to human. He stopped as he saw Shahly. His eyes consumed her.

A horse whinnied and a human shouted, "Ready that spear!"

The dragon's eyes turned behind her. His long, slender snout parted as his scaly lips drew up, baring many pointed teeth, some nearly the size of Shahly's foreleg, and a growl erupted from his throat.

He watched the humans for a long moment, then arched his back and stood. Beneath his armor scales he was very heavily muscled, and thick limbs betrayed strength Shahly had never even imagined. His arms were as thick as her body and ended in clawed hands not unlike the human's, yet very similar to a hawk's. His hindquarters were even bigger, his claws digging into the ground.

As his head turned one direction, Shahly got a good look at the horns which swept back from above and behind his eyes. Dorsal scales formed a rigid mane starting small between his eyes and growing larger and more armor like as they made their way down his neck and back, then smaller all the way to the end of his long, thrashing tail.

Standing fully, he was over five times taller than any of the humans.

Shahly glanced behind her, noticing the humans had regrouped and were holding their ground about ten paces behind her. They all had weapons in their hands, one holding the glowing spear. Nervously, they looked up at the dragon, mumbling amongst themselves.

She looked back to the dragon, seeing his attention on the humans, and a cold feeling swept through her again as she realized they meant to fight, and she was standing right between them.

Still staring up at the dragon, Shahly backed away a few paces, then turned and trotted to the canyon wall some fifteen paces away where she could safely watch the outcome.

A human waved his arm and ordered, "Spread out. We don't need to be givin' him a group of us to strike at once."

"He'll burn us all," one of the humans whimpered.

"No," the one with the spear corrected, riding even closer. "He'll not use fire so close to himself." He glanced at one of the others near the dragon's side and nodded.

The other human yelled and threw his axe at the dragon.

In the blink of an eye, the dragon caught the axe between his fingers.

The human with the spear hurled it at the dragon with a true aim.

Again, the dragon raised his hand, catching the spear on a green cushion of light in his palm. Fire and lightning exploded from his hand and the spear was gone in a puff of smoke.

The dragon's piercing stare bored into the human who had thrown the spear, and he pointed a clawed digit at him. A brilliant emerald light lanced from the end of the dragon's claw and slammed into he human's chest and through his body, rolling him backward from his horse. In that instant, the human's life force was gone.

Shahly stared down at the lifeless, smoking body of the human for long seconds. The dragon had killed him so easily, and with a power the elders had never spoken of. She looked back at the humans, realizing they had no chance.

Silently, the other humans and horses backed away as the dragon's attention returned to them.

Shahly still could sense nothing from the dragon, but she felt levels of fear from the humans that she did not even know they could feel, something more than prey fearing a predator.

She looked back up to the dragon.

His chest swelled as he drew a deep breath, then his jaws gaped, baring those menacing white teeth and he roared, fire exploding from his gape and reaching over the heads of the humans like an ominous cloud of doom.

They turned and fled, screaming.

The flames quickly thinned and died as the dragon's jaws closed, and he growled deeply, striding toward the fleeing humans with heavy, ground shaking steps.

Then he stopped, turning his huge head, his teeth bared. Powerful muscles tensed, drawing the scale mane from his head to the end of his tail more erect as he looked right at Shahly.

Vinton's capture, the humans chasing her, even the giant scorpion in the desert seemed miniscule at this particular moment.

With another deep growl, the dragon turned fully, stomping toward her.

Shahly found herself cornered and facing her kind's deadliest enemy, and for the first time in her life she knew absolute terror! Her wide eyes darted to one side, then the other, and she realized that she could never get around this great beast. She tried to back away, stopped by the canyon wall. Staring up at him with fear filled eyes as his scaly lips drew away from his sword sized teeth, her heart thundered and she tried desperately to back away further as she pondered what to do, and could find no way out, but for one.

Though the elders had taught her seasons ago that her essence was deadly to dragons and that her horn could easily penetrate a dragon's armor-like hide where little else could, Shahly knew nothing of combat. Sparring with the other unicorns of the herd had always been something of play, something to be enjoyed with another. The dragon was so huge, so powerful.

The dragon's scaly lips parted again, baring those horrible teeth as he growled. The red glow of his eyes became brighter, even against the light of day.

Trembling, Shahly channeled her essence through her horn, which began to glow emerald, and she directed its tip at the dragon's chest.

With another growl, the dragon shook the ground with a single step wide and toward her. His wings opened and his jaws gaped. Long, sharp claws curled. Muscles tensed and bulged beneath his scales. Somehow, he seemed even bigger.

Shahly knew she had little chance against him, but something much more important was at stake: Vinton. She did not want to die, nor did she want to live without the stallion she loved, even if he was not to choose her. What horrors must he be facing? Somehow, she had to survive and save him.

Setting her fear aside, she glared up at the dragon and channeled as much of her essence as she could muster into her horn, arching her neck to bring her horn to bear on the dragon's heart, then she snorted and kicked at the ground.

The dragon responded with an ear shattering roar.

Shahly reared up and lunged at him.

He flinched away, then opened his jaws and slammed them shut half of Shahly's length away from her.

Startled, she leaped aside, then whinnied, reared up again and jumped at him.

With a single step back, the dragon was out of range, yet was still close enough to strike at her.

Shahly ducked and watched the dragon's claws swipe closely over her in a quick blur, then she dodged away as he struck again and tried to circle around him.

He turned fully, crouching to strike at her again.

Shahly knew she would have to brave his claws and strike at his hand when he swung at her again. Then came a horrid thought. She would have to kill him. Projecting her essence at him would only stun him at best, if she was even strong enough to contend with his armor. She would have to plunge her horn into him, through his armor and loose her essence inside of him. The thought sickened her. Killing was something she could never do.

Though terrified, Shahly bravely raised her head and met the dragon's eyes with her own.

The dragon drew his head back, raising a scaly brow as a soft growl rolled from his throat. He just stared back at her for long seconds, then demanded in a booming voice, "Why did you lead humans here?" His words echoed through the canyon.

She cringed at the authority and volume of his voice and timidly answered, "I did not mean to disturb you! They chased me here from the forest and I just ran to get away from them!"

He nodded. "I see. So you led them here to get me to kill them for you."

"No!" Shahly gasped. "I wish death on no one!"

"Not even me?" the dragon bellowed.

"Why should I wish death on you?"

The dragon bent toward her and roared, "Because we're enemies!"

Shahly retreated, shaking her head as she confessed, "But I don't want to be your enemy."

The dragon leaned his head. "Because you don't want me to kill you? Is that it?"

"Yes," Shahly admitted shakily.

Drawing his head back, the red glow in the dragon's eyes fading until all that remained were the true colors of his eyes; round black-red pupils within pale blue. He glanced aside, then looked back to her and said, "I suppose I couldn't ask for a more honest answer than that." He looked down at her hooves. "You know, your stance could use some work."

Her ears swiveled toward him. "My what?"

"If you are going to fight a dragon then you need to have your hooves planted more firmly and further apart, that way you can outmaneuver him when he comes at you."

She leaned her head. "Outmaneuver him? What do you mean?"

"Dragons are too big to be very nimble on the ground," the dragon explained, "so it's an advantage you need to exploit. You should also avoid getting yourself cornered." He retreated a few steps. "All I would have to do is back away and use fire. Unicorns have no defense against that."

Shahly nodded.

The dragon approached again and seated himself catlike before her. "Never fought a dragon before, have you?"

She raised her head, answering, "No. You are the first dragon I have even seen this close."

A hint of amusement touched his eyes. "You don't say? Well, there's still much you need to learn before you challenge any more dragons, little unicorn."

She glanced away and admitted, "Well, I never intended to challenge a dragon."

"Just like you never intended to be chased by humans?"

Shahly nervously laid her ears back. "Some say humans are evil. They also say dragons are evil. Is it true?"

The dragon shook his head. "No, little unicorn. Good or evil is a choice made by individuals, not an inborn trait of a species."

She leaned her head. "You don't seem evil."

He reached to her, gently loosened the ropes around her neck and pulled them over her head. "I'll take that as a compliment."

"The humans didn't either, yet they hunt unicorns."

The dragon carelessly tossed the rope from him and informed, "Humans are weird. You shouldn't trust them or the legends about them."

Shahly watched the ropes land some distance away, then sighed, "They captured Vinton."

"Who?" the dragon asked in a half-interested tone.

Feeling tears well up in her eyes, Shahly turned and paced around the dragon. "My... He is a stallion of my herd. The other humans took him."

"How unfortunate," the dragon observed.

Shahly looked back at the dragon. "I have to go. Thank you for saving me and for your advice. I won't forget you." She turned and bolted away from him, running hard down the canyon and back into the desert.

Following her own tracks in the sand, now fully shadowed by the mountain, she ran the way she had come, slowing to a trot, then a walk.

Too far. Too much time to think.

Though her thoughts raced around Vinton and his freedom, new thoughts invaded her weary mind, bringing her to a stop.

How would she find Vinton? How would she rescue him?

Her throat was dry; her body ached.

Thirst was a more immediate concern.

Looking ahead of her, she knew she would have to find water soon. She knew where to find it. It was not far away, nor was the nightmare that guarded it.

She started forward again, then trotted toward the scent of the water, following her own tracks in the sand and the two sets left by the scorpion. She knew it would be waiting there for her, but so was the water that could save her life.

A short trek later she stopped some thirty paces from where she had encountered the scorpion before. Its tracks stopped at a bulge in the sand where it had buried itself to wait for its next victim.

Shahly stepped very lightly around where she knew the scorpion to be, keeping her eyes locked on the bulge in the sand. She could feel its presence in there, resting, yet strangely alert.

The sand moved.

Shahly froze.

Hesitantly, she continued on, gingerly ascending the shallow slope.

As her hooves found stone again, she turned ahead and looked over the pool, drawing a deep breath as the beauty of it warmed her.

Delicate ripples glided across the surface of the clear water. It appeared to be very deep, its bottom made of jewels and shiny stones. She did not see fish or moss living in the water and could smell no life in it. All around the water grew lush grasses, ferns, tiny shrubs and small fruit bearing trees. The water itself smelled pure, like spring rain and was too inviting to wait for any longer.

As she approached the pool and bent her nose to it she felt her hoof strike a rock. Looking back, she watched as it rolled from the stone ledge and down the slope of sand, and she winced as it struck the bulge there.

Her heart jumped as the scorpion rose from the sand and turned toward her, its claws held ready.

The dragon had spared her, had shown mercy.

This monster could feel no such things and only seemed to be interested in its next meal.

Cornered again, Shahly remained still and waited for the scorpion to approach, or charge, or something!

It, too, remained motionless.

Shahly's body ached and her throat burned from thirst. She had to drink, but she dare not take her eyes from the scorpion.

It rose up, widening its pincers, then quickly pivoted to one side, toward the canyon and the dragon's lair.

Shahly looked that way, then heard the thump. Another shook the ground. Another, closer. Another.

Shahly turned fully as she saw the dragon stride around the mountain, walking upright and hunched over as dragons would walk. His tail was not dragging behind him, rather it swayed back and forth as he walked. She backed away a few steps, wanting to flee but still very fearful of the scorpion, and still needing to drink. Coldness swept through her as he looked down at her.

He raised a brow, then looked down to the scorpion and tossed the body of one of the humans he had killed toward it.

She looked to the scorpion as it quickly seized the human and seemed to slam it into what could only be its mouth, right between its arms, then it turned and pushed itself beneath the sand, scurrying out of sight with its prize.

Slowly, she turned her eyes back to the dragon, who had stopped a few paces away and stared back at her.

"I thought you might come here," he informed.

Shahly looked back to the buried scorpion.

"My sentinel," the dragon explained. "Water is scarce here in the hard lands, so I find it best that I guard what little I have."

She looked up at him. "But what about the other creatures who live out here? They need to drink too."

"Not those who get eaten by my sentinel. Only the quick and clever get to drink—and those who are in my favor." He motioned toward the water with his head and ordered, "Drink your fill, little unicorn. I doubt you will make if far if you don't."

Shahly looked back to the water and took one final step toward it, then looked up at the dragon and softly said, "Thank you," then she lowered her head to drink. The water was very sweet, the purest she had ever tasted, and she could feel its soothing coolness all the way down her throat and into her belly.

Sand and gravel crunched beside her.

Still drinking, Shahly looked that way.

The dragon's clawed hand settled onto the ground beside her. His jaws gaped as he lowered his head to the pool and scooped a quarter of Shahly's weight in water into his lower jaw, then retreated, his throat sagging under the weight of the water.

Shahly watched him rise up slightly, water raining down from his jaw as he raised his nose and easily swallowed the water in one gulp. She quickly noticed the water level of the pool had dropped.

Turning her eyes back to the dragon, she saw every reason she needed to fear him, yet the terror she should have experienced in that moment was absent. He was not like the fierce predators she had been told of. Clearly, the elders were wrong about them.

"You're thinking awfully hard about something," he observed.

She flinched at the booming sound of his voice and raised her nose from the water, staring at him for a moment, then admitted, "I was wondering about you."

The dragon raised his brow. "Oh?"

"You are different than the dragons I have been told about. The elders say a dragon's instinct is to kill unicorns when you see us."

"Do they, now?" The dragon sounded amused. "Well, perhaps I am unique among dragons."

"It isn't true, is it? What the elders say."

The dragon shook his head. "No, it isn't. Dragons won't kill without a reason."

Shahly looked back to the pond, feeling her faith in her elder's words was no longer so absolute.

"Don't get discouraged," the dragon said sympathetically. "There are at least as many misconceptions about dragons as there are about unicorns."

Shahly nodded, then she looked up at him again and asked, "Why didn't you eat the human?"

He snarled and drew his head away from her. "Have you ever tasted one of those?" When she grimaced, he finished, "I see you haven't. If you had, you would understand."

She nodded again and took another drink, then turned away from the pond and paced down the slope, now even more curious about him, though finding Vinton was a far more immediate concern. "I should be going. Thank you for your help and for allowing me to drink."

"Watch your step," the dragon advised quickly.

Shahly froze, remembering the buried scorpion. She heard the dragon stand and looked back at him.

"You need to be careful traveling through the hard lands," he informed. "There are dangers out here you would not think to look for."

"I will be," she assured, then turned and paced on, circling wide around the buried scorpion.

She felt the dragon's eyes on her for some time, but when she looked back, he was gone, though his presence lingered somehow.

A long journey was ahead, and too much time to think.

Shadows grew long before her as she trekked back toward her forest. Her belly groaned, demanding food, but she barely noticed as Vinton occupied her every thought. She missed him and her heart ached at the thought of never seeing him again.

Hours later, as the sunlight grew dim and the shadows melted together, Shahly paced through the scrub country, wandering aimlessly until she glanced up and noticed something she recognized.

Ahead of her she saw the grove of trees and brush she had visited before, smelled the water and lush grass within it. Birds sang their songs of night and the clicking of bats danced on the air all around.

She paced around the thicket and found the trail that led into it. Without the sun above, the trail was very dark and she could barely see where she was going, and was thankful for the brightness of the moon.

Walking carefully and feeling her way along with her essence, she paced to the center, to the pond, and took a long drink. Having quenched her thirst, she nibbled at the grass near the pond, then lay down in the tall grass near the trees and tried to sleep.

Half the night passed.

A nearly full moon illuminated the pond and clearing in a soothing blue light.

Shahly's weary mind could find no rest. Still in her memory was the horror of her one true love's capture, and the knowledge that she might never see him again. Tears escaped from her eyes as she closed them and she sobbed, "It isn't fair. It just isn't fair."

A restless sleep claimed her some time later and she was finally swept into dreams.

Vinton was not to be found here, either.

CHAPTER 3

Footsteps.

Shahly opened her eyes slowly, squinting against the sunlight that was already over the trees.

A human strode into view and stopped.

Shahly sprang to her hooves and faced him.

Long white hair hung from his jaws. Bushy white eyebrows shaded dark blue eyes. He was dressed in light blue material that smelled like sheep's wool and hung from the shoulders of his thin frame all the way to the ground, the same material covering his head.

Shahly took a step back, then felt his mind and emotions. Here, he was different than the other humans she had encountered, even the black haired human. He had quite a gentle mind, one that reminded her of the elders of the herd. He seemed devoid of many of the thoughts the other humans had and his emotions lacked the predatory thoughts of gain and lust that she had observed were unique to humans. In fact, he felt as if he belonged in the forest.

He smiled, and warmth radiated forth from his emotions.

"Well," he said to her in a very gentle voice. "I never expected to see a unicorn in these parts." He reached behind him, his hand returning to view with two leather sacks. "I'll not disturb you long. Just need some water."

Shahly blinked as she watched him approach the pond and kneel down at the water's edge. Unlike the dragon and the other humans, this human had knowingly opened his mind to her. It was as if he wanted her to know him. She lowered her head and studied his mind further. No tricks, nothing hidden, only his gentle mind. Still, there was a power about him, a connection to the land and elements that she had never sensed before. It was almost like another essence, though it was at rest.

She paced very slowly, noiselessly toward him.

He seemed to ignore her, yet she felt an eagerness about him. He wanted contact with her, but for much different reasons than the other humans she had encountered.

The human lifted the bottle from the water and held it before him. Shahly stopped.

He lowered the bottle back into the water. Bubbles rolled from the mouth of it and burst on the surface with funny pops.

Shahly approached again and peered over his shoulder for a better look. The human's scent was still somewhat pungent, but he smelled much less offensive than most of those who had pursued her.

The human looked over his shoulder and smiled at her. "Come to claim this little oasis for your own?"

She took a step back and leaned her head, studying him in appearance and essence.

"I have nothing to hide from you," he assured. He lifted the bottle from the water again and examined it, then shoved something into the opening, laid it on the bank beside him and took the other in his hand.

Shahly watched as he held the other one under the water, interested in what he was doing only briefly. Vinton soon returned to her thoughts, the humans who had taken him, those who had pursued her, and the confrontation with the dragon.

Perhaps...

"I am Shahly," she whickered to the human.

The human raised his head, then slowly stood and turned toward her. He was truly astonished at having contact with her.

"I understand you," he breathed. "I heard the sound you made, but I understand you in my thoughts." He dropped the water bottle and cautiously reached for her, gently stroking her nose. "You need my help, don't you?"

Though nervous about such close contact with a human, Shahly refused to retreat from him and instead looked him in the eyes and asked, "How did you know?"

He smiled, stroking her nose again. "I am neither blind nor deaf to the perceptions of those things not seen nor heard."

"But I thought humans could not sense such things."

"Most cannot," the human confirmed. "Only a gifted few can. I would consider it an honor to use this gift in your service if you need me."

Shahly looked away. Humans took Vinton, and perhaps only humans could free him. She lowered her head and took a deep breath. "Humans took my stallion yesterday." She knew he was not truly her stallion, but in her heart he was, and if she could rescue him somehow, perhaps he would be.

Something in the human's emotions changed. It was not quite anger, more betrayal and shame. Looking back to him, Shahly could clearly see he made no secret of his disapproval for the deeds of his kind.

"So this is what it comes to," he said grimly. "I have seen fewer and fewer unicorns and signs of unicorns north of the Sullee River over the seasons. None in the last three seasons." He sighed, shaking his head. "The fools have no idea…" Something in his mind changed. His heart jumped. He sidestepped and raised a hand toward the path that led into the thicket, breathing, "Oh, no."

Only then did Shahly sense the human hunters.

"They've found you," the human said straightly.

Shahly turned, looking to the trail. "What do we do? Should we hide?"

The human shook his head, staring blankly at the trail. "No. One among them is gifted in the inner senses. He would find you easily."

"The black haired one," Shahly confirmed. "He can even sense me when I conceal my essence."

"They have you trapped here." He closed his eyes, lowering his hand.

Shahly's heart thundered and she cried, "There has to be some way out!"

"No," the human said. "The underbrush is too thick. It would slow you and you would be taken easily."

Shahly backed toward the water and begged, "Please don't let them get me!"

The human opened his eyes and patted Shahly's neck, assuring, "Courage, girl. Help is on the way."

They watched in silence as the hunters filed into the clearing, led by the black haired man.

Trembling, Shahly raised her head, her eyes locked on his.

Expressionless, he stared back. His mind had already found hers, yet remained silent to her.

Her eyes darted to the rest as they emerged from the trees. They were nine strong this time and formed a line as they had done before, but this time two remained back to guard the path out of the clearing.

The black haired human and two others dismounted and walked ahead of the other four riders. The black haired man stopped half way, staring with expressionless eyes at the older human who stood at Shahly's side while the other two readied their ropes.

"Careful," the white haired human warned. "Those things could bite you."

Shahly felt fear jump into the humans as they looked to their ropes and quickly dropped them, one man shouting, "Snake!" as he backed away.

"No," the other growled, turning his eyes angrily to the white haired man. "A wizard's mind trick." He drew his sword and took a step forward. "Aside, old man."

Smiling, the white haired human folded his arms. "And if I refuse?"

Pointing his sword at the older human from half a pace away, the armed human ordered, "Off with you! We'll be takin' this beast."

The white haired man shook his head. "You'll be taking no unicorns today. You must understand they are sacred animals and not to be hunted for food or trophies, barter or bounty."

With another step forward, the other human pushed his weapon against the wizard's chest, ordering, "I said off with you!"

Shahly took a step back. She did not want to see this kind human hurt or killed by the others. But what to do?

With a smile on his lips, the white haired man shook his head and laughed softly, informing, "Threatening a wizard is not a wise thing to do."

"Nor is standing between us and our bounty," the armed human countered. "Move aside!"

The wizard looked to the sky, sighing, "I so rarely resort to violence."

Don't, Shahly thought to him, more afraid for him with each passing second. She knew he heard her, yet he would not respond in thought or action.

The human still with the black haired man strode forward and reached for his sword, ordering, "Enough of this! Unless you mean to fight us all, move aside!"

"Oh, I don't think I could defeat you all," the wizard admitted, then smiled. "But I'll wager my apprentice can."

A moment of silence, then many of the men laughed and the one holding the sword to the wizard's chest ordered, "Be gone, old man, or you and your apprentice can both die today."

The wizard's voice hardened as he said, "You will *not* take the unicorn."

The black haired man suddenly became very uneasy, and looked up to the sky.

Rage welled up in the armed human as he stared at the wizard with death in his eyes. "Find this boy he teaches."

"Don't bother," the wizard advised.

Shahly's heart jumped as she felt a familiar presence sweep into the clearing and she wheeled around as the black dragon dropped from the sky and slammed into the water about twenty paces behind her and the wizard.

Crouched on all fours in water that came halfway up his legs, the dragon's jaws gaped and he roared loud enough to shake the very air all around. He was a nightmarish sight!

Terrified, Shahly turned to flee, then noticed most of the humans and horses already were.

The human with the sword had fallen to the ground, his weapon still in his hand as he stared up at the dragon with eyes that looked like they were going to explode from his head.

The black haired man stared up at the dragon without expression.

A long moment of silence passed, broken only by the babbling stream and the wind whispering through the trees.

She looked to the wizard.

He smiled at the human on the ground. "I'd like you to meet my apprentice."

The human whimpered, scrambled to his feet and fled.

The wizard looked to the black haired man and raised his chin. "If you still want the unicorn, you will have to speak to my apprentice."

Still staring up at the dragon, the black haired man said, "It is not a brave man who challenges the dragon. It is a foolish man." He turned eyes of stone to the wizard, adding, "And it is a strong man who can ally the dragon."

The wizard smiled and nodded to him. "We should talk."

Shahly slowly approached the black haired man, hesitantly asking, "Why did you take my stallion?"

His eyes widened slightly as he looked to her, then his lips tightened as he looked away. Finally, she felt some emotion from him: Shame.

With his defenses down, Shahly could clearly read his emotions, and feeling what he felt made her pity him.

"I don't understand," she said to him softly. "If you know it is wrong, why do you hunt us?"

"Gold," the dragon thundered.

Hearing a rush of water behind her, Shahly looked back and saw the dragon striding from the pond.

Once ashore, he seated himself on the bank, wrapping his tail around him on the ground as he stared down at the black haired man. "It is a pity you humans cannot see gold for what it is instead of what you have made it." He leaned his head. "You've been taking the unicorns to Red Stone Castle again, haven't you?"

Shahly looked back to the black haired man.

Staring at the ground, he took a deep breath and nodded, admitting, "They taught us how, and they pay a huge price for each unicorn we bring them."

"And you don't know why?" the wizard asked.

The black haired man shook his head.

Shahly's throat felt tight. It would hurt, but she had to know. "Will I ever see Vinton again?"

"No," the black haired man confessed softly.

Shahly took a deep, broken breath, her vision blurred by tears. The old wizard patted her neck and said, "We'll think of something, girl."

Her emotions felt like an avalanche within her. She turned fully and paced toward the trail, wandered from the thicket and walked aimlessly through the thin forest. Some time later she finally looked around her, not knowing where she was. Not caring.

"Such a pity," a voice boomed from one side.

She wheeled around, seeing the dragon's head before her, lying on the ground between the trees. The rest of him was sprawled in a clearing in the sunshine.

He drew a breath and said, "Your kind is becoming so rare nowadays."

"What will they do to him?" she asked timidly.

"They will kill him and take his horn," he answered straightly.

Breathing was difficult. Shahly's tail swished hard back and forth and she declared, "I cannot allow this to happen! How can we stop them?"

The dragon raised his brow. "We? Why should I care what happens to him?"

Shahly laid her ears back and protested, "But you just said—"

"I said it's a pity," the dragon interrupted, "not a tragedy."

Shahly felt very anxious and new tears welled up in her eyes. "I can't let them kill him!" She vented a deep breath and looked away as a tear rolled from her eye. "I can't save him either. I can't even fend for myself." She looked back to the dragon and begged, "I need you! Please help me. Please!"

"But I'm your enemy," he reminded.

"I don't care!" she cried. "I will do anything you ask. Please help me."

"Well," the dragon sighed, "if you think it's *that* important. There will, of course, be a price."

"Anything!" Shahly assured desperately.

She backed away and watched as the dragon stood to all fours and stretched, and she cringed as his spine popped loudly several times.

The dragon seated himself in the clearing before her and asked, "How important is this stallion to you?"

"He is my very life and my heart," she answered without hesitating, slowly approaching him.

The dragon nodded. "I see. You must understand this will be no easy task and will be fraught with hazards you cannot even imagine now. Humans are strangely unpredictable and one calling himself friend could easily turn on you without warning. Are you willing to face these dangers?"

Shahly bravely raised her head, answering straightly, "Yes."

"You seem confident. Good. Typically, the unicorn is taken to their arena to fight another beast before they take his spiral. Humans consider this entertaining."

"How horrible!" Shahly declared

"It's their odd nature," the dragon informed dryly. "Before this happens, you must take human form and go into the castle. Find a human female named Falloah. They are holding her in their dungeons. Free her."

"Take human form?" Shahly questioned. "Free a human? How will this help me rescue Vinton?"

"Too many questions," the dragon scolded. "I will provide you with the spell you will need to change your form and you will need Falloah to help you free your Vinton and return you to your true form."

"But how do I find her? Where do I look? What if I'm caught? When must I—"

"Enough!" The dragon interrupted. He lifted his hand and, from nowhere, produced an amulet suspended by a thin gold chain, a perfect emerald sphere gripped by a golden dragon's talon. It sparkled magically, almost unnaturally, and as the dragon slipped it over her head and around her neck, the chain tightened itself around her neck, but not uncomfortably so.

"What is this for?" Shahly asked.

"It channels my power. You will use it to take human form. Just speak Falloah's name, then the incantation, *transformatus de corporum unicornu Abtontae intro humanus.* You should travel to the castle as unicorn but you must transform before you are seen. The prince there is seeking a mate and already has many prospects, so you should be able to enter easily and have your run of the place.

"Once you are inside, do not allow yourself to be drawn in to the sensations you will feel as a human and do not assume the forest tricks you use as a unicorn will work. The world you will enter can be very dangerous, so stay on your guard and control your emotions. They could very likely be your undoing, and if something goes wrong while you are in the castle, I will be unable to help you."

Shahly nodded. "I understand. How do I change back once I find this human mare?"

"You will call my name and a reverse incantation."

Shahly's ears perked toward him and she asked, "Which is?"

The dragon shook his head. "Falloah will tell you what you need to know when you find her. Now you'd better be on your way. You have a long journey ahead of you and you'll have to hurry if you are going to arrive before dark."

"Right!" Shahly agreed eagerly, then turned and started to run, only to stop, turn back and trot back to the dragon to ask, "Where am I going?"

The dragon closed his eyes, growled and shook his head, then looked down to her and asked, "Do you know where the castle of red stone is?"

"It's in the Northlands," she answered. "I have seen it from a distance. The elders have warned me not to go too close because humans live there."

"That is exactly where you are going," the dragon informed. "Just travel north until you find one of their roads, a wide, well traveled path cut through the forest. Follow it away from the heart of the forest and it will take you right to the castle. Just remember to change form before you are seen."

Shahly nodded and said, "I understand." Then she turned to leave.

"One moment, little unicorn," the dragon summoned.

She stopped and looked back at him.

He raised his chin. "The moon will be full for three more nights. When its cycle ends, that spell to make you human will become permanent. Just be certain you are unicorn again by that time."

Something cold swept through Shahly and she just stared up at the dragon for a moment, then she turned and trotted on her way.

"Little unicorn," the dragon called.

She stopped and looked back at him again.

He pointed the other direction.

She looked, then glanced at the dragon, turned, and ran the other way, racing toward this human stronghold, and Vinton.

Though the journey back through the forest was exhaustive, Shahly pushed herself on without mercy, concentrating on Vinton's freedom. She ran or trotted most of the way, dodging between the trees more by reflex than conscious action.

Thoughts of how to rescue her stallion were a blur and thoughts of taking human form and trying to be human were frightening.

Untold hours later she found the road that the dragon said would lead her to this castle and trotted steadily down it, her thoughts still whirling around Vinton and how to rescue him.

She slowed to a walk, then stopped. Something had escaped her, something very important.

"Transform..." she said aloud. "Transformus... Transforming into... Uh, oh." She paced forward again, staring at the ground before her as she struggled to remember. "Transformusing... Oh, I wish he had repeated that a few times. Transformation. Transformat. Transformus. Wait! *Transformatus!* Yes! *Transformatus* what? Into. Inter. Int... Intra... *Intro! Transformatus intro...* something." She snorted. "Shahly, you should have paid closer attention! That is what the elders always say." She sighed. "Something else."

She concentrated silently for some time, pacing steadily toward this castle with her thoughts not straying from the elusive words the dragon had given her. She barely took note of the sound of running water ahead, the forest road opening near the river, and the smell of horses.

Stopping at the river's edge, Shahly lowered her head to drink from the fast running water, her eyes tense and aching as she struggled to remember.

A scream caught her ears and she jerked her head from the water. Another scream, up river. It was not fear, more something playful like she had heard from the monkeys of the forest.

She looked that way, to a large structure of wood that lay across the river.

Humans!

They looked and felt female. Their thoughts were playful and carefree, innocent as many unicorns Shahly knew.

And yet, they were human.

One facing her, a golden haired female with a long, thin, pink covering over her swept her hand across the water and splashed it onto a darker haired one in a blue covering, who screamed again, then splashed back.

It looked fun.

Not now.

Shahly sprang into the river, finding the water very cold and just over ankle deep.

A few bounds later the bottom was gone and Shahly found herself swimming in water that felt as cold as ice! She angled into the current and swam harder as she felt herself being drug toward the humans downstream.

Nearing the other side, her hooves found the bottom again and she struggled through the river the rest of the way, wading into shallower and shallower water until she reached the bank. Not daring a look back at the humans, who surely had seen her by now, she launched herself into a gallop.

A time later, Shahly stopped and half turned, shaking the icy water from her fur. She looked back to see if any of the humans were following and stared behind her for a moment even after she was confident none did.

"I must be nearing the castle," she said to herself, then turned and paced on her way, once again putting her mind to the words that would make her human. Although her memory surrendered many of them, the incantation as a whole continued to elude her.

She vented a deep breath, trying to calm herself enough to concentrate without distraction. "*Transformatussss unicorn...* No, *unicornu corporum intro* human. No. *Corporum_transformatus uni-*No! *Transformatus corporum! Unicornu Abtontae intro* human. *Humanus.* That's it! *Transformatus corporum-* No, *de corporum unicornu Abtontae intro-*"

"Highness, look!"

A human's voice! Male! Right behind her!

Shahly raised her head and looked back.

Three humans followed about thirty paces behind.

One pointed, shouting, "I told you! It *is* a unicorn."

"Well, after it," another shouted.

They charged.

Fear surged through Shahly and she sprang forward, running hard down the road.

Ahead of her in the distance she could see the turrets of a castle.

Time to change.

She veered left and sprang over a clump of brush and into the forest, darting between trees and bushes.

Some distance later she stopped and looked behind her.

The humans were still in pursuit, and not as far behind as she had thought.

She turned and ran further, then darted behind a thicket of new leaves and orange blooms and laid to her belly. Concealing herself from unwary passersby or predators was easy enough, but these humans were actively searching for her. If one looked directly at her he may recognize her despite her deception.

They stopped nearby.

Shahly could not see them through the thicket as they approached, so she remained motionless, hoping they could not see her, either.

They were quiet, but their horses danced nervously.

A human finally spoke. "Lost her."

"I think she went that direction," another said.

"Are you sure it would not flee toward the river?" the third asked.

"Unicorns will not cross deep water. We may be able to cut it off and drive it toward the river where we can corner it."

Won't cross deep water? Shahly thought to herself, whickering a laugh, then cringed as she feared she may have given herself away.

"What a surprise this will be for the queen," one said as they rode away.

Hesitantly, Shahly stood and paced around the thicket, peering cautiously around it to see to it the humans were truly gone.

She trekked on, so close to having that incantation she could feel it.

She stopped, closed her eyes and took a deep breath, then slowly recited, "*Transformatus de corporum unicornu Ab—*"

"There it is!" a human shouted.

Shahly looked behind her, seeing the humans coming at her again from some distance away. Impatience began replacing fear and she snorted and sprang forward again.

With dizzying speed, Shahly swept around trees and bushes. Hearing rushing water ahead, she charged toward the river, confident the humans would not follow her across.

As the forest opened into the flood plain, she recited the words once more so as not to forget when the time came. "Falloah, *Transformatus de corporum unicornu Abtontae intro humanus.*"

The amulet began to hum and Shahly could feel the power and essence of the dragon as she galloped into the ankle deep water. The humming raced along her entire body and she stumbled on forelegs that suddenly felt very awkward, splashing head-first into the deep, icy water near the middle of the river.

The freezing current was strong and Shahly was pulled to the bottom, bounced off of the sand there and finally struggled upward. An eternity later she broke the surface and desperately gasped to fill her burning lungs. Water and air rushed in together. For some reason, swimming was very difficult and she felt she could barely keep her head above the water as she fought the current and struggled toward the bank. Never had she been so cold.

Feeling gravel beneath her feet, she pushed herself toward the shore, still coughing up water as she made her way slowly toward dry land. The current was still swift here and the water felt even colder with the wind blowing on her, and that cold quickly drained her strength.

Her lungs would not take air, no matter how she fought to breathe. The cold water burned in her nose and chest. Strength abandoned her. She was enveloped by the shallow, icy water. One last push toward the shore, feeble and futile, was all she could muster. The current pushed her relentlessly down river. Consciousness slipped away...

So cold.

Shahly moaned weakly, still unable to open her eyes. Tremors violently shook her and every muscle felt unnaturally tense. Her head ached horribly. Something warm covered her, soft and dry. Something gently stroked across her cheek.

She coughed and was rolled to her side as water was disgorged from her chest. Her breath returned with some difficulty but it did return. With a whimper, she rolled to her back and slowly opened her eyes, first focusing on the dark blue eyes of the human who knelt beside her. Suddenly afraid, she shrank away from him.

"Easy, maiden," he said in a soothing, gentle voice. "No one is going to hurt you."

His face looked much like the humans Shahly had already encountered, yet something was different. He was younger. His skin was smoother and free of hair, except for the dark auburn mane which covered his head and flowed to his shoulders. He had prominent cheeks beneath his eyes and a jaw which swept powerfully from behind his ears, meeting his face with full lips that parted slightly as his beautiful eyes glanced from hers to her body and back again.

His coverings were a shiny material of black and red and fit him more loosely than those of the other humans, whose coverings of the same colors more resembled those of the humans she had encountered in the forest, though much more appealing to the eye. The other two also wore shiny metal coverings on their heads.

The blue-eyed human reached for her and gently stroked her cheek. "You are safe, now. You have nothing to be afraid of."

Shahly reached up and touched her face, but not a face she was familiar with, then she looked at her hand.

Hand?

Shahly gasped loudly and sat up, holding her hands before her. She looked back and forth at them, then jerked the black and red covering from her lean, well muscled human legs and looked at them, running her hands down the soft, fair skin. She felt of her flat belly and slid her hands up to her chest, then looked down to find perfect human breasts there, the dragon's amulet dangling between them.

Raising her eyes, she stared ahead for a moment. The dragon's amulet worked! She was human! Her eyes darted to the human at her side.

His face turned a little red as he reached for the covering Shahly had taken from herself. "We found you like this in the river," he told her. "You weren't wearing anything then." He would not look at her eyes as he slid the cloak around her shoulders and tried to fasten it near her throat. "This should keep you warm until we can find you something more suitable."

Shahly just stared into his face as he fumbled with the buttons. He was a kind human and she felt none of the strange, predatory emotions from him that she had felt from many of the other humans she had encountered. Her breath caught as she realized she could feel very little from him. Her unicorn senses did not seem so sharp anymore.

He finally turned his eyes back to hers, asking, "Are you hurt?"

She shook her head.

"What is your name?" he asked gently.

Hesitantly, she whispered, "Shahly."

He raised his brow. "Shahly?"

She nodded, then looked back down to her body, still amazed at the new form she was in.

"A pretty name," he said softly. "How did you end up in the river? Naked and all, I mean. The water seems a bit cold to be swimming in."

A little surge of uneasiness swept through her. She could not tell him the truth, nor could she deny him an answer. She swallowed hard and answered, "I... Someone was chasing me." She recognized her own voice, though it seemed different somehow.

He cupped her chin and cheek in his hand and gently turned her face to him. She could see a mix of rage and concern in his eyes as he asked, "Who? Who was chasing you?"

She shrugged. "I didn't know them."

"Bandits," he growled, then looked up at the other two humans and ordered, "Ride up river and see if you can find these heathens."

"At once, my Prince," one answered.

Shahly watched as the other two humans—two rather big humans—mounted their horses and rode fast up river, then she looked back to the human at her side.

"We will find them," he assured. "You have nothing more to fear."

She smiled. He was so noble, so sweet. She turned her eyes down, reaching from within the cloak to pull it closer to her.

"You still look cold," he observed.

She nodded.

"And still you have such a pretty smile," he said softly, "a smile that could warm the coldest winter day."

Her cheeks went warm and she rolled her eyes from him, playfully ordering, "Stop."

"Sorry," he teased. "Didn't mean to embarrass you."

"Sure you didn't," she responded, not meeting his eyes.

He cleared his throat, then asked, "What brings you out here all alone?"

Another direct question. She drew a breath and looked into the forest, grasping for an answer, then turned her eyes to his and said, "I am traveling to Red Stone Castle. There is someone there I need to meet."

He raised his chin a little, obviously trying not to smile. "Really. Anyone I know?"

She shrugged.

His brow cocked up. "I should tell you that a number of maidens have journeyed to Red Stone on just such a quest."

Shahly's eyes narrowed as she wondered just how many others that dragon had sent to find this Falloah.

"You are still quite welcome to come," the human invited quickly. "I mean, uh, no choice has been made as of yet. I am just playing the situation... I mean..." He pulled a deep breath and asked, "So, where is your home?"

"I come from the forest," she answered, feeling more comfortable with him.

"The forest?" He laughed softly. "Then you must be a fairy."

Shahly giggled. "No, I'm a—" Her breath caught as she realized she had nearly given herself away. "I'm not a fairy."

He laughed again. "I see. Since you are going to Red Stone Castle anyway, may I offer you an escort?"

She just blinked, not knowing what he meant, then shrugged.

"Perhaps knowing who I am would make you more comfortable," he suggested.

"Perhaps," she agreed.

He smiled slightly and introduced, "I am Prince Arden, heir to the throne of Red Stone Castle."

"You are the Prince?" she asked, astonished. Perhaps this was the prince the dragon had mentioned.

"Fortune smiles on us both, today," he said, "mostly me." He stood and offered her his hand.

Surely it could not be this *easy,* she thought. Hesitantly, she slipped her hand into his and struggled to her feet, trying to stand as he did, which was not as easy as it looked. Her legs were strong and held her well, but balance eluded her and she fell into him, grasping his shoulder with her free hand as her face was buried in the soft red material covering his chest. She raised her eyes to him, feeling a little embarrassed.

He was smiling, and shook his head. "Your ordeal appears to have drained you somewhat."

Shahly nodded, then pushed off of him and stood on her own, holding onto his shoulder and hand for balance.

"Well, you'll have all the time you need to rest once we reach the palace." He glanced down at her cloaked body. "That and something nice to wear."

The two guards returned and one reported, "We could find no trace, your Highness, only our own tracks and the unicorn's."

The Prince nodded, his eyes still on Shahly. "I see. Well, they cannot elude us forever."

Shahly smiled, knowing that the bandits the Prince and his guards sought were the Prince and the guards themselves.

The Prince smiled back at her and assured, "Don't worry. We'll get them."

She looked away. "Oh, I am not worried."

Prince Arden looked to the guards and ordered, "Ride on ahead and inform the palace staff there will be one more for dinner."

"Another one?" the younger of the guards asked.

Shahly looked over her shoulder at them.

The Prince added, "And stables to be cleaned by guards who question their prince's orders."

The guard bowed and turned his horse back down the road.

Shaking his head, the older guard, a taller and heftier fellow with a graying black beard turned his horse and called back, "You are a letch, my Prince."

"And very good at it," Prince Arden responded.

Shahly watched the guards ride away, then looked up at the Prince.

He looked back down to her and smiled. "I trust you've ridden before?"

She leaned her head.

He shook his head and stroked a lock of wet hair from her forehead. "Very well, little Forest Blossom. We'll go slowly."

CHAPTER 4

H orses were nothing to be afraid of.
Similar in size and form to the unicorns, Shahly had always felt some kinship with horses. Their minds were very simple and they lacked complex thoughts and communication skills. They were known to be physically stronger than unicorns, though not as fast or as agile. Such free spirits they had as well, though they were easily taken by the humans as slaves, just as the elders had said.

The saddle Prince Arden's horse carried looked and smelled like the skin of another animal, though hardened somehow and shaped to fit the haunches of the rider. It was obviously made to carry just one, but somehow the Prince had managed to get Shahly nestled comfortably—and very closely—in front of him with her legs dangling over one side, his straddling the horse and his arms wrapped tightly around her. He held the reins in one hand and Shahly's arm in the other, careful about where and how firmly he touched her.

Traveling in this way was actually quite pleasant and Shahly took the time to enjoy the scenery. The formerly talkative Prince spoke very little and Shahly felt he was thinking very hard about something, though she could not tell what, nor was she interested.

The ride was uneventful, but as they encountered more and more humans, Shahly became increasingly uneasy, her eyes darting about at them as they all turned and shouted when she and the Prince passed.

Ahead was the castle, with many, many more humans within.

Seeing the open gates and all of the activity within, Shahly leaned into the Prince a little more, nervously drawing her shoulders up.

His grasp on her tightened.

They neared the tall, timber gates which were open before them. More humans were on the wall that surrounded the mountainous castle of red and pink stone and still more were just inside. More horses as well. Five towers reached for the sky, four at the corners of the palace and the tallest at the center.

As they entered the gates, many humans ran toward them, shouting greetings to the Prince as they saw him.

This frightened Shahly and she turned toward him, looking into his eyes for some reassurance.

He smiled and said, "Relax, Shahly. You are among my people now. There is nothing to be afraid of."

She looked back to the humans who seemed to mob them like vultures approaching a kill.

Prince Arden pulled on the reins and the horse stopped, then he tossed the reins to one of the humans on the ground and swung down from the saddle.

Shahly glanced behind her, then down to the Prince and grabbed onto his arms as he seized her by the waist and lifted her down from the horse. Before she realized she was down, she was standing before the Prince, staring up at him.

"Feeling stronger?" he asked.

Still clinging to his shoulders, she nodded, then nervously looked to the crowd of humans who still gathered around them and pulled herself closer to him.

Arden slipped his arm around her shoulders and led her toward the palace. "Perhaps we should find you something to wear."

Shahly walked with him for only a few steps before something stabbed into her foot and she barked, "Ouch!" as she stopped and leaned into him, looking down to see what had gotten her.

"Ah, yes," the Prince added. "Shoes would be in order, too."

Shahly gasped and threw her arms around his neck as he swept her from the ground and cradled her in his arms, then she looked toward the palace as he carried her toward it.

Other humans, dressed much as the Prince's escorts had been, stood flanking the timber doors of the palace, and as he approached, they simultaneously reached to the doors and pulled them open.

When they entered, Shahly lost her breath at the sight of the cavernous room within.

So many colors! Long tapestries hung on the red stone walls, each showing a different picture: One a mountain, one a river and trees, still another an open field surrounded by trees with animals grazing peacefully. There were so many. Shields and swords were mounted between them. Suits of armor guarded the five doorways. Five huge crystal and brass chandeliers hung from the ceiling, which was very high and sky blue with many small, round windows that allowed the sun to light the huge room very brightly. Red, black and white tiles were laid in intricate patterns on the floor, giving way to a huge circle of alternating red and black in the center of the room. Two levels of balconies lined the walls above the tapestries. Many humans were standing on them, looking down at Shahly and Arden.

Many differently clad humans, some with buckets, rags, or other items, milled around the room, bowing to the Prince as they saw him.

The Prince stopped near the center of the room and allowed Shahly to study it a bit longer before saying, "Welcome to my home."

"This is beautiful," she breathed, her eyes still sweeping the spectacular room.

Arden asked, "Would you like to walk on your own now, or may I carry you a while longer?"

A smile touched her lips and she looked to him. "Perhaps you should put me down. I would not want you to hurt yourself carrying me."

He playfully raised her up as if to toss her in the air. "Oh, you aren't so heavy."

She raised her brow. "I used to be much heavier."

He laughed and tossed her again. "Sure you were. I suppose the next thing you'll try to tell me is that you eat like a horse."

Shahly rolled her eyes away. "Well…"

The Prince laughed and gently set her on the floor.

The tile she stood on was very cold and she cringed as her feet touched it, but she stood on her own, still clinging to the Prince's arm. Somehow, he made her feel just a little safer in this strange world.

One of the doors ahead of them closed, its sound bouncing off of the walls and ceiling all around in ever decreasing volumes until it faded to nothing. Activity in the huge room stopped and all of the humans faced the tall female who strode toward Shahly and the Prince, bowing their heads as they saw her.

Her footsteps sounded like miniature hooves, strangely two clops per step. The tall human's frame was clad in a red covering that was trimmed in black and gracefully swept the floor as she walked. Her black mane was pulled tightly to the back of her head and restrained in a long braid which was carried over one shoulder. Her face was thin and lightly painted red at the cheeks, darker over her eyes where a darker purple set off the green of her eyes. She seemed to squint as her eyes found Shahly, but not from the light in the room. A gold chain hung around her neck, suspending a sparkling medallion of gold and clear crystals.

Shahly glanced at the Prince, who bowed his head to the approaching female as she neared. Clearly, this woman was an important member of the human's herd, so Shahly nodded once to her as she would when greeting a herd elder.

The tall woman regarded her almost coldly for a second, then looked to the Prince and said in a deep, female voice, "I see you have found yet another one, Prince Arden."

The Prince met Shahly's eyes, smiling proudly. "That I have, Mother. The prettiest yet."

Shahly's cheeks felt warm again and she smiled, turning her eyes down.

The Queen nodded. "And I am sure you have seen enough of her to know that for certain."

"That I have," he answered.

Shahly looked back to the tall female, meeting her eyes. Something felt wrong.

The Queen stared at her for a second longer, then asked, "Where did you find this one?"

Prince Arden answered, "Would you believe a river current brought her to me while I was chasing a unicorn?"

A second more of that cold stare, then the Queen nodded. "Yes, somehow I could."

"Prince Arden," a younger female's voice summoned from behind. Shahly looked behind her as the Prince did.

The female who approached was a very attractive, black haired girl of Shahly's height, darkly complexioned with her face painted much as the Queen's was. Her hair was restrained behind her, flowing down her back in even locks. She wore a long, ruffled covering, red with white and silver trim which fit tightly around her waist and complemented a generous bust line, revealing much of it.

As she reached them, she curtsied low to the Queen and bowed her head, greeting, "Your Royal Grace." Then she stood and bowed her head to the Prince. "Your highness."

He offered her a nod, saying, "Nillerra."

Nillerra smiled, looking into his eyes as she slowly, gracefully glided toward him, angling herself between Arden and Shahly, and said in a sweet, girlish voice, "I have been waiting for your return all morning." She gingerly placed her hand on his arm, her brow raising slightly to show concern. "You said you would be back by high sun. I was worried something terrible may have happened."

He smiled and patted her hand. "Your concern is appreciated, as always."

She looked back at Shahly looking her over with scrutinizing eyes, and said with no kindness in her voice, "Who is that?"

Arden took Shahly's hand and pulled her to him, grasping her shoulder as he introduced her. "Nillerra, I would like you to meet Shahly."

Shahly smiled and offered, "Hello."

The black haired girl was clearly displeased and just stared for a moment. The look in her eyes told Shahly that the black haired girl felt threatened by her presence.

With tight lips, Nillerra finally looked to the Prince, making no secret of her disapproval as she spitefully asked, "Another one?"

"Yes," he confirmed sternly.

Nillerra glanced at Shahly again, then looked up to the Prince with childlike hopefulness on her features. "The moon is full tonight." Something much more experienced replaced the innocence on her face and in her nearly black eyes.

To Shahly, the pheromones Nillerra was broadcasting were almost pungent with the smell of her perfume, which was itself a strange but sweet odor.

Nillerra's voice was much more seductive as she told Arden, "I had hoped we could take a walk this evening. I love walking with you at night and I always enjoy your company."

Shahly heard the Queen vent a deep breath and glanced back to see her shaking her head.

Arden smiled. "Another time, perhaps."

Nillerra's lips tightened. Arden's response had clearly angered her.

With a somewhat forced yet pleasant smile, Nillerra bowed her head to the Prince and acknowledged, "As you wish, your Highness." She then turned almost malicious eyes on Shahly and said, "Nice dress."

Not recognizing the tone, Shahly smiled and replied, "Thank you, but it is really Arden's cape."

Nillerra's neck drew taut. She stiffly turned to the Queen and curtsied to her, strain in her voice as she said, "By your leave, your Grace?"

The Queen nodded to her, responding, "Of course, child."

The black haired girl turned and stormed away.

Watching Nillerra as she disappeared through one of the doorways, Arden raised his brow and observed, "Well. She seems a bit irked."

"I cannot imagine why," the Queen said dryly.

Shahly had never been disliked before. She had been stalked by forest predators, pursued by humans and that giant scorpion. Then there was her run-in with the dragon. But none of them just disliked her. She looked back to the Queen, whose eyes were difficult to read at best, though she still got the impression the Queen disapproved of her as well. Arden and the other male humans all seemed to like her. Perhaps such rivalries among females were common in humans.

As Shahly pondered this latest curiosity, Arden turned to the Queen and said, "I would like Shahly to dine with us this evening."

The Queen nodded, confirming, "Of course you would." Her eyes narrowed slightly as she stepped toward Shahly.

Shahly cringed as the Queen reached for her, but she did not retreat, and she was somewhat relieved when the Queen reached into the cape at her chest and took the dragon's amulet gingerly in her fingers.

The Queen examined it intently, then turned those dark eyes on Shahly's.

Reasoning that this ritual must be the way human females bond, Shahly took the Queen's necklace in the same way, looked it over, then looked up to her and smiled, innocently saying, "Pretty."

The Queen turned less than pleased eyes on her son.

Arden swallowed hard and took Shahly's hand from his mother, backing away with her. "Uh, perhaps we should get her ready for dinner."

The Queen nodded, looking Shahly up and down again. "Yes, Prince Arden. Perhaps you should." She then turned and strode gracefully toward the door she had emerged from.

Shahly watched after her nervously, sensing something very cold about her. Two less than successful encounters with human females, both of whom seemed to consider her a threat somehow, even the matriarch. She decided right then and there to avoid human females in the future, and find Vinton and this Falloah as soon as possible.

"This way, Shahly," Arden said as he turned her and led her toward one of the doorways.

She looked up to him, asking, "Where are we going?"

"To find you something to wear," he replied. "You must be freezing."

"I am a little cold."

"Well, we can't have you getting sick your first day in the castle, now can we?" He ran his hand up and down her arm a few times. "That and you need some nice things to wear."

She smiled and leaned into him, softly saying, "You are so kind."

He smiled and held her more tightly to him.

They ascended a flight of stairs, then walked slowly down a seemingly endless, lavishly decorated corridor which was flanked by colorful tapestries and paintings on the walls and had a plush carpet on the floor, then up still more stairs to a place that was not as well decorated, not as colorful. The stone walls had few tapestries, few decorations, and were illuminated by metal lamps which hung on the walls every five or six paces.

Shahly walked with the Prince in silence for a time, then turned her eyes up to him and said, "Arden."

He looked down at her and smiled. "Yes, Forest Blossom?"

"Where are we going?"

He looked ahead again. "We are going to see Ihzell, the castle steward."

Shahly nodded and turned her eyes ahead, wondering what a castle steward was.

They approached one of the doors and Arden pulled down the latch, pushed it and peered in, asking, "Everyone decent?"

"Prince Arden!" a woman's voice enthusiastically greeted from the other side.

Shahly turned her eyes down and groaned, "Not another mare."

As the Prince pulled her by the hand through the doorway, Shahly looked up and saw a tall, pleasant looking woman who was rather plump and wearing a heavy blue dress with long sleeves and a white, pocketed apron. Graying red hair was worn in a bun behind her head as green eyes looked to the Prince. "I haven't seen you all day. What have you—Gadzooks!" she suddenly declared as she saw Shahly.

Arden smiled. "Ihzell, this is Shahly. I realize this is short notice but I—"

The steward rushed toward them and took Shahly's hand, pulling her into the room. "My goodness, child. You can't go running around the castle half naked! You'll catch your death of chill. Come with me."

Shahly looked back to the Prince as she was pulled into the sewing room.

Arden followed. "Uh, I was wondering if you could—"

"That cloak does nothing for you," the steward raved. "Arden, this must have been your doing."

"Well, it *is* my cloak. Ihzell, can you—"

"You call yourself a gentleman," the woman scolded. "You could at least have allowed her to bring some of her own things to the castle with her!"

"She didn't have any," the Prince defended. "That is why I brought her to you. She will be joining me for dinner tonight and will need a gown."

The steward turned exasperated eyes on him. "Another one?"

He looked up and sighed, "Yes, another one."

Ihzell shook her head and began unbuttoning the cape Shahly wore, then stopped and turned her eyes back on the Prince. "Do you mind?"

Shahly watched him roll his eyes and turn around and Ihzell removed the cape from her. A second later it flew across the room and hit the Prince, wrapping around his head.

"Here you go, dear," Ihzell said, helping Shahly into a thin white robe. "This should keep you warm until we can get a wardrobe started for you." She took Shahly's hands and shook her head. "Oh, you are freezing."

Arden folded his cape over his arm and turned around. "Do you think you can fit her by this evening?"

"Not to worry, Highness," the steward assured. "She will be a pleasure to work with. You just leave everything to me and she will be stunning by dinner time."

"You have my every confidence, Ihzell."

"I know I do," the steward sighed, then backed away from Shahly, stroking her chin as she looked her subject over intently. "Now, lets see. What color? The style will be easy. Several to choose from, but it must compliment your figure." She laughed to herself. "What am I saying? You would look smashing in burlap. Yellow? No, something to make your golden hair stand out." She reached to Shahly and took a handful of her hair. "We also need to do something with it." She turned to an open doorway and roared, "Engash!"

Shahly flinched. This woman had the voice of a dragon!

A younger woman with light brown hair and dressed much as the steward was entered from the doorway and looked to Ihzell, responding, "Yes, Miss?"

"Get the girls together," the steward ordered. "We have only two hours to get this young lady ready to dine with his Highness."

Engash looked to the Prince and curtsied, then asked, "Another one, Highness?"

His lips tightened and he turned his eyes up.

"Now!" the steward ordered.

The younger woman looked to Shahly, smiled, and nodded, saying, "At once, Miss." She then turned and hurried out of the room.

Ihzell turned back to Shahly and suggested, "Let's go look at some dresses."

Shahly hesitantly nodded.

The steward looked to Arden. "No princely duties to perform?"

He raised his brow and nodded. "I suppose there are a few things I could take care of. I'll just take my leave of you ladies." He turned slowly toward the door.

Leave?

Shahly spun toward him, feeling near panic as she barked, "Arden!"

The Prince turned back, his eyes finding hers instantly.

He was the only human she felt comfortable with and the thought of him out of eyeshot was somehow terrifying. She managed enough breath to ask, "Aren't you going to stay with me?"

He smiled and walked to her, taking her hands. "Relax, Shahly. Ihzell will take good care of you."

She glanced into the smiling face of the steward, then looked down and nodded.

He reached to her face and gently raised her chin with his fingers, meeting her eyes. "You will be fine, Forest Blossom. We just want you to be ready when you meet me for dinner this evening."

She nodded, trying to resist the tears which already blurred her vision.

When he bent to touch his lips to her forehead, the steward pulled her away from behind and informed, "We'll make certain she is, your Highness. Don't let us delay you further."

Ihzell took Shahly under her arm and led her to the door the other woman had emerged from. "Don't you worry about a thing, child. We will have you ready to awe everyone in the dining hall before you know it.

Shahly glanced back as the Prince closed the door behind him, then looked into the room she was led into.

It was larger than she had anticipated with high tables, several chairs and two dressers with mirrors distributed around the room. Many bolts of brightly colored fabric were everywhere, as were the tools of a seamstress. In the middle of the room there was a small square stage covered with a white cloth. Metal bodied lamps with clear, black stained chimneys were abundant on the walls and sitting on several of the work tables, though most of the room's illumination came from the three huge windows.

The steward led Shahly to one of the dressers, pulled the chair out and invited, "Have a seat, dear."

Shahly looked the chair over for a moment, then looked to the steward and asked, "Huh?"

Ihzell took her firmly by the shoulders from behind, maneuvered her around the chair and pulled her back, saying, "Sit."

Shahly fell back and was sitting perfectly in the chair before she realized what had happened. The mirror was directly in front of her and she just stared at her reflection for a time, raising a hand to her face as if to be certain of what she saw. Her own brown eyes looked back at her and golden locks of hair framed the fair, smooth skin of her face.

Ihzell took a brush from the dresser and began running it through Shahly's hair. "So," she began, "where were you when the Prince found you? And why were you not wearing anything?"

Shahly's eyes darted to the steward's reflection, then back to her own as she answered, "He found me in the river."

"Oh, my," the steward exclaimed. "You weren't swimming in that freezing water, were you?"

"No," Shahly answered straightly. "I was drowning." The brush encountered resistance and her head was jerked back a little.

Ihzell shook her head. "My goodness, child. How did you end up in the river? You could catch your death this time of year."

"Someone was chasing me."

"Poor dear. The forest is thick with bandits these days. You should never travel out there alone. There is no telling what could happen, what with all the bandits, wolves and forest cats out there."

Shahly's head was jerked back again and she winced as her hair was tugged. "I usually have little problem avoiding them."

Ihzell held a handful of Shahly's hair as she stroked it rapidly with the brush. "I've heard that before, child, but it only takes once. They didn't catch you, did they?"

This human was full of questions! Shahly simply answered, "Not exactly."

The brush finally went through Shahly's hair easily, though Ihzell continued to run it through for some reason and asked, "So what do you think of His Highness?"

Shahly pondered for a second, then, "Whose highness?"

Ihzell stopped brushing and leaned her forearms on Shahly's shoulders, meeting her eyes in the mirror. "Prince Arden."

"Oh, Arden." Shahly glanced away, feeling something awkward within her. "He is very sweet."

The steward smiled. "And quite the looker, too."

Shahly nodded. "He does seem to look at me a lot."

Ihzell pursed her lips, then, "No, dear. I mean he is an attractive young man."

Shahly nodded again. "Yes. He is very much so." These people had a strange way of talking.

The steward began running the brush through Shahly's hair again, slowly, her eyes trained on it. "So what brought you to Red Stone Castle?"

"Arden's horse," Shahly replied.

Ihzell stopped brushing and just stared down at Shahly's hair for a moment, then looked at her reflection in the mirror. "You haven't been around other people much, have you?"

Not if you mean humans, Shahly thought, then she shook her head.

The steward smiled patiently and patted Shahly's shoulder, saying, "We have a lot of work to do, child."

⚜

The steward and her helpers labored very fast, yet progress seemed slow to Shahly, especially since her part entailed standing on the small stage with her arms out while the four women made subtle adjustments to the gown she wore. This was accompanied by the endless tutoring in how to conduct herself in the presence of the Queen and Prince, especially in front of others.

Ihzell stepped back, looking her up and down repeatedly as she asked, "How does it wear?"

Shahly shifted her shoulders. "It's kind of heavy and very tight around my middle."

"It's supposed to fit you tightly around the waist, dear," the steward confirmed. "Just don't fidget much. You'll get used to it. And remember not to eat too much."

Shahly nodded and looked down to the full skirt which covered her legs, a shimmering white material striped with a silver lace. All of the material she wore beneath it made it bell out, and very heavy.

Ihzell tugged on Shahly's hand and ordered, "Come to the mirror, dear. See how it looks on you."

With her skirts shuffling loudly, Shahly hopped down from the small stage and followed the steward to a large, full length mirror across the room, staring awestruck at her reflection. The dress *was* very tight around her waist. The neckline was very low and revealed much of her chest, leaving the dragon's amulet dangling in plain view. It had no sleeves, but was supported by a broad strap that was suspended by large, puffy pieces over her shoulders. The gown seemed to change her shape somewhat, enhancing certain areas of her body while strategically concealing others. Her hair was restrained behind her with a silver tiara, worn crown-like above her forehead.

Shahly stared for a moment, then smiled and said, "It is beautiful!"

Ihzell also smiled and patted Shahly's back. "In this case I'm afraid it's the woman who makes the gown. Now, do you remember what to do when you meet the Queen?"

Tight lipped, Shahly looked down and replied, "I curtsy and bow my head and wait for her to acknowledge me before I stand, then I stand up straight and don't speak until she does."

"Very good," the steward commended. "We'll keep you out of the dungeon yet."

Another of the steward's helpers entered and frantically reported, "They are sitting down to dine!"

At that point Ihzell became very excited, almost frantic. "Oh, I lost track of time again. Come on, dear. Let's get you downstairs." She took Shahly's hand and dragged her toward the door.

Shahly kept the steward's pace with some difficulty as they raced down corridors and stairways, finally ending up at a set of double doors flanked by two guards.

As they reached the doors, Ihzell turned and took Shahly's shoulders, looking her over once more, then asked, "Do you remember everything you are supposed to?"

Shahly nodded. "I think so."

Ihzell's eyes widened. "I don't want to hear *think*, Shahly. Do you remember?"

Hesitantly, Shahly nodded.

"Good," the steward commended, then turned to the guards and nodded to them.

They reached to the handles and pushed the doors open.

Shahly strode past the threshold and stopped, suddenly feeling overwhelmed as she looked into the large room.

A very long table covered with a white cloth sat in the center of a huge room which was illuminated by three chandeliers that hung directly above from the high vaulted ceiling. Two smaller tables sat at each side of the large one, also covered with white cloths.

Five other young women, all dressed in evening gowns of various colors and designs, were already seated at the table and all staring at her, though she barely noticed. Her eyes had found the Queen's, and the Queen's had found hers.

Once again, Shahly felt an uneasy quake in the pit of her stomach.

The Queen's gaze was locked on her in an unblinking, expressionless stare.

A hush fell over the room.

Very, very awkward. Shahly glanced around at the others in the room. Her eyes finally found Prince Arden, who was standing beside the Queen's chair, and just seeing him washed away much of her anxiety. Something seemed wrong with him, though, as he only stared at her like a deer staring down a wolf.

Shahly smiled and strode gracefully into the dining hall, now oblivious to all but Arden. Walking as Ihzell had instructed, she approached the Queen's chair and stopped about two paces away, greeting the Queen with a perfect curtsy and bowed head.

"Rise, child," the Queen commanded.

Shahly stood straight up, demonstrating perfect posture, smiled at the Queen, then turned and curtsied to the Prince, raising her eyes to him.

For long, uncomfortable seconds, he just stared at her.

Shahly waited a few seconds more, then whispered, "You are supposed to nod to me to let me know I'm supposed to stand."

Arden drew a deep breath. "Oh, yes. Of course." He finally nodded to her.

Shahly stood and looked back to the Queen.

Her eyes were on the Prince and she was shaking her head, smiling slightly, then she looked to Shahly and said, "You look stunning, dear. You compliment the gown you wear."

"Thank you, my Queen" Shahly responded softly, smiling.

"Clearly Ihzell's work," the Queen continued. "How does it wear, dear?"

"Very tightly around my waist and hips," Shahly replied, "but it is supposed to."

Still wearing a pleasant smile, the Queen turned those eyes on her son once again.

Arden cleared his throat and offered his arm to Shahly. "May I escort you to your seat?"

Unsure what to do, Shahly looked down at his arm, then back into his eyes. Ihzell had not covered this. In the forest, hesitation could mean death. Here, it felt much the same. Slowly, she reached up and grasped his hand with her own.

He smiled.

Yes! This human stuff was not so difficult. Confidently, she walked toward the other end of the table with him, grasping his hand just a little tighter.

They stopped at a chair near the end of the table and Arden pulled it out a little for her. Remembering Ihzell's instructions, Shahly brushed her skirts aside and gently settled herself into the chair, then looked ahead of her and froze as her eyes found the black haired girl she had encountered earlier.

Nillerra stared coldly back, making no secret of her disapproval of Shahly's presence.

Shahly tried to offer her a friendly smile, but the black haired girl just looked away. Glancing around, Shahly noticed several of the young women staring at her, but none with the malicious look Nillerra had given her.

The silence in the room was almost deafening, broken only by muffled noises behind the door which was across the room, behind the Queen. After a few agonizing moments, this door opened and many women in white filed out, each carrying a platter which was laden with crystal bowls or some other thing Shahly did not understand.

One of the women set a bowl before Shahly, then the next girl down the table.

Shahly looked into the bowl and raised her brow. It was filled with chunks of apples, grapes, and shreds of carrots, all bathed in a sugary syrup that made it smell wonderful. She loved apples, but restrained herself enough to recall her instructions from the steward.

She scanned her eating ware and found the little spoon on the far right, picked it up as instructed and worked with it for several seconds until it felt comfortable in her hand, then daintily scooped a rather large portion into the spoon and managed to get it to her mouth without spilling any. Ihzell had told her to bring the food to her, not go to the food, and this seemed to work out nicely. As she chewed, the fruit salad only seemed to get sweeter. It was wonderful!

She went for another spoonful, then froze as she noticed many eyes on her, and met the Queen's.

The queen looked anything but pleased.

Shahly swallowed her salad and smiled at her. "It is very good, my Queen. Go ahead and try it."

The Queen looked down to her salad, picked up a spoon and turned her eyes back to Shahly, an artificial smile on her lips as she said, "Thank you so much, dear."

Shahly nodded to her and took another bite.

Everyone else started eating right after the Queen did.

Slowly, the tension in the room diminished and the other girls began casually chatting among themselves. Even Nillerra seemed more docile and conversed with the dark haired girl in the blue dress beside her.

No one seemed interested in talking with Shahly, and for a moment she felt a little hurt, then she made herself remember why she was at the castle. While she had to fit in with these strange creatures, she still had to formulate a plan to get to this Falloah and free Vinton. Three days was not a long time.

"Where did you say you are from, Shahly?" the Prince asked.

Shahly froze with a mouthful of fruit salad and slowly turned her eyes to him. All other conversation stopped and Shahly felt many eyes on her. She glanced around, somehow managed to swallow, and answered, "I come from the Southlands."

Brows went up and people nodded their approval, and Shahly heard someone mention one of the rich kingdoms of the South.

Nillerra raised her chin slightly, almost glaring at Shahly. "Really. Which kingdom?"

Shahly met her eyes nervously, then looked down to her bowl, answering, "I don't come from a kingdom. I come from the forest."

The black haired girl nodded. "The forest. You live in the woods with the animals."

Shahly felt herself becoming anxious again and did not know what to say. She knew she had to fit in, yet somehow felt more of a need to do so than her purpose for being at the castle. After a long moment she looked to Arden and asked, "There is nothing wrong with that, is there?"

The Prince took the time to finish chewing his fruit salad, then leaned back in his chair and seemed to stare at nothing in the center of the long table. "I don't see anything wrong with it, getting close to nature and all that. Quite the contrary. Most of us don't take the time to do such things." He turned his eyes on Nillerra. "Too many of us are so consumed with being prim and proper that we forget about our little neighbors who live among the trees."

The black haired girl looked away from him.

Shahly was nudged from the other side and looked to the attractive young blond woman in the blue dress who sat beside her.

The other girl leaned to her and whispered, "Do not let what she says get to you. I don't come from a kingdom, either."

"Still," Nillerra sighed as she picked at her fruit salad with her spoon, her eyes locked on it. "A cottage in the woods does not sound very attractive, or very safe."

Shahly shrugged, realizing that the black haired girl just might not understand. "It is as safe as anywhere else, if you know the secrets of the forest."

With a quick glance at the Prince, Nillerra scooped up a spoonful of her salad and looked to Shahly. "Secrets like how to avoid being eaten alive by Dreads or wolves, or how to avoid bandits and barbarians?"

Shahly nodded, finally feeling as if she was getting through to the black haired girl.

"And I suppose you know what to eat out there? Like twigs and worms?" Nillerra slipped her spoonful of salad into her mouth.

Shahly shrugged. "I cannot say I've ever eaten worms, but if you like eating those things I guess you can."

The other girls laughed softly.

Arden smiled and took a bite of his salad.

Nillerra raised her chin somewhat, then took a deep breath and looked back down to her bowl. "It must have been hard out there in the wilderness, fending for yourself." She turned malicious eyes on Shahly. "Living like an animal."

"Oh, no," Shahly corrected. "It is a wonderful life, though it can be challenging at times, especially in winter when food is not easy to find. It is nothing like living here in the palace with everything brought to you."

Arden dropped his spoon into his bowl with a loud clank and covered his mouth with his napkin. He seemed to want no one to know he was smiling, but his eyes gave him away.

The girls at the table were not so subtle.

Nillerra just stared at Shahly for a moment, then looked back down to her salad and dipped her spoon back into it.

"Tell me," the Queen started.

Silence swept through the dining hall and everyone looked down to the Queen.

When Shahly looked, she found the Queen's eyes on her.

The Queen set her spoon down and folded her hands on the table, casually asking, "What brought you to the Northlands, dear?"

All attention was focused on Shahly.

She answered hesitantly. "I have heard about the beautiful forests and castles here."

The Queen nodded. "I see. Did you know of Prince Arden's search for a bride?"

Shahly nodded. "I was told about his search. Has he found one, yet?"

Several of the girls laughed under their breath.

Smiling, the Queen glanced at Arden and answered, "He has a few in mind. Do you find the beauty here that you were told of?"

Feeling some of the tension drain away, Shahly smiled and answered, "Yes, my Queen. Your home is very beautiful."

The blond haired girl sitting next to Shahly took her arm and anxiously said, "I have always heard there are unicorns in the forests of the Southlands. Have you ever seen one?"

Shahly nodded and answered, "I have seen many of them."

Whispers of excitement swept through the young women.

Glancing at the Queen, Shahly saw her quickly look away, clearly disturbed by the talk of unicorns. This was a curiosity, seeing as how everyone else was so excited about them.

Nillerra rested her chin in her palm, staring at Shahly with a disbelieving look. "You have actually seen unicorns?"

Shahly nodded to her.

The blond girl looked to Shahly with fascination in her eyes. "Have you ever had one approach you?"

"Many times," Shahly answered.

"What's it like?" another girl sitting down from Nillerra asked.

"I've always heard it is a magical experience," a red haired young woman in a yellow dress said. "They say once you have been touched by a unicorn, your life will be changed forever."

"That's true," the brown haired girl sitting two chairs down from Shahly declared. "A couple of seasons ago my cousin was approached near Caipiervell. I think she was about fourteen at the time. Anyway, right after that she seemed... Well, she was different. She seemed much happier and more at peace with herself."

Shahly took a big mouthful of her fruit salad as she listened intently and very amused at the stories and tales of her kind. Much of what they were saying was laughably inaccurate, but Shahly felt no need to disillusion these poor people. Besides, they were too much fun to listen to.

The brown haired girl in the bright red and white dress sitting beside Nillerra leaned toward them. "I heard if you see a unicorn your first child will be a prince."

"I saw one today," the blond haired girl beside Shahly cut in, looking directly at Prince Arden. "She was magnificent."

The brown haired girl rolled her eyes. "Audrell, we've been over this. It was not a unicorn."

"I'm sure it was," the blond haired girl defended.

"It couldn't have been," the brown haired girl countered. "It was swimming. Unicorns don't swim." She looked to Shahly. "Do they?"

Shahly had a mouthful of salad and just looked at her and nodded. This sparked fresh excitement.

"Unicorns will not even approach you if you aren't a virgin, will they?" the red haired girl asked.

A hush fell over the room and all eyes were trained on Shahly again. This made her feel uncomfortable, but she maintained her bearing, swallowed her salad and answered straightly, "It helps to be, but what is most important is that you be pure of heart."

Nillerra nodded. "You say that like you actually know for certain."

"I do," Shahly assured.

"What did your unicorn look like?" the Prince asked.

Shahly looked timidly to him, unsure of how to answer, but finally replied, "I've been approached by many of them."

"Of course you have," Nillerra chided. "I suppose you *don't* have to be a virgin, then."

Shahly looked to her, feeling somewhat shocked at such an accusation. "I am a virgin. Everyone without a mate should be. Aren't you?"

Nillerra's neck straightened and she almost gasped aloud. She met Prince Arden's eyes briefly, then looked back to her bowl.

Clearly, she was not a virgin, and this made Shahly feel that much more awkward.

The blond girl beside Shahly nudged her, then nodded, a subtle smile on her lips.

Talk of unicorns resumed as the servants emerged again and began placing silver goblets before everyone at the table. Others filled the goblets with what looked like the juice from fruit, though it smelled a little odd.

"Try the wine, Shahly," the Prince said.

She glanced at him, then picked up her goblet, sniffed the liquid within and took a sip. It was definitely grape, very sweet, yet there was a sharp taste she did not recognize. Still, it tasted very good and she took another sip.

"What do you think?" Arden asked.

She nodded to him and drank more.

Discussion of unicorns dominated the conversation and Shahly listened intently to the humans' tales of her kind, tempted to clear up some to their unfortunate misinformation, but too amused by them to speak up.

The red haired girl shook her head, looking impatiently at the blond girl sitting next to Shahly. "That is silly, Audrell."

"Well, it's true," the blond girl defended. "The white unicorns are the purest of all animals." She looked to Shahly and almost demanded, "Aren't they?"

Shahly smiled slightly and turned her eyes down. "I like to think so."

"See?" Audrell pressed.

Shahly finished off her wine and a servant immediately refilled her goblet, then turned to fill the next. She took a big gulp of her wine, then noticed Arden watching her.

"I trust you like the wine?" he asked.

She nodded. "Yes. It tastes very sweet."

He smiled. "I'm glad you like it. I thought you might prefer it to a dry wine."

Shahly looked into her goblet, then turned her eyes to the Prince and asked, "Dry?"

Noticing everyone looking toward the door behind the Queen, Shahly also looked and saw a human pushing a cart before him. On top of the cart, nestled among orange and brown roots and many green things was a juvenile pig. Its eyes were closed and seemed empty behind its eyelids. It was motionless, not breathing, and was an unusual red. Steam or smoke rose from the vegetation around it, and from the pig itself.

It was dead!

The human pushed it to the Queen, then stabbed a fork into its body and began cutting its flesh away with a large knife.

Shahly gasped loudly, then tore her eyes away and turned away from the grotesque sight, clamping a hand over her mouth.

Arden grasped her shoulder and asked, "Shahly? What is it?"

Shahly's stomach churned sourly within her and she was barely able to breathe. Her eyes found the Prince's, then she closed them to try and collect herself, though the vision of the pig would not leave her mind.

"Shahly?" Arden's voice beckoned again.

She finally turned her eyes to his, feeling some comfort there, and nodded to him, assuring, "I'll be fine."

"What happened?" he asked softly.

Shahly managed a deep breath and replied, "I am just unaccustomed to seeing animals that way."

"You don't have to eat any," he assured. "We could get you something else."

Shahly's eyes widened. "Eat it?" She suddenly felt a little more nauseous and turned her eyes down.

"You don't eat meat?" he asked.

She nodded.

"How perfectly charming," Nillerra chided.

Venting a breath through pursed lips, Shahly looked to the Prince and offered a strained smile, assuring, "I'll be fine."

"Would you like to lie down for a while?" he asked, his voice soft and sympathetic.

She just stared into his eyes for a time, then nodded.

He took her hands and pulled her to her feet.

Balance eluded her and she lurched toward him, barely keeping her feet under her. She shook her head and admitted, "I feel dizzy."

"Would you like more wine?" Nillerra asked dryly.

Arden shot a very displeased glance at the black haired girl, then looked down the table to the Queen and asked, "By your leave?" Then he nodded and took Shahly under his arm. "Come on. Let's get you to bed."

Strange emotions crept into Shahly's mind, emotions not her own. They felt like anger, sadness, and loss. Somehow they were a mix of many things she knew, yet were mated as one emotion, and came from many different minds. Her unicorn insight seemed stronger within her, yet remained elusive.

She looked up to the Prince's face as he led her from the dining hall, still unable to accurately read what she felt from him, though he was clearly attracted to her. This was certain.

He led her slowly through the castle, one arm around her, his hand grasping her arm. His other hand gently held hers.

Somehow, their journey seemed endless, but before long they turned toward a door and Arden pushed it open.

Inside, three humans were still hard at work preparing the spacious room, tending the little things a young woman would need. The curtains and bedspread were pink, as was the canopy over the bed and the huge rug on the floor beside it. Oil lamps lit the room from the tables flanking the bed, the dresser across the room from the bed, and the water lavatory table.

Arden scanned the room and the activity within, then loudly cleared his throat and asked, "Are you about finished?"

The young women within spun toward him and bowed.

Ihzell came from behind, pushing past him as she informed, "No, we are not. Why are you finished eating so soon?" She had a long pink cloth draped over her arm which she laid on the bed as she reached it.

The Prince gently caressed Shahly's shoulders. "Shahly is not feeling well."

Ihzell turned and strode to her, taking her hands. "Are you ill?" She smiled. "I know. You are in a strange place and you have every right to be uneasy." She gently patted Shahly's cheek and assured, "Not to worry. I will take good care of you."

Shahly smiled back and offered, "Thank you." She scanned the room again and declared, "This is pretty."

Ihzell patted her shoulder. "You are such a sweetheart. I should have it finished soon, but you look as if you want to rest."

"Finished?" Shahly asked.

"Of course." The steward sounded exasperated. "There will be tapestries on the walls and more rugs. This floor is going to be freezing in the morning." She glanced around. "Oh, yes. Flowers. I should already have had them here."

"It's all right," Shahly assured. "I'm really not all that hungry, anyway."

Arden cleared his throat softly, sounding as if he was trying to disguise a laugh, then he looked to the steward and said, "Everything is fine, Ihzell. I'm not even sure how you do it on such short notice."

"I am glad you think I can work miracles," she replied. "Heavens, I hope her nightgown fits."

"I won't need one," Shahly assured. "You said it is important to dress in public."

The steward raised her brow. "I don't know about the forest, Shahly, but here at Red Stone you wear a nightgown."

Shahly shrugged. "Well who is going to see me in here?"

Ihzell's eyes snapped to the Prince.

He drew back and raised a hand to his chest. "What are you implying?"

Feeling very light-headed, Shahly raised a hand to her eyes and drew a deep breath, the words spoken by the Prince and steward echoing in her thoughts like a dream. She heard her name and slowly opened her eyes, looking to Ihzell, who looked back with concern in her features.

The steward shook her head. "You look exhausted, dear."

Shahly nodded. "I feel dizzy."

Ihzell looked to the Prince and asked, "Wine?"

He nodded.

She vented a deep breath and looked back to Shahly. "We need to talk. But let's get you ready for bed first." She looked to Arden. "If you wouldn't mind too terribly, your Highness."

He sighed, turning to look down into Shahly's eyes. "If I must. But leaving such stunning beauty for a second time will be no easy task." He raised her hand to his mouth and gently touched his lips to her knuckles, then smiled at her and said, "Good night, little Forest Blossom."

She smiled back. "Good night, Arden."

He was brutally pulled away from her by the steward who said as she drug him out the door, "Allow me to make the task of leaving a little easier. Good night, your Highness."

He blew Shahly a kiss.

She smiled at him.

Ihzell slammed the door in his face, then turned and walked to Shahly. "Now, let's get you ready for bed."

"Why does everyone keep calling Arden *Highness?*" Shahly asked.

Ihzell stopped right in front of her, staring at her with blank eyes, then patiently raised her eyebrows and answered, "That is his title, child."

Shahly waved her hands in front of her. "Wait, wait, wait. I'm getting confused. You said his title is Prince."

Ihzell took a deep breath. "All right. Once more. He is a prince, therefore he is to be addressed as *your Highness.*"

Shahly watched the steward stride toward the bed, then turned fully toward her and asked, "Why not just call him Arden? That is his name."

Ihzell took the nightgown from the bed and turned back to Shahly. "You ask a lot of questions."

"I'm curious," was Shahly's reply.

Laughing softly, the steward laid the gown over her shoulder and strode to Shahly, taking her shoulders as she advised, "You need to stay away from that wine. Come, come, now. Let's get you ready for bed."

A short time later, Shahly was changed and tucked into her huge bed, watching the steward scurry back and forth to complete little tasks.

Ihzell finally stopped near the foot of Shahly's bed and scanned the room once more, mumbling, "I suppose I can finish in the morning." She looked to Shahly. "You get some rest, dear. I'll be back in the morning to finish up and bring you something to wear."

Shahly glanced around. "Finish what? I don't see anything left to do."

The steward shook her head. "You are very sweet, but I see a hundred things at a glance."

"Well, you look very tired," Shahly observed. "Perhaps you need to sleep a while."

Ihzell smiled and strode to Shahly's bedside, kissed her forehead and patted her hand. "I'll be back in the morning with a few more gowns. Good night, Shahly."

Shahly smiled back and said, "Good night, Ihzell." She watched the steward make one last lap around the room to blow out the lamps on the end tables, dresser and lavatory, then smiled at her once more as she left the room.

She just stared at the door for a moment after, then looked to the window.

The curtains were a strange blue in the moonlight and puffed out as the evening breeze caught them.

She stared at them for a time, then laid the sheet and blankets back one by one and swung her feet to the thick fur rug which lay on the floor near the bed. Slowly, she strode to the window, soon feeling the cold stone floor beneath her feet.

She brushed the curtains aside and gingerly placed her hands on the wooden windowsill, staring up at the bright full moon, which shined blue in the night sky, a constant reminder of just how little time she had to complete her mission. Though inside the castle, she still felt an eternity away from her Vinton.

Taking a deep breath, she reached out into the night with her essence to search for her love. Human form was making this difficult. When she tried to reason out why, she realized it was her own inhibitions, not her physical form that stood in her way. With another deep breath, she closed her eyes and tried again.

An unknown time later she found him. Her elation was brief.

He was very sad and so alone. She could only sense hopelessness from him, an empty pain that numbed him. She tried to touch him, to contact him, but he could not hear or feel her.

She opened her eyes and looked down into the torch-lit courtyard below, a blooming garden paradise that made her long for the forest. Her vision was blurred by tears, her chest quaking as she breathed.

"No!" she ordered herself. "This will not do. I have to be strong." She looked back to the full moon and insisted, "I will be strong for you, Vinton. Just do not give up. I'm coming for you. I promise I will find you and we will go home and be together forever." She closed her eyes and bowed her head as more tears spilled forth. "I promise."

CHAPTER 5

Until recently, nightmares had been absent from Shahly's dreams.

Jolted from what had started to be a peaceful dream, Shahly sat straight up in her bed with a shriek, glancing around the room that the morning glow barely illuminated. In a moment, dream and reality separated completely and her heart slowed to normal.

She slipped from her bed and went to the window, staring at the pre-dawn glow on what horizon she could see past the kingdom's wall. Somewhere, her Vinton waited, empty and alone. Two more dawns were all she had left here, and time already felt short.

She heard activity outside her door and turned as it opened, seeing Ihzell and two of her helpers enter the room with a glowing lamp and armloads of dresses.

The steward turned back to the door and ordered, "Just be sure it is up here within the hour." She then closed the door with her foot, wheeled around and strode to the bed, her eyes locking on Shahly as she dropped her arm full of dresses. "Shahly, dear. So glad to see you are an early riser."

"I'm not usually," Shahly admitted.

Ihzell walked to her and took her hands, pulling her toward the bed. "Well, you don't have to be. Come, come, child. I want you to try on these dresses. We need to find out what works on you and what does not."

Shahly stopped where the steward directed her to and just watched the three women go about their tasks of separating dresses, lighting the lamps, making the bed and so on. They stayed so busy all of the time that Shahly felt a little more out of place. Wanting to be more involved, Shahly asked, "What do you want me to do?"

Ihzell looked up from the dresses she was sorting through and ordered, "You can get out of that nightgown. I have a robe here for you. Are you hungry?"

Shahly nodded.

"Engash will be here shortly with some breakfast for you," the steward assured. "Come, come. Out of that nightgown. We have a lot of work to do."

Shahly sighed as she began to struggle from her soft pink nightgown. Truly, this promised to be a long morning.

As expected, time seemed to move along at a snail's pace and Shahly found herself standing in the middle of the three women once again with her arms extended as minor adjustments were made to the white dress she wore. This one was not a full skirted formal but more of a spring dress with thin material that fit her tightly from her chest to her hips, conforming well to her body. It was full sleeved with lace around the cuffs, the deeply cut neck line and the bell of the skirt. Her hair was down and shimmering like gold in the morning sunlight.

One of the steward's assistants, a younger, dark haired girl of about Shahly's height, stood behind Shahly, brushing her golden locks with steady strokes, and finally said, "What I wouldn't give for hair like this."

"How about that fullness?" the other assistant, a red haired girl slightly older than the first replied. "That is not something we can do in the salon."

Shahly looked to her. "But you both have beautiful hair."

"It isn't blond," both assistants pointed out in one voice.

The girl behind Shahly stopped brushing and grasped her shoulder. "You are so lucky to have the Prince's eye."

Shahly's eyes widened. Surely that did not mean what it sounded like.

"Of course," the other added, "there are the other five."

"You mean the other four and Nillerra."

"Yeah. I thought Urcean and Namleuf were bad."

"They are bad."

"Well, you don't see them in bed with half of the palace guards, do you? I mean, they are tramps and all, but Nill—"

"That will do, ladies," Ihzell interrupted, a recognizable tone of warning in her voice.

"Sorry, Miss," they answered together, then the girl behind Shahly added, "But it is all true."

Ihzell tugged down one of Shahly's sleeves, then stepped back to examine her work. "I know it is, but it is not proper to speak of openly."

The girl with the brush stepped around Shahly, looking to the steward. "Then I suppose you are not interested in Nillerra's latest conquest?"

Ihzell glanced at her, then looked Shahly up and down again and said, "Later."

Shahly puzzled for a moment, then looked to the girl behind her and asked, "Her what?"

Someone knocked on the door and Ihzell instantly roared, "What is it?"

All four women were silent for a moment, waiting for some response.

The girl with the brush nudged Shahly and whispered, "I'll wager it's the Prince."

"Oh, I'm confident it is," the steward assured, then turned to the door and barked, "Answer or go away!"

Long seconds later, the door swung open and Prince Arden strode in, freezing as his eyes found Shahly. His black and red attire was very clean and perfectly pressed. All of the metal buttons and buckles shined like mirrors. The red and black cape he had used to cover Shahly the previous day hung from his shoulders, buttoned neatly at his chest.

Shahly smiled at him and offered, "Good morning, Arden." A nudge from Ihzell had her quickly correct, "I mean Highness."

The Prince slowly shook his head and managed, "You look absolutely stunning."

Shahly looked away, unable to keep herself from smiling even more.

Ihzell folded her arms and asked, "And what brings his Highness up this way so early?"

He looked to her, then straightened himself, tugging down on the front of his cape and answered, "I came to see if Maid Shahly would care to have breakfast with me."

"Oh, dear," the steward sighed. "I had Engash bring her something earlier. I apologize if I botched up any plans you may have made."

He shook his head. "Oh, no. No. That's fine." He raised his brow, his eyes on Shahly's. "Perhaps we can take a walk and I can show you around the castle."

The idea was delightful! This could make finding Vinton and this Falloah that much easier, that and she liked Prince Arden's company for some reason.

Shahly turned to Ihzell and asked, "May I?"

The steward smiled at her and shook her head. "I am not your queen or keeper, love. You just do as you wish."

Shahly threw her arms around Ihzell's neck, hugging her tightly as she said, "Thank you!" then she spun back to the Prince and eagerly said, "I would love to!"

"Shahly," Ihzell summoned.

Shahly turned back, seeing the steward holding a pair of white slippers before her, then she looked down to her bare feet and confessed, "I thought the floor felt a little cold." She took the slippers from Ihzell and sat on the edge of the bed, pulling them onto her feet as she had been shown, then sprang back up and almost danced to the Prince's side and wrapped her arms around one of his.

"You two behave yourselves," Ihzell called to them as they walked out the door.

Arden rolled his and answered, "Yes, Auntie Ihzell."

Shahly stayed close to the Prince as he led her downstairs and into some lavishly decorated halls. She held tightly onto his arm as she studied the many colorful tapestries which hung on the walls, tapestries which depicted various scenes of battle and building around the castle.

"Do you like them?" the Prince asked.

Shahly nodded. "They're pretty. What do they mean?"

He stopped and looked at a tapestry. "They are a pictorial chronicle of Red Stone Castle's history from its construction nearly to the present."

She glanced away and hesitantly asked, "Do they mention anything about unicorns?"

Arden smiled at her. "You really have a fascination with unicorns, don't you?"

She shrugged, looking back to the tapestry before her. "A lifelong interest."

"I can tell," he observed. "As you can see, unicorns are shown in many of them, mostly watching from the forest. It is said the unicorns used to have quite a fascination with the castle."

Shahly nodded. "We still do." Her heart jumped and she drew a deep breath. "I mean I've seen them watching human places before." She nervously looked up to him.

He eyed her almost suspiciously. "*We* still do?"

"Are these in order of when they happened?" Shahly asked suddenly, looking back to the tapestry.

He nodded. "Yes, they just happen to be."

"Where are the later ones?" she asked innocently.

"Ahead of us," he answered, then extended his hand down the corridor. "Shall we?"

As they slowly made their way down the gently turning hallway, Arden interpreted what the tapestries meant as they came across them.

Shahly stopped at one that showed a large black dragon swooping down on the castle, fire lancing down from his jaws. Much of the castle was in flames and people fled in terror. A faint violet glow enveloped the top of the highest tower. Somehow, she knew the dragon shown here was the black beast from the desert.

"Ah, yes," Arden declared. "This is one of my favorites. It shows the black dragon attacking the castle about three seasons ago. As you can see, he wreaked havoc here for some time. It seemed like we were always repairing the damage left from his visits."

"Why did he attack you?" Shahly asked. "Surely, a creature of that dragon's intelligence must have some kind of reason."

Arden shrugged. "I'm not sure. It started about three seasons ago, when I first came of age. That was about the time the Talisman was completed."

She looked over her shoulder at him. "Talisman?"

He nodded. "It is our defense against dragons, our *only* defense. Some say his ire was against our army. Many think he was looking to destroy the Talisman." He turned his eyes down. "And my mother insists he sent Falloah here to do just that."

Shahly's heart jumped. "Falloah?"

He smiled and looked into Shahly's eyes. "No one you should be concerned with."

"Tell me about her," Shahly insisted.

Arden raised his brow. "You mean you actually want to hear about my past loves?"

Past loves? Shahly thought, then said aloud, "Of course."

He smiled. "You are the first one to truly care."

Shahly turned fully to him and leaned her head, looking up at him attentively.

Arden took a deep breath, clearly uneasy about telling anyone of Falloah, but finally spoke. "She was the first woman to come to the castle as I came of age. She was strong and beautiful, and I was so taken by her. You see, I was not well acquainted with the ways of women at that time and I felt things for her I had never felt before." He looked away. "Naturally, Mother did not approve of her and seemed determined to drive a wedge between us. She finally had her arrested, something about trying to sabotage the Talisman or some nonsense of the like."

"Why would she want to do that?" Shahly asked softly.

Arden shrugged and shook his head. "I'm not convinced that she did. Of course, several guards did say they caught her in the tower that night, and one guard was found dead near the door to the tower." He shook his head. "I don't know. I suppose I just did not want to believe it."

Shahly nodded. "Do you love her?"

The Prince laughed under his breath. "I'm not sure." He looked to Shahly. "The way things are now, I am glad I could not finally choose her."

"Why?"

Arden stroked her cheek. "Because I would never have met you."

She smiled and turned her eyes down, then looked back up to him and asked, "What finally happened to her?"

He sighed. "She is being held in the dungeon."

Shahly raised her chin slightly. "Do you ever go and see her?"

Arden shook his head, softly answering, "No."

"Why not?"

He shrugged. "I don't know. What I feel for her confuses me, and I'm not entirely sure she feels anything for me."

Shahly's lips tightened and she took his hand in both of hers. "I wish I could help somehow."

He smiled at her, cupping her cheek in his hand. "You already have, Forest Blossom."

She closed her eyes and leaned her head into his gentle touch, feeling a warmth within her she had almost forgotten about.

Vinton!

She blinked her eyes back open and lifted her face from his hand, looking into his eyes. "There are many questions that need to be answered. I think we should go and see her."

Arden shook his head. "No. No one is allowed to see her, especially considering the circumstances."

"Because of the Talisman?" she asked.

"Because of what they say she was trying to do to it," was his answer.

Shahly glanced away, then turned her eyes back to his and asked, "What is this talisman, anyway? What does it do?"

"It defends us against dragons."

"You already told me that. How does it work?"

He raised his chin, staring down at her with a hint of suspicion in his eyes. "Why so interested in it?"

She shrugged. "Well, very little can hurt a dragon. Something that can defend you against them must be something that is very amazing."

Arden considered, then smiled at her and asked, "Would you like to see it?"

She nodded.

He turned and offered her his arm. "This way, Forest Blossom."

Shahly smiled at him as they slowly walked down the hallway. "Why do you call me that?"

He laughed softly. "Well, you remind me of a Forest Blossom, beautiful and innocent."

She turned her eyes ahead. "You remind me of a unicorn."

He looked down at her. "Oh? How so?"

She glanced up at him and answered, "You are kind, noble, you are honest and you have a good heart."

Arden grasped her hand, smiling at her. "I believe that is the sweetest compliment I have ever received, Shahly. Thank you. I would love to be your unicorn."

She smiled at him, then turned her eyes away. He was not her unicorn. Her unicorn, her stallion was a captive in his castle.

A truly frightening thought was when she realized she had to remind herself of her quest, Vinton's freedom, and that this human she had become so comfortable with was her enemy. Things no longer seemed as simple as they had a day ago.

The door to the Talisman tower was some distance away, at the very center of the castle, and Arden seemed to take his time as he led Shahly to it, telling her more of the castle's history, very little of which actually interested her.

A time later they reached the tower hall.

The base of the Talisman tower was independent of the rest of the castle from floor to ceiling. No other walls contacted it, giving one the impression it was at the center of a huge room. It seemed to grow out of the stone floor like a huge tree trunk and measured at least twenty paces across, meeting the ceiling of the chamber very cleanly and without apparent seams. No decorations adorned this chamber, which had three other corridors opening into it. It was well lit with many torches and lamps and a large number of guards slowly patrolled the halls nearby and the common area which surrounded the tower. All of the guards were heavily armed with sword or axe and wore polished plate steel over their arming tunics and trousers.

Two guards, the larger with graying hair and beard, stood at opposite sides of the single door into the tower itself.

As Shahly and Arden reached the door, the older guard stepped forward, snapping to attention, then reported, "I'm sorry, Highness. Her Majesty wants only herself and the Talisman keepers beyond this point."

Arden raised his chin. "Is that so? Do your orders also involve detaining your Prince?"

The guard stiffened. "No, Highness." He glanced at Shahly. "But she was very specific as to who should and should not enter."

Shahly felt very uneasy about continuing on this course. She gently placed a hand on the Prince's arm and softly said, "It is all right, Arden. We can—" She cut off as he patted her hand.

The Prince's stare was unyielding as he sternly informed, "I will take who I like where I like. Move aside."

The guard seemed unable to breathe well and Shahly could sense the conflict within him, but he finally answered, "Yes, Highness," as he backed away and allowed them to pass.

Arden pulled the door open and invited Shahly to enter.

She cringed slightly as she walked through the doorway, still feeling as if they should not go to this place against the wishes of the Queen.

They slowly ascended the stone and steel spiraling staircase that led to the top. Fewer lamps illuminated the tower inside, but there was plenty of light for them to see where they were going.

What felt to be about half way up, the staircase emptied into a small room where two more guards sat at a small table, occupying themselves with several multi-character cards. They looked directly to the Prince and his guest, appearing somewhat surprised to see them.

Slightly winded, the Prince looked down to Shahly and asked, "Do you need to rest?"

This level of exercise was minuscule to a unicorn, even a unicorn in human form. Shahly was barely winded, so she just smiled at him and shook her head.

Arden glanced at the guards, took Shahly's hand and led the way as they continued up.

The corridor that enclosed the stairs narrowed to half its former width and with fewer lamps was darker than the rest of the trek, then terminated at still another timber door that had a lamp hanging on it, the only source of light.

Arden pushed the door open and led the way into the sizeable room which contained the Talisman, a room that seemed unnaturally large for a tower of the width they had just ascended. Light was offered by the five tall windows that stood open around the circular room. No breeze was blowing and the air in the room was still and hot.

Shahly entered behind the Prince, then froze as her eyes found the beautiful, horribly macabre work in the center of the room.

Two thick timbers supported the ring of black iron which was a man's height in diameter. The Talisman itself was an intricate web of gold braided threads woven inside the ring of iron. It resembled a spider's web and suspended twelve unicorn spirals near its outer edge near the iron ring, each horn woven into the golden braids and pointing toward the center. Closer to the center of the web, woven into the same strands as the horns were twelve sapphires, with emeralds woven in closer to the center and rubies forming an even tighter circle surrounding a complete unicorn skull which was woven into the direct center. Amethyst stones were set perfectly into the eye sockets of the skull.

Shahly was sickened at the sight of it, her eyes wide with horror as she tightened her grip on the Prince's arm.

He looked down at her and smiled. "Magnificent, isn't it?"

She just stared at the horrible thing before her for a moment, then looked up to the Prince and softly said, "But it is made with unicorn spirals."

His smile quickly faded as he looked away, out the window to his right. "I'm sorry, Shahly. I just didn't consider your fondness for unicorns when I brought you here. I guess I was too eager to impress you."

"Why is it made with the horns?" she asked her voice barely more than a whisper.

Arden took a deep breath. "That is the secret of its power, the unicorn horns. It was said that when a unicorn dies, traces of its essence are left in its horn. That power retained in the horns is channeled along the gold strands, through the jewels to the intact skull in the center where the power is brought together." He turned and walked to the window, staring out of it for a time before he spoke again. "I confess that I do feel a certain sense of pride at the accomplishment, but at the same time…" He sighed and turned his eyes down. "I hate seeing anything's life sacrificed like that, even to defend the thousand souls who live here."

Shahly watched him as he spoke, wanting to feel angry with him, yet she could sense his honesty, that he really did not like the killing of the unicorns to build this monstrosity. Somehow, this soothed the pain she felt for her brethren, though she knew it should not.

She looked back to the Talisman and stepped closer to it, reached up and touched one of the horns. Much of the essence was still there, part of the unicorn's being and its final emotions.

This unicorn died in terror!

She quickly withdrew her hand and backed away, looking back to the Prince.

He just stared out the window, and finally shook his head. "I cannot say that it is justified, but it did save hundreds of lives when it drove those dragons away."

As he continued, Shahly looked back to the Talisman and approached again. She reached up and placed her hand back onto the horn, feeling the essence, then slowly ran her fingers up the golden strand to the first, perfectly spherical jewel.

It was just as Arden had said. The unicorn's essence was being slowly channeled through it and focused, though it was strangely at rest.

She glanced at the Prince again, then looked back to the Talisman and ran her hand up to the next jewel, the perfectly spherical emerald.

Something was different here. The essence seemed magnified many times and focused into a power Shahly had never felt before. Suddenly, her hand cramped as a surge of this power lanced into it, causing her fingers to clench together.

She winced as the emerald popped out of its thinly made cocoon, her eyes following it down to the floor where it struck with a sharp clack and rolled to a stop near her foot. She managed to take a shallow breath and turned very wide eyes to Prince Arden.

He did not seem to hear the stone strike the floor as he continued to stare out the window and tell her of the Talisman's history.

Her stomach suddenly felt very tight. Breathing was a little difficult as she looked at the empty bulge in the gold braid, then turned her eyes back to the Prince and slowly knelt down to retrieve the stone. Her dress made this difficult as it restricted such movement of her legs. When Arden looked as if he was going to turn toward her, she quickly stood back up and turned slightly toward him, feeling her foot hit the gem.

He just glanced at the door, then looked back out the window and continued to tell her of the Talisman. "It is quite a responsibility, I suppose, being the only castle with the capability to repel dragons. It makes many who fear them seek sanctuary here."

Shahly looked down, her eyes darting around the floor until they found the stone. It was behind the Talisman, at least a pace away. She glanced at the Prince, then knelt down and reached under the Talisman to retrieve the elusive stone, not wanting to touch the Talisman itself. It seemed just beyond finger's reach.

She turned her eyes back to the Prince.

He shook his head. "I just don't understand why they would be so interested in burning this place to ashes after five generations of our presence here. It is almost as if they want to get at something. Or get rid of something."

Shahly looked intently back at the stone and stretched as much as she could.

Her middle finger bumped the stone.

It rolled a hand width away—and dropped into a crack in the floor.

Shahly's whole spine pulled taut and her mouth fell open as she stared at that crack in the floor. It was just a pace on the other side of the Talisman. From where she knelt, it was out of reach.

Slowly, her eyes turned toward the Prince.

He was still staring out the window, still talking.

With her eyes locked on him, Shahly stood and walked slowly toward one of the timbers supporting the Talisman, the one closest to the Prince.

He turned!

Shahly quickly folded her arms and leaned against the timber, raising her brow attentively.

Arden looked to her and sighed. "We've had no aggressions against them that I know of. I just wish they would allow us to live in peace." He leaned his head slightly. "You know a great deal about unicorns. Would you know anything about dragons?"

She shrugged, admitting, "A little."

He smiled slightly. "Perhaps you know a better way to stop them, something that does not involve killing unicorns."

"I wish I did," she said sympathetically.

His brow tensed. "You don't look well all of a sudden. Is anything wrong?"

"No!" she barked, quickly shaking her head. "Just listening." She had to keep his eyes from the empty cocoon, so she turned toward the Talisman and looked it over, then casually walked around the timber and asked, "When did they decide to build it?"

"About five seasons ago, I think," he replied.

She slowly stepped around the back of the work and looked to the top of it. "I guess your people tired of the dragon attacking."

"Very quickly," Arden confirmed. "Even the most loyal guards were talking about leaving."

"That is not good," she said sympathetically, then looked to the Prince. "Where did the dragon come from?" She suggested to his mind that he should look out the window, not certain that even such a simple trick of her essence would work in this human world.

He looked out the window. "The West, I think."

Good! She thought, turning her eyes to the floor.

There was the crack! It was very deep.

Now, where was the stone?

She knelt down and reached down into the crack. She could feel the smooth surface of the stone on the end of her finger, but could not get to it as the crack narrowed a finger length down and would not permit her to reach further. It was barely out of reach, yet frustratingly close.

One thing was certain: The stone was gone.

She slowly turned her eyes to Prince Arden, then sprang to her feet and folded her hands behind her as he turned around.

"The other one was not quite as big," The Prince continued, "and often attacked from the opposite direction."

Shahly slowly walked toward him again, casually sidestepped and leaned back against the timber. "And you still don't know what they wanted with you?"

The Prince shrugged. "I'm at a loss."

She looked to the window behind him. "What did they strike at first?"

His brow lowered. "Good question." He turned back to the window and pointed down to the defensive wall. "They seemed to go after the battlements first."

Shahly turned and walked back to the middle of the Talisman, her eyes immediately finding the empty cocoon. Feeling somewhat paranoid that Arden would also notice it, she pondered her very few options, one of which was fleeing the castle.

She stared at it for a time, wringing her hands together. The Queen! If *she* found out....

The thought was a horrid one and Shahly raised a hand to her throat, feeling the chain around her neck.

She looked down to the amulet, took it in her fingers and gazed at the perfect emerald sphere in the golden talon's grip, looked back to the Talisman, then wheeled back to the Prince and snapped her free hand to her chin.

Arden folded his arms as his eyes found her. "I am not certain where the idea of using unicorn horns to repel them came from, but it does seem to work."

"That is truly fascinating," she said, her eyes locked on his. "Have you ever seen a dragon?" *Look out the window,* she urged in her mind. *Just turn away a moment longer.*

His eyes widened and he nodded. "The huge beast that attacked the castle was the first one I ever saw. He was an awesome sight. I had nightmares for a month."

"Where did he come from?" she asked, still begging him in her mind to look out the window.

He did turn back toward the window, and pointed straight out. "From the West and a little south, I think. They say he comes from the desert and has a lair in the mountains there."

With much effort, Shahly pried the talon fingers of her amulet open and popped the stone out, then worked frantically to put it in the Talisman stone's place, glancing at the Prince as she worked. "Did you see him coming?"

Arden leaned on the window sill, staring out the window. "He was flying rather high the first time I saw him, and roaring loudly. It was as if he wanted us to know he was coming."

The amulet's stone was slightly larger than the Talisman's and would not fit easily into the cocoon. Shahly glanced at the Prince again and said, "That's amazing. Do you think he knew about the Talisman?" She winced as a strand of the cocoon broke.

"It was not finished at that time," Arden informed.

Shahly impatiently sighed, still trying to wrestle the threads over the stone. "How did you drive him away?"

"We didn't," he answered. "He just left much of the castle in ruins and departed on his own."

The last thread slipped over the stone and Shahly wheeled back to the Prince, folding her hands behind her as he turned from the window.

Arden leaned back against the window casing and shook his head. "He seemed to want to blast our castle from the land a piece at a time."

Shahly raised her brow. "That was not very nice of him."

The Prince smiled. "Well, I understand he is not a very nice dragon." A hint of concern took his features and he slowly approached her, taking her shoulders. "Are you sure you are feeling all right? You look a little pale."

Tension drained away and Shahly vented a deep sigh, offering him a reassuring and very relieved smile. "I'm fine." She fanned her face with her hand. "It's a little hot up here."

He nodded. "Perhaps we should venture back downstairs."

Shahly took a deep breath. "I think you are right."

She took his arm and walked with him toward the door, glancing back at the Talisman once more. She stopped as her eye caught a glass orb sitting on a small wooden table beside the Talisman near one of the windows on the far side of the room. Something red was suspended inside of it.

Arden looked down to her. "Shahly?"

"What is that?" she asked, pointing to the orb.

The Prince turned. "Oh. That is a scale from one of the dragons that attacked a couple of seasons ago. They say he cannot return here so long as some part of him is so close to the Talisman."

"A *red* scale?" Shahly breathed, her thoughts shifting to the black dragon.

Arden patted her hand. "Shall we?"

She nodded, her eyes still on the orb, then she turned with him and they left the chamber.

As they descended the stairway, Arden looked down to her and asked, "Would you like to visit the marketplace?"

She looked up at him and smiled. "I would love to. What is it?"

CHAPTER 6

Nillerra had never known such comfort, nor had she known such anxiety. For the other girls, marrying a prince was their final goal in life, comfort and security for as long as they lived, or as long as their husband could tolerate them. Nillerra wanted more. Happiness seemed to lie with power, security with those loyal only to her. Prince Arden was a stepping stone, the first of many goals.

Now, something was in her way.

Her thin red dress, full sleeved, low cut in the front and trimmed in white, shuffled gently as she strode toward her room. She would find security and privacy there, but also unspeakable horrors. What had happened to her so long ago still loomed over her. It had shattered who she had been, who she would have become, and each shard of her fractured psyche had grown in its own way, never healing, never rejoining her. They seemed to come when she needed them. They were not her, and yet they were.

No one knew. No one had to.

As she reached the door to her room, she grasped the door handle, closed her eyes and bowed her head. Fear surged within her. Horrible things could lie just beyond, as before. Still, she *had* to enter.

Nillerra's other hand slowly slid down to the single pocket on her skirt and wrapped tightly around the hilt of the small dagger within. With a deep breath, she slowly turned the handle and pushed the door open, peering inside.

Her room was much like those of the other girls, though it lacked all things pink and remained well lit at all times with no fewer than eight lamps. The heavy curtains remained closed as if to ward off something horrible from the outside. Many comforts were distributed around the room, including a single plush chair of red, cushioned material that sat in front of the huge vanity and four thick pillows on the bed. The bedspread itself was red with golden trim around the edges and did not dangle to the floor. Instead, it stopped at the bottom of the wooden frame, leaving the space beneath the bed in full view. No pictures hung on the walls and only one tapestry decorated the room, a tapestry showing the completed Red Stone Castle with a throne visible in the open gateway. The wardrobe stood open and full of dresses.

Slowly, carefully, she crept into the room, her eyes darting around as she studied every corner and shadow, especially near the window, in and behind the wardrobe, and under the bed.

Moving as silently as she could, Nillerra circled the entire room, and, as she reached the door again, was finally confident that she was alone.

She strode to the vanity and sat down in the deep cushions of the chair, her long black hair shimmering in the light of the lamps as she stared into her almost black eyes in the mirror.

"Conniving little tramp," she said to her reflection. "As if I didn't have enough to worry about." She picked up her brush and began slowly stroking it through her hair. "What can he possibly see in that witless little hussy? Surely no one believes she is the sweet little virgin girl she makes herself out to be, and I know he isn't *that* foolish." She slammed her brush down and glared at her reflection for a moment, then turned her eyes to the perfume bottle at the corner of the dresser and gingerly picked it up. "Zelkton assured me this would work. No man yet has been able to resist me so long as I wear it."

For some time she just sat and stared at the elegant crystal bottle as it cast mesmerizing rays of light about in intricate patterns. Slowly, delicately, she pulled the stopper from the bottle and upended it, holding her middle finger over its tiny mouth, then she closed her eyes as she gently stroked her finger from behind her ear to her throat, then repeated this on the other side.

She opened her eyes, nearly smiling at her reflection. "Arden can't resist me. He is just a little distracted. Perhaps she *is* a virgin. If so, how can she possibly satisfy him the way I can?"

Again, she stared at her reflection, her eyes blank and her mind wandering. She leaned her head and turned her eyes down to her brush, picked it up, and began slowly stroking it through her hair.

Someone knocked on the door.

She did not take notice. She just kept brushing her hair.

A second knock finally distracted her and she blinked, staring at her reflection as she set the brush down and bade, "You may enter."

The door opened and a palace guard strode onto the room, stopping just a few paces inside the door. She could see him in the mirror, staring at her, and she cringed as he asked, "Maid Nillerra?"

She closed her eyes and took a deep breath to calm herself, then looked at his reflection and snarled, "Do you see anyone else in here?"

He cleared his throat, then reported, "Her Majesty Queen Hethan has sent for you. Come with me, please."

Nillerra's eyes widened a little. Fear fluttered around in her belly. The Queen had never summoned her before, and the last of Arden's girls she had called to audience had not been seen at the castle since.

She drew another breath and slowly blew it out through pursed lips, then looked down at her collection of cosmetics, brush, and hair pieces and softly said, "I should make myself presentable."

"You look fine, maiden," the guard assured. "Please come with me. It is not wise to keep her Majesty waiting."

She looked back to her reflection and nodded. "We should go, then."

Hesitantly, Nillerra stood and walked to the guard, looking innocently up to his face. "I have never had an audience with her Majesty before."

He half turned and extended his hand to the door, offering, "Shall we?"

She turned and strode elegantly out the door, freezing just outside as she saw the second guard out there waiting for her.

The second guard turned down the corridor and ordered, "This way," in a burly, less patient voice.

Hesitantly, she followed, hearing the footsteps of the first guard behind her.

Many moments passed. Neither of the guards spoke.

This did not feel encouraging. She was terrified, but refused to let them know she was.

Finally, Nillerra slowed her pace and turned to the guard behind her. He had been kind and patient with her and she felt more comfortable talking to him. Almost like a little girl, she asked, "Did her Majesty say why she wants me?"

He shook his head. "Only that she wishes to see you."

She looked ahead again, turning her eyes down as she said, "I hope I have done nothing wrong." Memories assaulted her. She had seduced the Prince on many nights during her time at the castle, but not just him. Hopefully, Queen Hethan had not found out about this.

Some time later, they reached the Queen's study. Two *more* large guards stood at the doorway. The feel was not good. Beyond that door was a dark world she had hoped not to enter as long as the Queen lived.

The guard behind Nillerra said to the guards at the door, "Maid Nillerra to see her Majesty."

One of the guards at the door nodded and confirmed, "She is expected."

The first guard stepped around her and knocked on the door.

"You may enter," came Queen Hethan's voice from the other side.

The guard opened the door and strode in a few paces, then snapped to attention and reported, "Maid Nillerra, as you commanded, my Queen."

Nervously, Nillerra strode in behind him.

The study was not so dark, yet it was not as lavishly furnished as she had imagined. On the walls to the left and right, dark wooden shelves were burdened with many books and reached to the ceiling. Two small tables sat down from the bookshelves with parchments piled on them, each with a crystal weight keeping the parchments down. Light was offered by the single, large window on the wall to the right.

Queen Hethan's huge desk was directly ahead, neatly organized with two lamps at the corners, pen and inkwell on one side and a variety of parchments and other things on the other.

The Queen sat behind the desk, dressed casually in a light, black and red gown.

After several seconds, she looked up from the parchment she was reading and right at Nillerra, then to the guard and ordered, "That will be all."

He bowed and backed from the room, gently closing the door.

The Queen looked to the black haired girl.

Still standing near the doorway, Nillerra stared back quietly, nervously.

Queen Hethan watched her a moment longer, then finally raised her brow and asked, "Do you intend for me to shout at you from across the room?"

Nillerra gulped a breath, rushed to the desk and curtsied deeply, her head bowed.

"Done as if you actually meant me respect," the Queen observed. "Very impressive."

Nillerra stood, feeling even more nervous as she met the Queen's eyes with her own. "Your Grace?"

Queen Hethan had the appearance of someone who knew she had nothing to fear. She was in control of all around her and knew it, and seemed to be sure Nillerra knew it as well. Her eyes were as stones, locked on Nillerra's in a predator's stare as she slowly slid the parchments before her away and folded her hands on her desk, informing, "You may dispense with the formalities and the demonstrations of your experience in royal courts. I saw right through you from the moment you arrived at Red Stone."

Tension piled up and Nillerra felt herself near panic. Something innocent and childlike tried to emerge from within her. She suppressed it with great effort, slowly shaking her head as she confessed, "I do not understand, your Grace."

The Queen's eyes were very, very cold and unwavering. "Just save it for Arden. Not that he believes your petty acts any more than I do."

Nillerra looked away from her, out the window.

"Let us cut through the thick of it, shall we?" the Queen advised. "It is quite clear you do not like me."

Nillerra's eyes snapped back to the Queen, her lips parted slightly as she breathed, "What?"

The hint of a smile barely curled the corners of the Queen's mouth. "Oh, don't look so shocked. It is all too obvious, and you fail miserably as an actress. But it is all right, dear. I don't like you especially well, either. I have only allowed you to stay here as long as I have because I am so very amused at watching you over-act for my son. Of course, I can hire a simple player to do that, one who is not hungry for my throne."

Nillerra raised her chin slightly, her eyes locked on the Queen. The words were as daggers, each finding its mark.

"But," the Queen continued, "that is really not my concern. No one gets the throne until my death." Something sinister touched her eyes. "But you already know that, don't you?"

"What are you implying?" Nillerra asked coldly.

The Queen shook her head. "I am not blind, girl, and I am not quite as naïve as my son. You may be able to seduce your way around him and a few palace guards, but you need to remember that the real power is in my hands and mine alone, power enough to see you married to my son, banished from my kingdom, rotting in the dungeon with that other tramp, or…." She raised her brow and looked aside, then turned her eyes back to the black haired girl with a blink.

That feeling of panic was almost overwhelming and Nillerra felt her hands clench into tight fists. She forced herself to relax somewhat, to breathe normally, and asked, "What do you want of me?"

"Much better," the Queen drawled. "You are finally learning." She leaned back in her chair and locked her eyes on Nillerra's in a deadly stare. "You have all of the faculties you would have needed to win my son, except that one thing that draws him like a bee to honey to our newest guest."

With a shallow breath, Nillerra tightened her lips and looked down.

"A pity you gave that up so long ago," the Queen said almost sympathetically. "You might have been truly innocent at one time, but now you are no better that what my son could buy in the marketplace. Of course, this new girl… What is her name? Shahly?"

Just hearing the name drew every muscle in Nillerra's body taut and she turned her eyes back to the Queen. Anger began replacing fear.

"She is a very sweet girl," Queen Hethan observed, "Much more than any of the others. Especially you." She looked to her fingernails. "Still, she seems to lack the wits to be Arden's princess, much less the Queen of Red Stone."

Nillerra raised her chin. "So are you going to have her banished? Or imprisoned, maybe?"

Hethan shook her head. "Oh no, I could not do that. Arden is much too fond of her for me to do that."

"But you can," Nillerra pressed.

The Queen smiled slightly. "Of course I can. But that would put Arden and me at odds, now wouldn't it? And we really don't want that to happen. Besides, she is hardly a threat of any kind to me, whereas she is your most dangerous rival. It appears to me as if she has already won his heart in the short time she has been here, something you have failed miserably to do in the months you have been here. You see, Arden is a bright lad, much more so than any of the men you are used to dealing with."

Nillerra turned her eyes down, the anger within her swelling.

Queen Hethan looked back to her parchments, picking one up to read. "I suppose as long as she is here you can kiss the throne and any chance of marrying my son good-bye. Perhaps you should think about what you intend to do about it. That will be all."

Nillerra considered for a moment, her eyes on the Queen, then she started, "But even if—"

"You are dismissed," the Queen interrupted more loudly with her eyes still on the parchment and a noticeable tone of warning in her voice.

Nillerra stared at her a second longer, then bowed and backed from the room.

She closed the door, then just stood there and stared at it for a time, stewing over the obvious change in her status.

"Do you require an escort, maiden?" one of the guards asked.

Nillerra looked up at him and shook her head, answering, "No. I just want to take a walk." She turned quickly and strode down the corridor, feeling numb inside as she pondered her situation. She wandered for some time, her mind brewing. She had not thought the Queen to be so perceptive or devious, or the Prince so intelligent. One thing was all too certain, though.

They both knew exactly what she wanted.

The throne was so close, yet just out of reach. The Prince was her only way into it, and it was he who had provided a seemingly impassable obstacle. The throne had not seemed this distant since she had arrived.

Her next objective was all too clear.

Shahly would have to go!

Barely noticing her surroundings, Nillerra stormed up to the second level, down the corridor, up to the third level.

She stopped as she saw a group of palace guards, her eyes locked on one.

He looked back at her, then took his leave of the others and walked in her direction.

Nillerra turned and strode quickly to her suite, entered, and left the door slightly ajar. She stood only a few paces inside, staring at the window across the room, her eyes tense and aching.

She heard the door open, the hinge creaking ever so slightly, then it closed. The sound of boots on the stone floor behind her drew closer and she tensed as they neared, then finally wheeled around and wrapped her arms around the guard, burying her face in his shoulder.

Gently, he slid his arms up her back, then held her tightly and asked, "What is it?

She drew a shaky breath. "I do not know how much more time we have together."

"What do you mean?" he asked hesitantly.

She raised her head slightly, rubbing her smooth cheek to the scruff of his. "That new girl Prince Arden has brought to the castle could threaten everything we have worked for. I may have to go soon."

She felt him vent a heavy breath and almost smiled.

"I cannot allow this to happen," he growled.

"What can we do?" she whimpered. "He spends most of his time with her now, and I am sure he will choose her soon."

"He may just be testing you," the guard tried to assure.

"No," Nillerra softly said.

He stroked her hair. "Then, no matter what happens, stay here at Red Stone. Many of the girls will, chosen or not."

She shook her head. "If I do not marry Prince Arden soon I will be called back to Ravenhold, and I will never be allowed to see you again." She slid her hand up his back and to his neck, angling his face toward her nape. She felt his lips gently kiss her neck and she felt the cool passing air glance across her skin as he breathed in. The strong effects of the perfume were quick and obvious as he tensed slightly, and held her more tightly.

"There has to be some way," he insisted.

"Not so long as she is here," Nillerra whimpered. "She has doomed us both to a future of loneliness."

"Then she will not be here long," the guard informed sternly.

Nillerra slowly opened her eyes, staring blankly ahead.

He pushed her away slightly, gazing down into her dark eyes as he said, "Leave everything to me."

Her brow arched and her lips parted slightly, then she breathed, "What are you going to do?"

He smiled, slowly running his hand over her hair. "Nothing you should be concerned with. It is just time for this new maiden to take her leave of us." He bent toward her and touched his lips to hers, then turned and stormed from the room, closing the door as he left.

Nillerra stared at the door for some time, then slowly turned and walked to her dresser, sat down and picked up her brush. As she slowly ran it through her hair, she smiled at her reflection and said as if to the guard, "Obedient fool."

She laughed under her breath and set the brush down, smiling at the face that smiled back at her.

"Good-bye, Shahly."

CHAPTER 7

Such sights and smells the marketplace offered. Humans called minstrels made the most wonderful sounds with their wooden instruments. Colorful tents and booths were scattered everywhere as humans peddled their goods. Shiny things abounded. Many humans wandered the marketplace in search of one thing or another, or just to enjoy themselves.

Escorted by two palace guards, Shahly and Arden wandered the marketplace without a given direction or plan. Holding hands the whole time, they visited many booths and tents, tasted some of the most wonderful foods, and watched small groups of humans in comical exploits.

From one booth, Arden traded copper discs for a large white and pink flower that he mounted skillfully in Shahly's hair just above her ear. It smelled wonderful and made her feel good just having it there.

They spent much of the afternoon just enjoying themselves until they were approached by a young man in a black and red tunic. He bowed to the Prince and said something to him Shahly could not hear.

Arden nodded to him, then turned to Shahly as the young man departed. He took her hands in his and smiled at her, though his eyes betrayed stress as he informed, "I have some duties at the castle to attend to."

Shahly's brow arched slightly. "We have to go?"

He nodded. "I'm afraid so. We can always come back if you like."

She smiled. "I like."

"Perhaps we could take a ride in the forest," he suggested.

Shahly nodded. "That sounds fun, too."

Arden held her hand tightly as they made their way back to the palace. He talked to her the whole way as they entered the castle and slowly walked toward her suite. Shahly listened intently as the Prince told her of his exploits as a younger man. By the time they reached her room, she was giggling almost uncontrollably, and in tears from doing so.

"I swear it was not my intention to make Ocnarr's horse stop like that," he confessed, "but seeing him sail head-first into that pile of stable sweepings was well worth the thrashing he gave me in battle training later."

"You were such a young scamp," she laughed.

"Yes," he confessed, then laughed himself. "Something tells me you were not always so sweet and innocent yourself."

She glanced away. "I did things that lost the favor of the elders from time to time."

"So here we are," the Prince announced. "Two scamps on a rampage." He sighed. "I wish I could spend the whole day with you, but, alas, my princely duties await."

"I understand," she assured.

He stroked her hair and softly said, "Somehow I knew you would, Forest Blossom." He gently took her chin and touched his lips to hers.

Shahly's heart raced and her thoughts whirled as she stared up into his eyes for many long seconds after, then she finally, softly asked, "Why did you do that?"

"Kiss you?" He shrugged. "Something about the moment, I suppose."

She reached up and touched his lips gently with her fingers, then her own and breathed, "That was a kiss?"

Arden smiled. "Well, not really." He slipped his arms around her back and pulled her to him, holding her tightly as he informed, "This is." He pressed his lips to hers much harder, not painfully so, but passionately.

This was a very new experience and Shahly had no idea what to do. She was briefly repulsed, then found herself more and more drawn to him. She was terrified, exhilarated, somehow even aroused. Unicorn instinct urged her to push away and run, but something else was in control. Human response proved much more powerful than she had anticipated, and Shahly found these strange feelings within her to be overwhelming.

Her heart thundering, Shahly closed her eyes and slowly slid her hands up his sides and to his shoulders, holding him as tightly as she could.

Time passed so slowly.

Arden finally pulled back slightly, rubbing his nose to hers, then he smiled at her and stroked his fingers through her hair. "Something tells me you have never been kissed before."

She slowly shook her head. "No. Never before."

His brow shot up. "Oh. I am your first, then?"

She nodded.

"Would you like to try again?" he asked.

Her unicorn instincts spoke up again, telling her this was not such a good idea, but it was such a wonderful experience, touching in this way. Innocence and wonder still glowed from her eyes as she stared up at him and fumbled with such a simple answer.

An answer which he did not wait for.

She drew a deep breath, then whimpered as he kissed her again. The sensation was tenfold what it had been the first time and Shahly melted into his arms, turning her head slightly as he pulled her closer. She held him as tightly as she could and slipped one hand up to his neck as if never to part from him, and finally realized she was nearly gasping for each breath.

Again, time seemed to pass very slowly.

Someone cleared her throat behind them, unmistakably Ihzell.

Arden pulled away, appearing to be very tense as he looked behind Shahly and declared, "Oh! Ihzell. Didn't see you there."

Shahly turned and smiled at her.

"Clearly," the steward said, folding her arms. She glanced at Shahly, then looked back at the Prince and asked, "So what are we up to today?"

"We were kissing," Shahly answered with a big smile on her lips, feeling giddier than she had ever felt in her life.

Ihzell nodded. "I could see that."

"Well," Arden announced, tugging his shirt down, "if you ladies will excuse me, I've a hundred things that require my attention." He looked to Shahly and asked, "How about a walk in the gardens this evening after dinner?"

She looked up to him and eagerly nodded.

He touched his lips to hers, then pulled away, nodding to Ihzell as he hurried past her.

The steward shook her head as she walked to Shahly. "I see he is showing you all kinds of things."

Shahly sighed loudly and grasped the steward's arm with both hands, leaning her head on Ihzell's shoulder as they entered her room. "It was wonderful! I have never felt anything like it in my life!"

"At your age you should not be feeling any such things at all," the steward insisted. "The very idea. You two have only known each other two days. You need more time to get acquainted. I mean, you barely know anything about one another."

"It doesn't matter!" Shahly declared as she spun around and threw herself back-first onto her huge bed. "Arden is so wonderful!" She took a deep breath and immersed herself in the feelings that were still very strong within her, barely noticing the shuffling of the dress Ihzell worked with across the room at the wardrobe.

"You know," Ihzell started slowly, "he is going to be a very powerful man some day."

Shahly giggled. "He is awfully strong, now."

"No," the steward corrected. "I mean he is going to be the ruler of Red Stone."

Shahly turned over, laying on her belly as she looked to the steward and said, "But you said he is the Prince."

Ihzell shook her head and looked to Shahly. "Sweetheart, that means he will be King one day."

Shahly leaned her head, asking, "What does that mean?"

With pursed lips, Ihzell drew a breath and answered, "That means he will be one of the richest, most powerful men in the land."

With a broad smile, Shahly rolled to her back and laughed. "Oh, it doesn't matter. He will still be Arden." She closed her eyes, savoring recent memories.

"I suppose riches and power mean nothing to you?" Ihzell asked.

"No," Shahly answered. "Freedom and love are everything."

Shahly heard the dress hit the floor and the steward said with a sharp tone of surprise, "I do believe you mean that. You really don't care about his power."

"Why should I?" Shahly asked. "I have no need for such nonsense." She sighed. "I just like to be close to Arden."

Ihzell walked to the bed and sat down. "Shahly, every girl who came here was looking for something. They all wanted to marry a Prince."

Shahly sat up and looked to the steward, asking, "Why?"

Ihzell smiled and shook her head. "He has been so happy since you came here. I just hope his eyes are open enough to see that you are the perfect choice for him."

"Choice for what?" Shahly pressed, a slight smile on her lips.

Ihzell grasped Shahly's hand and answered, "To be his wife, child. To be his Princess."

Shahly felt something within her collapse. It hurt. She blinked and glanced away, breathing, "His wife? His—His mate?" She slid from the bed and wandered around it to the window. This had been such a beautiful day, a day of discovery and fun. Now, she felt so much pain and confusion.

"I know it seems like a fairy tale," the steward continued, "but you could very likely be the next Princess of Red Stone."

Staring down into the gardens, Shahly gingerly placed her hands on the windowsill, feeling as if she was being choked. Everything had been so wonderful before, feeling happy and carefree at Arden's side as he showed her the wonders of his world. Now, she hurt badly inside, feeling she had betrayed someone else.

Ihzell gently grasped her shoulders from behind and asked, "What is it, child?"

Shahly's vision was blurred by tears and the many colors of the garden seemed to melt together. A life with this strange and wonderful human was all so appealing. Too appealing.

"He loves you dearly," Ihzell informed. "Don't you feel the same?"

It was finally apparent—and all too painful.

Shahly bowed her head, and nodded.

Ihzell squeezed her shoulders. "Then what is wrong, child?"

Shahly closed her eyes and softly breathed, "Vinton."

Ihzell patted her shoulders. "You sound like you have some thinking to do. I will be in the sewing room if you need me. Just have a guard take you there."

Shahly nodded.

The door opened, then gently closed again.

Her thoughts bounded about like a week-old foal and refused to offer her any answers.

She gazed out over the gardens for a time, then past them, over the wall which protected the palace and into the forest beyond. For some time she just allowed the memories to pass through her mind, memories of a childhood in the forest, running and playing with the other young unicorns, growing up with them, and the ever growing feelings she had for Vinton.

Newer memories and feelings invaded her mind, memories of her human prince bringing her to the castle, his affectionate words to her, how he touched her and looked at her, the fun they had together, and her first kiss.

This human place she was growing so comfortable in was not her home.

"I came here for a reason," she told herself aloud. "I must free Vinton."

But as the unicorn she loved had occupied her every thought, those thoughts now included another, a human prince.

Trying to deny what she felt for Arden was impossible. Even in human form, she was unicorn and could not lie, not even to herself.

With a deep sigh, she turned and strode to the door.

Her own feelings would have to wait. Vinton needed her.

She pulled the door open and strode out, intent on searching this human stronghold for Vinton, but froze as two guards standing at her door turned to her.

"May we help you, maiden?" one asked.

Clearly, the search was not going to be so easy.

Shahly forced a smile and assured, "Oh, no. No. I just thought I would step out for a stroll while I wait for Vint—uh, Ar… I mean Prince Arden to come for me. We are taking a walk in the gardens later and I am feeling a little restless in here." She looked to the other guard. "I am from the forest. We wander around a lot out there."

The guard nodded. "I see." He looked to the other guard and informed, "I will escort her."

"Oh, no!" Shahly said quickly. "I don't want to be a bother. I know my way around. Arden… Prince Arden and I went walking earlier. He showed me around the castle and took me to the marketplace."

"By Her Majesty's command, maiden," the guard told her sternly, "I must escort you."

Shahly turned her eyes down a little and nodded. "Oh. That was very sweet of her." She looked back to him and assured, "But it really isn't necessary."

"Still, maiden, you must be escorted. It is the wishes of the Queen."

She nodded. "Okay, if you must. I just don't want to be a burden."

He smiled. "Not at all, maiden."

She smiled back at him, then turned and walked slowly down the corridor, her lips tightening as she pondered how to go about finding her Vinton with this man watching her. Unicorns could easily elude unwanted eyes in the forest. Unfortunately, this was not the forest, Shahly was no longer a unicorn, and the guard was watching her like a hawk watches a rabbit.

Even in human form, Shahly found her unicorn senses growing stronger, and she could feel the thoughts and emotions of the guard behind her.

He was not thinking of her safety or the security of the castle, rather his thoughts were more like those of a rutting stag. She could feel his eyes on her almost constantly. His emotions were strange and unfamiliar, even for a human.

There was definitely something predatory about him, something wicked.

Rather than exploring uncharted areas of the castle, Shahly wandered down the same corridor she and Arden had walked that morning, feeling a little more secure in a place she was familiar with.

She took the time to study the tapestries while she reached out with her essence to find another unicorn, praying she would find Vinton.

Looking ahead, she saw Nillerra enter the corridor and quickened her pace, feeling a little safer with someone familiar in sight.

"Hello there," Shahly greeted with a smile. "I see you are exploring as well."

Nillerra hesitated as she saw Shahly, then strode toward her, smiled and said, "Shahly. What a surprise."

Shahly stopped a pace from the black haired girl, who also stopped, and tried to make conversation. "I had not expected to see you here."

"Nor I you," Nillerra responded. "Learning your way around the castle?"

Shahly nodded. "This place is much larger than one would think. Prince Arden showed me around this morning, but he was called away."

Nillerra nodded.

They were both silent for a long moment.

The presence of the guard behind Shahly seemed to magnify, as did her uneasiness about him, so she invited, "Would you care to walk with me?"

"It sounds fun," Nillerra admitted, "but I have so much to do today. Another time?"

Shahly nodded and conceded, "Sure. Another time."

Nillerra smiled at her again, then looked up at the guard and nodded once as she walked past.

Shahly looked back at the black haired girl, then up to the guard, not liking what she saw in his eyes, or the sinister thoughts she sensed from him.

She turned forward again, resuming her walk down the corridor, and quickening her pace.

The guard behind her did not allow her to put much distance between her and him.

Glancing around, Shahly realized the corridor she was in was empty of other people, and only this guard for company made her feel uncomfortable. Very uncomfortable.

Ahead, a set of double doors sprayed light from between and around them. Clearly, they led to the outside. She could faintly hear activity out there. Just knowing someone was close by made her feel safer and she headed that way.

"Wait," the guard ordered.

Shahly froze, staring at the doors only ten paces away.

He firmly took her shoulder and turned her toward him, sternly informing, "You can't go out there. The guard's stables are that way."

She looked fearfully back at him. His eyes betrayed him. The way he looked at her frightened her and she wished she was anywhere else.

"I'm sorry," she said softly, then looked behind him and added, "I did not know. Perhaps I should be getting back now."

He nodded and stepped aside. "Very well. This way."

Noticing how short he was with her, Shahly strode by him cautiously, only wanting to get back to her room, or anywhere where there were people around.

He took her shoulder again and directed her down another corridor, informing, "This way will be shorter."

Shahly felt she had no other choice, so she hesitantly went the way he directed her to go. Something felt horribly wrong.

This corridor was darker and did not appear to be used much. There were no tapestries on the walls, only an occasional display of sword and shield or a rusted suit of armor. Lamps were scarce and barely illuminated the corridor. Shadowed doorways were invitingly open, yet ominous and terrifying as they seemed to have no limit of depth and no light to drive away the night-dwelling horrors that might be waiting within. Just the feel of the place was dreadful. The damp, still air was a little difficult to breathe and smelled of wet stone and fungus, rusty metal and rat leavings.

Shahly could see little light ahead. The corridor did not seem to end and the guard behind her offered no comfort, rather he seemed to be almost a part of this horrid place.

She turned her head slightly, panning her eyes as if to see him. She could feel his mind and presence with little effort, and easily felt his eyes on her.

Everything she felt was confusing, horrifying. He had a wanting, and what he wanted was more than just her life!

Not knowing what to do, Shahly felt near panic. Blood was in his thoughts, blood and that horrible wanting of her.

She quickened her pace.

The guard did as well.

She felt him reach for her, and braced to run when she felt his touch.

"Maid Shahly," came a man's voice in the distance behind her.

Shahly sidestepped and wheeled around.

The guard behind her was gone!

She glanced around, unable to see well in the poorly lit corridor, but feeling his presence nearby, frustration in his thoughts.

"Maid Shahly," the voice summoned again, closer.

Booted footsteps approached, and a much gentler mind

Shahly walked cautiously toward the sound of the approaching footsteps and anxiously replied, "I am here."

The other palace guard, a slightly older, larger man, strode up to Shahly and folded his arms. "What brings you down here? His Highness has been looking all over for you."

Shahly glanced around again, still feeling the presence of the first guard, then she looked up to the man before her and answered, "I'm a little lost."

The guard laughed softly and shook his head. "Well, that can happen when you explore a castle this size without an escort. Just let one of the guards know when you want to go wandering and we will be glad to show you around. Meanwhile, his Highness is anxious to see you again." He turned and offered her his arm. "Shall we?"

She grasped his arm with both of hers and walked with him back the way they had come, glancing behind her.

"Something of interest back there?" the guard asked.

She glanced up at him, then looked ahead and replied, "It's dark and scary back there."

He patted her hand. "I certainly am glad I ran into that traveler when I did or I might never have found you." He looked down to her. "You are very tense. Is anything wrong?"

She looked up to him, asking, "What are you called?"

"I am Ocnarr," he answered, "Captain of the Royal Guard."

"You were with Arden when he found me," Shahly remembered aloud.

"That I was," he assured. "We all prayed we were not too late when we pulled you from the river. I thought for sure we were, but was relieved to see you are such a strong girl."

Shahly smiled at him. "Thank you for saving me."

He smiled back and patted her hand again. "My great pleasure, maiden. Thank you for being there to be found. I don't remember seeing Prince Arden happier than when he is with you."

She looked ahead. "I feel happy with him, too."

Vinton crept back into her thoughts and her own words stung. She had come here to find him, and somehow Arden still occupied her thoughts. What she felt for this Prince was not natural. He was human. She could not allow these feelings to grow nor could she allow herself to feel even more comfortable with him.

Still, rejecting him now might jeopardize her mission to find and free Vinton and the dragon's Falloah. As long as she was close to Arden she had a much better chance of finding them, and a much better chance of losing Vinton forever.

What a vicious circle.

"You are suddenly very quiet," Ocnarr observed.

She looked up at him, then ahead. "Just thinking."

This guard was so different from the last. She sensed a longing for her that was similar to the first guard's, but no predatory sensations. In fact, he had quite a gentle, disciplined mind, and she even felt trust for him.

They finally entered the better lit corridor and Shahly looked to the doors to the outside and stopped. "Another guard would not allow me to go out there."

"That is where the guard's stables are," he informed.

"That is what the other man told me," Shahly said, then looked up to Ocnarr. "If there are just horses and guards out there, why can't I go and see them?"

"There are more than just horses out there, maiden," he answered, turning and leading her away from the door. "That is where the captive unicorns are kept."

Her eyes widened. "Unicorns?" *Vinton could be out there!*

He nodded. "Oh, yes. That part of the stables is restricted to only a few people."

She tugged on his arm. "Oh, can we go and see them?"

He glanced down at her, looking somewhat uneasy.

"Oh, please?" she persisted.

Ocnarr reluctantly shook his head. "I'm sorry, maiden. I'm afraid I cannot take you there." He raised his eyebrows as he looked fully down at her and continued, "But I will wager if you ask his Highness as nicely as you asked me, he might just be willing to show you himself."

"Do you think so?" she asked hopefully.

"Not for me to say," the guard answered, "but he may. Just don't tell him it was I who advised it." He winked at her.

Shahly smiled and assured, "I promise."

Ocnarr also smiled. "I certainly hope you are the one."

Shahly turned her eyes ahead as she realized she thought of Arden almost all the time now, much the way she had once thought of Vinton. This was awkward and painful and she felt something she had not even known of until she had entered this human world.

Guilt.

After a long trek back through the castle, they arrived at her suite to find the steward already there.

Ihzell turned from the dress she had laid out on the bed and set her hands on her hips, asking directly, "Just where have you been?"

"Exploring the castle," Shahly answered hesitantly.

The steward turned her eyes to Ocnarr, saying, "You are on the arm of the wrong man, Shahly."

Ocnarr laughed softly.

"He came to find me," Shahly defended, then glanced around. "I thought Arden would be here."

Ihzell glanced at the guard, then raised her chin and informed, "He had something to attend to. He should be along shortly. Now let's go and try on that new dress before he arrives."

Shahly sighed and turned her eyes down. "That seems to be all I do."

Ihzell folded her arms. "Well, you have to be fitted properly with the proper wardrobe. You do want to look your best for dinner tonight, don't you?"

"I suppose," Shahly sighed.

A seamstress who had assisted on Shahly's first fitting hurried into the room, calling for the steward.

Ihzell turned and warned, "It had better not be bad news."

The seamstress cringed and timidly reported, "I am afraid it is. The light blue silk we were going to use for maid Shahly's dinner gown is— Um, we have run out."

Ihzell threw her hands up and roared, "How in the world can we run out? I've told those girls again and again to keep those...." She sighed and grumbled, "Must I do everything myself?"

Shahly gently grasped the steward's arm, softly assuring, "It is okay, Ihzell."

Ihzell patted Shahly's hand and said, "You are such a sweetheart." She shook her head. "I had the most spectacular gown designed."

"Why not just use another color?" Ocnarr suggested.

"Another color," the steward growled.

"We have many colors still in the sewing room," the seamstress informed. "Perhaps yellow, or teal."

Ocnarr nodded. "I rather like teal, myself."

Ihzell looked to him, her brow low over her eyes as she asked, "What could a man possibly know about a woman's gown?"

He raised his chin. "I know what I like to see on a woman."

The humans were very occupied with their conversation and eluding their minds and attention was easy.

Shahly folded her essence around herself, concealing herself from notice as she slowly backed away. She did not take her eyes from the people in front of her until she was out of the room, then she turned and hurried back down the corridor, down the stairs to the first level, and strode down a corridor that looked familiar.

After a brisk walk, and some time later, she realized they all looked much the same. The search for the stables was not going to be as easy as she had hoped.

She rushed into a very elaborately decorated, carpeted hallway, well lit with many lamps. The servants who milled about the castle, going about their routines of cleaning and maintenance did not concern her, but the dozen or so palace guards who approached from ahead did.

She doubled back and found the corridor that branched off of the hallway. It emptied into the cavernous room where she had first entered the castle. She found a large collection of humans filling lamps, scrubbing the floor, cleaning the tapestries and ornaments and carrying different things to and fro.

It was time to act human, calm and dignified.

Trying not to draw attention to herself, Shahly strode casually through the great room, looking around her as if interested in the decorations. The females seemed to take little notice of her. The males stared at her with great interest.

She tried to ignore them.

The doors leading to the outside were ahead of her and wide open, and once she was outside she knew finding the stables was going to be easy. They were to the left, upwind.

Shahly circled around the castle, following a group of riders who slowly paced the way many others were coming from.

The walk to the stables was considerable, as Red Stone Castle was not a small place, and when she finally got the stables in sight, she froze as she also saw the many, many palace guards who led the horses in and out of the long, stone structure. She could not see behind it and it was too far away for her to make out anything within, but the scent of the horses was unmistakable, and very strong.

With a deep breath, she slowly approached the stable, her hands folded behind her as she glanced around wondrously and hoped no one would take notice of her. She reached out with her essence, searching for her stallion. Unicorn scent was here, but faint, and smothered by the scent of the horses and humans. With so many creatures gathered in one area, she had a difficult time sorting out the different life forces, like trying to spot a certain pebble in a pile.

Many of the guards looked her way.

She pretended not to notice them and instead looked to the huge horses which paced by, carrying riders who watched her closely. As expected, they were all a little tense, yet not as alert as she had thought they would be. She had feared that her presence would cause some degree of alarm, but she was feeling quite a different reaction from each of the humans who looked at her.

As she looked to one side, she noticed a human approaching her from the stable. Only forty paces away, she was determined not to be stopped so close to finding Vinton.

Before he reached her, she reached toward him with her essence and looked into his thoughts, finding strong, fatherly emotions as well as the common human male wanting for her. He seemed to expect her to give him problems, question his authority and cause him no end of anguish. Where he got these notions Shahly could only guess, but she knew immediately such conduct from her would only anger him, and that was something she could not do as provoking him would jeopardize what she came to do.

"Excuse me, maiden," he finally greeted.

She stopped and looked toward him, smiling innocently as she looked up into his eyes.

He was a tall man, lean built beneath his well decorated tunic and armor. He wore short hair on his head and a graying blond mustache on his lip. His eyes were wrinkled at the edges. The skin of his face was very red, betraying much time in the sun.

He raised his chin commandingly and rested one hand on his sword as he asked in a deep, authoritative voice, "What brings you this way, maiden?"

Shahly leaned her head and looked past the guard, asking, "Aren't they beautiful?"

He glanced over his shoulder. "The horses? I think so. Is that why you ventured this way, to see the horses?"

"I really like horses," Shahly told him, trying to sound girl-like and very naïve, which was really no stretch for her. "Do you get to ride them?"

His chest puffed out a little as he answered, "Of course I do. I belong to her Majesty's mounted guard."

Shahly's brow popped up. "Really?" What he said sounded impressive, so it had to be something important.

A proud smile took his lips as he informed, "I have been for over fifteen seasons, now. In my humble opinion, we are the elite, the best part of the guard to serve in."

Shahly looked past him, determined to investigate the stable. Vinton had to be there somewhere. She smiled and looked back to the guard like a wanting child, asking, "May I see your horse?"

His forehead tensed and wrinkled a bit as he seemed to consider, then he stroked his mustache and answered, "I don't think that would be such a good idea. I would not want you to get hurt in there."

She clasped her hands together and raised them to her chin, widening her eyes beneath an arched brow as she pleaded, "I promise I will not be any trouble. Please?"

He vented a deep breath and smiled slightly, then nodded. "Oh, very well, maiden. I will take you to see him."

"Thank you!" she squealed.

"But," he added quickly, "you must stay close to me. I do not want you getting yourself hurt or accosted by some young stable hand."

Shahly grasped his hand with both of hers and assured, "I will be right at your side."

Getting into the stable was much easier than Shahly had anticipated. No one stopped them to ask of her presence, though glances turned to long stares. It seemed as if this practice of bringing maidens into the stable took place all of the time.

Many windows lit the stable, as did many lamps hanging from the timbers that ran down the center of the stable. Dozens of horses were in the stalls or standing in the wide walkway between them as they had their hooves worked on or their coats brushed.

Near the center of the stable, Shahly and the guard stopped and turned to one of the stalls and the guard looked proudly at the shiny brown stallion within.

The guard glanced at Shahly, then raised his chin and looked back at his mount as he said, "I call him Thunderhooves."

In size and form the horse looked much like Vinton. His dark mane and tail were almost black. Had he a beard, a horn and more intelligent eyes, he would look just like Vinton to Shahly's human eyes.

Vinton's image came into full focus in the back of Shahly's mind and she felt herself almost in tears as she stared at the beast before her. Slowly, she shook her head and breathed, "He's beautiful."

"Isn't he?" the guard agreed. "And with the exception of only three others, he is the fastest animal at Red Stone."

The horse snorted and fidgeted, clearly growing agitated at Shahly's presence. Though not born in the wild, he was still a creature of nature and Shahly knew the insights humans had lost long ago were still very much alive in him, and he could feel her essence.

Shahly stepped forward, touching the horse with her essence to assure him she meant him no harm.

"Careful," the guard warned. "Thunderhooves is a tad anxious around strangers."

The horse understood Shahly and stepped toward her, reaching his head over the stall gate to get closer to her.

Shahly smiled and gently stroked his nose.

The guard laughed softly and patted the horse's neck. "Then again, I suppose he can see that you are a lovely, gentle maiden."

Shahly smiled and declared, "He likes me."

"I can see that," the guard observed.

Feeling the horse's emotions, Shahly was astonished at what she found there. "He really loves you," she said softly. "He is actually happy here."

The guard chuckled. "You say that like you know what he is thinking."

"Well I do," she responded absently, then stiffened, her eyes darting to the guard as she realized she had slipped again. "Uh," she stammered, seeing his eyebrows lift, "just look at how shiny his coat is, how clear his eyes are." She looked back to the horse. "He has very perky ears. That is the easiest way to tell." She looked back to the guard and touched his mind with hers, hoping against hope she could find some way to distract him. "But I do know he loves you. Very much so."

The guard smiled and looked back to his horse. "I do believe you are right, maiden. I feel quite a bond with him." He patted the horse's neck, then nodded. "You are quite a beast, Thunderhooves. I am a lucky man."

The horse turned his attention to his rider, nudging him with his nose.

The guard laughed and stroked the horse's snout.

Shahly slowly backed away and concealed herself from his mind. With a little subtle persuasion, she convinced him to forget about her and concentrate on his new, deeper relationship with Thunderhooves.

When she was confident that the guard's attention was fully occupied with his horse, Shahly turned and wandered silently through the stable, working to conceal herself from the rest of the humans there.

As she passed by them, the horses in the stalls grew agitated at her presence, but did not panic and were quickly calmed by their tenders.

In human form, such a mind trick seemed even more exhaustive and Shahly looked for a way out of the stable, finding an open door at the far end.

She exited slowly, peering around her.

Few humans were present, just a couple of guards talking and a rider adjusting his saddle.

Another stable was behind the guard's stable, built much the same but only half the length. The windows were closed with gray wooden shutters and the door Shahly could see was also closed.

Shahly peered inside the smaller stable with her mind and found unicorn essence. It was obscured by strange and powerful emotions which masked the unicorn's mind. She had never felt such things from a unicorn before, such anger, such conflict. The unicorn seemed at odds with himself, emotionally restless, though his mind was asleep.

She squinted her eyes, just staring at the stable ahead of her for a time. There were no guards around it. Entering would be easy. Something told her it looked too easy. No matter.

Shahly rushed to the door and took the handle in her hands, glanced around once more, then pulled the door open, her heart jumping as the hinges creaked.

She entered and slowly pulled the door shut, then turned and looked into the darkness within. Very little light entered, only stray bands of sunlight lancing through cracks and seams in the shutters. The air seemed very cold and heavy.

She shuddered and slowly crept forward. Something else was here, something of unicorn essence, yet very, very cold. This was the essence she had sensed a moment ago, but inside the stable it seemed clearer, backward somehow.

Moving forward slowly, Shahly bumped into the door of an open stall and the hinges creaked loudly as it moved away from her.

Movement ahead and a rustling in the hay caught her attention. A dim, eerie violet light illuminated the far end of the stable.

The awakening mind was unlike anything Shahly had ever felt in her life or even imagined, yet it was familiar, something from many seasons ago.

Something stepped heavily toward her, crunching hay into the earth and a deep, raspy voice, a strangely familiar voice cruelly demanded, "What do you want here?"

She quickly backed away, into a wall that stopped her retreat.

It advanced, the violet glow of its eyes drawing nearer as it demanded, "Answer! What are you doing here?"

A breath shrieked as Shahly forced it in and she fearfully replied, "I'm sorry. I didn't mean to disturb you."

It snorted, eerily horse-like, then sneered, "Still another prospective mate for the Prince, I see. I am sure he would be rather disappointed to find you dead in here."

Shahly swallowed hard, fighting terror as she made her way along the wall behind her and each second feeling closer to panic as she heard the beast before her drawing steadily closer.

It snorted again and rasped, "You still have not told me what you are doing here!" It kicked something metal in the darkness.

Shahly flinched as a bucket slammed into the wall right next to her. She breathed in short, shrieking gasps. Terror was nearly in control of her. The essence she had felt before was fully awake, alert, and so horrible.

Finally, her shoulder brushed the wooden door, the way out she hoped.

"I am sorry," she apologized. "I will not disturb you again."

"See that you don't," it warned. "Do so again and I shall kill you for it. Now get out."

Shahly whimpered as she fumbled with the door latch, fearing she would not be able to open the door in time.

"Go!" it roared.

The latch finally gave.

Shahly turned and slammed her hands onto the door, screaming as it held firm. She pulled harder on the latch and beat on the door hard with her palm. When it finally opened, she burst out and ran toward the castle, tears obscuring her vision as she fled. Something of that horrible mind lingered in hers. Surging fear was panic and she felt as if she could not retreat from the beast fast enough. Only escape was in her thoughts, and finding refuge in the safety of Prince Arden's arms.

Horrible images of death and darkness, pain and unimaginable evil flashed through her mind.

She ran toward a door on the palace wall and slammed into it, grasped the latch and tugged hard on it, sobbing as she tried to pull it open many times before it finally let her pass.

Shahly burst into the palace and ran aimlessly down the corridor, her heart racing away within her, her mind whirling and her vision blurred by tears. She had no destination. She just ran, trying to get away.

She ran into something, someone. Her wrists were tightly seized and she looked up into his face. Focusing was difficult, but she did not have to. She recognized his mind, cold and predatory.

Her eyes widened as his face finally came into focus.

He was smiling at her, a horrible, wicked smile.

Shahly tried to back away.

He pulled her back to him.

Her death was in his eyes, his thoughts, and something worse, something demented and sickening.

Panic burst from her in a scream and she jerked her arms back, somehow breaking his grip. She wrenched herself free and fled down the corridor again.

An unknown time later she was grabbed again and easily subdued by strong arms which wrapped around her and held her tightly.

Her weary mind could endure no more and she shielded herself from his thoughts and kept her eyes from his as she struggled to pull herself away.

"Shahly," he called to her as if from a distance.

His voice tugged at her memory, but she could not overcome the fear which still had its grasp on her.

"Shahly!" she heard again, then was seized by the shoulders and shaken. "Stop it! Shahly, look at me!"

Not quite of her own will, she looked up. Her struggling ceased as she saw Prince Arden's eyes. Her defenses collapsed and his emotions poured into her. He was very concerned, very frightened, and his mind scrambled around how to protect her.

Arden gently brushed her hair from her face and asked with a compassionate voice, "What is wrong with you?"

She wanted to tell him, yet knew she couldn't. With tears streaming from her eyes, she wrapped her arms around him and nuzzled into his shoulder, holding him as tightly as she could. When she felt his arms around her, tightly holding her, she finally felt safe, and vented a long, broken breath.

He gently laid his cheek on her head and stroked her hair. "Shh. Nothing is going to get you. You are safe now."

"I know," she whispered, tightening her grip on him.

The sounds of many booted feet came toward them at a run and Shahly could hear the clanking of metal weapons and one human barking orders. His sudden silence came when Shahly felt one of Arden's hands leave her back.

The Prince pulled away slightly and stroked Shahly's cheek, asking, "Are you okay now?"

She looked up at him and nodded.

Many more guards and servants arrived, the red haired girl from dinner the night before among them. Ihzell rushed to them.

Nillerra also approached from down the corridor.

Shahly felt a whirl of curiosity and concern from everyone present but the black haired girl. Fear was in Nillerra's thoughts, concern for herself.

Ihzell slipped an arm around Shahly, gently stroking her back as she sympathetically said, "Poor dear. What has happened to you now?"

Nillerra laughed under her breath and sneered, "Perhaps she lost a few more of her wits."

Arden looked up, but not at the black haired girl as he said, "Nillerra, I have never struck a woman before, but I advise you not to provoke me today."

The black haired girl's mouth fell open.

Shahly still could not understand why Nillerra felt the way she did about her. The impressions she got from her mind were not quite anger, but close, more threat, but not quite fear.

Arden turned and took Shahly under his arm. "Come on. Let's get you back to your room."

Still clinging to him, Shahly walked easily with him and glanced around at the many people who still stared at her. She felt uncomfortable with all of the attention, almost threatened, even with the Prince. The urge to get away was almost overwhelming.

"Arden," she asked. "May I leave the castle for a while?"

She felt his grip tighten around her.

"Of course," he answered softly. After a long silence, he asked, "How about a ride in the forest?"

Shahly nuzzled his shoulder as she answered, "I would like that."

CHAPTER 8

rden had said he would be right back for her. *Right back* for humans was a broad spectrum of time and he had been gone for what felt to be over an hour.

Still, as she stared into her open wardrobe, Shahly was somewhat thankful he was taking his time, as she had no idea what was appropriate to wear when riding a horse through the forest with the Prince. Ihzell had made it clear that she must dress appropriately, but she had never been very specific about this.

Someone knocked on the door, unmistakably hard, unmistakably Ihzell.

Shahly turned and bade, "Come in," then watched the steward swing the door open and stride in with a white cloth draped over her arm.

Ihzell smiled and asked, "Are you ready?"

Shahly shrugged and admitted, "I don't know."

"Well," the steward comforted, "We haven't any proper riding attire for you as of yet so you can just go as you are."

Shahly felt very relieved and loosed the tension in a long breath through pursed lips.

"I brought you a shawl," Ihzell continued, taking the cloth from her arm and wrapping it around Shahly's shoulders. "There is still a chill in the air."

The shawl was soft and warm and Shahly pulled it close to her and looked to Ihzell, smiling. "This is nice."

"I thought you would like it," the steward sighed. "You just tell his Highness if you get too tired out there to have him bring you right back to the castle. I have arranged for a few guards to accompany you to keep those bandits and monsters at bay, so you will be quite safe out there."

"I am not afraid of the forest," Shahly informed. "I grew up there."

"Still," Ihzell insisted, "we must not take any chances. Bandits do not care if you are a prince's prospective bride or just a maiden lost in the forest."

"I understand," Shahly conceded. Ihzell was at least partly right. As a unicorn such bandits would be easy to elude, but not as a human.

She shuddered and cleared her mind of such thoughts.

Someone else knocked on the door.

Ihzell turned and roared, "What do you want?"

"It's me," Prince Arden answered from the other side.

The steward smiled at Shahly, then bade, "Come in, Highness. Come in."

He opened the door and proudly strode into the room. He was dressed much the way he had been when Shahly had first seen him, but his red silk shirt was different this time, more open at the neck line and revealing much of his chest. The black laces which should have held it closed were very loose, their short ends dangling carelessly near the collar. The normally puffy shirt seemed much tighter around his waist, making his chest and arms look bigger. His hair, of course, was perfectly groomed and his lips curled up slightly in a smile as his eyes found Shahly.

Shahly's heart raced for some reason and she felt hot and a little out of breath. Still staring at the Prince, she pulled the shawl from her shoulders and handed it back to Ihzell, informing, "I don't think I will need this after all."

The steward flung it back around her shoulders, scolding, "Put that back on, you little flirt."

Arden strode to Shahly and took her hands. "Sorry I'm late."

"Late?" she asked, still staring at him, then blinked and shook her head. "I had not noticed."

Ihzell loudly cleared her throat and informed, "I want you two back before dinner time and well before dark."

The Prince glanced at her and answered, "Yes, Auntie Ihzell."

"Stop that!" Ihzell barked, then gently pushed Shahly toward Arden and ordered, "You two go on now, and behave yourselves."

Prince Arden led Shahly by the hand out the door where they were met by two guards who followed them down the corridor.

They descended to the castle's ground level in silence and slowly made their way toward the door at the side of the castle which led to the stables.

Shahly felt uneasy about going out there again as memories of that unpleasant encounter were still fresh in her mind, but she felt safe with the Prince and knew in her heart he would allow no harm to come to her.

She looked up at him.

His eyes were forward, his face tense.

"You are very quiet," she observed.

He looked down at her, his eyes betraying that he felt uneasy about something as he replied, "I just feel like I am forgetting something." He sucked a breath and stopped, his eyes widening somewhat. "I *am* forgetting something! Uh, can you excuse me for a few moments? I'll be along shortly. I just have one last matter to attend to." He bent to her, touched his lips to hers, then turned and hurried back down the corridor.

Shahly watched after him, then looked up at one of the guards.

The guard shrugged. "If you will forgive me for saying so, maiden, he has been a trite flighty since he came of age."

"He's still a bright lad, though," the other quickly interjected. "Just got a lot on his mind."

"I can see," Shahly confirmed with a smile, then took each guard's arm and proceeded on with them. "He is still very sweet."

"I suppose he is," one guard agreed. "He has always been kind to those beneath him."

Shahly pondered, then looked up at the guard and asked, "Beneath him?"

The guard nodded. "Oh, you know. The guards, the servants, the peasants and people of the like."

"Should he not be kind to everyone equally?" Shahly asked.

"All should," the other guard answered, "in my humble opinion, anyway. Sadly, not all are."

Shahly looked ahead, her brow tense as she observed, "How odd." She turned and looked to the other guard. "Why would some not be kind to those of lesser status?"

"They feel they don't have to be," he answered.

The first guard cleared his throat and mumbled, "Here is a prime example of that, now."

Shahly turned her eyes ahead and saw Nillerra approaching. Behind her was that guard with the strange, predatory thoughts. Just his presence made Shahly feel uneasy and she felt the hair on the back of her neck stand up, but the guards at her sides made her feel safe.

Nillerra raised her chin as she saw Shahly and greeted her with a nod, then she stopped and asked, "Are you going out?"

Shahly also stopped and answered, "Arden and I are going to take a ride in the forest."

Nillerra nodded, clearly annoyed at something, though she tried to conceal it. She glanced at the guard behind her, and something changed in her thoughts, clearly betrayed in her eyes. "I see. Well, enjoy your ride." She proceeded on, the strange guard following.

"Thank you," Shahly responded, watching her. She wondered if she should warn Nillerra about the guard who followed her, but decided this would not be the time. Nillerra seemed well able to take care of herself in this human world, anyway.

Shahly and her guards walked on, and some time later one of the guards said, "You would do good to keep your distance from that one, Maiden."

Shahly looked up at him and asked, "From what?"

"Nillerra," he replied.

"Why?" she asked.

The guard tensed up a little and glanced away, then looked back to Shahly and said, "She is just not the kind of person a nice girl like you should associate with." He looked ahead. "I should say no more about it."

Shahly nodded.

"For your own well being," the other guard advised.

Humans seemed so protective at times, yet their behavior was confusing and erratic, just like the dragon had warned. Some acted like predators, some like nurturing parents, still others like nervous deer. They were so diverse in their personalities that Shahly wondered if they were all truly the same species.

They finally reached the door to the stables and one of the guards rushed ahead and opened it, allowing Shahly and the other guard to exit before he closed the door and joined them again.

"Will this be your first ride with the Prince?" the other guard asked.

"Not really," Shahly answered hesitantly. "He brought me home on his horse yesterday. We had quite a nice ride then."

"I heard," the other guard chuckled.

The first guard loudly cleared his throat, much the way Ihzell did when she disapproved of something, then he said, "We will be along to see to it you do not get chased by bandits again, Maiden."

She looked up at him. "You can call me Shahly if you like."

He smiled back at her. "As you wish, Shahly."

They finally reached the stables and one of the guards excused himself and went inside. The place was still bustling with activity, and even through it Shahly could sense that strange essence that she had encountered before, though it seemed to be at rest.

A moment later, the guard sighed loudly and asked as if to himself, "I wonder where his Highness is?"

As if summoned by the guard's question, Prince Arden ran right up to Shahly, out of breath and still looking very concerned about something.

Shahly tried not to notice his plight and greeted, "There you are."

"Yes," he confirmed. "I'm back."

"Your Highness," someone called from the stable, unmistakably the young voice of Audrell.

Arden's face suddenly got very grim and fear seemed to seep from him as he looked toward the stable, and tried to smile.

Shahly turned and saw Audrell striding toward them in a yellow spring dress that fit her very tightly around her waist with a neckline that finally stopped half way down her chest. The loosely fitting sleeves were very large at the cuffs and stopped at the middles of her forearms.

She reached them and curtsied to the Prince, then looked to Shahly and asked, "What brings you out here today?"

Shahly smiled pleasantly and answered, "Arden and I are going to take a ride in the forest."

All of the pleasantness in Audrell's face seemed to just wash away as she stared into Shahly's eyes for long seconds, then she looked away and softly said, "Oh. That sounds fun." Clearly, she was disappointed, hurt. The pain which flowed from her was something Shahly had never sensed before, almost loss but tainted with something else.

Shahly looked up to Prince Arden, sensing much the same feeling from him, though she also felt guilt and pity from him.

Audrell would not look at him, but clearly did not want him to know how she felt, though it was obvious.

The moment was very tense, very awkward.

Feeling she could do something to cheer everyone up, Shahly grasped Audrell's shoulder and offered her a warm smile, inviting, "Why don't you join us?"

Venting a deep, broken breath, Audrell simply shook her head and turned her eyes down, saying, "No. I do not want to be a burden."

"No!" Shahly insisted. "We would love to have you along. It would be fun." She looked to the Prince. "Wouldn't it, Arden?"

He raised his brow and nodded. "Yes. Of course it would. The more the merrier." He still clearly felt uneasy for some reason.

Hearing the Prince say it seemed to perk up Audrell's feelings and she finally turned her eyes up to him. She was obviously very fond of him and she was the only one of Arden's female guests who Shahly felt truly loved him.

She looked to Shahly and said, "If you are sure I will not be in the way."

"Of course not," Shahly assured. "We can have all kinds of fun out there together."

Audrell's smile finally returned and she said, "I would love to, then."

"Splendid!" the Prince exclaimed. "Shall we find our mounts?" He strode toward the stable, beckoning to Shahly and Audrell as he walked past them.

Shahly still sensed he felt awkward about something, but she also sensed he would rather it remain a secret, so she said nothing and acted as if she did not know.

A boy in a long red and black tunic and a bowl-like red hat on his head ran to the Prince, calling, "My Lord!"

Arden turned to him, then bent down to allow the boy to whisper something to him. When he nodded, the boy turned and fled and the Prince turned to Audrell and Shahly, shaking his head as he informed in a voice of disappointment, "I am truly sorry, ladies. My duties have called me away unexpectedly." He seemed more relieved than disappointed.

"I understand, your Highness," Audrell quickly said, then glanced at Shahly and asked, "May Shahly and I still go?"

Arden smiled and looked to Shahly.

She raised her brow as if to silently ask the same question.

He nodded and said, "Oh, I suppose."

Audrell curtsied to him and said, "Thank you, Highness," then took Shahly's arm and pulled her hard toward the stables.

Shahly stumbled a little before she took a trotting pace to keep up with Audrell.

They rounded the stable and Audrell stopped suddenly, her eyes locked on the buggy before her which already had a horse ready to pull it and four guards on horseback ready to follow. A fifth guard sat in the first seat of the buggy. The rear seat, plush and satiny red, was empty and waiting. A stable hand stood by the buggy, holding the door to it open.

Audrell slowly turned her eyes to Shahly.

Shahly looked back at her and shrugged, admitting, "I don't know how to ride horses."

Audrell laughed and said, "Fair enough," then she pulled Shahly to the buggy and invited her to enter first.

Once they were nestled in, the driver turned around and asked, "Will his Highness not be joining us?"

"No," Audrell replied. "He was called away. Shall we go?"

The driver nodded, then turned and snapped the reigns.

The horse snorted and pulled the buggy forward with a jerk.

Audrell turned to Shahly and asked, "You can't ride a horse? How did you get around in the forest without a horse?"

"We walk," Shahly answered straightly.

Audrell blinked, then asked, "Aren't you afraid of being eaten by wolves?"

Shahly giggled. "Wolves will not hunt unicorns. They prefer much smaller animals or very sick deer."

Audrell's eyes widened a little.

A chill ran throughout Shahly. That was another careless slip of the tongue. She took a deep breath and added, "Many unicorns live in that part of the forest where I come from and the wolves cannot find much to eat."

Slowly, Audrell nodded.

"Wolves don't really eat humans much, anyway," Shahly continued. "Very few forest animals do."

Audrell nodded again, then asked, "Are Dreads real? You have seen unicorns, and I think I have, but I have heard only a trite about Dreads." She seemed to be looking for reassurance.

Shahly leaned her head inquisitively. "What have you heard?"

Audrell took a breath and looked ahead as they exited the main gate. "They found parts of a man near where I used to live. The men who brought him home said he was attacked by Dreads. There was not much left of him. I was not supposed to go and look, but all of my brothers went and I did not want to be left out. It was horrible." She shuddered, then looked back to Shahly. "For two nights before it happened and several nights after we heard some unholy howling in the forest, not quite like a wolf but not quite human. We had to keep our doors and windows barred and many men had to stay out with the animals and keep fires burning to keep the Dreads away."

"Have you ever seen one?" Shahly asked.

With another shudder, Audrell shook her head, then looked to Shahly and asked, "You?"

Shahly glanced away, then looked back to her and nodded.

Audrell's face turned a little ashen and her eyes widened slightly as she whispered, "They *are* real."

"Do not be concerned with meeting any today, though," Shahly assured. "They are mostly night creatures and do not usually approach groups of other animals, especially big animals like horses and humans."

"You sure know a lot about forest animals," Audrell observed.

"It comes from living out there with them," Shahly replied.

Audrell looked ahead again. "So, aren't you going to miss living in the forest if Prince Arden chooses you?"

"I don't think he will choose me," Shahly said confidently, also looking ahead.

"Why do you say that?" Audrell asked. "He spends a copious lot of time with you and I have heard the servants talking." She looked to Shahly. "They say you occupy his every thought."

Shahly's quest flashed into her mind and she looked down to her hands, human hands folded neatly in her lap, and she softly said, "That will change."

They were silent for a moment, then Audrell took Shahly's hands and said, "If it comes to not being chosen by him, I would much rather it was you instead. At least he would be happy."

Shahly looked to her and asked, "You love him, don't you?"

Tears welled up in Audrell's eyes and she replied, "With all my heart." She sighed. "If only he knew how I love him."

"Why don't you tell him?" Shahly suggested.

"I can't."

"Why?"

Audrell folded her arms and snapped, "Could you?"

"Yes," Shahly answered.

For long seconds, Audrell was silent and just stared into Shahly's eyes, then she looked ahead, almost wishfully saying, "You are braver than I am."

"Why do you say that?"

Audrell shook her head. "To just come out and admit that to someone, to lay your heart out and let them know how you feel."

Shahly puzzled for a second, then, "Why should I keep how I feel about someone from them?"

Audrell looked down and shrugged, murmuring, "Rejection."

How odd, Shahly thought. These humans were so preoccupied with trivialities that it was no wonder they could not sense the feelings of others. Of course, she had always been afraid to admit to Vinton how she felt, and for the same reason. She smiled and shook her head, comforting, "I do not think rejection is something you should be so concerned with."

"Why not?" Audrell asked dryly.

"Because if he is going to reject you he will. Your feelings for him will not change that."

Audrell turned her eyes to Shahly.

Shahly raised her brow. "However, his knowing how you feel about him might. Being honest with him about how you feel cannot hurt what the future will bring, but it might just make your future much happier."

"Does it work for you?" Audrell asked.

Shahly shrugged.

"Then why tell me?" Audrell demanded. "Why help me?"

"Would you not help me?" Shahly countered.

Audrell turned away. "I wish I could truthfully say yes."

"I think you would," Shahly assumed.

"I am glad someone has confidence in me." Audrell looked to Shahly and continued, "My brothers seem to think I will never amount to much, maybe just the wife of a farmer or something of the like."

"Why do they think that?" Shahly asked.

"I'm the youngest," Audrell replied in a sigh, "and I am the only girl of five. Papa is a blacksmith and metal forger. He is teaching this to all of his sons so they will have some way to make a living. All I was taught was how to tend a home and garden."

"Is that bad?"

Audrell sighed again and looked up at the trees. "I just wanted more. I thought when the village sent me here to marry the Prince I would have a chance at it." She turned her eyes down. "My first meeting with him didn't go well."

"What do you mean?" Shahly asked.

Audrell was slow to answer, but finally replied, "I didn't know it was him. We met during my journey to the castle and I thought he was just another soldier on patrol. I wasn't wearing the gown the village made for me; I wasn't wearing any make-up... I had just woken up. I must have looked a fright." She shook her head. "I spoke a little too freely, and said things that probably were not proper to say to a prince." A smile managed to touch her lips. "We had a wonderful time, though. I feel like I fell for him before I even knew who he was. I just wish...."

"Is it so bad that he got to know who you really are?"

Audrell looked away and shrugged. "I don't know. A prince is supposed to have a proper lady at his side. I'm the daughter of a blacksmith and his peasant wife. We live in a peasant village. I don't know how to be a lady of the court much less a princess." She turned her eyes to Shahly. "Just be glad Prince Arden found you *after* the spring ball."

"Why?" *And what is a spring ball?* Shahly wondered.

Turning her gaze back to the forest, Audrell was again slow to answer, but finally said, "Everyone there knew how to dance in the ballroom but me. The other girls were kind of ruthless that night. Prince Arden had to teach me some steps in the next room. I just don't fit in here and everyone knows it."

Shahly smiled and nudged Audrell with her shoulder. "You fit in better than I do. And no matter what, you should always try to be happy. That should be first and foremost."

"Aye," Audrell conceded softly, then looked to Shahly and smiled. "You seem to have a lot of answers."

Shahly raised her brow and admitted, "I wish I had a few more."

Time seemed to pass quickly and Shahly hardly noticed how far they had traveled until she heard water running ahead and looked to see the river and structure spanning it that she had seen on her journey to the castle.

Audrell pointed down river and declared, "That is where I saw the unicorn. I have always heard unicorns cannot swim, but I'd wager she could out-swim you or me."

So I was seen, Shahly thought, then just nodded when Audrell looked at her.

"You believe I saw a unicorn, don't you?" Audrell asked hopefully.

"Yes!" Shahly confirmed, nodding and trying not to smile. "Of course I do."

The buggy stopped and the driver announced, "Here we are, maidens." He jumped down and opened the door, offering his hand to Audrell first.

She took his hand and gingerly stepped to the ground, then turned to Shahly.

Shahly mimicked Audrell's moves as best she could, but still stumbled slightly as she found the gravel beneath her feet. Before she even had her footing, Audrell grabbed her hand and pulled her toward the water, shouting, "Come on!"

Without hooves, running on gravel was a little uncomfortable, but in no time they were at the water's edge and Audrell stopped, smiling as she stared out over the water.

Shahly also looked, scanning the forest on the far side as if for the first time. Her absence from the forest only seemed to heighten its beauty and she looked on it with new eyes. Humans perceive colors differently than unicorns and in human form Shahly was no different. The smells of nectars and green things still seemed to be blunted in this new form, as were the sounds of the forest, the wind whispering through the trees and even the flow of the water over the rocks. Her home seemed somewhat alien to her, yet even more enchanting than she remembered.

"Isn't it beautiful?" Audrell asked dreamily.

Shahly nodded.

"Prince Arden and I come here every free moment we both have," Audrell informed. "I often come here just to get away. I can think of no more beautiful place in the whole world." She looked at Shahly and asked, "Do you want to go across?"

Shahly glanced at the river. "The water is awfully cold."

Audrell laughed. "We can cross on the bridge, silly." She took Shahly's hand and bade, "Come on," as she pulled her along again.

The wooden structure which spanned the river was much more solid than it appeared to be and offered a good look at the water from above.

Shahly stopped and leaned on the waist-high rail, looking down into the deep part of the river that she had almost drowned in. Watching the water rush by beneath her was dizzying and she shook her head.

Audrell pushed her from behind.

Shahly screamed as she felt herself falling toward the river, her arms flailing, then someone pulled back hard on her dress and she stumbled to the center of the bridge, soon realizing Audrell had a firm grip on her shoulders.

Laughing, Audrell released Shahly and playfully slapped her back, advising, "You should be more careful."

This was surprising, but all too clear that it was done in play.

Audrell turned and fled.

Shahly pursued.

Audrell jumped over the rail of the bridge and landed very close to the water's edge, then faced Shahly and backed away.

Her heart racing, Shahly also jumped over the rail of the bridge but landed way off balance and fell into the shallow, near freezing water, screaming as the chill penetrated to her bones.

Audrell covered her mouth and laughed hysterically.

Shahly sucked a breath, her mouth wide open, then her eyes narrowed as she saw Audrell laughing at her again. This did not seem funny, but she smiled and struck the water with her hand, sending icy drops of water all over Audrell, who screamed and laughed even harder.

Scrambling from the river, Shahly continued to pelt her hysterical attacker with water, but when Audrell knelt down and splashed back, Shahly found herself laughing too as she cringed against the onslaught of cold water.

The water war continued for an unknown time, and finally ended when Audrell backed up the bank and shouted, "Okay! Okay! I give up!" She fell back and sat down on the sand, wrapping her hands up in her skirt.

Shahly joined her there, sitting down beside her, then declared, "Ow!" as she looked down to her hands, which were red, cold, and aching horribly. Wrapping them in her skirt as Audrell did seemed to be a very good idea.

Audrell vented a deep breath as she looked down to the river. "I'll wager this place is wonderful in the summer time. I would spend all of my time every day here if I could."

"It seems a little cold right now," Shahly observed.

Giggling, Audrell pushed her shoulder and said, "Aye, you would definitely be the one to know."

Shahly nodded. "That I would. Twice, now."

"Wouldn't it be grand to live out here?" Audrell asked dreamily. "Not a care in the world, no need to be prim and proper for the royal court, no one telling you where to go, when to eat, how to dress... No order. Just freedom."

Shahly sighed. "I have lived that life. Someday, I hope to live it again."

"As princess?" Audrell asked softly.

With another deep breath, Shahly stared blankly into the running water, remembering how her life had been only two days ago, what seemed like an eternity now, then she shook her head and answered, "No. As my old self."

"Do *you* love Prince Arden?" Audrell asked straightly.

If only these humans understood how difficult that question was.

Shahly bowed her head, closed her eyes, and nodded.

Audrell vented a deep breath and shook her head. "At least two of us do. Those other tramps just want him because he is a prince. Oh, Urcean claims to love him, but her true feelings are all too obvious, especially since she has such an eye for several other men around the castle."

Shahly looked to Audrell and asked, "Why would she want more than one mate?"

Audrell shrugged. "I don't know. If I had Arden as my husband, no one else would even appeal to me." She drew a deep breath and sighed, "He is so beautiful."

Shahly turned her head slightly as Audrell went into detail about Arden's attributes. Something was wrong. The birds in the trees and underbrush behind them had stopped singing. An odd odor was there, not the scent of forest animals. This was the odor of unkempt humans and leather. Faint was the smell of at least one horse. Sulfur and char found her senses, too, very, very faint on the breeze.

The hair on the back of her neck stood up and every muscle in her body tensed. She sat up straight, her heart pounding, her legs taut and ready for flight. Breathing shallowly through her mouth, Shahly slowly looked toward the river, trying to listen behind her.

Whoever was back there was very still, not wanting to be noticed.

She reached back with her essence and felt them, four male humans. Their thoughts were predatory, like that guard from the castle.

Her essence touched something else, something powerful and distant, then it was gone.

The humans!

Slowly, Shahly planted her palms on the sand and drew her feet up to her.

"Shahly?" Audrell called softly to her.

"We need to go," Shahly informed, "very quickly."

"What's wrong?" Fear was in Audrell's voice.

Shahly scanned the river bank, seeing three of the guards leisurely talking with one another on the other side while two others tended the horses. She knew she could trick the minds of the humans behind her, but Audrell's presence would complicate that as she lacked a similar defense.

"Run for the bridge," Shahly ordered. "Run as fast as you can and don't look back, no matter what."

"If something is wrong then we need to get the guards' attention," Audrell informed in a low voice.

"You must get closer to them, first," Shahly insisted.

"Me?" Audrell asked nervously. "What about you?"

A faint rustling in the brush behind them alerted Shahly and she felt their minds quicken. "Just go, Audrell. Now!"

Audrell went to stand, then hesitated and looked to Shahly.

"They are coming!" Shahly hissed, her teeth clenched. "Go!"

Springing to her feet, Audrell ran toward the bridge, screaming for the guards.

Shahly also sprang up, wheeling around as the four men burst from the underbrush. They were less than ten paces away. She thrust her essence at them, suggesting a horrible threat.

They stopped. One retreated. Two glanced behind them. The fourth shielded his eyes.

Shahly glanced back at Audrell, who had fallen on the bridge and was just getting back to her feet. She had to buy her more time, so she darted around the bewildered men, found the road she had traveled earlier and sprinted down it.

Half a moment later she heard them in pursuit.

Running down this dirt and gravel road in slippers on human feet was painful and Shahly found herself slowing. Running in human form was also quite different than as a unicorn and, try as she may, she just could not attain the speed she was accustomed to.

Something sharply cut the air behind her and a second later her legs were snared at the knees by thin, weighted ropes.

Shahly fell forward, instinctively breaking her fall with her hands, one hitting something sharp in the road. She cried out as pain ripped into her palm, and she pulled her hand to her, tightly holding her wrist. She looked down at it and saw the deep gash from the middle of her palm nearly to her wrist, then her breath caught as shadows fell over her.

Slowly, she looked over her shoulder.

The four humans who loomed over her looked and smelled much like the hunters who had pursued her before, yet she did not recognize them. All of them had hair on their faces, wore leather and steel armor, and had predatory looks in their eyes.

She cringed as two reached for her, but she knew it was futile to struggle against them and allowed them to pull her to her feet.

One, with red hair on his face and head, smiled and grasped her throat, bent close to her and said, "Aye, we got the better of the two, I think." His breath really stank.

"Those guards will be along in short order," another informed. His voice was familiar, though Shahly did not recognize him.

The red haired man drew his dagger and snarled, "The others'll hold 'em off until we finish with this little vixen." He drew the side of the dagger along Shahly's cheek. "Aye, we'll not let this one go to waste."

His thoughts were horrifying. He had an evil wanting of her and no discipline, nothing to stop him. He slowly grasped a handful of Shahly's dress at the neckline, then brutally jerked on it, ripping the material from her shoulder.

Tears welled up in Shahly's eyes and her heart pumped terror throughout her. She knew what he wanted. He would ultimately kill her. Knowing what he wanted, she prayed he would kill her first and wished now that she had gone with Audrell.

"Let's take 'er to the woods," another suggested. "I don't want to be busy with 'er and have them guards find us."

The red haired one nodded and sneered, "Aye."

Shahly felt and heard a thump on the ground, then another. Another, closer.

The humans were too preoccupied with their horrible thoughts to notice.

A louder thump shook the ground, then another.

As they took her toward the trees, one holding her stopped, looked around and asked, "What was that?"

They all looked around and another asked, "What?"

A dragon roared, loudly and nearby.

Shahly looked behind her, shrieking a gasp as the black dragon strode around a bend in the road, hunched over and looking like a predator on the hunt. His eyes found them and narrowed, then his jaws gaped and he bared his many sword-sized teeth and roared again.

The humans screamed and ran back down the road, toward the river, dragging Shahly along with them.

The dragon growled, quickening his pace as he rapidly overtook them.

"Give 'im the girl!" one human shouted. "She'll slow 'im up and give us some distance."

The red haired man grabbed her arm and brutally jerked her sideways.

Shahly stumbled and rolled to the ground, coming to her senses quickly as a talon-like foot slammed onto the ground a pace away from her, then another on the other side. She looked to the humans who had left her at the mercy of the dragon, then slowly turned her eyes up to his.

The dragon drew his head back and growled, "Well, that's chivalry for you, nowadays." He took two steps back and shook his head as he looked down at her. "Do you just enjoy being chased by humans?"

"No," Shahly answered timidly.

"Well," he countered, "you seem to be making a habit of it." He seated himself before her and asked, "So how are things going in the castle?"

Shahly struggled to her feet, still cradling her injured hand, which stung horribly, and she replied, "Not as well as I had hoped. I have had little time to look for your Falloah or Vinton."

"Well, you have little time left," he informed, then looked down the road where the humans had disappeared. "But I see you are taking time to make some friends."

"I don't know who they are," Shahly admitted.

"You should think about staying closer to the castle," the dragon advised. "You might live longer that way. And you need to find Falloah soon and get your stallion out of there. Time is growing very short for you both."

Shahly's throat felt tight and she asked, "Did you attack them?"

"Who?"

Shahly raised her chin. "Arden said you attacked the castle. That is why they started building the talisman of unicorn spirals."

The dragon leaned his head. "So. You found out about the Talisman."

"Yes," Shahly answered sharply. "They built it to keep you away. And they killed my people to build it!" She felt herself near tears, but refused to break down. She needed answers.

He shook his head. "You don't seem to understand. My objective is to get rid of the Talisman and those building it as well as those who hunt your kind. They use the Talisman to defend themselves against dragons, but they are building a second to attack dragons. I knew about this even before they completed the first, and they can't be allowed to complete it."

Shahly looked away, then back to the dragon. "Falloah was trying to break the Talisman, wasn't she?"

The dragon looked toward the castle, his eyes glowing red. "That is why I sent her there. That is why she must be freed."

"So you can attack them again?" Shahly snapped.

"Of course," was his dry answer.

"There must be another way," Shahly insisted.

"There is no other way," the dragon growled, then looked back down to her. "You don't worry about the Talisman. Just free Falloah and get your stallion out of there before they kill him. And remember my warnings."

Vinton. Arden.

Shahly glanced away, then bowed her head and nodded, conceding, "I will."

"They're coming," the dragon warned.

Shahly wheeled around. "But you chased them away!"

"No," the dragon corrected, "these humans are on your side, I think."

She looked up at the dragon and asked, "What should I tell them?"

The dragon turned his eyes to her and informed, "You won't need to tell them anything." He waved his huge, clawed hand before her.

Everything went black.

CHAPTER 9

"Shahly?"

Arden's gentle voice.

Dreamless sleep.

Someone grasped her hand; something wrapped around it and someone gently stroked her cheek.

Shahly moaned, recognizing her own human voice. With much effort, she opened her eyes. The visions she saw were blurry. She took a deep breath and blinked. Finally, Arden's face came into focus and she woke fully, smiling back at him.

He stroked her cheek and gently said, "Welcome back."

"You had us worried," Audrell's voice informed from the other side.

Shahly turned her head and saw Audrell sitting on the bed, smiling down at her, though a little strain was in her eyes. Ihzell sat beside Audrell and had Shahly's hand in her lap. She was neatly tying a white cloth around her hand and was concentrating very hard on what she was doing.

Shahly drew a deep breath and managed, "Ihzell?"

The steward glanced at her, then went about her work. She was eerily silent. Something was wrong.

"I was so afraid for you," Audrell said. "I just knew those bandits had gotten you. Then we heard that horrible roar."

"I am okay," Shahly assured. "I just cut my hand when I fell. Nothing else happened to me."

Ihzell finished with the bandage, laid Shahly's hand across her belly and patted it, asking, "You are certain you are hurt nowhere else?"

"Positive," Shahly confirmed.

The steward smiled slightly, then suddenly grabbed Shahly's dress and brutally pulled her up, shouting, "Are you out of your mind? You could have been killed out there!"

"Ihzell!" Arden barked.

Shahly fearfully stared into Ihzell's eyes, knowing she was angry about something but also seeing concern there, and plenty of fear.

"What were you thinking?" Ihzell ranted. "You must never run off alone like that! Do you understand?"

Tears welled up in Shahly's eyes and she offered with trembling lips, "I'm sorry."

The steward drew a breath, then tightly embraced Shahly, rocking her back and forth as she gently ordered, "Just don't every scare me like that again. I thought the worst when they brought you back."

"I'll be more careful," Shahly whispered. "Thank you for caring about me."

"It's my job, dear."

Audrell grasped Shahly's shoulder and said, "Thanks for saving me out there. I owe you my life."

Shahly smiled at her, correcting, "No you don't."

Audrell smiled back and insisted, "Sure I do."

Ihzell pulled away from Shahly and stood, grumbling, "Okay, enough of this dribble. Audrell, dear, you need to go and get yourself changed for dinner. And I want you to bathe."

Audrell rolled her eyes and turned for the door, sighing, "Yes, Miss."

"I have that blue gown finished and in your room," the steward informed. "It would look just smashing on you with the pearl ensemble."

Audrell spun around, smiling as she squealed, "Thank you." Her eyes caught the Prince and she bit her lip, drawing her hands to her, then offered, "I will see you at dinner, your Highness."

He smiled and said, "I always look forward to seeing you."

She smiled back, turned and almost danced out the door.

Arden took Shahly's hands and helped her from the bed, then gently grasped her waist and gazed into her eyes, the corners of his lips curling up slightly as he said, "I am glad you are feeling better."

She slid her arms around him and smiled back, looking up into his eyes and feeling that familiar warmth grow within her.

Ihzell loudly cleared her throat.

Arden glanced at her, then looked back to Shahly and said, "Perhaps I should allow you to change out of this torn gown."

"I suppose I should," Shahly agreed dreamily.

When the Prince bent to kiss her, Ihzell pulled him away by the arm and toward the door, saying, "And perhaps his Highness also needs to get ready for dinner."

He stumbled at first, then turned and pulled his arm away as he made his way to the door, sighing, "Yes, Auntie Ihzell."

"Stop that!" Ihzell barked as he left. She slammed the door behind him and turned back to Shahly, striding to her. "You do not appear to be very traumatized by your ordeal."

"I'm fine," Shahly assured, somehow barely remembering anything that had happened, anyway. "I am sorry I frightened you so."

"Never mind that," Ihzell ordered. "We do not want this little incident to be common knowledge, so do not speak of it openly at dinner."

Shahly nodded.

"Well, come, come. Get your slippers on. I have a new gown waiting in the sewing room. We have a few alterations to make before dinner tonight."

Shahly sat down on the bed and pulled her slippers on. "If you keep making all of these dresses we are going to run out of room to put them."

"You just let me worry about that." The steward took Shahly's hands and pulled her to her feet. "You are going to look absolutely heavenly."

Shahly smiled and wrapped her arms around one of Ihzell's, leaning into her as she sighed, "I always feel that way when I am around Arden."

Ihzell eyed her suspiciously. "I need to have you two supervised more closely."

Shahly giggled as they left the room.

⊘

This dinner gathering did not feel as tense as the last, but Shahly still did not feel very comfortable. Her dress was light blue satin with a broad white ribbon around her midriff. The low neckline and bell of the skirt were accented with white and silver lace and long, uncomfortable sleeves ended in white lace cuffs.

Many of the other girls seemed fascinated with her and questions were in abundance as Shahly was milked for information on unicorns.

Formerly one of the most talkative of the bunch, Audrell, seated beside Shahly and dressed in a darker blue gown, was silent for the most part.

Nillerra, seated across from Audrell and dressed in red and black, was also silent, but her eyes darted to Shahly many times, though she refused to make eye contact even once. Something about her seemed amiss. She would not even look in Prince Arden's direction.

The brown haired girl in yellow sitting next to the Prince and across from Shahly shook her head and insisted, "That is simply impossible.

Unicorns are afraid of deep water and cannot swim." She looked to Audrell. "And before you say it, that was a horse you saw, not a unicorn."

Audrell raised her brow and picked at her fruit salad, retorting, "I don't think so, Urcean."

The red haired girl in white down the table leaned toward the brown haired girl and asked, "How do you know they fear water?"

Urcean rolled her eyes and vented a deep breath. "Everyone knows that. Have you not read any of the scripts on unicorns?"

"What do you think, Shahly?" the red haired girl asked, looking at her.

Shahly looked back at her and answered, "There are many misconceptions about unicorns and many truths." She looked to the brown haired girl. "They do swim, though."

"Have you seen this?" Urcean asked.

Shahly nodded, then took a big mouthful of her fruit salad.

"Why should we believe you?" the brown haired girl spat.

Shahly could not understand why this human constantly challenged her knowledge of unicorns, so she just shrugged.

Staring down at her bowl, Nillerra unexpectedly said, "Because she is from the forest, and you have not spent enough time in the forest to know for yourself."

"So what difference does that make?" Urcean snapped.

Nillerra slowly turned her dark eyes on the brown haired girl. "Do you know any different?"

Urcean stared at her for many long seconds, then looked back to her bowl.

"Didn't think so," Nillerra chided.

The last thing Shahly expected was for Nillerra to come to her defense.

The servants emerged from the kitchen with trays of cheese and bread and pitchers of wine. The Queen was served first and the others began working their way down the table.

Nillerra looked to Shahly and pleasantly said, "So. I hear you and Audrell had quite the little adventure today."

Ihzell had been very specific about not speaking of this matter openly and Shahly felt a tremor within. She looked to Audrell, noticing she, too, felt uncomfortable.

Everyone was quiet. Attention was on Shahly.

This awkward moment felt worse than the incident itself.

Still, with Nillerra finally acting friendly toward her, Shahly did not want to provoke her by denying her an answer. Not now.

She looked to Nillerra, answering straightly, "It was very frightening. I am glad just to have survived."

Nillerra turned her eyes to one of the servants approaching from the far end of the table, nodded once, then looked back to Shahly, asking, "What happened to your hand?"

Shahly glanced down at her neatly bandaged hand, then back to Nillerra as wine goblets were distributed before them. "I fell. It is not bad." Shahly's instincts warned of something sinister in the black haired girl's voice.

A servant filled Nillerra's wine goblet.

Nillerra picked up the goblet and stared at it for long seconds, then turned her eyes to Shahly and advised, "You should be more careful."

Shahly nodded, timidly assuring, "I will."

Another servant, a dark haired girl who looked to be not quite a woman, reached around Audrell and poured wine carefully into her goblet, then turned to pour wine into Shahly's.

Shahly looked to her just as an older, larger, dark blond servant with a tray of bread and cheese bumped the girl hard on the back with her elbow.

Red wine splashed onto the table and into Shahly's lap.

Shahly drew back with a jerk as the wine cascaded off of the table and onto her dress.

The servant girl dropped the near empty pitcher.

Shahly took her napkin and tried to wipe some of the wine from her dress. The smell of it was very strong and it darkened the blue of her gown to purple. Hearing a sob, Shahly looked up to the servant girl.

The servant backed away, her hands covering her mouth as she stared with wide eyes at Shahly's dress. She looked to Shahly, lowered her hands and whimpered, "I am so sorry."

The taller woman, the one who had caused the accident, seized the girl's arm and pulled her brutally toward the kitchen, scolding, "Clumsy fool!"

"Please," the girl begged. "I am sorry. I didn't mean—"

"You are going to be very sorry, you clumsy little wretch."

The girl was very frightened. The larger woman clearly meant to do something awful to her.

Shahly turned to the Prince, pleading to him with her eyes, though she could only say, "Arden."

The Prince nodded to her, then stood and bade, "Wait."

The servant woman stopped and turned, then, still dragging her helper along, approached him and bowed, responding, "Your Highness."

Arden looked down to the servant girl.

She also bowed, tears dropping from her eyes.

"It is all right," he assured.

Timidly, she raised her head and looked to him, still sobbing.

A fatherly smile curved the Prince's lips and he ordered, "Go about your duties. We will overlook this tonight."

Her jaw quivering, she curtsied deeply to him and whimpered, "Thank you, your Highness. Thank you."

He nodded to her, then looked to the older servant and sternly informed, "It is forgotten."

She bowed to him. "I understand, your Highness." She glanced toward Nillerra as she turned and strode back into the kitchen.

Shahly looked that way, noticing the black haired girl was watching the servants return to the kitchen as she took a sip of her wine. Clearly, she would not have been as forgiving.

Arden looked down to Shahly's dress and shook his head. "You are a mess."

She looked down at the stains, then up to the Prince and suggested, "Perhaps I should go and change."

He nodded. "I agree."

Audrell stood as Shahly did, approached the Prince and curtsied to him, asking, "May I go too, Highness?"

He folded his arms. "So the two of you can exchange thoughts about me?"

Shahly looked up to him and raised her brow, informing, "Yes, and it would be easier if you were not around listening to us."

He laughed under his breath, shaking his head as he agreed, "Fine. Go on."

They turned and curtsied to the Queen and Audrell said, "By your leave, your Grace?"

She casually waved them away, then raised her goblet to her lips.

Shahly turned and followed Audrell out of the dining hall, smiling coyly at the Prince as she walked past him.

They reached the top of the stairs and Audrell looked back to Shahly, slowing to allow her to come abreast as she warned, "She is going to kill you."

Shahly smiled. "I am sure she will understand. It was just an accident, after all."

"Aye, but still. She worked very hard on that dress."

"She also very much enjoyed doing it. She told me so herself."

They arrived at the door to the sewing room and Audrell reached for the latch, then she turned to Shahly and took a deep breath, offering, "Good luck."

Shahly rolled her eyes and entered behind Audrell, greeting, "Hello, Ihzell."

The steward turned from the dress she was working on and said, "Shahly, I didn't expect—oh my god!"

Shahly held up her stained skirt and reported, "I had a little accident."

"I can see that!" the steward ranted. "And I told you not to drink so much wine. Look what has happened!"

Shahly's brow arched. "Well, I didn't actually drink any."

"No, you swam in it!" Ihzell shook her head and strode to Shahly. "Audrell, would you be a sweetheart and help me get her out of this dress? And close the door."

Audrell complied, saying, "Yes, miss."

Ihzell shook her head again as she worked. "Goodness. You are definitely going to need a bath before you go out again." She glanced around and sighed. "And I already sent the girls home for the evening."

"I can help," Audrell offered. "What do you want me to do?"

Ihzell smiled at her and said, "Thank you, dear. I need her soaps and perfumes. They are in her room on her vanity."

"Will you need more towels?" Audrell asked eagerly.

"No, no," the steward answered. "Just bring what I asked for, and hurry, child. The Prince is likely to come out of the woodwork any moment."

Shahly giggled. "No, he was still eating dinner when we left."

"That does not matter," Ihzell informed. "That boy would gladly skip a course if there is something he would rather do." She looked to Audrell. "Go on, dear, and get back here quickly."

Audrell nodded and fled the room.

The steward tossed the stained dress aside and helped Shahly into a soft, terry robe, then backed away and sighed. "You are a mess."

"That is just what Arden said," Shahly informed.

Someone knocked on the door and a hinge creaked as it slowly opened.

Shahly turned and saw the servant girl who had spilled the wine on her peer into the room.

"Miss Ihzell," she said timidly. "May I come in?"

"Yes, of course," the steward sighed.

The girl hesitantly entered, her eyes finding the wine stained dress crumpled on the floor. She instantly welled up with tears and sobbed, "I am so sorry, miss. I really did not mean to." She looked to Shahly and apologized again, "I am sorry."

Shahly smiled at the girl and took her hands. "There is no need. It was just an accident."

"You did this?" Ihzell bellowed.

The girl cringed, looked up at the steward and nodded.

Staring down at the girl, Ihzell sighed, then shook her head and, in a much calmer voice said, "Well, the least you can do is help us clean this mess up."

"Please forgive me," the girl sobbed.

"Help me here and it will be forgotten," the steward assured, suddenly sounding very motherly. "Now, we will need water for a bath and we need to clean that dress before the stain sets in too badly. Come now. Get to it."

The girl glanced away and timidly informed, "Miss Verrta said I should go right back to the kitchen after I apologize."

Ihzell set her hands on her hips and raised her brow. "Did she, now? Well, if Miss Verrta has any objections you can tell her to voice them directly with me, and find herself another place to work. Come, come. Get to the back and throw some wood in the stove so we can heat some water."

The girl nodded and hurried off.

Shahly looked to Ihzell and assured, "There is really no need for all of this trouble. I can just swim in the river. That usually gets me pretty clean."

Ihzell smiled and stroked Shahly's cheek, saying, "You are such a sweetheart," then she took Shahly's hand and pulled her toward the back room. "But you *are* going to have a bath tonight."

A hot bath was soon prepared in a large, white marble tub and Shahly approached it slowly. The water had thin ribbons of steam rising from it and she was hesitant to test its temperature, but finally ran her hand across it and found it hot, but not uncomfortably so. She glanced at the door, wondering if she should wait for Ihzell and her helper to return.

She turned her eyes back to the water and stared at it a moment longer, then opened the robe and allowed it to slide from her arms to the floor, then she hesitantly stepped in. The hot water was very soothing, very relaxing, and she settled herself all the way in and slouched down, leaning her head back against the rounded rim of the tub. All of the day's stresses seemed to melt away and she felt every part of her body slowly going limp, so she closed her eyes and settled herself into sweet daydreams, instantly finding Arden there.

She opened her eyes an unknown time later as she heard the steward stride into the room carrying a red flask. The servant girl was behind her with an armload of towels and a small white bucket.

Shahly dreamily smiled at Ihzell.

"Well," the steward said. "You look comfortable."

"This is wonderful," Shahly sleepily replied.

Ihzell approached and patted Shahly's head. "I thought you might like it. Deep breath."

"Deep what?" Shahly asked, then winced as Ihzell pushed her head under the water. She gulped a deep breath and grasped the sides of the tub as Ihzell pulled her back up by the hair.

"Be still, dear," Ihzell ordered. "Keep your eyes closed."

Something thick and cold oozed onto Shahly's head.

"What are you doing?" she asked a little fearfully.

"I am washing your hair," the steward answered straightly.

"But I didn't get any wine on my hair."

Ihzell laughed softly. "You are getting your hair washed anyway. Be still."

Shahly finally relaxed and settled herself against the back of the tub, then breathed in deeply as she finally smelled the sweet aroma of the shampoo, observing, "It smells good, like strawberries."

Ihzell began working the lather through Shahly's long hair. "The shampoo, you mean? Well, it is made with the extract from strawberries. Makes your hair smell good. Bring me that pail, dear."

Shahly opened her eyes and saw the servant girl dip the pail into the water and hand it to the steward. A second later the water was dumped over her head. She closed her eyes and squealed as the water cascaded down her face, then she brushed her hair from her face and laughed, insisting, "Do it again!"

"Gladly," Ihzell agreed, then dumped another bucket of water over Shahly's head.

Shahly giggled and shook her head, sending water everywhere.

"Enough of that!" Ihzell scolded.

Smiling, Shahly looked to the servant girl and shook her head again.

The servant girl laughed and tried to shield herself with her hands.

"Stop that!" Ihzell laughed.

Shahly looked up to the steward with a big, mischievous smile.

"Little scamp," Ihzell said, then looked toward the door and asked aloud, yet to herself, "Where is Audrell? She should have been back some time ago." She shook her head and looked back down to Shahly. "No matter. Let's get you out of that tub and find you some clothes."

Shahly stood and stepped out of the tub and was instantly wrapped in the terry robe by the servant girl while Ihzell put a towel to her head and violently rubbed the water from her hair.

"We should put a comb to this before someone sees you," the steward ordered, then growled, "Where is that girl? She should not have been gone so long."

"Perhaps she could not find what she was looking for," Shahly suggested.

"Perhaps," Ihzell sighed. "Well, let's get you to your room and find you something to wear. Does Prince Arden still want to wander the gardens with you tonight?"

Shahly nodded.

Ihzell turned her and gently pushed her by the shoulders toward the door. "Then you will need a shawl. It is chilly out. Where are your slippers?"

Shahly glanced back at her. "They had wine on them and you threw them out the window."

The steward sighed again. "Oh, yes. So I did. Oh well. We will find you another pair. Come along."

The door burst open and a young guard stormed in, out of breath and slightly pale. His eyes were wide and his pupils big, his face suspended in a fearful pose. He looked directly to the steward and started, "Miss Ihzell…"

"What is the meaning of this?" the steward barked. "Weren't you taught better than to barge into a room where a young lady is bathing?"

He glanced at Shahly, then looked back to Ihzell, shaking his head as he stammered, "I am—You had best come, Miss."

"Well what is it?" Ihzell demanded.

Shahly looked deeply into his eyes and saw the image there in his memory. It was horrible. There in his most recent memory was Audrell, lying on a colorful rug. Part of the rug around her head was stained darker than the rest, purple where it should have been blue and crimson where it should have been white.

Shahly's throat tightened and she could feel her heart pounding hard within as she breathed, "Audrell."

The guard looked to her and hesitantly nodded.

Ihzell took Shahly's shoulder and asked, "What about Audrell? Shahly?"

"Oh, no!" Shahly cried, then she screamed it again as she bolted out the door.

She ran at a full sprint all the way to her room and froze in the doorway as her eyes found the horror she had seen in the young guard's mind.

Audrell lay face down and partly on her side a few paces from the door, sprawled on the floor like a doll which had been dropped. She barely breathed and the rug around her head was stained dark, just like in the guard's memory.

A palace guard was kneeling beside her. He looked up to Shahly. The pain he felt for the stricken girl was in his eyes.

A pace away from Audrell's head was a small metal mallet with blunt spikes on both sides. It was stained red.

Shahly slowly approached and knelt down beside her fallen friend, gingerly laying a hand on her back. Audrell's life force was weak and Shahly could sense the recent memory repeating over and over in her mind.

Ihzell, the servant girl and the guard finally caught up and ran into the room, stopping just inside the doorway.

The servant girl shrieked and covered her mouth, her eyes wide and locked on the horrible scene before her.

Ihzell slowly shook her head and breathed, "Dear God!"

Tears streaming from her eyes, Shahly looked back down to Audrell, then looked up as the steward knelt down beside her.

Ihzell felt of the fallen girl's throat, then looked up to the older guard as she demanded, "What happened?"

He shook his head and reported, "We found her like this when we came to post at Maid Shahly's room. The door was ajar and most of the lamps had been blown out."

The steward's breath caught and she looked fearfully at Shahly. There was a different fear in her eyes, not the concern for Audrell that Shahly expected; rather it was something that warned of danger. This was a fear that Shahly remembered from when she was very young, a fear that was in her mother's eyes when a predator would stray too close to the herd. It fed Shahly's uneasiness.

Ihzell shook her head, then folded a towel she still held and pressed it to Audrell's wounded head, ordering, "Find something to tie this in place with."

The servant girl ripped a piece from her skirt, then handed it to the steward.

Ihzell tightly tied the makeshift bandage in place and looked to the guard again. "We need to get her to her room."

He nodded and slowly slid his arms beneath Audrell's shoulders and knees and gently picked her up, cradling her tenderly in his arms.

As he stood, Ihzell supported her head and laid it against the guard's shoulder, saying, "Gently now." She crossed Audrell's arms in her lap and stroked her hair, offering, "We will get you to your room now, dear. Just hold on a while longer." She looked to the younger guard and ordered, "Go find Captain Ocnarr and tell him what happened and that I require his presence at Maid Audrell's suite, then inform Prince Arden." She seized his arm as he turned to leave and swung him back around. "And I want this incident kept quiet. No one else is to be told, understand?"

He nodded, responding, "Yes, Miss," then he turned and fled the room.

The older guard looked to Ihzell and informed, "The corridor on this level should be relatively clear this time of the evening. We should go ahead and take her to her room now."

Ihzell nodded, then took Shahly's hand as he turned to leave and ordered, "Come along, Shahly."

The walk to Audrell's room was not that far, but it seemed to take an eternity to get there. No one spoke and only footsteps could be heard.

The servant girl rushed ahead of them and opened a door, standing out of the way as the guard and Ihzell hurried through.

Shahly followed, wringing her hands together as she watched Ihzell pull the sheet and blanket of the bed back and the guard gently laid Audrell on the bed.

The white towel was already red where it touched Audrell and Ihzell pressed on it gently, then looked to the servant girl and asked, "Do you know where my bandages and healing agents are?"

Hesitantly, the girl nodded, then assured, "I will get them for you, Miss," as she fled the room.

Ihzell turned to Shahly and ordered, "Bring me the basin and pitcher, dear." She pointed to the lavatory.

Shahly blinked, then looked that way. Water! Ihzell wanted water! She rushed to the lavatory and picked up the basin and water filled pitcher that sat in it. It was heavier than it looked and awkward as the water moved in it. Carefully, she turned and carried her burden to the steward, her eyes locked on it.

"On the night stand," Ihzell ordered, moving a lamp to make more room.

Shahly awkwardly set the basin down and backed away as Ihzell worked.

"More towels, please," the steward said, trying not to sound concerned, though Shahly knew her to be.

The guard rummaged through Audrell's wardrobe, producing and armload of towels and a terry robe.

Ihzell worked for many moments longer, removing the make-shift bandage and holding a clean towel to Audrell's wound as she carefully cleaned around it. She was quiet, telling Shahly that she was indeed very, very worried.

The servant girl returned with a wooden box and rushed to the bed with it, laying it down beside the steward.

Bandages and powders were repeatedly applied, but the wound continued to stubbornly bleed.

Long moments drug on.

Frustrated, Ihzell vented a long breath and shook her head.

Ocnarr, with a half dozen guards behind him, burst into the room, glanced around, then stormed to the bed and demanded, "What happened?"

Long seconds passed as the steward continued to work with the bandages and powders, then she finally answered, "She was attacked."

"Do you know by whom?" Ocnarr growled, his eyes on Audrell.

"We can talk about it in a moment," Ihzell said dryly.

Ocnarr nodded, still staring down at Audrell, then he turned to the other guards and ordered, "You two post outside this door, you two at opposite ends of the hallway."

Four of them turned and strode from the room.

Ihzell glanced back at Ocnarr and informed, "I would like someone at Maid Shahly's door as well."

"Already done," the Captain assured, then looked to the guard who had found Audrell and asked, "You were there with her?"

He nodded, replying, "I found her."

"Come with me," Ocnarr ordered.

They turned and strode from the room, the guard who had found Audrell glancing back at her as he left. He, too, looked concerned and Shahly knew he wanted to stay with her.

As they left, the two remaining guards took up their positions flanking the inside of the door, watching Ihzell's efforts to control the wound.

Many long moments drug by as before.

Finally, a bandage was in place and tied neatly around the girl's head. The bleeding finally seemed to have stopped.

Ihzell leaned back and vented a deep breath as she rubbed her eyes, then she looked to the servant girl and ordered, "Help me get her out of this gown and ready for bed." She looked up at Shahly. "Can you help?"

Shahly nodded, finally feeling that she could be of some assistance.

"Gently," Ihzell ordered as she worked, then she looked to the guards and raised her brow. "Do you mind?"

They glanced at each other, then looked back at the steward, turned and stepped out of the room.

"Close the door, please," Ihzell called after them, turning her attention back on her patient.

Soon, they had Audrell out of her dress and comfortably beneath her sheet and blanket, covered to her shoulders.

Some time later, they sat on the bed with the injured Audrell, Shahly on one side and Ihzell on the other with the young kitchen maid.

Never had Shahly felt so absolutely helpless.

Through it all, the servant girl stayed nearby, seated on the foot of the bed much of the time and assisting the steward when she was called upon.

No one spoke for what seemed like hours.

Shahly grasped Audrell's hand in both of hers, willing her to be strong, willing her to heal. In unicorn form, such a healing would be difficult and tiring, though much more productive than what the well-meaning humans were doing at the moment. Shahly wondered if she could even work her natural healing abilities in human form, yet she knew she dare not even try in front of the humans.

Her reason for coming to Red Stone Castle tried to weigh itself on her, but even it, even thoughts of Vinton could not seem to distract her from the crisis at hand.

The door latch clicked and the hinges creaked slightly as the door opened.

Shahly looked to the door and saw the Prince, still dressed as he had been at dinner, slip into the room with the younger guard right behind him. His eyes were locked wide on Audrell and Shahly could easily see the concern he had for her.

Through it all, his true feelings for Audrell pushed forth.

He loved her. His feelings for her were much like those he felt for Shahly, but somehow they were much more deeply rooted.

Ihzell checked the snugness of the bandage, then stood and took the Prince's arm, leading him back toward the door.

Shahly watched them for a moment as they stood by the door and whispered to one another. She could not clearly hear what was said, but she knew they spoke of what happened to Audrell, and she heard her own name at least once.

She looked back down to her injured friend. With her essence, she could see into Audrell's mind but could make out little more than fear and pain, and the awful memory that repeated over and over.

Moments later, Arden approached and sat on the bed across from Shahly, taking Audrell's hand as he looked tenderly to her sleeping face.

"Why would anyone do this?" Shahly asked softly.

Slowly, the Prince shook his head and replied, "I don't know, Love. I wish I could tell you." He looked to Shahly and took her arm. "I am going to stay with her for a while. You look as if you could use some rest."

She looked back down at Audrell, staring at her for a moment, then shrugged.

"Go on," the Prince ordered. "I will be here if you need me."

Shahly sighed and nodded, then stood from the bed and walked to Ihzell, who waited by the door.

Ihzell slipped an arm around Shahly's shoulders and led her toward the door, comforting, "It will be all right, child. You can come back and visit her in the morning."

Shahly stopped and looked back at the Prince, at Audrell. As she saw him sitting there beside her, something within felt uneasy, an awkward feeling that she had never experienced, yet it was strangely familiar. She felt threatened, afraid, almost betrayed. These feelings, so alien, yet so familiar.

Nillerra! She had felt this from Nillerra!

She turned back toward the door, struggling to sort out these strange sensations.

Ihzell squeezed her shoulder and asked, "Are you all right, dear?"

Hesitantly, Shahly shook her head and admitted, "I am not sure."

"I am certain she will be fine," the steward comforted. "Just have faith, child."

"I hope she will be," Shahly wished softly, while something awful, something human contradicted her words.

As they reached the door, the older kitchen servant, the very woman who had caused the accident that night, stormed into the room with two guards behind her. She appeared to be very angry and almost oblivious to what was around her. She strode in past Shahly and Ihzell and stopped, scanning the room. She locked her eyes on the younger kitchen servant and sharply said, "There!" as she pointed at the girl.

The guards strode to the frightened girl and took her arms.

The older servant slowly approached, her eyes locked on the servant girl in a predatory stare as she sneered, "You treacherous little wretch."

With tears streaming from her eyes, the servant girl shook her head and whimpered, "I don't understand."

The older servant slapped her very hard, brutally snapping her head around.

Shahly flinched.

"Be silent!" the servant woman ordered harshly, loudly.

Prince Arden sprang to his feet and shouted, "Enough!"

The woman spun around and gasped as she saw the Prince, then bowed deeply to him. "Your Royal Highness!"

He strode to her and folded his arms. His face was as stone and was a little red, his brow low over his eyes as he demanded, "What is the meaning of this barbaric display?"

She stood up straight and timidly answered, "Forgive me, Highness. I did not know you were here."

"Clearly," he growled. "Now answer my question." He looked to the guards and ordered, "Release her."

"But, Highness," the woman protested. "You cannot!"

Arden's lips tightened and he raised his chin. "What I cannot do is grow accustomed to kitchen maids questioning my orders. Now answer my question!"

She cringed, then straightened herself slightly and reported, "I was told of the attack on Maid Shahly." She turned a glare on the servant girl. "I sent this insolent little wretch to apologize for spilling the wine on her. Apparently, she had thoughts of revenge against one of her betters who she had wronged to begin with."

Crying, the servant girl shook her head and whimpered, "But I did as you said."

The woman looked back to Prince Arden and continued, "I noticed after she left that a meat tenderizing mallet was gone. When I heard of the attack on Maid Shahly and what had been used, everything came together quickly and I came looking for her. I am just—"

"An interesting tale," Ihzell interrupted, slowly walking toward the older kitchen servant. "Unfortunately, your story is not well put together. It was not even Maid Shahly who was attacked."

Still staring up at the Prince, the servant woman's neck grew taut, her eyes widening slightly.

Ihzell folded her arms, staring at the servant's face from half a pace away. "You do not seem to know much about what happened here tonight, and yet you know a little too much. I instructed the guards who found her to keep this little incident quiet, and they have hardly left my sight since our struck maiden was found."

The servant woman looked away from the Prince and swallowed hard.

Ihzell took a step closer to her. "You seem to know what was used to attack her and who was supposed to be attacked, even though no one else did. That is amazing."

The servant woman trembled slightly, turning her eyes slightly toward the steward.

Ihzell raised her chin. "You even knew where to find the girl, Verrta. That, too, is amazing. How do you do it?"

The servant woman finally looked to Ihzell. "Well, who else could have gotten a utensil from the kitchen without my knowledge? She was the only one who could have. I mean, her clumsy mistake earlier in the dining room—"

"Was supposed to have been forgotten," the Prince reminded.

"What was the motive again?" Ihzell taunted. "Oh, did I forget to mention that she came to the sewing room half a moment after Audrell left?" Her lips tightened, her brow growing tense. "When the attack occurred, your suspect was in the sewing room with me. Would you care to explain that?"

The servant woman looked away. "I... Perhaps I have made a mistake."

"I would say so," Ihzell confirmed. "Your little scheme is riddled with mistakes. Is there anything else you would like to share with me now?"

The servant woman just stared across the room.

Ihzell smiled. "I did not think so."

Prince Arden looked to the guards and ordered, "Take her to the dungeon until she remembers a few more details about tonight."

The servant woman looked helplessly into the Prince's eyes and pleaded, "Mercy."

He nodded. "Of course, if you deserve it."

Shahly stepped aside as the guards escorted the servant woman from the room, then she looked to Ihzell, who was walking toward her.

The steward took Shahly's arm and gently pulled her from the room, saying, "Come along, Shahly."

What had been said in Audrell's room repeated in Shahly's mind over and over and she finally asked, "Why did she think it was me who was attacked? I was not even in my room at the time."

Ihzell patted Shahly's hand and assured, "She was just mistaken, dear. It is nothing for you to worry over."

Shahly shrugged and looked ahead, seeing Nillerra with that guard behind her enter the corridor from another.

The black haired girl froze as she saw who was in front of her and declared, "Shahly!"

Ihzell tensed, not nervously but defensively, almost angrily. Her eyes narrowed as she stared at the black haired girl and she said suspiciously, "You seem surprised to see her, Nillerra."

The black haired girl glanced at Ihzell, then replied, "I just did not expect to see her in this part of the castle. I thought she would be in her room changing."

Ihzell folded her arms. "Really. What brings *you* to this part of the castle?"

Nillerra glanced at Audrell's door. "I came to see his Highness. I heard he was up here."

The steward folded her arms and asked, "For what purpose?"

Nillerra finally turned her eyes fully on Ihzell and snapped, "That is none of your business. I do not answer to you. Now tell me where the Prince is."

In that instant, Shahly sensed a shift in Nillerra's thoughts, her very personality. At the same time she felt rage well up within the steward, and she took a step back as Ihzell strode forward.

The guard also stepped back as Nillerra met the steward half way.

Ihzell raised her chin, glaring at the black haired girl from less than half a pace away and sneered, "You are not on the throne yet, you conniving little tramp."

"How dare you," the black haired girl hissed.

"It is time you learned a little respect," Ihzell informed coldly. "It is also time you looked reality in the eye. You are a long way from the throne, and until you get there—and don't count on it—you *do* answer to me. Do not ever forget that."

Nillerra smiled evilly. "I don't think you know who you are dealing with, old woman."

Nodding, Ihzell corrected, "Oh, I think I do. You are nothing but a plotting, treacherous nobody, hungry for power and wealth and willing to murder to get it."

"Oh really," Nillerra sneered.

Ihzell smiled slightly. "It is fortunate for those who are better than you that you are nothing more than a bungling little whore child who can barely wipe her own nose, much less eliminate her rivals."

Nillerra's brow stiffened as she warned, "Watch that tongue, old woman, or you may just have it fed to you."

The steward laughed. "I might take you seriously if you were a real woman."

"Then take this!" Nillerra swung hard at Ihzell's face.

Ihzell was much quicker than she appeared to be and easily caught the black haired girl's wrist, digging her fingernails in as she gripped like a hawk.

Nillerra whimpered and her knees seemed to nearly buckle, her eyes growing wide as she reached up and tightly grasped the steward's wrist, pulling back to free her arm.

Ihzell twisted the girl's arm and pulled her closer, bringing their noses a finger length apart. "That was your first mistake, little girl. Now you listen good and make certain you remember. I am going to be watching you like a hawk watches a snake. I eat little vixens like you for breakfast and I can take you apart without winding myself. One wrong move from you, one more act of treachery and I will feed your broken body to the pigs. Do I make myself clear?"

"Let go of me!" Nillerra cried, then sucked a hard, shrieking breath as the steward twisted further, her fingernails nearly drawing blood.

Ihzell watched the black haired girl sink to her knees, then she repeated, "Do I make myself clear?"

Nillerra tightly closed her eyes, and finally nodded.

Long seconds passed.

Ihzell threw Nillerra's wrist from her, watching her struggle to keep her balance as she cradled her arm. With a deep breath, the steward folded her arms and raised her chin slightly, staring down at the whimpering young woman before her. "That was only a warning, little girl. Next time I break it." She turned and ordered, "Come along, Shahly," then she glared down at Nillerra once more and strode past her.

This was a very stressful, very awkward moment and Shahly did not know whether to comfort Nillerra or just follow Ihzell.

Following Ihzell seemed to be the wise thing to do, so, hesitantly, she did, her eyes on Nillerra as she walked gingerly past.

Ihzell paused next to the guard, staring ahead as she softly informed, "You are also being watched, so I would suggest you tread very lightly from now on, and be very careful where your loyalties lie."

She continued on.

Shahly hurried to catch up to her and walked at her side in silence for a time.

Humans could be so hostile toward one another at times.

Thoughts of her feelings about seeing Arden worry over Audrell returned. For the first time in her life she actually felt hostility toward another, and could not reason out why. With some effort, she pushed it from her mind, only to have something else invade, something that needed an answer as well.

She looked to the steward and asked, "Why are you so angry with Nillerra?"

Ihzell sighed and answered, "She is a troublemaker, Shahly. You would do well to stay away from her."

Shahly nodded. "Many people keep telling me that, but I still do not understand why. Is she bad?"

"To the core," Ihzell growled.

Shahly looked to the floor ahead of her and said, "I hate to think that anyone is just naturally bad. There must be a reason for her to act so."

"She wants power, child," Ihzell informed grimly, "and she will do anything to acquire it."

Power. Vinton had always said freedom was power. Perhaps humans had a different perspective on this.

Shahly looked to Ihzell and guessed, "I have the feeling you think she had something to do with what happened to Audrell."

Ihzell sighed again and confirmed, "I know she did."

"How?"

The steward shrugged. "Woman's intuition, I suppose."

Shahly nodded. "Oh. But why would she want to hurt Audrell?"

Ihzell was silent for long seconds, then she looked to Shahly and answered, "She did not want to hurt Audrell, child. She was after you."

Shahly stopped, feeling as if something was tightening around her throat. Her lips parted as she stared back at the steward and shook her head, whimpering, "Me? But why?"

Ihzell turned fully. "Shahly, Nillerra is a jealous, vindictive little girl. Sometimes people like that see other people as a threat to what they want and when that happens they only know to hurt them to get them out of the way."

Breathing was hard and Shahly shook her head again and whimpered, "But I have done nothing to her."

Ihzell took Shahly's shoulders and comforted, "I know you haven't, child. It is not your fault."

Feeling tears coming on, Shahly turned her eyes down, still trying to reason out why Nillerra would have such intentions toward her.

Ihzell took Shahly's hands and said, "Just stay clear of her. If she tries anything I will be waiting to pounce."

Her mind still whirling, Shahly shook her head. "I need to think."

"I understand, dear," the steward comforted. "Let's get you back to your room."

"No!" Shahly barked, backing away. "I cannot go back there. Not after..." She closed her eyes and shuddered.

"It is all right, dear," Ihzell said sympathetically. "You don't have to. I will have another room prepared for you."

Shahly nodded, then looked up to Ihzell and said, "Arden and I were supposed to walk in the gardens tonight. I know he will not be coming with me, but may I go there? Just to think?"

Ihzell offered her a smile. "Of course you can. I will have Ocnarr send along an escort. We should also find you something to wear. That bathrobe just will not do in this chilly air." She took Shahly under her arm and led her the other way down the corridor, toward the sewing room.

Shahly leaned against the steward as they walked slowly down the hallway, feeling comforted by her presence. She drew a deep breath and softly said, "Thank you."

Ihzell patted her shoulder and held her more tightly.

The gardens of Red Stone Castle were indeed spectacular. As in the forest, everything was in bloom and the nectars of the many flowers filled the air with their sweet aromas, though they could not fully mask the unusual smell of the castle and its inhabitants. The trails which led between the miniature thickets of heavily flowered plants and small trees were flat laid, white stones of differing rectangular sizes that seemed to fit together like a puzzle. The sound of running water emanated from every direction.

Shahly, attired in a light pink spring dress and soft white shawl made of lamb's wool, slowly walked down the stone path between beds of retiring flowers, small fruit-bearing trees and lush bushes. She glanced around casually at the rainbows of color and the many statues and stone benches which dotted the area. She would run across an occasional fountain which fed the artificial creeks that snaked their way along the gardens, casting thin mists into the air that made small rainbows of their own as torch and lamp light hit them just right.

The trail came to a small wooden bridge with high rails which arched over one of the creeks and Shahly walked to the center of it, leaning onto one of the rails as she looked down to the water which ran below. This place right in the middle of a human stronghold reminded her of home, the forest she missed so much that now seemed an eternity away, even in the gardens.

She glanced back at the ever-present guard.

He seemed to sense that she wanted to be left alone and kept a discreet distance, and an attentive eye on her.

She looked back to the creek and scanned the gardens again.

A few other humans slowly wandered down the garden paths, all in pairs who walked very closely to each other. This was clearly a place of emotional freedom, of lovers.

Shahly did not feel threatened by them. Quite the contrary. They seemed to give her a sense of security, something she thought she would never feel from humans.

She felt someone approaching from the other side of the creek, then heard the footsteps. She tried to ignore him, but finally sensed that he was approaching with her in his thoughts.

She glanced at the guard again, her heart pounding as she recognized the mind of the human who approached her.

The black haired human stepped up onto the bridge, leaned on the rail a pace away and also looked over the creek.

Nervously, Shahly glanced at the guard again.

After long seconds, the black haired man finally spoke. "Much like the forest, is it not?"

Hesitantly, she nodded, still not looking at him.

"You were not easy to find in this place," he informed. "It would seem the guards and tenders keep you moving, and you are watched every moment."

She nodded again, hoping he would get bored with her and just go away.

"Already the Prince's favorite," he observed, then finally turned his eyes on her. "I know who you are. I know what you are."

Breathing was a little difficult. Her heart pumped fear throughout every part of her and she found herself bracing for flight.

"Why did you come here?" he asked.

Shahly drew a trembling breath and timidly answered, "My stallion is here."

"The other unicorn?"

She raised her chin and answered, "Yes."

He looked out over the creek again and nodded. "At least you have not forgotten."

Shahly's eyes darted to him.

He looked to her. "You have many enemies here and few people you can trust while you are in human form, probably none as a unicorn. Guard your secret well and finish your task as soon as possible. Time is running dangerously short."

"I wouldn't even be here if not for you," she reminded coldly, pain in her voice.

He stared back at her, then looked over the creek and lowered his eyes, admitting, "I know."

"Why did you come to find me?" she asked, almost demanded.

He drew a breath and admitted, "Like you said. I am responsible for you being here. That wizard I found you with is a wise man. He and I had much to talk about."

The clank of armor and weapons drew their attention to the other side.

Shahly's guard approached with long strides, his eyes on the black haired man, his hand on his sword as he demanded, "Maid Shahly, is this man bothering you?"

She slowly looked to the black haired man.

His dark eyes were as stones as they met Shahly's and he said in a low voice, "I am called Traman. You will see me again." Then he turned and strode back the way he had come, disappearing into the gardens.

Shahly watched after him, trying to sort out the few feelings she had received from him, feelings that were much different now.

She glanced back at the guard as he walked up behind her, also looking to where the black haired man had disappeared, then she looked back that way herself.

"Someone you know?" the guard asked.

Shahly nodded, answering, "I'm beginning to think so."

CHAPTER 10

The full moon was at its apex and shining very brightly on the forest road, lighting the way brightly enough for the two horses to easily see where they were going. An eerie blue glow bathed everything the moon could touch and cast frightening, cavernous shadows beneath the trees and underbrush. The sounds of unseen night creatures were frightening, from the clicking of bats overhead to the occasional chorus of wolves somewhere in the forest. A Dread howled somewhere in the distance.

Nillerra wore black riding trousers and a loosely fitting red silk shirt beneath a black, hooded cape. Her horse was also black. Her dark eyes were forward and as stones in her face. The horrible images running through her mind paled even the terrors she should have anticipated and imagined in the forest night. Still, she pressed on without fear of attack, only fear of her arrival. This was necessary. Things at the castle were not going well and it was time to act.

A single guard rode with her, the same guard who had sought her favor from the beginning. He would kill for Nillerra and had, in fact, done so on her wishes. For reasons he could not understand he had to have her near him and could not allow her to lose her bid for the throne.

But this night he glanced around nervously, waiting for an attack from bandits, wild animals or monsters that may never come, and he finally protested, "This is madness, riding into the forest in the middle of the night."

Nillerra glanced at him and reminded, "Wespard, you did not have to come."

He huffed back, "Well, I could not very well allow you to come out here alone and get yourself eaten alive by Dreads or mountain cats, either."

She turned her eyes ahead again and spat, "I can take care of myself." She squinted, seeing the light of a window ahead. "There's the cottage. It is time for you to turn back. And remember to tell no one where I am."

"I do not think allowing you to go alone is a wise idea," he informed. "At least let me—"

"Wespard!" she barked. "I told you before we left that I have to do this alone! Do not argue with me about it further."

He shook his head. "I still do not like this."

"Then leave," she ordered. "Leave anyway."

He took a deep breath and admitted, "I am afraid for you."

Her lips tightened as she stared back at him, then she maneuvered her horse close to his, slipped a hand around his neck and pulled him to her, kissing him for a long, passionate moment before drawing back and saying, "Don't be. I will be fine. Now get back to the castle before you are discovered missing and wait for me there."

He raised his brow and asked, "Are you certain about this?"

She glared at him and ordered, "Just go!"

He looked away, then reluctantly turned his horse back toward the castle and rode away, not looking back.

Suddenly feeling very alone, Nillerra called back to him, "I will be back some time tomorrow morning."

He waved over his shoulder, not looking back at her.

With a deep breath, Nillerra turned back toward the small cabin and swallowed hard, then dismounted and walked her horse the remaining fifty or so paces, tying the horse to a nearby tree as she arrived. She trembled as she approached the door, drew another deep breath, and hesitantly knocked.

A deep, ancient voice beckoned from within, "Enter if you will. Leave if you will not."

Nillerra vented still another deep breath, then slid the door bolt back and slowly pushed the door open.

The door hinges creaked like something from a nightmare and she shied away from the spider webs that tore away as the door opened.

Hesitantly, she stepped into the cottage, glancing around nervously and holding onto the door handle even after she was inside. This was not her first visit to this cabin, but previous visits made things no easier for her now. Quite the contrary. It was a dreadful place, worthy of her worst nightmares.

The walls were lined with shelves which bore the weight of books and bottles of potions, flasks of powders and dried animal parts. To her left was a work bench covered with more bottles and flasks, a couple of books and a candle burning on the corner. To her right were a cluttered desk and an old bed just down from the wall from it.

Something growled a nightmarish growl.

Her eyes snapped ahead to the fireplace which illuminated the room in a soft orange glow.

A large, deep cushioned brown chair sat between her and the fireplace with its back to her. A Dread was crouched beside it.

The Dread growled again, leering at her with featureless black eyes. It shifted, looking as if it was preparing to leap at her.

Nillerra's eyes widened and she took a step back.

A thin hand reached from the chair and stroked the creature's head.

The Dread seemed placated, but its eyes remained locked on her.

Nillerra swallowed hard, pondering what to do. This would be her last opportunity to turn and flee back to the castle.

She could not. This was too important, horrible as it was.

"Close the door," the voice commanded. "You are letting the night in."

She complied, slowly pushing the door closed and sliding the bolt back into place.

"Come closer, Nillerra," he ordered. "Let me see you."

Hesitantly, she approached, wringing her hands together, then she stopped when the Dread growled at her again.

The hand smacked the Dread's head, then went about stroking it again and the voice informed, "Do not worry about him. He'll not bite you until I tell him to."

Trembling, her hands held to her chest, she circled wide around the Dread, her eyes locked on it.

Its eyes remained on her and it turned as she circled around it, breathing loudly through its nose.

"Easy," the voice commanded, his hand scratching the Dread between the ears.

She gingerly stepped to the front of the chair, approaching to within a pace of it and knelt down, looking up at the man who sat in it with timid, almost child-like eyes.

He was very old and wore the tattered brown and white robes of a warlock. He had no beard on his skeleton-like face. Thin lips were stretched over large teeth. His white eyebrows were thin, as was his very long white hair. He smelled very bad.

He smiled at her, an evil gleam in his eyes. "Living among royalty certainly agrees with you. It is a far life from such humble, humiliating beginnings."

Nillerra raised her chin slightly and said, "I need your help."

"Again?" He seemed amused. "You said you could do the rest on your own."

"There is a problem, now," she informed. "Things are starting to go very badly."

He smiled broadly, showing his yellow teeth as he raised his head. "Ah, a rival."

Patience left her features. "You said the perfume would draw him to me. You said he would not be able to resist me, and now he pushes me away as if I am a commoner."

"You mean he has found another?" the warlock asked, amusement in his voice. "Are you jealous of his attentions toward her?"

Nillerra's brow tensed and she harshly asked, "Did you give some to that other girl?"

"I give to no one," he snapped. "And, no. You are the only one with spells that will work over Prince Arden." He turned his head slightly, scratching his chin. "That is, unless you have found some way to botch them."

"I haven't!" she assured. "I have done everything you told me, and yet he spends all of his time with this new girl."

The warlock looked away, clearly in thought, then said, "Perhaps it is something she has naturally which holds power over him. Or perhaps she is just more attractive to him than you are."

Nillerra's face turned slightly red, her features hardening as she demanded, "Tell me what to do about it."

He turned his eyes to the Dread, scratching it almost tenderly between the ears. "And what do I get in return for helping you this time?"

"I have gold," she answered. "And if it is not enough I can get you more once I am on the throne."

"Do you think me so foolish, girl?" he laughed. "Once you have what you want, you will gladly forget that I ever helped you."

"I won't!" she assured, desperation sharpening her voice. "I would not want you holding any debts over me once I am queen." She raised her chin slightly. "And perhaps I would need your services again. You could be useful to me once I am on the throne."

The warlock looked back to her and complemented, "A twisted wisdom, lacking in gratitude and honor." He nodded. "Very good, Nillerra. Those qualities should serve you well once you are on the throne. I will take the gold you have with you. It should pay for what I will give you to return to the castle with. Almost."

Her eyes widened slightly as she softly, timidly asked, "What more do you want?"

He leaned forward and reached to her, gently cupping her cheek in his bony hand as his eyes bored into hers and he answered, "You will stay with me tonight, as before."

Nillerra cringed and shakily snapped back, "Before, you assured me the potion would work, yet I am back now and further from the throne than ever."

"Through no fault of mine," the warlock pointed out, leaning back in his chair. Silently, he eyed her for a moment, then said, "This new girl you speak of, this rival. Clearly she has something natural about her that draws him more strongly. It could be experience in the ways of men which is beyond yours."

Nillerra shook her head. "No, she lacks the wits."

"Or," he continued, turning his head slightly, "Possibly her innocence, something which you cannot compete with."

Nillerra glanced away.

The warlock smiled. "That may just be it. He has reason to spend such time with her, to want her. He has a need to protect her that he does not even realize, and she has a distance from him that he must close. The perfume you have to captivate him will not be enough against such a natural allure."

Something changed in Nillerra's thoughts and showed in her face as features of stone took over and she turned commanding eyes on him and stood, saying with more authority, "Tell me what to do, how to defeat her and I am yours tonight."

Looking patiently up at her, the Warlock folded his bony hands in his lap and informed, "You can do nothing so long as she is in his company."

"I have already tried to get rid of her," Nillerra snapped.

The warlock raised his brow. "Oh? Yourself or by another's hand?"

"I had someone try for me. He failed miserably."

He nodded. "There lies your problem. If she is protected somehow, then she will have to die by your hand and no other. You must spill her blood yourself."

Nillerra's eyes narrowed and she reached into her skirt pocket, her hand finding the small dagger there, and she snarled, "That will not be a problem."

His eyes narrowed. "There is more. Much more."

"What else?" she demanded, her teeth clenched.

The warlock smiled and replied, "After you have paid in full, as before."

She shuddered and turned her eyes away from him, a horrible chill running up her back.

"Will you pay?" he asked.

Nillerra just stood there, staring blankly across the room for long seconds, then she nodded and looked back to him. "Very well. I will pay." She quickly produced the dagger and pointed it at him. "But if your tricks fail me again I will spill more than her blood."

The Dread growled and snapped at her.

With the dagger in her hand, she looked at the Dread without the fear the young woman who had entered felt and snarled, "And keep that disgusting thing under control or it dies first!"

The warlock laughed. "Spoken like true royalty, Nillerra. Very, very good." He raised a hand and the door to his cabin opened, letting in a rush of cool air, leaves and the sounds of the wind in the trees and the night creatures outside, then he looked to the Dread and ordered, "Out!"

It turned and fled on all fours.

He looked back to Nillerra as he lowered his hand and the door closed and asked, "Shall we begin?"

She slowly put the dagger back in its place, then turned her eyes down and nodded, suddenly feeling very ill.

A longer, more grueling night Nillerra could not remember. Part of her wept. Part of her felt ill. Part of her wanted to kill that warlock!

Now is not the time for any of that, she kept telling herself.

An early morning glow illuminated the forest and finally displayed its colors. The air was still very cool and smelled of all of the green things that slowly awoke. A thin mist slowly crawled along the forest floor, parts of it snaking into the road to join other parts which would eventually blanket even the road.

Nillerra's face was blank as she stood in the doorway of the cabin and stared out over the road that would take her back to the comfort of the castle. She held a leather sack in her hand, gripping it tightly. It was not heavy. She was just on edge.

She finally looked toward her horse and strode toward it, not looking forward to the long journey back to the castle, but she could barely wait to arrive.

She threw back the flap on the saddle bag as soon as she reached the horse and stuffed the sack into it, then she froze and stared blankly ahead as she heard the warlock approach from behind and she cringed as he placed his hands on her shoulders.

Barely as tall as she was, he drew in close to her and whispered, "I will hold you to the promises you made."

She raised her chin and closed the flap on the saddle bag, countering, "And I will hold you to yours."

He laughed softly. "Oh, not to worry, girl. Fulfill your responsibilities and I have not a doubt you will be on the throne by summer. Just remember. A drop of your blood and the potion in his wine and he will be powerless against your wishes when he drinks it."

"I remember. And that vial of other stuff? What does it do?"

He seized her arm and brutally turned her, staring like a madman into her eyes as he rasped, "It is vengeance! Use it only if all else is lost. Once you drink it there will be no return from its power!"

Nillerra stared back at him for a moment, then slowly nodded and said, "I will try to remember that. You never did tell me what it is supposed to do for me, though."

He raised a finger. "I will only tell you this. Once it is a part of you, there will be nothing to stop you from your quest of vengeance, of blood against your enemies. It does, however, come at a high price."

Her lips tightened and she hissed, "I have paid you all I intend to."

He smiled and shook his head. "No, girl. Not a price for me. A price for vengeance."

A chill ran throughout Nillerra. Without another word, she turned and mounted her horse, riding fast away from the warlock and his dreadful cabin.

"Remember my warnings," he called to her from some distance behind.

Nillerra would not look back. She kicked her horse's flanks and rode as fast as it would go until she saw the towers of Red Stone Castle rise above the trees in the distance.

She brought the horse to a stop, just staring at the towers for long moments. Security was there, safety, comfort.

Power.

She kicked the horse forward again, riding until she found the road which led to the castle's main gate, then she took a moderate pace toward the palace, fantasizing about a future on the throne, servants when she wanted them, many men at her disposal.

Respect.

A smile touched her lips.

Shahly out of the way, out of the castle, out of her life.

Dead!

The main gate opened before her and she allowed her horse to trot through it, then she rode to the doors of the castle's spectacular entry hall and finally stopped.

Several guards approached, a few stable hands behind them.

She gingerly dismounted and handed the reigns to one of the guards, then turned to the saddle bag, opened the flap and removed the leather sack.

"Where were you off to so early, maiden?" one of the guards asked.

She turned to him, smiling pleasantly as she answered, "That is none of your damn business. One side."

As he sidestepped, she strode past him and into the entry hall, up the stairs and straight to her room.

Gently, she closed the door to her room and scanned the place. As she had instructed before she left, the lamps were still burning. Very quickly, she went about her ritual of checking under the bed, in the wardrobe, behind the curtains and so on. Finishing that, she scanned the room once more, turned and strode to her bed, kicked off her riding boots and laid on her belly on the bed where she dumped out the contents of the leather sack.

Lying innocently on the bed was the vial of red potion which she would mix with her blood in Prince Arden's wine. Beside it was a ring, which she picked up and gazed at, then pulled on the stone, opening the hollow beneath it to reveal the fine powder which could quickly rid her of the enemy of her choice.

She looked down to the remaining object, a small glass vial which lay harmlessly beside the vial of love potion. Something about seeing it, about knowing what it was, made her feel strange inside and she turned her eyes from it.

Someone knocked, breaking her train of thought and she sprang from the bed, jammed the vials and ring into her pocket and bade, "You may enter."

The door opened and Wespard slowly entered. Seeing her, he closed the door and strode to her, extending his arms.

She pushed him away and took a step back, barking, "Don't touch me!"

Startled by her reaction to him, he also took a step back, just staring at her for a moment before softly offering, "I am sorry. I was just glad to see you."

Nillerra looked away from him. She wanted to be held, yet could not allow herself to be touched, not yet, not after that horrid night with the warlock.

She shook her head and strode wide around him, to her vanity where she opened a drawer and, piece by piece, emptied the contents of her pocket into it.

Her dagger went in as well.

Slowly, Wespard approached her again, not daring to touch her this time. "Are you all right, Love?"

She closed the drawer and leaned on the vanity, closing her eyes, then finally answered, "I will be. It was just a long, horrible night." She turned and strode to her bed, to the night stand and opened the drawer, looking into it for a moment, then she shook her head. "My wine is gone."

"We finished it a couple of nights ago," he reminded, then slowly approached her yet again.

She sighed and nodded. "I should have known. Can you get me more?"

"Of course I can," he assured. "Anything you want."

Disgust and anger drained away as something else in Nillerra emerged. She looked up from the drawer, then turned and slid her hands up the guard's chest and to his shoulders, smiling as she said, "You promise?"

He smiled back, gently taking her waist in his hands as he answered, "Anything."

She grasped the back of his neck and pulled him to her, leaning her head over to kiss him as she ordered, "Then satisfy me."

CHAPTER 11

This had never happened before.

Shahly had always been able to fall asleep at will, but with her mind so overwhelmed and her emotions strained to their collective limit, sleep was an elusive prize that would not be won. She tossed and turned in her bed most of the night and finally rose and went to the window, staring out over the wall and into the forest as the sun slowly illuminated the countryside and castle.

Normally by this time, Ihzell would already have arrived, but she was absent, no doubt tending Audrell.

Arden, too, was absent and she knew he would be at the injured girl's side.

Vinton's capture, the chase, the dragon, the mysterious black haired man called Traman, the bandits who meant to do horrible things to her, that guard with the predatory thoughts about her, and now this. A human, one of the few she actually considered her friend, was injured and probably dying because of another human's jealousy. Shahly felt responsible, knowing that if she had not come to the castle then Audrell would never have been mistaken for her and would never have been attacked. If she had not come to the castle then Vinton would have no chance and would surely die soon.

Vinton's life or Audrell's life? An innocent or an innocent?

She shook her head, knowing she could never reason it out, then she went to her wardrobe and pulled the doors open, took a blue spring dress out and slipped into it.

She could not lose Vinton, but she had to see Audrell one last time first.

Dressed and with her hair combed and white slippers on her feet, she left her room and strode down the hall toward Audrell's room, barely noticing that one of the guards at her door was following.

When she reached Audrell's door, she saw a guard there as well and slowly approached him, tugging on her finger as she looked up into his eyes and softly asked, "How is she?"

"No change, Maiden," he answered.

She turned her eyes down, then looked at the door and asked, "Is Prince Arden in there?"

The guard shook his head and reported, "He stayed with her through the night, but finally left about a half hour ago. He said he would be back shortly."

Why did he stay with her? Shahly asked herself, already knowing the answer. She had never felt selfishness before and she felt shame along with it, more so when she realized she almost wanted Audrell to die, just so Arden's attention would not be so focused on her.

This could not be! She was still unicorn, human form or not.

She looked up to the guard and asked, "May I go in and see her?"

The guard took a deep breath and stroked his chin, looking down at Shahly with his brow raised. "I don't know, Maiden. I am not supposed to allow anyone in there."

Shahly's lips tightened, her brow arching as she stared up at him with begging eyes.

The guard smiled and added, "Oh, I do not see you causing her harm." He stepped aside and opened the door for her. "Go on in, Maiden, and call me if you need anything."

Shahly tried to smile back at him, but could not, so she just said, "Thank you," then entered the room.

The door closed gently behind her and she slowly padded to the bed, afraid of making any sound that might wake the injured girl. For long moments, Shahly just stared down at her friend's face, seeing none of the radiance that always seemed to be present there.

Audrell had not moved from the night before, still covered to her shoulders with the sheet and blanket. A clean bandage bound the wound on her head. She appeared to be sleeping peacefully, but Shahly could sense her pain and horrifying dreams.

She gingerly sat down on the bed and gently placed a hand on Audrell's forehead, shuddering as she felt her pain. With a quick glance at the door, Shahly carefully removed the bandage and examined the wound.

It was much worse than she had expected. She turned her eyes away and raised a hand to her mouth, fearing she would be ill. After a moment to collect herself, Shahly looked back to her unconscious friend and whispered, "Why would anyone do this?"

Audrell's mind feebly responded.

Shahly could feel her growing weaker by the moment and a tear spilled from her eye as she realized the dreadful truth.

Audrell would not be alive much longer.

Such a terrible reality this was. This race, these humans were so different from the creatures she had grown up with in the forest, even the predators. The Dreads, the wolves, whispers, tree leapers, water demons and forest cats all killed to eat, to survive. They killed for a purpose.

But the humans... They killed their own for power and spite, and others for games and greed. Most unicorns in the forest knew nothing of this race other than to avoid them. Shahly found herself possessing knowledge she had never even imagined, and wanted nothing to do with now.

And now, a human Shahly called her friend, an innocent among a species of barbarians lay dying before her because of another's jealousy of her.

Shahly did her best to compose herself, but soon her tears were flowing freely and she raised a hand to her eyes and whimpered, "This is all my fault. I am sorry, Audrell. Please forgive me."

Still crying, Shahly stood and walked slowly to the door, stopped, and turned for one last look at her friend.

Audrell's life force was very weak, and still Shahly felt her fighting hard to stay alive, even for a moment more.

A few moments more was all she had left.

New tears streamed forth and Shahly turned quickly, seizing the door handle as if to escape this room and the horrible feelings which burned inside of her.

She could not pull the door open. After a moment, she looked over her shoulder, then slowly turned and walked back to the bed. She sat down and took Audrell's hand. "I know this is frightening for you. In the forest I would know what to do. I could heal you. But then you would know me, who I am and what I am." Shahly drew a deep breath, sobbing as she confessed, "I am a unicorn. I'm the same unicorn you saw cross the river. You believe in my kind and I feel you love us because of what we are and what you want us to be." She glanced away. "But I must think about Vinton. He is to be killed by your people soon. I cannot do anything that would jeopardize my quest to free him." She shook her head, looking back down to Audrell. "I cannot allow you to die, either. Forgive me, Vinton."

With a deep breath, Shahly placed her hands over Audrell's wound and asked, "Please do not betray me," as she channeled her unicorn essence for the first time in human form.

An emerald light sprayed from between her fingers.

Shahly closed her eyes and easily saw into Audrell's mind.

Audrell fought back hard. Very hard. She believed, she trusted, and when she was touched with unicorn essence for the first time, she truly loved.

An unknown time later, a nearly exhausted Shahly raised her head and drew back, removing her hands from Audrell's head.

The wound was gone.

Shahly rubbed her eyes. Much of her own life force had been channeled to Audrell and she felt even more exhausted than the lack of sleep the night before had left her.

She moaned, fighting off the urge to just faint, then blinked her eyes and forced herself back to consciousness, looking down to Audrell.

Audrell stared back at her, bewilderment in her wide eyes.

Shahly looked away.

"How can this be?" Audrell breathed.

Shahly sighed and said, "It would take too long to explain. How do you feel?"

Audrell was silent for a moment, then she whispered, "I can hardly believe this. You healed me?"

Shahly nodded.

"I had heard somewhere that unicorns could take the shape of people," Audrell informed. "Human people, I mean."

Shahly smiled and finally looked to her. "We normally cannot. I had a little help."

With some effort, Audrell sat up and leaned back against the headboard, then took Shahly's hand and looked into her eyes. "I owe you my life yet again. Anything you need, anything, and I am yours. I promise."

"You owe me nothing," Shahly assured. "I only ask that you tell no one."

Audrell shook her head. "No! Never! They could not torture it out of me!"

Shahly patted Audrell's hand and assured, "I do not suspect they will think you know."

"I suppose not," Audrell agreed, then smiled at Shahly. "I did see that unicorn, didn't I?"

Shahly nodded.

Dreamily, Audrell looked away and smiled. "I wonder if the legend is true, then, the one that says your first child will be a prince if you see a unicorn." She looked back to Shahly and raised her brow. "Is it?"

Shahly turned her eyes up, then looked back to Audrell and answered, "I think in this case the possibility is very much there. Do you love Arden?"

"Yes," Audrell whispered.

"Then he must know," Shahly insisted.

"What if he has no such feelings for me?" Audrell asked fearfully.

"He does," Shahly informed straightly. "He stayed here with you all night. He was very worried about you."

"He stayed with me?" Audrell asked, a little surprised in her voice.

Shahly smiled and nodded.

Audrell stared across the room for a moment, her lips parting as this news sank in, then she looked back to Shahly and smiled as she asked, "Are you sure you see nothing in him?"

Shahly glanced away and smiled herself, answering, "Well, I would not say I see nothing."

"He is beautiful, isn't he?" Audrell pressed. "You feel something for him. And I am not talking about just loving him. Just seeing him makes you feel all mushy inside, right?"

Smiling, and trying not to, Shahly turned her eyes up and admitted, "Well, a little."

"A lot?" Audrell prodded. "Come on, Shahly. I can see you blushing. Admit it. You want him."

Shahly laughed. "Would you stop? I can't want him. We are not even the same species."

Audrell folded her arms and said, "Really. Well right now you look every bit as woman as I am. You can't tell me you don't feel something like that for him."

Shahly giggled and could not answer.

Audrell nudged her and persisted, "Come on, Shahly. Unicorns can't lie, so just admit it. You have lustful thoughts for him."

Taking a deep breath, Shahly finally confessed, "Not on purpose."

"I do!" Audrell said straightly.

They stared at each other for a moment, then exploded into girlish giggles and laughter, slapping clumsily at each other.

The door burst open and the guard and Prince Arden strode into the room, stopping half way to the bed.

Shahly looked back at them, then looked back to Audrell.

The girls just stared at each other for long seconds, then started giggling again.

Shahly raised a finger to her lips.

Audrell did the same, then looked to Prince Arden as he approached and greeted, "Good morning, you princely stallion."

Shahly laughed very hard at that and fell into Audrell. One could never guess what had just transpired between them, the secrets that had been exchanged. No, the guard and the Prince merely saw two close friends sharing a moment of absolute joy.

The girls finally regained their composure and looked to Prince Arden as he sat down on the bed beside Shahly and reached for Audrell.

Gently, he brushed the hair from her face, looking for the wound left by her attacker the night before. His eyes were wide, betraying confusion at its absence and he shook his head and remarked, "You look much better."

Audrell wiped some tears away and looked to Shahly and smiled. "Shahly helped me pull through. She used some things she learned in the forest to help me heal." She threw her arms around Shahly's neck and hugged her tightly.

Shahly hugged her back and whispered in her ear, "I have to try to find my stallion."

"Go," Audrell whispered back. "I will distract them for you."

They pulled apart and Shahly stood, backing away a step as she stared into Audrell's eyes.

The Prince shook his head, saying, "But how—"

"Shahly said you stayed with me all night," Audrell interrupted. "That was very sweet of you."

The Prince smiled slightly, taking her hand as he confessed, "I could not just leave you like that."

Shahly folded her essence around herself and slowly backed away. She peered into the guard's mind first, noticing that he was already distracted with Audrell, but she nudged his mind more toward her anyway. She turned to Arden next and suggested to his mind that he should do what he could to comfort Audrell.

Everyone but Audrell was distracted and would not notice her leave, so she slowly turned and silently padded to the door.

Another guard was already posted outside the door. Problem.

Before he noticed her, she suggested to his mind that he should look down the corridor the other way, just to see.

He did, and did not notice her even as he looked forward again.

Slipping by him was as easy as it had been in the forest.

She strode down the corridor, her mind focused on her next objective.

It was time to find this Falloah, and get her and Vinton away from the castle.

Dungeon. What exactly did that mean? And where would the humans put it?

The dragon had said that she was being held there, no doubt against her will. The least he could have done was tell her where to find this dungeon.

She wandered along, descended a flight of stairs, down the corridor further, down more stairs.

And still more.

Shahly found herself in the lower levels of the castle where there were no windows and little ventilation. The air was heavy and still, and a little difficult to breathe. The pungent aroma of unwashed humans was very strong. Light was offered only by a few rusty lamps, many of which looked like they should have been lit but were not.

This lower level was a labyrinth of dark corridors which twisted and wound their way in a seemingly endless journey for those not familiar with them, and Shahly's frustration grew more with each turn.

She stopped and glanced around her, listening for any clue as to where this dungeon might be, but not even sure what to look or listen for.

The smell was becoming almost unbearable.

She trekked on, found another flight of stairs and descended them into a deep, dark place under the palace, almost like a cavern. The walls were not stones so carefully laid on top of one another here, rather they were solid stone, carved right out of the rock the castle sat upon. Water dripped somewhere. Even fewer lamps lit the place.

Torches up ahead offered more light and an inviting way to go. The smell of human sweat and refuse was quite potent here, as if many humans were behind the doors which lined the corridor ahead.

Slowly, she walked toward the torches, noticing that the corridor opened into a larger room.

As she entered the room, a large, somewhat over-fed and dirty guard with the scruff of an early beard on his face stood from a table in the center of the room where four others sat and met Shahly half way with folded arms and eyes of stone, asking, "What be bringing ye here, maiden?"

"Hello there," she greeted timidly. "I am a guest of Prince Arden."

He raised his chin and prodded, "And?"

She took a deep breath, ready to call upon her unicorn essence as she answered, "I must speak with Falloah."

The other guards at the table stood.

The guard standing before Shahly shook his head and coldly informed, "I do not think so, maiden. Guest of his Highness or not, no one sees that prisoner unless sent by her Majesty the Queen."

Shahly gazed into his eyes and bored into him with her essence. "Don't you think the Queen wants something of her?"

He blinked, appearing to grow dizzy and confused. "Her Majesty was very specific that no one sees her."

Shahly leaned her head and reached into his mind further. "You are obeying the Queen very well. I think you should be rewarded. Would you like to be?"

Hesitantly, he nodded and answered, "Aye, I would."

"Then perhaps you should be." Shahly raised her brow and asked, "Would you like for me to tell the Queen?"

"I live to serve her." The guard was suddenly a little afraid, almost as if he thought the Queen was watching or listening. "My rewards are in her service."

"But you want more," Shahly observed sympathetically. "You want something more than watching these doors from day to day. You want to be out in the sunshine, don't you?"

He nodded.

She bored into his mind even deeper, whispering, "If you obey the Queen's wishes, then perhaps you will get what you want. Perhaps she will allow you to spend more time outside."

"What must I do?" he asked softly.

"I must speak with Falloah," Shahly said directly. "It is very important that I do so."

"Of course," the guard assured. "Right this way."

She smiled and followed him. What simple minded creatures these humans could be.

A smaller, older guard stopped them and harshly asked, "What is the meaning of this? Where are you taking this woman?"

The fat guard raised his chin and ordered, "By her Majesty's wishes. Move aside."

The smaller guard stiffened, then returned to the table.

The big guard led the way to a timber door at the far end of the room, a door with a small, barred window near eye level. He took a ring of keys from his belt and shoved one into a hole near the door handle, then looked to Shahly, asking, "Do you need me to go in there with you?"

She shook her head, reassuring, "I will be fine."

He nodded and turned the key, then turned to Shahly again before he pulled the door open and said, "I will be nearby. If you need anything just shout and I will come. And be on your guard, lass. That woman is dangerous. She has killed three men already."

Shahly gazed into his eyes once again and smiled. "Thank you, but I am sure I will be fine. Just do not listen to what is said in there. It would be bad for you to hear."

He nodded and pulled open the door, saying, "I understand."

Shahly took a few steps into the small room and stopped. There was not an abundance of light within and colors were difficult to make out. The room itself, three or four paces in any direction, was furnished only with a flat, low table that appeared to be what the prisoner was supposed to sleep on. The floor was hay and rock.

Slowly, the tall, muscular woman who stood in the center of the room turned to Shahly and met her eyes in an unkind glare with beautiful amber eyes of her own. Her eyes almost glowed in the dim light offered through the window of the door and were amazingly intense for a human, focusing more like an angry predator. Her hair was fiery red and very long, worn loosely to her mid-back. Her tattered gown appeared to be lavender, was low cut in the front and had one of its sleeves and shoulders torn away.

Very slowly, Shahly took a step toward her, feeling something that was not human essence. This woman was very strong in body and immensely strong in essence, and was very intimidating. Shahly knew fear of her in that first moment.

"What do you want?" Falloah asked coldly.

Shahly cringed, holding her arms close to her as she stared fearfully back at Falloah for long seconds, then finally, timidly answered, "We need to talk."

Falloah's features were like stone as she snarled, "I do not want to talk."

"I am Shahly."

"I don't care."

Clearly, this Falloah was not going to be so easy to talk to.

Shahly took a deep breath and said, "Please. It is important that I speak with you. We haven't much time."

"Just go away," Falloah ordered, turning her back to Shahly.

"But I must speak with you," Shahly insisted.

"Why?"

Shahly glanced at the door, then softly said, "The dragon told me to find you."

Falloah half turned her head.

"He said you know things that will help me rescue Vinton," Shahly continued. "You also know the words that will return me to my true form."

Falloah turned fully and demanded, "What dragon? What was his name?"

Shahly backed away a step. "His name? He said you are supposed to tell me."

Falloah shook her head and informed, "You should have prepared yourself better. This is not going to work."

Shahly leaned her head. "What do you mean?"

"I will *not* tell you his name," Falloah said coldly. "Your queen's interrogators could not break me and neither will this little act you are performing for me."

"I don't understand," Shahly whimpered, starting to feel anxious. "You must tell me! I don't want to be like this the rest of my life. And we must find Vinton. He is to be killed soon!"

"Who is this Vinton?" Falloah questioned. "Another traitor against the Queen?"

"No," Shahly replied softly. "He is a unicorn, my stallion." She turned her eyes down, trying to compose herself.

"Your stallion?"

Shahly nodded, then looked back up to this tall, red haired woman. "I am unicorn. The dragon changed me to human form so that I could come into the castle without attracting attention and get you and Vinton out."

Falloah slowly shook her head. "You are either very sick or very imaginative."

Shahly felt a subtle choke in her throat and asked, "What do you mean?"

Falloah folded her arms. "Do you really think I believe a word of this?"

"I don't understand," Shahly confessed. "Why would you not?"

"Just leave," Falloah ordered as she turned away. "Go and tell your Queen she has failed again, and to leave me alone."

"She does not know why I am here," Shahly informed. "Everyone thinks I am here to marry Prince Arden. Please help me. I cannot rescue Vinton alone and the dragon told me to free you first. He said you would know what to do."

"I don't think so," Falloah said, no feeling in her voice. "Just get out."

Shahly vented a heavy breath, frustrated and near tears as she whimpered, "But he said you would help me."

Falloah swung around and shouted, "Prove it, then! Prove what you say or get out before I tear you apart!"

Shahly shrieked and backed away, stopped by the heavy timber door. Her eyes were wide and locked on Falloah's and she knew this woman meant what she said. As Falloah strode toward her, Shahly raised her hands to her chest and felt the chain there, looked down and pulled the amulet from inside her dress, turning her eyes back to the red haired woman's.

Her eyes locked on the amulet, Falloah raised her chin, slowly reached to Shahly and took it gingerly in her fingers, then turned wide eyes on Shahly's and asked, "Where did you get this?"

"The dragon gave it to me," Shahly answered.

Falloah glanced down at the amulet, then back to Shahly. "You say you were once unicorn. What form were you in when he gave this to you?"

"My true form."

"Unicorn?"

Shahly nodded.

Falloah glanced away, her brow low, then she looked back to Shahly and asked, "If so, why would he help you, a unicorn?"

"I asked him to," Shahly replied. "Well, I begged him to. He said something about a price but I don't know what he meant by that."

Falloah nodded, her eyes very intense on Shahly's. "That sounds like him. What else did he tell you?"

Shahly felt as if she was finally getting through to this woman. Almost happily, she reported, "He told me to find you and free you. You are to give me the words that will change me back, then we must find Vinton and make our escape."

Again Falloah's eyes narrowed and she said, "By trusting you I would be taking an awful risk, but this story of yours is far too bizarre to have been concocted by someone."

"I understand what you are going through," Shahly sympathized, "but I implore you to help me. Please!"

The red haired woman considered a moment longer, staring suspiciously down at Shahly, then she finally nodded and said, "Okay. I will trust you. I only pray I will not regret it."

"You will not!" Shahly assured.

"Very well," Falloah sighed. "Before we can even think about getting me and your stallion out of here there is something you must do, something very important."

Shahly raised her brow, hoping at least this task would be reasonably easy.

Falloah continued, "There is a tower at the center of the palace, the tallest of the five. At the top you will find a talisman made of jewels and unicorn spirals woven into a web of gold."

"The talisman the humans use to defend themselves against dragons," Shahly confirmed. "Arden showed it to me yesterday."

Falloah nodded. "All fine and well. That talisman must be destroyed."

"What?" Shahly demanded, despair and shock in her voice. "I know nothing of this thing! What can I—"

Falloah clamped a hand over Shahly's mouth and glanced at the window in the door. "Just listen. The sequence of jewels and spirals must be perfect. If it is disrupted in any way then the Talisman is useless. You must do this and bring the dragon. If you fail then they will take it throughout the land and kill all of the dragons." She raised her chin. "And they will keep killing the unicorns to build more talismans."

Shahly looked away. "With the Talisman gone, the people here would be defenseless against dragons."

"That *is* the idea," Falloah said, sounding almost frustrated.

Shahly looked back to the red haired woman, shaking her head as she admitted, "I do not want anyone to get hurt. I have friends here."

"Now is not the time for a moral debate!" Falloah hissed.

Shahly looked away again and shook her head, saying, "I just don't know."

"Look," Falloah growled. "You can destroy that talisman by sundown or you can watch your unicorn friend die in the arena tomorrow. Eventually the humans could kill off your entire herd! What sounds better to you?"

"Tomorrow?" Shahly breathed, then hesitantly nodded and admitted, "I understand." She looked to the red haired woman. "What about the words to change me back?"

Falloah sighed and looked away. "I am not very familiar with the language he uses for his incantations. However, I would assume you would use the same words he used to transform you to human and reverse the subjects of the incantation."

Shahly blinked and asked, "What?"

The red haired woman's lips tightened and she appeared to grow even more frustrated, then she looked Shahly in the eyes and asked, "Do you remember the whole incantation?"

Not again, Shahly thought, looking away. She considered, then recited, "*Transformus... Transformatus corporum...* No, *transformatus de corporum unicornu Abtontae* into...Wait! *Intro humanus.*" She looked back to Falloah. "He had me call your name first, then those words."

Falloah rolled her eyes and mumbled, "No doubt to make certain you found me. He always has to make things so damn complicated. Look. The words *humanus* and *unicornu Abtontae* should be reversed when you speak the incantation. Just say them in the opposite order. That should change you back when the time comes."

"And what if it does not?" Shahly asked grimly.

With a sigh and a shrug, Falloah shook her head and admitted, "I don't know. I guess that would leave you stuck as a human."

Shahly moaned and turned her eyes down.

"But no matter what," Falloah continued, "destroy the Talisman, or just damage it and bring Ralligor."

Shahly's eyes snapped to Falloah. "Ralligor?"

"The dragon who made you human," the red haired woman informed. "Once the Talisman is gone he will be my only hope for freedom, and your only hope to save your Vinton and rejoin your herd." She took Shahly's shoulders, some desperation in her eyes, though hope now glowed there very deeply. "The whole land now depends on you."

Shahly nodded, feeling very, very important for the first time in her life, and assured, "I will then. Somehow, I will." She turned and knocked on the door, calling, "I am ready to come out, now."

The guard peered in through the little window, then unlocked the door and pulled it open.

Shahly glanced back at the red haired woman once more, then strode out of the door and back the way she had come.

The large guard caught up to her and asked, "Everything went well? Didn't give you no problems?"

With a quick glance at him, Shahly sighed, "Only one."

Shahly got away from the dungeon and back to the upper levels without incident and ended up wandering aimlessly through the halls of the castle with an aching head.

She half turned and leaned back against the wall, her arms folded as she stared ahead with blank eyes. An angry sigh escaped her and she shook her head, mumbling, "Destroy the Talisman. I cannot even get close to it without Arden." She shook her head, frowning. "And I used the stone out of the amulet the dragon gave me to fix what I *did* break."

The Prince crept back into her thoughts and she closed her eyes as something tugged at her heart. She did not want to admit to herself what she felt for him. He was human; she was unicorn. Her human form was all just a trick to free Vinton. It was all just a lie.

Still, she wondered absently if such a life with this human prince would be so terrible.

Shahly gasped aloud. Vinton. Her parents. The herd. The forest. She was unicorn, not human. Not human!

Thoughts were painful and confusing.

She breathed heavily, shaking her head, then she turned and ran blindly down the corridor, barely able to think. Her mind whirled. She needed answers. Someone had to help her put things back into perspective.

Only one could. She just had to find him.

There was one obvious place Shahly had not searched for her love, one place close to where she had experienced that horrible mind the day before.

Only a few obstacles were in her way.

Four guards: Four weak and unsuspecting minds.

The first man guarding the third stable was already very consumed by his wishes for advancement in the royal guard. The second had a woman in his thoughts, very strange behavior with her, and was very easily pushed even deeper into those images. The third guard's mind wandered from thought to thought. He could be distracted easily when the time came.

The fourth, however, was the senior guard among them, and was actually vigilant and concentrating somewhat on what he was there to do. He would pose a problem.

Shahly took a deep breath and crept toward the stable, staying close to the wall of the second building as she watched the men before her at the gate of the stable.

With her help, three men daydreamed carelessly.

The fourth warily scanned the area.

Shahly froze as he looked her way, and instinctively she folded her essence around her, concealing herself from his mind.

Just as in the forest, he did not see her.

However, now was not the time to take chances. She dare not move for attracting his other senses may mean she would be discovered.

Finally! A stray thought from him!

She concentrated hard on it and finally brought it to his full attention, the image of him and Queen Hethan.

Shahly's eyes widened a little and she felt a little embarrassed at what he was thinking.

Slipping past them was fairly easy when she controlled what they saw of her and she went unnoticed all the way to the door of the stable, padding lightly so as not to make a sound that might attract their attention.

She gently pulled the bolt of the door back, hoping the sound of metal and wood rubbing together would also go unnoticed.

"Maiden!" one of them shouted.

Shahly's heart felt as if it was going to burst from her chest. She managed to gulp one last breath of air before everything in her body just froze.

"I am afraid you cannot come here," another of them informed sternly, walking away.

Walking away?

"I just want to see the horses," Audrell's voice argued playfully.

Audrell? What was she doing here?

Shahly risked a look back, surprised to see her friend thirty paces behind her and surrounded by three of the guards.

She looked to her right.

The fourth man, the senior, vigilant guard, was still at his post, watching the confrontation before him.

She looked back to Audrell.

The girl met Shahly's eyes, and winked.

Shahly smiled, then she turned back to the door, slowly pulled it open and slipped inside.

This stable was dark as well, the windows covered with shutters which allowed in only thin ribbons of sunlight. The far end, however, was more brightly illuminated by a window with a broken shutter. Unicorn essence was very strong there.

Something moved at the far end and Shahly's heart jumped as she remembered her first encounter in just such a place.

Hesitantly, she started forward, wringing her hands together as she looked for any sign of her stallion. The stalls in this end were more like cages with iron bars mounted securely from the stall walls to the ceiling. The faint scent of carrion lingered in the air.

The essence grew stronger as she approached. She recognized it!

Moving a little faster down the stable, she reached out with her mind and searched for the mind of her stallion, her eyes also searching.

She reached the last stall, the one with the broken shutter, and gingerly placed her hands on the gate, looking hopefully inside.

There, standing at the far end of the stall in the sunlight was the unicorn she sought.

Elation was short lived. He did not look well.

There was little shine to his coat and mane and his head hung low, facing away from her. He just stood there.

Shahly could sense very little from him, but what she did sense was painful. He seemed to have lost all hope. Something in his heart was bitter, cold. She had never sensed this from another unicorn before and was sure it was painful to him. This could not be. This would not be.

She leaned toward him and softly called, "Vinton."

He did not respond. He did not even move.

"Vinton," she summoned again. "It is me. It's Shahly."

Still nothing.

Shahly's frustration began to grow. "Vinton, please say something to me. Please. I need to know that you are all right. Vinton." She vented a deep breath, then calmed herself and reached out to him with her essence, pouring everything she had, every feeling for him to his mind.

Here, too, he rejected her, and did not even feel who she was. He was consumed by his loneliness, his despair, and would allow no contact.

Shahly stared at him a moment longer, then fumbled with the latch to the gate, trying to work it open.

He still did not respond to her openly, but an ear twitched, drawn by the sound of the latch opening.

Shahly pulled the gate open, glanced at the door to the stable, then slipped into the stall. She was hesitant to approach him, feeling strange things in his mind. Such anger. Such hopelessness. He seemed numb to all around him.

A pace away, Shahly reached out to touch him but retreated as he jerked his head up.

Vinton just stared ahead. He would not even acknowledge her presence.

"I have come to get you out of here," she whispered. "Can you not understand me? Vinton!" She gently placed a hand on his back.

He snorted and moved away from her, still not looking at her.

This hurt. Shahly found herself near tears. For two days she could not wait to see him again, to rescue him so they could return home. Now, he did not seem to know her and she felt that he wanted her to just leave.

Her mouth trembling as she tried not to cry, Shahly whimpered, "Vinton, why won't you talk to me? Don't you know who I am?"

"I know what you are," he finally said.

A little elation returned to Shahly's heart and a smile was almost to her lips as she prodded, "Yes! You know me!" She stepped toward him, urging, "Vinton, you only have to reach to me. Please!" She retreated from him as he turned his horn on her.

Vinton turned fully and advanced on her, keeping his horn trained on her chest as he hatefully said, "So that is why you came here. You wanted to be touched by a unicorn. Why are you backing away, then? Don't you want me to touch you?"

Shahly knew fear of him for the first time in her life and instinctively raised a hand between Vinton's spiral and herself, begging, "Wait! Please!" She backed into the stall railing near the gate and shrank away from the tip of his horn, her eyes locked on it.

He glared at her for long seconds, slowly raising the sharp point of his spiral toward her face.

Shahly lowered her hand and looked into his eyes, begging with hers.

His eyes narrowed, then he backed away and snorted, chiding, "Unicorn, are you? A unicorn who looks and smells just like a human." He turned from her and paced back to the window. "You look human, you smell human, you respond human and you have a human's fear. You are no more Shahly than any of the others here. Now go."

"I am Shahly," she insisted timidly.

"Of course you are," he snorted. "A unicorn would have known not to fear the spiral of another unicorn. Shahly especially would not have feared my spiral. You responded just as a human would; fearfully, just as I predicted."

His cold words stung and Shahly looked away, feeling horrible tremors within. He was right. She even felt more human than unicorn now. She looked back to him, not willing to believe her own feelings and slowly approached him again, feebly arguing, "But it is me."

Vinton snorted again. "You are nothing more than a treacherous human who is trying to be touched by a unicorn. Well I don't want to know you that well. I want nothing to do with you at all. Now leave me alone."

Tears welled up in Shahly's eyes. "But Vinton, our chase by the river, everything you've taught me, all the time we've spent together... Don't you remember? Please remember."

He raised his head but would not look at her.

Shahly sniffed and wiped a tear from her cheek, sobbing, "You must remember."

"I remember those things," he confessed, then he turned his head and looked out the window. "You know much about my last moments of freedom. I sent Shahly away, but they must have captured her as well."

"No!" Shahly assured. "They did not get me!"

"And Bexton tore the memories from her," Vinton continued grimly. "He wants me to join him. You are just a tool to that end. Just go back and admit you have failed. Perhaps his hard heart can still show enough mercy not to kill you for failing him."

"Vinton, please! They did not get me!"

"You are not Shahly!" he insisted. "She is unicorn. You are just another of Bexton's loyal, misguided humans, evil and selfish."

Shahly stepped toward him, set her hands on her hips and cried, "I am *not* selfish, Vinton! I came here to free you and take you home! Now quit being so stone headed, feel my essence and let's get out of here!"

"Just go," he said dryly.

"Not without you!" she insisted.

He turned his head to her, glaring as he shouted, "Go!"

Shahly flinched. She could only feel hatred from him now, hatred of her. She had never felt hatred from him before. To be hated by someone she loved so absolutely.... The feeling stabbed at her, and stabbed deep into her.

Slowly, and still clinging to what composure she had left, she turned and left the stall, closing the gate behind her.

She just stared at the ground for a moment, then looked to him once more and swore, "I will come back for you, Vinton. I promise. I will come back and free you."

He turned away from her.

Shahly could still sense only hatred from him, hatred and loneliness.

She slowly turned and walked away from the stall, each step an agonizing journey through the pain he had left her with, his rejection of her, his hatred of her.

Consumed by the pain she felt and still bewildered by his rejection of her, Shahly pushed the door to the stable open and wandered out, angling toward the palace.

One of the guards approached and asked, "Maiden, what were you doing in there? How did you get in there?"

She just shook her head and walked faster, her fragile heart crumbling more with each step.

"How did you get in there?" the guard asked again.

"Please!" she begged, sobbing. "Just leave me alone." She ran blindly toward the palace, running from her pain.

CHAPTER 12

So much to do; so little time.

Shahly did not eat or rest the whole day. She wandered the grounds outside of the palace, oblivious to everything happening around her.

When she had come to Red Stone Castle, everything seemed so simple. Now, nothing made sense, nothing was in perspective, and nothing was simple. Everything she had to do was a blur, an overwhelming set of impossible obstacles which were too far away to reach and too threatening to overcome. Even her goal, the very reason for her quest, was obscured.

She loved Vinton, the unicorn she wanted as her stallion. She also loved Arden, her enemy. Vinton had rejected her, hated her. Arden loved her deeply, absolutely, just as Vinton once had.

She shook her head, not wanting to remember what had transpired between them only a few hours ago. She could not seem to sort anything out.

Only one thing was clear.

Vinton would die tomorrow if she failed.

She finally stopped and looked up to the open gate which led outside of the palace wall. Somewhere, out in the world she knew, a dragon waited for her, and the red haired woman, Falloah.

She longed for the simple days in her forest, frolicking with the herd, a mind and heart unburdened by such strife and free to be happy.

Shahly finally acknowledged her aching legs and dry throat and realized the sun was quickly approaching the trees on the western horizon. Another day gone and nothing accomplished except for more problems to overcome.

Still, all she had to do was walk out of that gate and try to forget everything that had happened. It would be so much easier, so much less painful.

She stepped toward the gate and the home and life she missed, then stopped and stared into the forest with despair in her eyes, knowing she would never truly be happy or at rest with Vinton in the hands of the humans, with the mission given to her by the dragon incomplete, and with a unicorn stallion and a human prince at odds in her heart. She could not just run away.

Close to tears once again, she turned and walked slowly back to the palace.

Once inside, she found she still had no destination and just wandered for a time, trying not to think about what she had waiting ahead of her.

Shahly had nearly succeeded in losing herself in pleasant memories when someone seized her arm and a gruff voice harshly demanded, "What are you doing here?"

With a gasp, she looked up to the burly guard who had a firm grip on her arm. He was a large, powerful man with a full beard and anger in his eyes.

His lip curled up slightly as he snarled, "I said what are you doing here?"

"I am not doing anything," she answered. "I'm—I'm just wandering the palace."

"Of course you are," he drawled. "Just wandering about to see what kind of sabotage you can get away with."

"What?" she breathed, then looked around her, her eyes locking on the door to the Talisman chamber, ten paces away!

Many guards were converging.

And her mission to destroy it came fully to bear on her.

She swallowed hard and looked back up to the guard. "That is where the Talisman is kept."

Still firmly, painfully holding her arm, the guard led her back the way she had come, saying, "Yes, that is where the Talisman is kept, an area where you do not belong. I think you have some explaining to do."

"But I just did not realize where I was," she tried to explain. "I don't know my way around the palace very well."

"And yet you knew where we keep the Talisman," he pointed out.

"Where are we going?" she asked fearfully.

"Where do you think," was his reply. "The dungeon."

Shahly cringed and suddenly did not walk so willingly with him now. "But I did not mean to do anything wrong!"

"I've dealt with the likes of you before," the guard snarled, pulling harder on her arm.

Wincing from the pain, Shahly reached for his hand.

"See here," another, younger man called from behind.

The guard stopped and turned, swinging Shahly along with him.

The younger guard, one who had guarded the door to Shahly's room before, stormed to them and right up to the much larger man, informing, "I think you should explain why you are assaulting his Highness' favorite maiden."

"I do not answer to you, boy," the older man growled.

"You do answer to others," the other man informed, "so I would advise you to release her and allow her to be on her way."

"Your advice means little to me, boy. Now go stand my post until I return."

The younger guard raised his chin, snapping back, "Go and stand your own post."

With a scowl, the larger man growled, "That is an order, boy."

"And how will your orders stand when his Highness finds his favorite maiden in the dungeon? I think he would come down very hard on Captain Ocnarr, and Captain Ocnarr would come down very hard on you."

"You think so? Because of this saboteur?" The large man jerked on Shahly's arm, digging his fingers in."

She winced and tugged on his hand, crying, "Please! You are hurting me!"

"You are in deeper trouble by the second," the younger man informed. "I would suggest you do as I say if you do not want to be in over your head with Captain Ocnarr."

"You leave Ocnarr to me, boy, and do as I told you." The large man turned and dragged Shahly down the corridor.

Still tugging on his arm, she pleaded, "You are hurting me! Please, just let go and I will go with you. I promise!"

"Quiet!" he barked.

He was very brutal with her and she could feel from him that he was enjoying this as he dragged her with him. He was enjoying her pain.

She was taken down flights of stairs, down to the lower levels of the palace where light was becoming sparse and the odor was so bad, the air so heavy.

Back into the dungeon, but this time not of her own choosing.

With the guard still firmly holding her arm, Shahly was taken to a different area than what she had visited before. Many black timber doors held together with heavy iron lined the corridor on one side and blocks of tombs lined the other. The place reeked of old carrion and death.

Shahly was taken into one of the cells, one which was better illuminated than the corridor outside. There was a table in the center of the room and two chairs to each side of it. Knives, whips and other instruments of torture, things which Shahly did not understand, lay on the table. A black cauldron of hot coals sat beside it with two iron bars stabbed into the coals. Closer to the far wall was a tall timber A-frame with finger width braided leather cords hanging from the joint at the top between the timbers.

This was far from a pleasant place to be. The damp, still air in the room made it feel close, very confining, and, close to panic, Shahly found she could barely breathe.

Still, she knew she had to keep her wits about her. Judging from the large guard's reactions, he was easily brought to anger and she knew it would not be wise to provoke him and risk getting herself hurt.

Another man entered the room behind them, a fat man wearing only wool shorts, a thick leather belt and dark boots. He was dirty with a few days growth of beard and a bald head, and he did not smell good at all.

The bald man folded his thick arms, his dark eyes on Shahly as he asked, "What do we have here?"

The guard jerked on her arm and answered, "A saboteur, one who thought she could get to the Talisman, just like the last."

Shahly shook her head, protesting, "But I—"

"Quiet!" the guard barked, jerking on her arm again. "You will talk when you are told to!"

"One of the Prince's?" the fat man asked.

"So she would like to think," the guard sneered as she shoved her into the room.

The fat man watched Shahly stumble to a stop, shaking his head as he said, "This could be delicate."

The guard pointed a finger at her and ordered, "Wait here," then he and the fat man turned and left the room, closing the door behind them.

Shahly could hear the two men talking outside but could not make out what they were saying, though it was obvious they spoke about her.

She crossed her arms, holding onto her shoulders as she turned and scanned the room again. It stank here, the damp, heavy air betraying many unpleasant odors, one of which was unmistakable.

Blood.

She shuddered, slowly walked to the table and gingerly sat in one of the chairs, still looking around her. Her eyes snapped to the door as it opened and she tensed slightly as the fat man entered and closed the door behind him. For long seconds he just stood there and stared down at her with cold eyes, feeding her fear.

Eerie, deafening silence thickened the very atmosphere of the room.

After what felt like a day of staring back at him, Shahly took a deep breath, her brow arched as she asked, "Am I in trouble?"

He nodded. "You're in trouble."

She turned her eyes down, nervously wringing her hands together as she said, very child-like, "I did not mean to do anything wrong."

Shahly heard him slowly approach her and she felt his eyes on her as he asked, "Then why were you trying to get into the Talisman chamber?"

"I was not," she corrected softly. "I was just wandering the castle."

The fat man reached to the table and picked up a short whip, one with a half dozen thick pieces of leather dangling from the end. "Is that so? What were you doing there, then?"

Shahly shrugged. "Just wandering, trying to think."

"About what?"

"Why I'm here."

"Why are you here?"

She turned her eyes away from him. Direct questions were difficult, as they demanded direct answers. Still a unicorn within, she could not lie, nor could she answer.

"Well?" he prodded. "What brought you here?"

She looked up to him, and found the truth, answering softly, "Love."

The fat man raised his brow and nodded. "Love, huh? I can see making such a journey for love. You are here for the Prince, are you not?"

Shahly looked down, shamefully answering, "He does not know I am here."

"At Castle Red Stone?" he asked.

"In the dungeon," she replied

The fat man released a deep sigh and growled, "Why me?" Then he drew a breath and said, "Okay. Let's try something else, shall we?"

Shahly looked up to him, sat up straight and agreed, "Okay."

He sort of smiled and commended, "Good. What is your interest in the Talisman?"

The Talisman. Definitely a sore thorn in Shahly's side.

Her brow arched again and she asked, "Have you ever seen it?"

The fat man shook his head. "No, I haven't. Do you want to see it?"

"I already have," Shahly answered straightly.

The fat man drew his head back. "You have?"

She nodded. "Ard... Uh, Prince Arden took me to the tower and showed it to me." She shuddered and looked away, feeling her heart grow heavy. "It is made with unicorn spirals. They killed unicorns to make it."

He just stared down at her for long seconds, then nodded and asked, "This saddens you?"

"It should sadden anyone," Shahly replied.

The fat man shrugged and halfheartedly agreed, "I suppose so. Then, perhaps they should be avenged."

Shahly puzzled for a moment. Avenged. What was that supposed to mean? She blinked and looked up to the guard, asking, "What do you mean?"

"Oh, you know what I mean," he said as if patronizing her. "You want to get back at those who made it for killing the unicorns."

"Get back at them?" Shahly questioned.

"Revenge!" he said more loudly. "The unicorns died so those responsible must die and the Talisman must be destroyed, correct?"

Shahly winced.

"You avenge their deaths," he continued. "Destroy that talisman, allow the dragon to level the castle and kill everyone within, that way you get even with those who killed the unicorns. You have made them pay for their crime."

"That is horrible!" Shahly declared. "Why would I disgrace the spirits of those unicorns by killing in their memory?"

The fat man raised his eyebrows.

"And what about the people here who had nothing to do with it? What would they die for? It just isn't right to even think about."

The fat man just stared at her for a time, then shook his head. "You are a strange girl."

"*I* am strange?" she barked, her brow high over her eyes. "Your talk of *avenge* and killing everyone here for the acts of a few people sounds very strange to me."

He laughed, heartily and in a jolly way Shahly did not know he could. After a moment to collect himself, he wiped tears from his eyes and drew a deep breath, shaking his head again as he managed to say, "You are truly an unusual one." He seemed to try to compose himself further, but a smile was still in control of him as he looked to Shahly and said, "Okay. Let's be frank with one another. You were brought down here so that I could get the truth and a confession out of you. So just be absolutely honest with me so that we don't have to go on further."

Shahly nodded.

He nodded back and directly asked, "Were you trying to gain access to the Talisman?"

Shahly shook her head and answered, "No."

"Good," the fat man accepted. "Why were you near the door?"

"I was just wandering the palace," she replied. "I wanted to think and be by myself for a while. That is all."

"And you just happened to end up near the only entrance to the Talisman tower."

Shahly nodded, answering, "Yes."

The fat man drew and then vented a deep breath, looking to the floor, then he shook his head. "Normally, I would have you in tears by now, begging me for mercy." He turned his eyes to her. "But somehow I feel you are telling me the truth."

"Why would I not?" Shahly asked, leaning her head. She flinched as the door burst open and looked to it, her eyes widening with her mouth as she saw the black haired man enter the room.

The fat man spun around, demanding, "What is the meaning of this? I am in the middle of an interrogation!"

Traman folded his arms, glaring at the fat man. "I could ask you the same. Prince Arden has nearly every member of the royal guard and staff looking for this maiden." His eyes narrowed and he finished, "And I find her here."

The fat man glanced down at her, then looked back to the black haired man. "A palace guard brought her here and told me she was trying to get at the Talisman. Considering the circumstances—"

"Is that true?" the black haired man asked, turning his eyes to Shahly.

"It was just a misunderstanding," she assured. "I wandered too close to the door to the tower where the Talisman is kept and the guard thought I was someone called *saboteur* and brought me here." She looked to the fat man. "I promise there was nothing more to it than that."

Traman nodded. "A misunderstanding. Good." He raised his chin, meeting the fat man's eyes. "And fortunate for you. Clearing this up now may just have saved you from losing your head."

The fat man swallowed hard and raised a hand to his throat.

"Of course," the black haired man added, "if the Prince sees so much as a scratch on her then you may end up on the receiving end of what you have been employed to administer."

Shahly could feel the fat man's emotions very clearly at this point. He was terrified. She looked to Traman and assured, "He was very kind to me. All we did was talk. There was nothing more, really."

The fat man glanced down at Shahly, then looked to the black haired man and nodded, hiding the whip behind his back. "Just talked. That's all we did."

Traman looked to Shahly, then eyed the fat man suspiciously once more. "Very well. Her escort should be here shortly. See to it she is kept comfortable until then. Your hide depends on it."

The fat man nodded eagerly and assured, "Oh, she will be comfortable as I can make her. You just tell his Highness I will look after her and keep her well."

With one last glance at Shahly, the black haired man turned and left the room, leaving the door open.

Shahly watched after him for long seconds, a renewed curiosity about him growing within her.

With the situation over, the fat man tossed the whip back onto the table and vented a long breath, leaning on the table as he stared at it blankly. His scent changed slightly from the acrid smell of fear to a more metallic, salty odor usually associated with heat or exertion in animals that did sweat. Slowly, he turned his eyes to Shahly.

She stared back and asked, "Not feeling well?"

He shakily said, "You could have had me whipped to death."

She grimaced a little, inquiring sharply, "Why would I want to do that?"

The fat man shook his head and replied, "I am just glad you did not."

"That would be avenge," Shahly assumed, "wouldn't it?"

He nodded. "Aye, and I'll be thankin' God you have no taste for it."

The guard who had taken Shahly to the dungeon stormed in and bellowed, "Have you still gotten no confession from her?"

The fat man stood fully and turned to the guard, sternly informing, "There will be no confession. She did nothing. It was just a misunderstanding."

Appearing to grow irritated, the guard looked to Shahly, then back to the fat man and said, "You've not even scratched her yet."

"And I'll not be scratching her, either," the fat man retorted. "As I told you, she did nothing."

"You overweight fool," the guard growled. "She's got you believing her lies." He turned and reached for Shahly. "I'll get the truth out of you."

She shrank away.

The fat man grabbed the guard's arm, stopping him. "I said she has done nothing, and she will not be harmed."

The two men just stared at each other for a long, tense moment.

Jerking his arm free, the guard backed away a step and reached for his sword, growling, "Insolent fool!"

The fat man snatched a knife from the table and squared off against him, glaring back.

The younger guard who had protested Shahly's apprehension rushed into the room and declared, "Maid Shahly!" He strode past the men and offered her his hand. "I have been sent to escort you back upstairs, my Lady."

"She is going nowhere!" the older guard barked, drawing his sword. "And I told you to watch my post!"

The younger guard turned fully as Shahly stood, facing the older man as he defiantly said, "You should go and watch your own post."

"That is an order, boy," the older guard growled.

"And how will your orders stand when his Highness finds his favorite maiden in the dungeon to be tortured in your presence, huh?" the younger guard questioned.

Shahly's eyes widened and she looked to the fat man. "Tortured?"

He looked down at her and shrugged. "It's not a bad living, really."

"And on your orders, no less," the younger guard continued. "I think he would come down very hard on Captain Ocnarr, and Captain Ocnarr would come down very hard on you!"

The older guard stepped toward him, warning, "Boy, you are in way over your head."

"But nowhere near as far as you," the younger guard informed. "I would suggest you do as I say if you don't want to be in further trouble with Captain Ocnarr."

The older guard bumped the boy in the chest with his sword, ordering, "You just go mind that post like I told you before I whip you to death myself. I will handle Ocnarr."

"Will you, now?" Captain Ocnarr asked from the doorway.

The guard swung around.

So involved with the confrontation was Shahly that she did not even notice him approach the room.

Boring into the older guard with eyes of stone, Ocnarr snapped his fingers, then folded his arms.

The younger guard rushed to him and snapped to attention, loudly answering, "Yes, Captain Ocnarr."

Ocnarr took a long breath and looked away, blowing the air from him slowly, then he looked back to the younger guard and ordered, "Escort Maid Shahly to her suite and remain at her door until I arrive."

The younger guard glanced at the other guard, then looked back to Ocnarr, responding, "Yes, Captain Ocnarr. Will anything else be required of me?"

Ocnarr turned to the fat man and ordered, "Take the rest of the day off. I will send for you if I should require your services again today."

The fat man glanced at Shahly and nodded to her.

She smiled and nodded back.

Hastily, the fat man made for the door, nodding to Ocnarr as he offered, "Thank you," and left the room.

Ocnarr looked to the younger guard and said, "You have your orders."

"Yes sir," the young guard confirmed, then approached Shahly and offered her his arm again. "Maiden?"

She slipped her arm over his and followed him past the two men who faced each other again, then paused and glanced back at them once more.

The older guard looked considerably less confident at this point as he stared into the eyes of his superior, who more than matched his size.

The last thing Shahly heard from the room as she left was Ocnarr say, "Now. Perhaps you should explain just how you intended to *handle* me."

As if he sensed Shahly's eagerness to be out of the dungeon, the young guard kept the pace quick, but was careful not to allow her to stumble.

Shahly kept up with him well, but slowed as she felt the presence of the black haired man somewhere in the corridor.

The young guard looked to her and softly beckoned, "Maiden? Something wrong?"

She scanned the area once more and shook her head, continuing on with him as she assured, "No, nothing's wrong."

She knew the black haired man was watching, but still could not reason out exactly why he had decided to stay so close to her, to look after her. He knew who and what she was and had not betrayed her to the other humans, but still Shahly felt leery of him.

Soon, Shahly and her escort were outside of the dungeon, back to the upper levels in the warm, brightly lit ground level of the palace. The cleaner air tasted good, though memories of the sweet forest air were still strong.

They ascended a flight of stairs and the guard slowed the pace as they continued toward her room in silence.

Shahly finally turned to him and offered, "Thank you."

He smiled, not looking at her as he replied, "My duty and my great pleasure, Maiden."

"You were very brave," Shahly complemented. She could feel this embarrassed him, but she also felt that he liked it.

His face turned a little red as he informed, "Your words are way too kind, my Lady. Not that I object in any way."

Shahly laughed softly. "You are so modest."

Another young guard jumped out into the hallway before them and drew his sword, his eyes locked on Shahly's escort. He smiled fiendishly and declared, "I have you now."

Shahly's guard gently pushed her behind him, glaring at the challenger as he drew his own sword and warned, "Stand away, Maiden. I will take care of this rogue." With a cry of battle, he raised his weapon and charged.

Shahly raised her hands to her mouth as she watched the duel escalate. The ringing of steel stung her ears and she flinched each time a sword came too close to one or the other.

Someone grasped her shoulders from behind.

Shahly shrieked and spun around.

Surprised herself at first, Ihzell offered her a warm smile and said, "Sorry. I did not mean to startle you." She looked to the duel and asked, "Now what?"

"That other guard came out of nowhere and challenged him," Shahly reported frantically, turning back to the combatants.

"Oh, don't worry over them," Ihzell advised. "They do this all the time. It is all a ruse to impress the maidens around the castle and they usually do not hurt one another."

Shahly puzzled for a long moment as she watched the duel, then asked, "You mean they are fighting for me?"

Ihzell laughed. "They are not fighting for me, sweetheart."

Shahly just watched a moment longer, her mouth slightly ajar, then she looked back to Ihzell. "But won't Arden be upset?"

The steward laughed again and patted Shahly's shoulder. "I have so much to tell you about men and boys." She loudly cleared her throat.

The combatants stopped in mid parry/thrust and turned startled eyes to the steward, then straightened themselves and sheathed their weapons.

Shahly's escort strode to the women and reported, "Miss, we have found Maid Shahly."

"You are such a good boy," Ihzell complemented. "Now, go and tell Prince Arden you found her and return to her room."

He stiffened a little and informed, "Miss, Captain Ocnarr himself told me to personally escort Maid Shahly to her suite and wait there."

Ihzell smiled. "Tell me. Who do you fear more, Captain Ocnarr or me?"

The young guard raised his chin, his eyes widening slightly as he admitted, "Uh, you Miss. I will just go and find his Highness."

"Good boy," the steward commended, then turned to Shahly as both boys fled. "It is all a matter of knowing what to say and how to say it. Now where have you been all day?"

Watching the guards run down the hallway, Shahly nodded, glanced at the steward, then turned her eyes down and confessed, "A guard took me to the dungeon."

Ihzell turned fully to her and set her hands on her hips, demanding, "*Now* what did you do?"

Shahly folded her hands behind her and watched one of her feet as she kicked at the floor and answered, "I wandered a little too close to the Talisman door."

"Oh, Shahly," the steward scolded. "You really should stay away from that part of the castle."

"I did not mean to," Shahly defended, sounding much like a child who was trying to avoid punishment. "I was just wandering and…Well, I just sort of ended up there."

"Without an escort?" Ihzell questioned.

Shahly glanced up at her and raised a hand to her mouth, nibbling on her thumbnail, then finally admitted, "I just wanted to be by myself for a while."

Ihzell huffed a breath and ordered, "Well, next time you want to be by yourself you have a guard along, understand?"

Shahly nodded.

"No harm done this time, I suppose," Ihzell comforted, then took Shahly's wrist and pulled her hand from her mouth. "And stop chewing your nails. Come, now. Let's get you back to your room. I just finished the loveliest spring dress for you."

With a deep sigh, Shahly protested, "Oh, not another one."

"Stop whining," the steward scolded. "You need a wardrobe."

Shahly nodded, then her lips tightened as she stared at the floor before her. Ihzell was one of the few people she actually trusted. Audrell knew her secret and had not betrayed her. The strange black haired man who had once hunted her knew and even he had not betrayed her. Ihzell did not even have the chance to gain such trust, and continuing this lie with someone she felt so close to did not seem right.

Still, the dragon's warning about humans' loyalties was fresh in her mind. "One calling himself friend could easily turn on you without warning," were his words. Shahly did not feel that Ihzell would do this, but even Ihzell had proven to be unpredictable at times.

Should I tell her? Shahly thought. *How should I tell her? When?*

"We should stop by the sewing room," Ihzell suddenly announced.

Shahly flinched and looked up to her, then nodded and looked ahead again.

"I left my kit there," the steward continued, "and we must make certain that gown fits by dinner tonight. I hope you like yellow."

"Yes," Shahly confirmed softly. "I like yellow." Her lips tightened as she pondered whether or not to reveal her secret to Ihzell, fearing how she might react.

A long silence later, Ihzell nudged her with her elbow and asked, "So what are you thinking so hard about?"

Butterflies swarmed in Shahly's stomach and she finally turned her eyes up to Ihzell and answered, "Oh, I was just wondering if I should tell you that I am a unicorn in human form and came to the castle to rescue my stallion who is going to be killed by your people soon." She stiffened and waited anxiously for a response, dreading it at the same time.

Ihzell gave her a sidelong glance, then laughed and nudged her again. "Shahly, you are a strange girl, but I love you dearly anyway."

Shahly smiled a halfhearted smile and turned her eyes ahead.

They finally arrived at the sewing room and Ihzell opened the door, inviting Shahly to enter first.

When Shahly stepped into the room she noticed Prince Arden already there, wearing a silk shirt that was forest green in color and open at the collar, white trousers with green stripes down the outer legs and what looked like his riding boots. As usual, his hair was perfectly groomed.

Nillerra was also there, wearing a tightly fitting white casual dress that revealed much of her chest, and she was holding a wine goblet in each hand.

They both turned to the door as if startled and much of the wine in the goblets sloshed out, some of it finding the Prince's trousers.

Seeing what she had done, Nillerra winced and dropped both goblets, sending much of the rest of it onto his trousers.

He jumped back, looked down at the stained material, then turned highly upset eyes on Nillerra, asking with a stiff jaw, "Are you certain you do not want to live with my anger?"

She just stared down at the goblets for long seconds, slowly shaking her head, then she looked up to the Prince, turned and strode to the door, freezing as she saw Shahly.

A little fearfully, Shahly stared back into her eyes, not liking what she saw there.

Nillerra clenched her teeth, hissing, "I *will* get you for this," then she fled the room.

Shahly watched after her for a few seconds, knowing fear of the black haired girl and what she might be thinking, then she looked back to the Prince, feeling a little sorry for him as he just stood there and stared down at his stained trousers.

He turned his eyes to Shahly, looking very disappointed and a little embarrassed, then he looked to Ihzell and growled, "I think it is time I asked Maid Nillerra to leave."

"And about time," the steward added, striding into the room. "So what were you two doing in here?"

Shahly gently closed the door.

Arden took a deep breath and replied, "Well, I came to see if you would stitch up a loose seam in these trousers. Nillerra came in and was very insistent that I have a drink of wine with her. I am at a loss as to what has gotten into her of late. I just know I have tired of it."

"We all have," the steward agreed. "Well, I am afraid stitching those trousers would seem to be a lost cause at this time. Get out of them and I will see if I can do something with those stains."

He raised a brow and asked, "Here?"

Ihzell vented a deep breath. "Your Highness, I spent many a season changing your diapers and dressing you." She glanced at Shahly, then nodded and said, "Oh yes. Perhaps you should go to your room and change."

"Capital idea," he agreed, then turned and approached Shahly, taking her shoulders. "I was going to ask you for that walk in the gardens."

She smiled and assured, "I would love to."

He gently kissed her lips, then turned to Ihzell and offered, "Thank you anyway."

"Just leave them by the door," she ordered. "I will be along to fetch them in short order."

"Thank you, Auntie Ihzell," he said as he left.

"Stop that!" the steward barked, then shook her head and stormed into the sewing room, emerging a moment later with a fabric-covered box. "Come along, Shahly. Let's get you fitted into that dress."

Ihzell always seemed to be obsessed with perfection, especially where her dressmaking was concerned, and every tiny detail received the same attention. Not even the few small threads which hung defiantly from the seams in the dress were safe from the steward's sharp eyes.

Standing in the center of her room with her arms held out, Shahly took the time to reflect on the last few days, to study what she knew of the steward, and to ponder further whether or not to disclose her secret. Her greatest fear was that Ihzell might simply not understand, or that she might be angry at being deceived so. Shahly did not feel right about keeping such a secret from one so close, but even more she feared the consequences of such honesty.

What a horrible dilemma this is, she thought.

Ihzell stepped back and looked over her work.

Shahly watched her, urgency racing within, hesitation and fear keeping it at bay.

The steward stroked her chin and mumbled, "That neck line might be a tad too low."

"Ihzell," Shahly started, "there is something—"

"Too tight around the waist?" Ihzell asked suddenly. "I have a little room to let it out."

Shahly shook her head and assured, "The dress is fine. There has just been something..." She sighed, feeling frustrated with herself. How to say it?

Smiling, Ihzell took Shahly's hands and said, "Child, if something is bothering you then the best thing to do is just come right out and tell me what it is."

Perhaps she was right. After all, how bad could the consequences really be?

With a deep breath and great effort to calm herself, Shahly looked into the steward's eyes and said, "Ihzell, the true—" she hesitated again as someone knocked on the door.

Ihzell turned and in her own subtle way bade, "What!"

"It is me," Prince Arden's voice answered from the other side.

The steward glanced at Shahly, smiling slightly, then looked back to the door and ordered, "Come in, Highness. Come in."

Prince Arden slowly opened the door and peered in, then, sporting a white silk shirt and tight fitting red trousers, entered the room and slowly approached Shahly, his eyes locked on hers as he asked, "How can you be lovelier each time I see you?"

"I don't know that I am," she replied, staring back into his eyes. She noticed the thin, silver crown he wore, one studded with diamonds, two big rubies and a black jewel right in the center. He had never worn this before or anything like it.

She glanced at Ihzell, who stared back at the Prince with a proud look in her eyes. Strangely, she seemed near tears.

The Prince offered his hand to Shahly, reminding, "I believe we have a walk to take in the gardens tonight."

Shahly smiled and slipped her hand into his. Suddenly, all of the strife she had been facing seemed to be swept away.

Ihzell stepped forward and asked, "Are you certain about this?"

He looked to her and nodded. "I have never been so certain about anything."

"Certain about what?" Shahly asked.

Arden turned his eyes to her and smiled, answering, "You will see shortly, Love." Then he looked to the steward and advised, "Don't wait up. We will be back sometime tonight." He turned and led Shahly do the door, placing his other hand over hers.

"You two behave yourselves," Ihzell called after him.

Arden was silent and kept the pace very slow as they walked down the corridor, down a flight of stairs and down the hallway that led to the gardens.

Sensing that he was uncomfortable about something, Shahly looked up to him and observed, "You are awfully tense tonight."

He glanced down at her and shook his head. "Oh no. No. I'm just thinking."

"You are tense," Shahly corrected.

Arden laughed softly and admitted, "Okay. So I'm a little tense. I just have a lot on my mind."

"Like what?"

He grew even more uncomfortable and asked, "Do we have to talk about it just now?"

Shahly shrugged. "I suppose not."

Arden subtly quickened the pace.

They arrived at the torch-lit gardens and walked casually down the main path toward the center where the sky was open and the creek widened to form a pond. Unlike the night before, other people were absent. No matter. Walking in such a beautiful setting alone with Arden was much more pleasant and Shahly felt truly happy once again.

The grass was thick and lush and the bushes all around were fragrant with blooms which had not yet closed fully for the evening.

A marble bench sat on the thick carpet of grass which surrounded the pond and Arden took Shahly right to it, inviting her to sit, then he sat down beside her, fidgeting for a moment as if he was trying to make himself comfortable.

Shahly carelessly straightened and smoothed her skirt over her legs, then looked out over the moonlit pond, the moon's reflection over the water dancing in her eyes. She drew a deep breath, savoring the scents of the spring blooms and green things for a moment, then looked up to the stars and moon and dreamily said, "This is a beautiful evening."

"Yes, it is," he agreed, then looked to her and finished, "but nowhere as beautiful as my Forest Blossom."

She turned to him, raising a hand to her face. "You always know just what to say to make my cheeks feel warm."

He smiled back and stroked her cheek with the back of his hand. "I am glad I can. A woman as beautiful as you deserves such compliments." He just gazed into her eyes for a moment, then seemed to tense up again and looked to the sky, observing, "It is a clear night and a perfect full moon."

Shahly also looked. "It is very bright. I used to take long strolls in the forest on nights like this."

"That sounds pleasant," Arden sighed. "A pity tonight is the last night of its splendor for a whole month."

Shahly's breath caught and she gasped, "The last night?"

"Not to worry," the Prince assured. "We will have many more nights like this."

Shahly shook her head. "It has already been three days?"

"There is no need to be so anxious, Forest Blossom," Arden comforted. "We will have the rest of our lives to enjoy such simple pleasures."

Something did not feel right and Shahly looked toward the moon's reflection in the pond, then nervously panned her eyes toward the Prince and asked, "What do you mean?" She felt very uneasy as he stood, walked in front of her and knelt, taking her hand in both of his as he locked his eyes hopefully onto hers.

Arden took a deep breath and finally confessed, "Shahly, I love you with all of my heart. I have waited my whole life for you, someone who is as beautiful in spirit as she is in my eyes, and I finally feel complete where there was only part of the man you see." He took another deep breath. "Shahly, I wish to pledge my eternal love and devotion to you, my heart and my very soul. Will you be my wife?"

She gasped and slowly raised a hand to her lips, her eyes locked wide on his.

"Will you marry me?" he asked softly.

Shahly's heart thundered as her different emotions waged war with one another. This was a decision she had never counted on. Her quest had all but failed and now Prince Arden was offering her a new life.

She looked up to the full moon. A new life with this fabulous human or Vinton's life? This would be her last night to return. Something strong within her urged her to just give in to the love she felt for Arden while something else which was just as strong knew it could never be. She could never be truly happy with him. She could never be truly happy without him, or Vinton.

Pain was all she could sort from it.

She slowly looked back down to him, feeling his desperation for an answer, not knowing herself what that answer would be.

Until she heard herself say, "I'm sorry, Arden."

Instantly, she felt pain and confusion erupt from him.

The pain showed fully in his eyes as he breathed, "What do you mean?"

She slowly shook her head, tears dropping from her eyes as she told him, "I cannot marry you."

"But... Why?" he demanded. "Don't you love me?"

Her composure broke down quickly and she nodded, admitting, "Of course I do. I just... I ..."

"Did someone threaten you?" he asked suddenly, almost angrily. "Is someone trying to intimidate you? Do not be afraid to tell me. I can protect you."

"It is not that," she insisted, crying, "and it is not you. Please, just do not make this harder."

He stood and backed away, glaring down at her. "Harder? How could it possibly be harder? I love you, Shahly. I want you to be my wife! Is that so terrible?"

She shook her head and sobbed, "No."

"Then why?" he shouted.

She cringed, covering her ears as she begged, "Arden, please."

"I just do not understand, Shahly. Do you just need more time? We could have a long engagement."

"Arden," she sobbed, "you just do not understand."

"Then tell me!" he insisted.

Shahly raised her hands to her eyes and just sat there for a moment, trying to sort out what she felt, trying to compose herself. Finally, she stood and cried, "I can't!" as she fled down the garden path.

∘❈∘

Too much to bear.

Shahly found she could not stop crying no matter how far or how long she wandered down the garden trails. If she was truly human then this would be the best day of her life, a half hour ago the happiest moment.

She was not human. The dragon's warning about the emotions she would experience in this form crept back into her thoughts, though it was too late to act upon now.

"How could I have been so selfish?" she asked herself aloud. "How can anyone forgive what I have done?"

She found a marble bench and collapsed onto it, burying her face in her arms as she wept still more. *Arden must surely hate me now,* she thought, *and Vinton will surely die tomorrow.*

"I am so sorry, Arden," she sobbed. "I have made such a mess of everything."

"That you have," Nillerra's voice agreed from behind.

Shahly raised her head and slowly looked over her shoulder.

Nillerra stood behind her, flanked by four palace guards. Her arms were folded and hate was in her eyes.

Shahly pushed herself up and stood, facing the black haired girl as she wiped tears from her cheeks. Something did not feel right. She sensed danger, and something wicked in Nillerra's thoughts. She looked into the black haired girl's eyes and swallowed hard, feeling the urge to run and hide.

Nillerra raised her chin and observed, "You look upset, Shahly. Did Prince Arden turn down your advances?"

"I do not understand," Shahly admitted softly.

"Of course you don't," the black haired girl drawled. "Where is the Prince? Don't tell me he allowed you to come out here all by yourself. No escort?"

Shahly shook her head, feeling that something was dreadfully amiss.

Nillerra shook her head and sighed, "That is unfortunate, Shahly."

Two of the guards advanced.

Shahly retreated a step as they reached her and too late tried to elude them as they took her arms. She struggled against their grips for only a few seconds before realizing she was no match for them, then she looked fearfully back to Nillerra, sucking a hard breath as she realized that the guard with the predatory thoughts about her was standing at the black haired girl's side.

Nillerra approached slowly, her two escorts following.

Shahly was too afraid to feel the black haired girl's thoughts, though she recognized the look in her eyes and finally knew fear of her.

Nillerra just stared back at her for long seconds, then she shook her head and sneered, "I have not liked you since the first time I laid my eyes on you. I knew you would be trouble for me from the beginning and I should have taken care of you myself the first opportunity I got. Unfortunately, you have already cost me the throne. Prince Arden sent word that I am to leave by tomorrow." She leaned her head. "And I have you to thank for it."

Barely able to breathe, Shahly slowly shook her head and said, "But what did I do? I've tried to—"

Nillerra slapped her very hard and shouted, "Did I say you could speak?"

Shahly's head was snapped around so hard that her neck popped and her knees weakened beneath her, barely holding her up. Many seconds later she opened her eyes and looked back to the black haired girl, her cheek stinging almost unbearably. Fear had grown to terror as she looked to what was truly the dark side of humans, the true evil of this odd race.

Nillerra stared coldly back at her, and a small smile curled her lips as she asked, "Where is your prince now, Shahly? You seem to be out here all alone without anyone to protect you." Her hand darted into her skirt pocket and emerged with her dagger. "What a pity."

Her eyes fixed on the mirror-like steel of the blade, Shahly slowly shook her head, struggling just to breathe as she whimpered, "Nillerra, please. Don't do this."

The black haired girl looked down to her dagger as she ran her finger down the side of the blade and said in a perversely encouraging voice, "That's right, Shahly. Beg me for your miserable life. Let's see if you can sweet talk me like you did Arden." Her eyes snapped to Shahly's. "Remember? When you stole him from me?"

"But you do not understand," Shahly tried to explain. "I did not steal his attentions from you. He is not even the true reason I came—"

"Liar!" Nillerra cried suddenly, glaring back into Shahly's eyes. "You are no different than the rest! You would take everything from me if I did not stop you!"

Shaking her head, Shahly assured, "All I ever wanted from you was your friendship."

The black haired girl just stared pitifully back at her for long seconds, appearing to be near tears, then her eyes hardened and she hissed, "Liar," and slapped Shahly again. She spun around, her hands clenching into tight fists as she ordered, "Shut her up."

One of the guards clamped his hand over Shahly's mouth and jerked her head back.

After a moment of consideration, Nillerra turned back to Shahly, stepped toward her and pushed the tip of the blade against her throat, thoughtfully asking, "Now where do we begin?"

All of Shahly's muscles tensed as she felt the cold, sharp steel firmly against her throat.

The black haired girl smiled and slowly ran the blade down Shahly's throat, down to her chest where she hesitated and suggested, "Maybe I should cut your heart out and see what Prince Arden likes about it so."

Shahly tried to retreat from the blade but was held firmly in place by the guards.

The blade was slowly drawn up, cutting the fabric of Shahly's dress, and stopped over her throat again.

"Oh, this could be interesting," Nillerra observed with a smile. "If I shove the blade into your throat you will take much longer to die. That can be very messy, though, what with all of the blood spewing and the gagging and choking you would do, but it would do my heart good to watch you suffer so."

Shahly whimpered and shook her head, tears streaming from her terror-filled eyes.

Nillerra raised her brow. "No good for you? Well, perhaps I will let you live after all, and just cut your face up so badly that no one will want you, much less a prince." Something sinister took her eyes. "Maybe I could let the guards have at you while I come up with something even better."

"Or maybe you could rot in the dungeon for the rest of your life," Prince Arden added.

Nillerra and her escorts wheeled around.

The Prince stood two paces away, his arms folded and a menacing glare locked on the black haired girl.

Ihzell stood beside him, and smiled at Nillerra, reminding, "I told you I would be watching, you conniving little snake."

Combing a hand through her hair, Nillerra straightened herself and declared, "Prince Arden! I did not expect to see you this evening."

"I can see that," he informed. "What exactly is the meaning of this little display of yours?"

She glanced around her. "Display? I do not know what you mean. Shahly and I were just… We were, uh…"

"Never mind," Arden growled, striding forward. He took the dagger from Nillerra and looked to the guards who held Shahly, ordering, "Release her."

They just glanced at each other.

The Prince turned fully on them and barked, "Did you not hear me? Release her! Now!"

Wespard seized the Prince's arm and informed, "We heard you, Highness. No need to shout."

When Arden turned on him, the other guard took his other arm and the two men brutally pulled his arms behind him, holding him firmly.

Ihzell attacked the second guard, slamming her fist many times into his back and helmeted head as she fought to free the Prince.

One of the guards holding Shahly abandoned her and strode to Ihzell, wrestling her arms into his from behind and pulling her from the second guard.

The steward looked back at him and hissed, "You have just sacrificed more than your job here."

Nillerra looked around her and smiled, saying almost childlike, "This gathering is turning out even better than I expected. Everyone is coming."

With the Prince and steward under control, Wespard looked to the black haired girl and impatiently asked, "What now? If either of them goes free then we all rot in the dungeon." He looked to the Prince. "Or worse."

"Much worse!" Ihzell confirmed.

Arden glared back at him. "Right now your life is not worth much, but I would be willing to give you a head start and a sporting chance before I hunt you all down like animals!"

Nillerra took her dagger from the ground where Arden had dropped it, gazed down at it for a moment, then turned and slowly approached the steward, smiling at her. "You know, Ihzell, I am really going to enjoy watching you die." She turned and looked pitifully to the Prince, sighing, "But you, dear Arden. I am sorry it has to end like this between us. We could truly have been so good to one another." She shrugged. "Now, you are just one more liability." She reached up and stroked his cheek. "I will not allow you to suffer, my prince, but I do insist that you watch your little forest blossom die first."

"Nillerra," he warned.

She turned on Shahly.

The guard behind Shahly held her wrists firmly behind her with one hand and had the other around her throat. She did not struggle against him, even as she saw Nillerra approach with the dagger.

Before, there had been a choice between Arden and Vinton. Now, it appeared as if they both would die, and Shahly felt wholly responsible.

"Nillerra!" Arden shouted. "Stop this at once!"

She stared into Nillerra's eyes, fearing what was to come and knowing there was nothing she could do to stop it.

Until something touched her mind.

The black haired man was nearby!

"Wait!" Shahly barked.

Nillerra stopped, staring at her blankly.

"Do what you will to me," Shahly insisted, "but I beg you to let Arden go. I could not bear having his death in my memory in this life or the next. Please, Nillerra. Please."

Nillerra slowly raised her brow. "Seeing the Prince die would hurt you?" She smiled. "Well. That sounds absolutely delicious." She slowly turned and looked to the Prince. "Oh, Arden. I have changed my mind."

The guard behind Shahly seemed confused by this.

Quickly, Shahly peered into his mind, searching for any weakness or fear she could tap into.

There!

Spider! She thought to him.

He sucked a hard breath and pulled his arm from around her throat and retreated.

Shahly twisted away from him and jerked her wrists free of his grip, then charged the black haired girl while her back was turned and tackled her.

Arden stomped on one guard's foot, freed his arm and slammed his palm into the other's nose, freeing his other arm as he backed away.

Nillerra managed to push Shahly from her and swung her dagger, the blade slicing across Shahly's upper arm.

Shahly screamed and fell backward, grasping her wound. She scrambled to her feet and looked to the black haired girl, who was already standing and had the knife poised to attack.

"Okay, wretch," Nillerra sneered. "This will do just as well."

Traman burst from the bushes some distance behind Nillerra, drew his sword and slammed it into the helmeted head of one of the guards Arden was fighting.

The guard holding Ihzell threw her to the ground, drew his sword and swung it at the black haired man.

Blades met in mid-air, ringing loudly.

Nillerra wheeled around and surveyed the situation.

Prince Arden, locked up with one of the other guards, looked to Shahly and shouted, "Shahly, run! Get away and warn the guards!"

Feeling near panic, she stepped toward him and insisted, "But I cannot leave you!"

"Shahly, go!" the Prince shouted, throwing the guard he fought to the ground to engage another. "Get away from here and warn the guards!"

"Vinton!" she cried as an echo of a terrible memory grew louder.

Nillerra spun back to her, holding the dagger ready.

As she had done three days before, Shahly turned and fled, hearing Nillerra in pursuit.

Still grasping her wounded arm, Shahly ran blindly down the garden path, lost her footing and fell to the gravel and stone. Looking back, she saw that the black haired girl was already upon her and had the dagger raised to strike.

"Nillerra!" someone shouted.

The black haired girl looked up from Shahly, up the path.

Shahly also looked.

Audrell strode to them, glaring at the black haired girl as she snarled, "Okay, wretch. It's just you and me, now. Let's go!"

The black haired girl jumped over Shahly and yelled as she charged Audrell, swinging the dagger.

Audrell easily caught Nillerra's wrist, stopping the dagger, then she hit the black haired girl hard across the jaw.

Stunned, Nillerra stumbled backward, dropping the dagger.

Shahly stood and backed away, still grasping her bleeding arm.

Audrell advanced, something predatory in her eyes as she snarled, "That is for what you did to Shahly." She swung again with her other fist, slamming it into Nillerra's eye and sending her stumbling back further. "That is for what you did to me."

Nillerra dared another look at her.

Audrell pursued, cocked her arm back and delivered a quick, solid jab to the black haired girl's face with a sharp crack.

This time, Nillerra screamed as she was spun completely around and collapsed, holding both of her hands over her face.

Shahly did not need her unicorn essence to know that the black haired girl's nose had been broken.

Audrell rubbed her knuckles, chiding, "And that's for being such a bitch." She stepped over Nillerra and approached Shahly, raising her hands to see her wounded arm as she gently ordered, "Let me see."

Shahly took her hand down and allowed Audrell to examine her wound. She looked to Nillerra, who slowly rose from the path.

Audrell tore a piece from her own skirt and used it to bind the cut on Shahly's arm.

Nillerra glared back at Shahly, her hand darting to her skirt pocket. Blood poured from her nose and her face was already swollen. Shahly first thought she was reaching for a cloth to clean herself with, but the black haired girl produced a small vial of brown liquid and smiled, saying, "No, you don't. I *will* have my revenge against you. Both of you!"

Audrell turned around as the black haired girl swallowed the potion within the vial and she cried, "What are you doing?"

Breathing heavily through her mouth, Nillerra dropped the vial and doubled over, looking pitifully on Shahly, then she turned and fled down the path, looking as if she could barely keep herself upright.

Audrell stepped toward her, then shook her head and asked, "Did she poison herself?"

Shahly looked down to the vial, sensing something evil about it, something alive! Slowly, she shook her head and informed, "No, it is not poison." She took Audrell's hand and ran back the way she had come, fearing for Arden.

They found the Prince, the black haired man, Ihzell and the four renegade guards still by the pond, surrounded by Ocnarr and six other palace guards.

Shahly ran straight to the Prince and fell into his arms, holding him tightly as she whispered, "I feared the worst."

"As did I," he replied.

She pulled away and looked into his eyes, her brow arching slightly as she started, "Arden—"

He covered her lips with his fingers and comforted, "There is no need, Love."

Shahly took his hand from her lips and pressed, "But you do not understand."

Traman took the Prince's arm and insisted, "We have to get her out of here. Now!"

Arden turned his eyes to the black haired man. "Why?"

"She is in grave danger here and time is very short," Traman explained. "That is all I can tell you. It is time for her to go."

Despair in his eyes, Arden looked to Shahly, then tightly embraced her.

She hugged him back, never wanting to let go.

"Now!" Traman urged.

The Prince pulled back, his eyes low as he nodded, then he took Shahly's hand and they reluctantly followed the black haired man down the path.

"Your highness," Ocnarr called.

They all stopped and turned to the Captain.

"What about the prisoners?" Ocnarr asked.

Arden raised his chin, regarding Wespard with eyes of stone as he ordered, "Just lock them in the dungeon tonight. I will deal with them in the morning." He half turned, then stopped and turned back again, correcting, "No, my mother, the Queen will deal with them."

Terror took the features of the renegade guards.

Prince Arden glanced at Shahly, then turned and followed Traman down the path, holding tightly onto Shahly's hand.

Overhead, a horrible shriek echoed into the night, almost the tortured scream of a woman.

CHAPTER 13

Shahly, Arden and Traman hurried through the castle, trying not to draw attention to themselves. On their way to the main gate, Shahly tried to explain to the Prince who she was, what she was, and why she had really journeyed to Red Stone Castle.

By the time they exited the palace, Arden was still shaking his head, barely able to believe what he was hearing.

"We have to hurry," Traman urged, time and time again.

Arden's pace still slowed. "But how can this be? You mean you... This was all just a deception?"

"Much of it," Shahly admitted shamefully.

He would not look at her. He could only shake his head, then, "So you are a unicorn, and you came to free the stallion who is being held in the stables. The same dragon who has tried time and time over to destroy Red Stone Castle just happened to find you, give you human form and...." He shook his head again, then sighed. "And to think that I was actually convinced that you loved me."

"I do, Arden," Shahly assured. "I was not supposed to. It was something I did not expect." A tear rolled from her eye and she took a deep breath, trying to compose herself enough to say, "I understand that you are angry, but please do not hate me." She turned her eyes to him, begging with a look for him to understand.

Finally, many strides later, he looked at her, took her hand and pulled her to him, holding her tightly. "I could never hate you, Forest Blossom. Never."

Once they reached the main gate, which was closed for the night, many of the guards patrolling inside of it approached, the senior guard asking, "What brings his Highness out so late?"

"That is none of your affair," Arden countered sternly. "Open the gate and forget you ever saw us here tonight."

Hesitantly, he nodded, turned and shouted, "Open the gate!"

The huge timber gate swung open and Traman led the way outside.

Thirty or so paces down the road, Shahly and Arden stopped and faced each other.

Arden took her hands and gazed deeply into her eyes. "I do not want you to go, Shahly, but...." He looked away.

"I feel the same way, she admitted. "I never thought I could be this close to a human, much less fall in love with one. And then I met you."

He smiled and looked back to her. "Just do not tell me I will find another. I do not think I ever will."

"Stop looking," she told him with a smile. "She has already found you. You only have to open your heart to her."

His brow lowered. "What do you mean?"

"Shahly," Traman summoned softly.

She and Arden looked to him.

The black haired man raised his chin slightly and said, "We have to go now."

She nodded and turned back to her prince. "I have learned so much from you, things about your kind I had not even imagined." A tear spilled from her eye.

Arden gently wiped it away. "There is much you taught me as well, Forest Blossom."

Shahly just gazed into his beautiful eyes for a time, then, drawn by something that could only be felt in their hearts, they fell into each other, joining in one last, passionate kiss.

Traman moaned and turned his back to them, folding his arms as he tamped his foot impatiently.

An unknown time later, Shahly pulled away, her eyes locked on the Prince's as she reluctantly said, "I have to go now, Arden."

He nodded and choked out, "Good-bye, Shahly."

She shook her head, placing a finger gently on his lips as she ordered, "Never say good-bye, Arden. That is what you say when you never expect to see someone again."

"Will I?" he asked hopefully.

She just stared at him for long seconds, then nodded and assured, "Of course you will, my Prince."

Arden smiled, strained as it was. "I will wait for you every day." He pulled her to him and hugged her tightly. "I love you, Shahly."

She hugged him back as tightly as she could, her eyes closed and dropping tears as she answered, "I love you too, Arden." Then she pulled away and took Traman's side, looking up at him with glossy eyes as she said, "I am ready."

"And about damn time," he scolded. "Let's not waste any more time. We've a long journey." He started running down the forest road. Shahly followed, mercifully not looking back at the Prince.

⚜

A full league later, Traman stopped from a dead run and turned back toward the palace.

Shahly stopped four or five paces past him, a little winded as she approached and asked, "What is it?"

Traman's eyes narrowed as he replied, "A hunting party is already pursuing us."

"Oh, no," Shahly whimpered. "I suppose the full moon tonight is not a good thing after all."

The black haired man shook his head. "It will only make us easier to find. We will have to go faster."

"This road is hurting my feet," Shahly complained. "I can't go any faster."

He turned to her and informed, "You could as a unicorn. Transform back now."

She nodded, took the amulet in her hand and closed her eyes as she concentrated on the words. "*Transformatus de corporum unicornu...* No, wait. That is how I became human. Uh...."

"Whenever you are ready," Traman said, trying to sound patient.

"*Transformatus de corporum humanus intro unicornu Abtontae...* Oh, wait!"

Traman sighed heavily. "Now what?"

"His name," Shahly answered, then closed her eyes again and recited, "Ralligor, *transformatus de corporum humanus intro unicornu Abtontae.*"

For long seconds nothing happened. She looked at Traman, up at the moon, down at the amulet, then repeated the incantation.

Still nothing.

"But she said Ralligor is his name!" Shahly cried. "The moon is still full! What is wrong?"

"Are you certain you spoke the words correctly?" Traman asked.

"Yes!" Shahly confirmed.

"How did it happen the first time?" the black haired man demanded. "When you changed to human form, did it take long to change you?"

"I don't remember!" she snapped. "I was kind of drowning at the time."

Whoops and shouts behind drew their attention.

"They are too close!" Traman growled. "Sore feet or no, we have to run."

They sprinted down the road again, Shahly doing her best to keep up, but the horses behind were much too fast and in a few moments torchlight illuminated the trees bordering the road behind.

Then that horrible, tortured shriek echoed from overhead.

"What the hell was that?" Traman shouted, looking up.

Shahly's heart jumped as her essence touched it and she answered, "Something horrible!" She did not know exactly what it was, but it had thoughts, terrifying thoughts, and massive power that was fed by its hate and bloodlust.

She looked up to see.

There, silhouetted against the blue moonlight reflecting off of the clouds, a huge, winged form flew high above them. It strongly resembled a bird of prey in body, had a vulture's head and neck and a lizard's or dragon's tail trailing behind. She dared to touch the thing's mind and found death in its thoughts, the death of its enemies, of those who had hurt it, and of its very innocence.

The death of its former life.

Shahly gasped as she recognized the mind and looked forward again, kicking her stride longer as she shouted, "We have to get away from it!"

"I fully agree," the black haired man said.

The bird creature screeched loudly overhead, its horrible, sharp voice lancing through Shahly's ears like thorns, and she covered her ears against the painful sound.

A hiss from overhead rapidly grew louder, closer.

The road was illuminated in an orange glow, then something hit the ground and exploded only ten paces in front of them.

They stopped and shielded their faces against the heat of the fiery burst, a hot blast of air blowing them backward.

Shahly fell to the road and just laid there for long seconds, shielding her face. She was taken by the shoulders and pulled to her feet, hearing Traman order, "Get up! We must get out of here!"

They ran again, wide around the large, smoldering crater that was left by the explosion.

Shahly looked up, fearing the worst, and saw another ball of fire falling toward them. She gasped, took Traman's hand and pulled him hard across the road.

It hit the ground not far from where they had been, the hot air from the explosion slamming into them like a gust of desert air, though much more scorching.

"We have to get into the forest," Traman insisted. "It will not be able to see us there."

"No!" Shahly cried. "It will burn the forest to get to us."

"I do not see any other choice," the black haired man pointed out.

"I will not sacrifice the forest," Shahly insisted.

An arrow whizzed by.

Traman glanced back, then shook his head and growled, "This is hopeless."

Shahly also glanced back at the hunters, up at the bird creature above them, then forward to the road that led to freedom and grimly said, "It is me they want. Go into the forest and hide. They will follow me and allow you to escape."

"I cannot do that," he informed. "You are too important."

"Just go!" she shouted. "I cannot allow you to sacrifice your life for me. One of us must survive to rescue Vinton."

"What will you do?" he asked.

She looked to him, meeting his eyes, then ordered, "Just go."

He just stared at her for a time, then nodded and veered into the forest.

As he disappeared into the trees, Shahly suddenly felt alone, vulnerable and defenseless. She did not want to die, but knew she had little chance to escape her pursuers. Her only comfort was knowing that the man who had come to her aid in her time of need over and over would not die with her.

She heard chaos in the distance behind her, men shouting, horses whinnying, and the unmistakable voice of Traman in some kind of battle cry. The disturbance continued for some time, growing more distant as she ran as fast as she could down the road. *They must have found him,* she thought sadly, then reached back with her essence to know for sure, smiling as she found his mind. He was laughing at the hunters and had delayed them long enough to allow her to open the gap between herself and them, even slightly.

That loud hiss, growing closer! The orange glow illuminated the road.

Shahly veered quickly to the other side of the road, but the explosion still caused her to stumble.

The hiss and light of another approached.

Using an old unicorn trick, Shahly stopped and turned away from the fireball as it exploded on the ground about twenty paces in front of her, then she darted forward and ran around the crater.

The loud hiss of the fireballs and the glow they let off was her only advantage as she could predict when they were coming and evade them, though this was tiring her even more. Her feet hurt badly from the jagged road and her lungs burned, but she knew she dare not stop to rest, even for a few seconds.

The orange glow illuminated the road in front of her and she abruptly stopped, turning away as it hit the road some thirty paces away.

The hiss was still coming! The road grew brighter and brighter orange!

Shahly darted forward, barely moving three paces before another fireball slammed into the ground almost where she had been standing. Still too close to it, the blast tore into her back and knocked her forward an unknown distance, the searing heat like sunlight on a burn.

Barely conscious, Shahly lay face down on the road, moaning and fighting to stay awake. She bled slowly from numerous cuts and as she sluggishly raised her head she felt the sting of a long gash from above her left eyebrow to her temple which bled very freely.

Something large hit the ground hard behind Shahly, sending tremors beneath her.

She looked ahead of her, drawing a shaky breath, then slowly turned her head, revealing still another bleeding wound at the corner of her mouth, and looked over her shoulder. Breathing was difficult as her eyes fell upon her menace standing only ten paces behind her, a huge, bird-like creature with the head and hooked beak of a bird of prey, and solid black eyes that scrutinized her.

At the base of its vulture-like neck was a mane of feathers that looked dark gray in the blue moonlight. The feathers of the body darkened to black and were large, appearing to be almost armor. They covered a broad chest where powerful muscles drove its broad wingspread, which filled the road one side to the other with plenty of spread left. Its legs were long and thin and ended in the long clawed talons of a bird of prey. The long, scaly tail of a lizard thrashed behind it.

The bird creature hissed and leaned its head, asking in a raspy yet familiar voice, "Death or dungeon? What would suit my purposes best?"

A chill ran throughout Shahly and her eyes widened as she recognized the voice and mind of the bird creature and she breathed, "Nillerra."

"You remember my name," it cackled, some amusement in its tone. "How very touching, Shahly. And how very fortunate that you know who it is who will bring you down!"

Shahly turned over and tried to pull herself away. Before, reasoning with Nillerra had been unsuccessful at best. Now, it would clearly be impossible.

Nillerra stepped toward her, lowering her head slightly as she said, "Perhaps I should burn you to death, or maim you and leave you for the hunters." Something even more wicked took her eyes and she took another step toward her victim. "Or perhaps I should just eat you."

Shahly breathed in shrieks and tried to scramble away as the bird creature bent toward her, opening her tooth-filled beak.

Someone seized Shahly's shoulder from behind and a bright blue flash slammed into the bird creature's head and exploded.

Shahly turned and looked up, very surprised to see the old wizard she had encountered with the dragon in the forest three days before.

"I had a feeling something would go wrong," he sighed, staring up at the beast before him. "Ralligor simply *must* learn to anticipate encountering other magics." He looked down to Shahly and asked, "Why have you not changed back?"

"I tried," she answered, frustration in her voice. "The words he gave me don't work anymore."

His brow lowered and he looked up to the full moon, "Hmm," rolling from his throat as he looked back down at her. "Very strange. You recited the words correctly?" He offered Shahly his hand and pulled her to her feet.

"Twice," she confirmed, then wheeled around as the wizard looked back to the bird creature.

Nillerra shook her head once more, clearing her wits, then she turned a furious glare down to the wizard and roared, "You both die now."

"In time," was the wizard's response, "but not today."

The bird creature lunged at him.

The wizard thrust a hand at her and slammed another flash of blue light into her head, sending her stumbling backward. With Nillerra stunned again, the wizard raised his other hand, glaring up at her.

Shahly felt something hum along her essence, as if the very ground she stood on and the forest itself were generating huge amounts of power and focusing them on the wizard.

A blue tinted white mist swirled around the wizard's arm and toward his hand. Faster, faster it swirled until it formed a luminescent stream of cold light which lanced from his hand and slammed into the bird creature's breast.

Nillerra shrieked and retreated, flapping her wings as if to ward off the spell as ice began to pack on her chest.

The wizard was clearly concentrating hard on his spell, his eyes locked on the beast before him, yet he still ordered, "Go. Get out of here. I will hold it as long as I can."

Shahly turned to flee, looked back to the struggling bird creature, then to the wizard and shook her head, saying, "I cannot just leave you here like this."

Nillerra fell backward to the ground, the ice which encased her breast shattering as she struck.

The wizard turned his eyes on Shahly and commanded, "I said go. Do not worry over me. I can tend myself. Now run to the hard lands and find the dragon. He will be your only hope of not being captured by the hunters or this beast here."

She stepped toward him and protested, "But...."

"Just go," he ordered again, then raised a hand toward her. "Run, Shahly. Run to the hard lands."

She backed away, looking to his hand as it glowed pale blue and knowing fear of his power, then she turned and fled. Something struck her back and she felt enveloped in a warm light and a power which hummed throughout her body and essence. She stumbled, fell forward...

And landed perfectly on her hooves.

Shahly ran as she had not for many days and she felt strength and vitality pour into her body with each stride. The road no longer hurt her as she ran. Her wounds was gone. Her spirit soared. Her confidence and strength grew like wildfire.

It was like being reborn!

Shahly galloped fast down the forest road, knowing she could now outrun the hunters who pursued her and still she felt concern for the wizard. However, from what she had seen of him, he seemed more than able to take care of himself.

So near time. Vinton could be free by morning!

She reached out with her essence and felt the distant presence of a dragon, recognizing it as the dragon she had encountered before. He seemed to be growing nearer and she slowed her pace, glancing up at the sky as she called, "Ralligor!"

His essence seemed vague and distant, but she felt his mind respond as she called to him.

She stopped. Something else touched her mind, something....

Shahly sprang forward, dodging sharply as a fireball slammed into the road right where she had been standing. Looking to the sky behind her, she saw another one coming and leapt out of the way, barely in time.

The bird creature screeched somewhere in the night, behind and above.

Shahly bolted into a full gallop once again, running as fast as she could to the hard lands. The hunters she could outrun. Nillerra was a different story and she knew she could never match the speed of a flying creature.

Fully unicorn again, Shahly was able to sense the bird creature more clearly and was able to better anticipate when the fireballs would come and about where they would hit, a small advantage, but very useful considering she had no other defense against Nillerra's attacks.

As the fireballs came at her, she dodged to and fro, not realizing until too late that this was slowing her to the point where the hunters were catching up to her, and she glanced back as she heard the whoops and whistles of the hunters and the thunderous sound of many hooves on the ground.

An arrow whizzed by.

The hunters were already close enough to shoot at her!

"Ralligor!" she called, terrified and no longer able to feel his presence. "Ralligor, please help me!"

Her heart thundered, more from terror than exhaustion. She leapt aside to avoid a fireball and another arrow barely missed her. The arrows offered no warning of their approach and she could only hear them as they passed her.

Some time later she noticed an unusual smell, one she recognized as a desert bloom. It was faint and clearly some distance away but encouraging nonetheless.

Something deep within pumped strength into her legs and she managed to quicken her pace and lengthen the gap between her and the hunters.

Nillerra!

Shahly veered sharply aside.

The hiss drew close and the orange light a little too bright. Her maneuver came too late.

The fireball exploded a pace away from her, the force of it knocking her to her side.

Dazed, she struggled back to her hooves and started forward again, slowly at first, then accelerating to a full gallop.

Another arrow whizzed by.

She dodged right as a fireball slammed into the trees at the side of the road, debris pelting her as she charged ever closer to the scrub country that bordered the hard lands. She barely avoided another fireball, the blast sending her stumbling and slowing her pace yet again.

The whoops and whistles of the hunters drew closer.

She glanced back at them, seeing that they were alarmingly close, then turned ahead and heard still another fireball coming at her, leaping away from it.

It seemed to explode right beneath her and lifted her into the air. She landed on her side at the edge of the forest and rolled to a stop, realizing that consciousness was slipping away.

She forced her wits to return to her and struggled to stand before she was fully coherent.

The loop of a rope dropped over her head and brutally tightened around her neck, pulling her to one side and off balance again. Another rope caught a rear leg, pulling it behind her. Still another fell over her head.

Shahly struggled hard, whinnying and snorting as she kicked her legs to regain her footing.

This cannot be! She cried in a whinny. *I am too close!*

Finally too exhausted to fight further, Shahly went down completely, struggling just to catch her breath. She raised her head and helplessly looked to the three humans who approached on foot, the ten or so others who still sat on their horses, and saw Nillerra descending from the sky.

A tear spilled.

It was over.

She had failed.

Nillerra landed hard behind the hunters who were still on their horses, startling everyone. Half of them turned and drew their weapons, backing away.

Nillerra hissed at them and said, "Do not turn your weapons on me, fools! It was I who made possible the capture of this unicorn."

One of the men on foot stepped toward the bird creature and asked, "You are on our side, then?"

"I am vengeance," she shrieked. "I only want the blood of my enemies."

"We have been promised a large bounty on this beast," the man informed.

"And you shall have it," Nillerra assured. "I only wish to see her dead."

"You will then," the hunter agreed, drawing his sword. "May I?"

"Please," Nillerra hissed, seeming to smile. "I wish to see her suffer. I want her in pain. Break her legs, one by one."

The hunter laughed. Many of them did.

As the hunter approached, Shahly drew away as much as she could, fighting against the ropes that grew ever tighter around her neck. She whimpered as he drew closer, fearing what he was going to do to her.

He smiled and nodded, saying, "Aye, you led us a merry chase, didn't you? But now it's over. You'll run no more after this night." He raised his sword.

Every part of Shahly's being cried out and she whinnied and kicked against the ropes that held her as he brought the sword down.

Half way to her, the steel clanked as something hard and solid stopped it.

Air was pulled hard into something huge.

The hunter's eyes slowly turned up.

Shahly looked behind her to see the black dragon crouched down, his head right above her, and the sword lying firmly between his nostrils.

The other men quietly backed away, as did Nillerra.

A red glow could be seen deep in the dragon's eyes, growing brighter second by second until it illuminated his features and much of the road before him. He reached to the human and plucked the sword from his grip, then growled, his bared teeth shining bright white in the moonlight, and he stood, his head five men's heights from the ground.

The man was frozen where he stood, his breath coming in short gasps.

Holding the sword by the tip of the blade, the black dragon slapped the hilt into his other palm, doing this for many long seconds before he finally spoke. "Mighty, courageous hunters," he said, "tracking such dangerous creatures as rabbits and unicorns. And it only took twelve of you to subdue this one. Very impressive." He glanced at Nillerra, then growled again and threw the sword from him, into the forest as his wings spread and his eyes glowed crimson. "Why don't we see how you fare against bigger game?"

The hunters retreated, the one standing closest falling to the road and scrambling away on all fours.

Staring up at the dragon, Nillerra shrieked, "Back away. He is mine."

"You can have him," one of the hunters offered as they fled.

Nillerra's eyes narrowed as she sneered, "A moment of mercy for you, dragon. I only want the unicorn. I want her blood and her pain. Leave here. Leave her to me and I'll spare you."

A hint of amusement touched the dragon's eyes as he retorted, "Oh, I cringe in terror."

"I am vengeance!" Nillerra cried. "My wrath will find her wherever she may hide and any who dare to oppose me! Withdraw or you will die here with her!"

The dragon drew his neck back, raising his brow slightly as he said, "You mean you expect *me* to turn and run from the likes of you?"

The feathers around Nillerra's neck stood up, her eyes narrowing as she growled, "I am warning you, reptile. I have power you cannot even begin to imagine."

"You might be surprised at what I can imagine," the dragon countered. His voice and tone lacked anything that even resembled fear. In fact, he sounded as if he was trying to provoke her into attacking him.

Nillerra's eyes narrowed. "This is my last warning, dragon."

"And no more impressive than those that came before," the dragon mocked.

Slowly, Shahly pulled her hooves under her and she prepared to spring up.

"I have heard enough from you," Nillerra sneered. "Leave here now or die with the unicorn. My patience is at an end."

"How sad," the dragon drawled. "I am just getting started."

"Then your life ends now!" the bird creature shrieked. "You have signed your own death warrant in her blood!" Her beak gaped and she belched a fireball at him.

Shahly was on her hooves and darting away before she realized. She looked back at the dragon as the fireball struck him, wincing as it exploded on his chest near his shoulder and she wheeled around and stopped as he lurched backward and took a step back.

"One less problem," Nillerra spat.

The dragon's chest smoked and he stood motionless for long seconds, then, slowly, he turned back on the bird creature, baring his teeth as a thunderous growl rolled from his throat. "One less problem? Oh, no, bird. Your problems are only beginning."

Shahly backed away.

The dragon's jaws gaped and he belched fire of his own which struck Nillerra's chest and exploded with such force that she was blown from her feet and slammed hard onto the road.

Burnt feathers drifted to the road and smoke rose from what remained of her breast feathers. She moaned, slowly rocking her head as she tried to regain her wits, and just as slowly sat herself up and shakily tried to get back to her feet. She was illuminated in a green light from the dragon's eyes and looked back to him.

The green glow in the dragon's eyes went back to red and he nodded, mumbling, "Just as I thought. One of Zelkton's potions."

Nillerra stiffened, taking a step back.

"His services do not come cheap," the dragon observed, then he seemed to smile. "A pity you paid him so much only to fail."

That seemed to infuriate her and she huffed loudly, then looked down to Shahly and growled, "If nothing else happens tonight, even if I should perish doing it, *you* will die before the coming of the sun!" Her beak swung open.

Shahly's eyes widened and she backed away, seeing a glow from within the bird creature's throat.

A fireball burst from Nillerra's beak streaking right at Shahly.

She started to leap away.

The dragon's clawed hand swept overhead and batted the fireball down into the road between Shahly and Nillerra.

The dragon stepped toward the bird creature, his huge foot slamming hard onto the road as he growled, "I don't think so, bird. Your fight is with me now."

Nillerra's eyes snapped to him and she hissed, "You first, then." She opened her beak and screeched as she lunged at him, stroking her wings.

Shahly backed away again.

The dragon easily batted the bird creature aside and turned toward her as she slammed into the trees across the road. His tail swept over Shahly, almost close enough to touch, then slammed into the ground and thrashed like an enraged serpent.

With a deep growl, the dragon shook his head and mocked, "You are one of those who will never learn, aren't you?"

Nillerra pulled her talons under her, screamed, and lunged at him again, snapping her beak.

The dragon lowered his head and Nillerra crumpled against his horns and the heavy scales of his head, and she fell limply to the road. He raised his head and growled as he stared down at her. When she stirred, he reached to her and seized the back of her neck, tearing her from the ground as he roared, "Get up!"

She shrieked and stroked her wings, kicking at him as he easily hoisted her from the ground. Clearly, Nillerra had greatly underestimated the strength of this dragon.

He watched her struggle in his grip for long seconds, then he growled and slammed her back onto the road.

The dust settled slowly and Nillerra moaned pitifully, drawing her talons and wings under her. She raised her head and looked up at the dragon, no longer appearing to be the horrible monster that had once challenged him, rather she had the look of a terrified animal cowing from a predator. Her breathing came hard.

Shahly sensed her terror, but she also sensed a certain familiarity. Nillerra had been here before, not losing a mortal duel with a dragon, but laying beaten and helpless at the feet of a predator, a human predator.

The dragon bared his teeth, opening his jaws. His chest and arms swelled as powerful muscles tensed and readied for the killing strike. His eyes narrowed as he growled, "This ends now, bird."

Nillerra whimpered and shrank away.

"Ralligor, wait!" Shahly whinnied, sprinting toward them.

The dragon's head swung toward her and he roared, "Now what?"

Shahly stopped between the dragon and the bird creature, turning her eyes to Nillerra. "Must you kill her?"

The dragon rolled his eyes and mumbled, "Grazers." He drew a long breath and turned his attention back to Nillerra. "I'm going to do you a huge favor, bird, not because I am a compassionate dragon, but because I am curious to see what you really look like." He raised a hand and fired a bright emerald blast of light at her.

Nillerra screamed as the light enveloped her. It flashed brightly and briefly like lightning, then was gone, leaving Nillerra's naked human form laying in the bird creature's place.

The dragon looked to Shahly and hissed through clenched teeth, "Satisfied?"

Shahly looked up to him and offered, "Thank you."

Nillerra raised her head and looked back at herself, then sprang to her feet and crossed her arms over her chest as she turned terror-filled eyes up to the dragon, and slowly backed away.

The dragon leaned his head toward Shahly and murmured, "Watch this," then he took a step toward Nillerra, swinging his jaws open and bearing his teeth as he roared like something from a nightmare.

Nillerra screamed wildly and wheeled around, sprinting down the dimly lit forest road that led toward Red Stone Castle.

The dragon raised his head, watched her flee for a few seconds, then called, "Watch for that…" He broke off as he heard a splash, then finished, "Water puddle." He dropped to all fours as he turned back to Shahly, shaking his head as he asked, "Can't I leave you alone for a single day without you getting yourself neck-deep in humans?"

She glared up at him and snorted. "There were a few things you didn't tell me to expect. And your stupid amulet and words did not work! I didn't change back!"

He drew his head back. "Well, let's see. Horn, hooves, mane… You certainly *look* like a unicorn."

"That white haired human of yours changed me back," she snapped. "If it had not been for him, the humans and Nillerra would have gotten me!"

The dragon reached to her and pulled the ropes from around her neck, grumbling, "Complain, complain, complain." He paused as he saw the amulet, hooked it with one of his claws as he examined it, then turned his eyes back to Shahly's, asking, "Where is the emerald?"

She leaned her head. "The what?"

"Emerald," he said loudly. "There was a green stone in this when I gave it to you."

Shahly glanced down at the amulet, glanced at the dragon, then looked away, feeling a little awkward as she explained, "Oh, that. Yes. Um, Arden was showing me the Talisman, the thing that they use do defend themselves against your kind."

"I know what the Talisman is," he scolded. "What does that have to do with the stone?"

She cringed and looked down, almost feeling ashamed as she continued, "I reached up and touched it and a stone came out, so I put the one from the amulet in its place before he saw it was missing."

The dragon slowly drew back, raising his brow as he asked, "You what?"

She sighed and answered, "I put the stone…" The Talisman! "Oh no!"

"Now what?"

Shahly desperately turned her eyes back up to him. "Falloah told me to damage the Talisman so that it would not work. I forgot!" Her front legs seemed to collapse and she buried her nose between her hooves. "I have failed! We cannot get them out of there now!" Emotions poured from her as tears poured from her eyes, and she fully realized that Vinton would certainly die now.

"You haven't actually failed, little unicorn," the dragon informed.

She turned tear swollen eyes up to his and asked, "What?"

He raised his head and ordered, "You just let *me* take care of them now. You have done all you need to."

"But I did not damage the Talisman," she cried. "I did not free your Falloah and I did not free Vinton!" She looked away. "And Arden." She laid completely to her belly, looking toward the ground as she finished, "You cannot go close to the castle so long as that talisman is there and working."

"I'm afraid you don't understand," the dragon started. "The Talisman…"

She stood and walked around the dragon, toward Red Stone Castle as she insisted, "I have to get Vinton out of there, no matter what."

"No, you don't," the dragon corrected. "I said I will handle it from here."

"I don't see how," she spat, continuing on her way. "I'm going to free Vinton."

One of his hands gently seized her around her middle, just in front of her haunches, stopping her, and he advised, "That's not a wise idea."

She just glared ahead, feeling less and less patient with this dragon as she ordered, "Let go."

"You are going to get yourself killed," he said straightly. "Just let me handle this now."

Shahly wheeled around.

The dragon jerked his hand back.

She advanced a few steps and shouted, "What do you care if I live or die anyway? I *have* to get Vinton out of there! He is to be killed tomorrow!" Her eyes narrowed. "And you are not going to stop me."

The dragon seated himself before her, shaking his head as he stared down at her, then he conceded, "Oh, go on, then."

She stared back for a long moment, then turned and continued on her way.

"Little unicorn," he summoned.

She stopped and looked over her shoulder, annoyance still in her eyes.

Ralligor raised his head and instructed, "When you are captured, do not resist. Allow them to take you to the arena with your stallion. That will be the only chance for freedom for both of you."

Without responding, she turned back down the road and paced on.

Not even half a league was behind her when she stopped again, staring blankly ahead at the white haired wizard who stood twenty paces in front of her.

Slowly, he approached, smiling as he reached toward her to scratch her between the ears.

"Thank you for what you did," she whickered to him. "I was hoping I would see you again."

"Anytime you like," he replied.

"I was afraid for you," she informed.

He patted her neck. "No need. I can take care of myself."

She looked away. "I wish I could. If not for you and Ralligor and Traman… and others…. "

"And if not for you," the wizard pointed out, "your stallion would have no chance, would he? Don't discount your own bravery because you need help from time to time."

She huffed a breath. "I wish I was a dragon right now. At least then I would be strong enough to free him."

"You are a unicorn instead," the wizard assured. "I think your stallion has a better chance with his unicorn mate than he would with a powerful dragon like Ralligor."

Shahly turned her eyes back to him. "What if I do my best and fail? What if I get myself killed and never get him out of there?"

The wizard smiled at her and patted her neck again, then turned and walked into the forest, asking, "What if you never try and live a thousand seasons?"

She watched him disappear into a sudden mist, then continued on her way, pondering his words. A long life without her Vinton, without even trying to free him sounded more horrible than anything she could face at the castle. In her heart, she knew it would not truly be a life.

Hours later she was standing at the edge of the tree line, staring at the secured gate of the castle. Many guards milled about up on the battlements and several more just outside of the gate. Apparently, they expected someone to try and enter uninvited.

She stared a while longer, then walked along the tree line and found a large clump of grass. She nibbled some of the blades for a time, then lay down to her belly in the middle of it and turned her eyes to the gate. When the sun came the gate would open. She only had to rest.

And wait.

CHAPTER 14

Shahly slowly opened her eyes, focusing on the castle as she sluggishly raised her head.

The sun was not yet over the treetops but its glow illuminated the countryside, casting long shadows toward the castle. The gate was open and half a dozen guards milled about, talking with one another or checking their clothing and armor.

Shahly stood and stretched, shook her head and mane, then looked back to the gate, her eyes narrowing. In human form she had been plagued with a reluctance to use her natural abilities to conceal herself, only doing so when she had to and not confidant that she could do so effectively. Now unicorn again, her confidence was high and her determination was very strong.

She took her time surveying the gate and battlements, seeing immediately that there were too many eyes, too many minds to trick into not seeing her, especially while she was moving. Another plan would have to be used.

Turning back into the woods, she pondered what to do and exactly how to do it, then she stopped near the edge of the road leading to the castle as a small group of riders and several humans on foot passed by. In an instant, her plan was conceived.

Pacing onto the road behind them, she folded her essence around herself and suggested to any alert minds that she was merely a small white horse carrying a rider, a girl of no importance, dressed commonly like some of the servants around the castle and with no features that they should find attractive or interesting.

One of the men on foot glanced back at her.

Her breath caught, but she knew she dare not panic. No matter what, she *had* to act like an ordinary horse. Her suggestion of an ordinary looking rider seemed to help greatly here as the man turned forward again and gave her not another thought.

As the group approached the gate, Shahly following about two paces behind them. At this point, none of the guards seemed especially interested in her and only a few glanced her way.

"One moment, maiden," one of the guards behind shouted.

Her heart felt as if it was jumping into her throat, but she fought panic and just paced on.

Someone ran up behind her.

She closed her eyes.

They ran past and stopped one of the women on horseback in front of her.

The woman looked down at the two guards who had stopped her and smiled.

"Coming to see the spectacle?" one asked.

"Aye," she answered, "and maybe pleasure a gentleman who knows how to treat a pretty lady."

Shahly noticed the one guard smiling broadly as she paced by and chose to ignore their banter. Humans' liberal mating habits were something she could never grow accustomed to.

"Aye, this should be a good one," another guard shouted to a rider ahead of her. "This unicorn is bigger than the last, and a spirited beast. Should be a good match."

The rider laughed and replied, "Oh, it'll end as all the others do, and we'll enjoy every last drop of blood."

Shahly snorted, anger welling up in her. Her deception began to slip and she quickly drew a long breath to calm herself and keep her essence cloud from fading.

She continued on toward the stables, hoping she could find a way to get Vinton to safety before the humans came for him. There was little activity at the guard's stable, but the few humans she did see made her continue her exhaustive deception. Once out of everyone's eyeshot, she switched to a less demanding defense, and when she encountered humans again, she merely convinced their minds that they saw no unicorn, nothing out of the ordinary. Doing this while walking right past them was risky, but they were mostly young males, simple minded with more to think about than the tasks they were assigned.

As planned, no one saw her as she passed the entrance to the stable. She decided to keep close to the building as she made her way toward the stable where her Vinton was being held, that way she only had to worry about one side.

Ahead of her was the second stable. There were still no guards at the door, but considering the nature of the horrible, powerful mind within, there seemed to be no need for them.

She paused, staring at the stable before her for long seconds. She drew a deep breath and concealed herself even deeper, then slowly started forward again. The mind within was awake but did not seem fully alert. It was resting, waiting for something, and seemed somewhat disappointed.

Movement to her exposed side caught her eye and she stopped and looked.

The door to the palace had opened and humans were filing out of it, six large humans in armor and red and black tunics. Half of them carried crossbows; the other half carried halberds or swords. They seemed to take up defensive positions around the doorway, scanning the surrounding area intently.

Shahly's eyes widened as Queen Hethan exited the palace, followed by four more guards. The Queen was dressed in a long, red gown with black sleeves and collar and black lace around the bell of the skirt. Her hair was restrained by something metal, a crown or tiara with clear and red jewels set into it.

Once the Queen was outside, the guards marched toward the second stable, all of them keeping themselves between possible harm and Queen Hethan.

Shahly lay to her belly, remaining still and hidden from the searching minds of the guards as they drew closer. She just watched, wondering what the Queen could want with such a terrible mind as the one that lived in the stable. Curiosity was strong. This *must* have something to do with the killing of the unicorns, Vinton's capture, and perhaps the Talisman. It all seemed strangely connected, and revolving around the Queen, though Shahly could not quite put her hoof on why she felt this. Something, perhaps that woman's intuition Ihzell had spoken of before, told Shahly that many of the answers she sought were within that stable, and with the Queen herself.

One of the guards opened the door to the stable and scanned the area once more as Queen Hethan entered.

Shahly slowly stood, her eyes narrowing as she watched the door close. She thought a broad suggestion to the guards, something around the other side of the building that they should see, something that might be a threat, and when most of them were distracted, she folded her essence around herself once again and moved cautiously around to the other side.

Once on the side of the building and out of eyeshot, Shahly pressed herself against the cold stone of the shadowed side of the stable and listened for any hint that the guards knew she was there.

"What was that?" one guard asked.

"I could have sworn I heard something," another said.

"Forget about it," still another with a more gruff voice ordered. "Keep your eyes open and your mouths shut."

Slowly, Shahly drew a deep breath, then noiselessly made her way along the wall, piercing into the stable with her essence to find the Queen. Once she felt her, she followed, and listened.

The Queen stopped.

So did Shahly, right outside of a shuttered window near the end of the stable.

There was a rustling in the hay within, hoof-steps on the ground and a deep, raspy voice cruelly demanded, "What do you want?"

That voice! Something about it was very familiar. She had not wanted to admit it to herself before, that she recognized that voice when she had encountered the horrible presence in there. It was unmistakable, though different somehow, as if his very being was injured.

"There is something about that new maiden my son brought to the palace," Hethan answered, "something which disturbs me."

"Something about each of them disturbs you," the voice growled. "I thought you said she has departed."

"She has," Hethan confirmed. "I sent one of the unicorn hunting parties for her as you said to do."

"Have they returned?" the voice asked deeply.

Hethan was silent for a time, then, "Yes, but without the girl, and with talk of a battle between a dragon and a giant vulture."

"Their stories do not interest me," the voice growled, sounding annoyed. "There has been talk of another unicorn, a white mare. Send your hunters back out. I want her brought to me alive."

Shahly swallowed hard.

"But her horn," the Queen protested. "Will we not need it for the Talisman?"

"Do as I say!" the voice snapped. "You will find another for the second Talisman."

Second talisman? Shahly thought. *Just as the dragon said!*

Hethan became afraid, feeling as if she was a child being scolded. She sighed, then offered, "Forgive me. I will instruct the hunters as you wish." A short silence later the Queen continued, "Something about that girl still bothers me. Arden was too easily taken with her."

"Your son's mating habits do not concern me," the voice growled. "How many more spirals are needed to complete the second Talisman?"

"Three," Hethan answered softly.

He snorted, eerily horse-like, then ordered, "Continue the hunts, then. You will find the herds moving to the Northwest, toward the Spagnah River. There will be younger unicorns among them. They will be spared. It is the older ones I want for the Talisman, those with more power and experience." A long silence, then, "And bring Falloah to the games today. I have something special planned for her."

Shahly's ears perked. *Falloah?*

"I still do not understand what it is you need her for," Hethan said. "She can do us no more harm. Why not just kill her and have done with it?"

"It is not that simple," the voice informed.

Hoof beats drew closer and the shutter Shahly stood beside was bumped open.

She gasped and dropped to her belly, looking up at the open window as the shutters creaked to a stop.

Something tested the air and Shahly could feel a strange unicorn essence scanning the area, and quickly hid from it.

A moment later the voice answered, "He will be watching. Even dragons grow impatient after a time, and when he sees her in the arena with the unicorn he will come for her. He will think the Talisman will not be waiting for him, as the tenders will keep it silent until he lands." He snorted. "Then the Desert Lord will finally be at my mercy, and our plan can proceed without any further delay."

Hearing the Queen approach, Shahly pressed herself against the stone wall, fearing Hethan would look out the window and see her.

"Why this war against the dragons?" Hethan asked. "How could destroying them serve us?"

"The dragons are our enemies, Hethan," the voice impatiently informed. "They could be the undoing of all our plans, especially the Desert Lord."

Who is this Desert Lord? Shahly wondered.

"And the unicorns?" the Queen asked.

"They will be brought under a new order," the voice answered, "under me. Those who remain will flock to me, taste flesh and blood as I have, and they will know power. They will know the strength I have discovered. They will know the world."

"And we will always be together," Hethan said dreamily.

Whispering from within caught Shahly's ears, but she could not make out what was said, then she heard the evil voice say, "Yes, Hethan. Always. You should go and prepare yourself for the spectacle. This promises to be an eventful morning."

"Yes, Bexton," the Queen answered.

As Shahly heard the Queen stride to the other end of the stable, she turned her eyes down, her worst fears confirmed.

"How can this be?" she whispered to herself. "Bexton is.... He is part of the herd. How can he send the humans to hunt us?" She shook her head, not wanting to think about one of her own kind in such ways, then she got to her hooves and paced noiselessly toward the third stable where the humans kept her Vinton.

Something swept around her, numbing her senses.

She stopped, closed her eyes and shook her head.

She opened her eyes and looked ahead of her, her eyes widening as she gasped and retreated from the large, black unicorn in front of her. The three spirals of his horn had separated, becoming three pewter colored horns that spiraled loosely around each other and ended in sharp, gleaming points. His dark coat and mane reflected no light back, as if it absorbed all light that touched it. His eyes glowed violet and were locked on Shahly's.

She felt him withdraw his essence, evil and tainted, and the numbness which had distracted her faded away.

Bexton raised his head and mockingly asked, "Are you glad to see me, Shahly?"

Shahly took another step back, knowing fear of him immediately. She wheeled around to flee, but stopped as she saw three guards behind her, each with a crossbow aimed at her. She heard more approaching from behind the black unicorn and slowly turned back to him.

Three other humans, two with ropes and one with a halberd stood behind the black unicorn, staring at her.

She locked her eyes on the black unicorn, the full realization of all of her questions coming together and she breathed, "It was you! You sent the humans to hunt us!"

"Very perceptive, Shahly," he complemented. "Very perceptive. It just surprises me that you thought you could use your pathetic forest tricks to deceive even me. But I must congratulate you. I did not even sense you until you were right under my nose."

Shahly slowly shook her head and asked, "Why? How can you send the humans to hunt and kill your own kind?"

He stepped toward her, his eyes locked on hers as he answered, "Very easily, young mare. It is about power. And I did not just have the other unicorns killed as you think. There is a purpose to everything I do." He raised his head and the men with the ropes strode around him, toward Shahly.

Remembering the dragon's words, Shahly did not resist them as they slipped the ropes over her head and tightened them around her neck. She just stared back at Bexton.

"You and the entire herd had the chance to join me," the black unicorn continued. "Even so, I will not allow your journey here to be completely in vain. Guards, take her to the holding stable." He seemed to smile with his eyes. "I will allow you to die in the arena with Vinton today." He turned to leave.

"At least you still have *some* compassion," Shahly spat.

Bexton snorted and continued on without even a glance back.

As the guards took Shahly into the stable where Vinton was kept, Shahly's elation filled her more with each step. Surely he would recognize her this time.

Once inside, she was led down to the end of the stable and into the cage-like stall across from her stallion's where her ropes were removed and she was locked in before the guards left.

Shahly paced to the bars of her stall and saw Vinton lying in the hay below his window. He appeared to be asleep, though his mind was still restless.

Now probably was not the time, but Shahly felt compelled to take advantage of this first time when she knew his guard was really down. She backed away, reared up and whinnied as loudly as she could.

Startled, Vinton sprang to his hooves and snorted, stumbling to the middle of his stall as he wheeled around and faced her.

Shahly whinnied a laugh and approached the bars of her stall again, saying, "I finally got you!"

His eyes widened and he whinnied, "Shahly!" as he rushed to her, his horn sticking between the bars as he tried to get as close to her as he could. "I had so hoped they would not get you."

"They did not exactly get me," Shahly corrected. "I came to get you out of here."

He sighed and turned his eyes down, shaking his head. "Shahly, you should not have done that. They are just going to kill us both, now."

Shahly raised her chin, suddenly feeling very in control as she said, "Oh, no they are not."

Vinton loosed another deep breath and shook his head again, grimly asking, "Why did you come here?"

"This time or the first time," she asked back.

He turned his eyes to her. "First time?"

Shahly's ears twitched. "You do not remember, do you?" She looked away from him, finishing sadly, "Of course, you *were* awfully rude to me."

"When?" he questioned.

She looked back to him, her eyes teasing his as she answered, "When I visited you in human form yesterday. You weren't very nice to me."

"That *was* you?" Astonishment was in Vinton's voice. "How? How did you look and smell human? I—I didn't even recognize you."

"That was the idea, Vinton," she said with the hint of a laugh. "Are you happy to see me this time?"

He looked away from her, answering, "Well, yes and no."

Shahly blinked. "Okay."

Vinton looked back to her, despair in his eyes again as he replied, "Shahly, you should not have come here. They are going to kill us both."

"Vinton, no. I am going to get you out of here."

He nodded. "How do you propose to do that?"

She looked to the shuttered window, then to the stable door, then back to Vinton and replied softly, "I don't know yet, but someone on the outside has promised to help."

"Just great," the stallion laughed. "Good thing there are still plenty of empty stalls in here."

Shahly smiled and shook her head. "Just have faith, my Love, and leave everything to me."

His eyes shifted away from her. "There is still something I need to speak to you about, something very important."

"It can wait until we go free," she insisted, fearing the words he had for her.

"What if we don't?" he asked softly.

She just stared at him for long seconds, her eyes a little wide, then she raised her head and replied, "You only have to know that I'll always love you, Vinton. That is all that matters."

Vinton's eyes snapped back to her and showed a little surprise.

They both looked as the stable door opened and several palace guards entered, two with ropes in their hands.

Vinton looked back to Shahly and said, "Time for me to go."

Her ears swiveled toward him and she corrected, "Time for *us* to go, you mean."

The stallion shook his head and informed, "No, Shahly."

Shahly felt a choke in her throat and she protested, "But Bexton said we would go into the arena together."

"You should not have believed him," Vinton said grimly. "They will only put one of us in at a time."

She took a step back, frustration growing within her as she cried, "What?"

He just stared back at her for a time, then started, "Shahly, I…" He looked to the humans as they approached, stepping away from the gate as one opened it, then he looked back to Shahly.

"They can't," she whimpered as she watched them fight the ropes over his head and forcibly lead him from the stall. "Vinton!"

He managed to stop once more and look back at her.

Tears filled her eyes as she said to him, "Vinton, I love you."

Vinton raised his head and replied, "You have to get out of here if you can, Shahly. Get back to the herd and forget me."

Shahly stepped as close to him as she could, watching the humans take him from her once again, and she watched a while longer even after the stable door closed and darkness filled the stable once again.

"Vinton," she whimpered, then slowly turned and paced to the middle of her stall, feeling so alone, so afraid of the uncertain fate which awaited her, and so empty without her stallion. She ignored the stable door as it opened and shut again, and ignored the footfalls that grew closer to her.

That familiar, horrible essence filled the very air around her and her eyes narrowed as she slowly turned, locking her gaze on the black unicorn as he paced toward her.

He stopped at the stall gate, raised his head and asked, "How do you like the accommodations?"

"You beast," she spat.

Bexton laid his ears back and seemed to smile as he said, "Such harsh words from one so pure."

"Why?" she demanded. "Unicorns are your people!"

"And not one yet has chosen to join me," he informed, a little frustration in his tone.

Shahly's eyes narrowed slightly more and she half turned her head, asking, "Join you? I don't understand."

The black unicorn glanced casually behind him, then looked back to her as a burly guard stepped from the shadows, dragging a white clad human child by the hand.

Shahly stepped back, watching as the guard opened the stall door and threw the young boy inside. The boy could not have been more than four seasons old and he scrambled away from Shahly as soon as he looked up at her.

"A fitting sacrifice," the black unicorn observed, his eyes on the boy.

Shahly was filled with fear and suspicion as she looked to the boy, then she turned her eyes on the black unicorn and asked, "What do you mean?"

Bexton raised his head and ordered, "Kill the child."

Shahly gasped, backing away a step.

"It is very easy," Bexton explained calmly. "Stab your spiral into his heart, then drink his warm blood. It is not so unlike nursing from your mother when you were a foal. You will remember once you do it."

Shahly backed away, her eyes locked wide on the black unicorn's as she cried, "You are insane!"

"The blood will not poison you as was once thought," he informed. "It will simply make you powerful, as I am now."

"You don't know what power is," she retorted.

"Quite the contrary, Shahly. Right now I have the power to decide whether you live or die. I can choose whether Vinton lives or dies. I have the power over life itself. And death. Do you know another unicorn with such power at his disposal?"

"You are no unicorn!" Shahly barked. "You were once, but I have no idea what you are now. All I do know is that I would rather be human than you!"

Bexton smiled. "You were human, weren't you?"

Shahly's breath caught and she looked away from him.

"Tainted for life," he continued. "You will never truly be rid of it, Shahly. As a unicorn, it will nibble at you and eventually wear you down to the human's level. What I offer you is more than you will become. Join me and know real power."

"I would sooner die," she hissed, still not looking at him.

"That choice I leave with you," he offered. "I will be back after the spectacle. If the child still lives when I return, I will kill him myself. Either way, *you* will be responsible for his death, and if you do not join me you will die as well. Quite horribly."

Shahly heard him turn to leave and finally looked back at him, approaching the stall gate as she reminded, "You said you would allow me to join Vinton in the arena."

"I lied," the black unicorn admitted as he left.

Shahly snorted as the guard closed the door to the stable, then she laid down in the hay near the child and stared blankly ahead, trying to reason a way out of this predicament. When she heard the child whimper, she looked to him, seeing tears streaming from his eyes as he stared at her in horror. She leaned her head and drew a deep breath as she reassuringly said to him, "Do not be afraid of me. I will not harm you."

He appeared to understand, and after some time he crawled to her and hesitantly stroked her mane.

For some time she just stared into nothingness, struggling to devise a way to save herself and her stallion from their fates. Reasoning with her captors was clearly impossible and the guards would not be so easily tricked while they were under Bexton's influence, especially since they probably knew to anticipate anything she could do.

She loosed a deep breath, trying to alleviate some of the frustration she felt. Everything remained in the hands of the dragon, and with the Talisman waiting for him not even he could help her now.

She already missed Vinton. And Arden.

Arden!

Shahly closed her eyes, searching for the Prince with her mind. Her essence swept through the castle, not stopped by guards or stone walls, and she finally found him, resting and very sad. She poured her feelings into him, willing him not to feel so, and implored him to come to her.

Shahly? She heard his mind say.

She thought to him where she was and instantly felt his mind and spirit race.

An unknown time later she opened her eyes as the door to the stable burst open and she looked to see the Prince running toward her. Feeling elated at just the sight of him, she stood and approached the gate to the stall, greeting, "Arden!"

He reached her and wrapped his hands around the bars of the gate, staring at her for a moment. He looked down to the amulet she still wore, still minus the emerald, and breathed, "Shahly. It *is* you!"

"Of course it is," she confirmed. "Don't be silly."

"You are a unicorn now," he observed, appearing a little confused. "How is it I know what you are saying?"

"You are hearing me with your heart," she informed. "Only that way can you understand me." She drew a deep breath and looked away from him. "I am to die in the arena soon, Arden."

His breath caught and he slowly shook his head, protesting, "They cannot do that to you!"

"Well," Shahly started, trying to sound lighthearted, "Bexton did give me a choice." She motioned to the boy who still stared at her. "I can eat him or die in the arena. It has something to do with power and joining him."

Arden's eyes showed bewilderment as he turned them to the child and asked, "What kind of beast...."

"That is just what I called him," Shahly said, trying to sound amused at the coincidence, then she looked down and tamped the earth beneath her hoof, asking, "I do not suppose you can put a stop to all of this and get me out of here, could you?"

The silence that followed seemed deafening, then the Prince jerked on the latch and pulled the gate open, ordering, "Out. Both of you."

The boy scrambled to his feet and fled.

Shahly paced out and looked to the Prince, smiling as she offered, "Thank you, Arden. I owe you so much."

"You owe me nothing," he assured, then looked away, shaking his head.

"What?" she prodded.

He looked back to her and tried to smile. "I just wish... If only you would come back to me, the way you did before."

"Part of me wishes I could," she admitted, "But I cannot. I am unicorn and cannot truly change that." She nudged him with her nose and added, "But if I were human, you would be the only one I would want to be human with."

He smiled. "Thank you, Shahly."

"Arden, would you do one other thing for me?"

He stroked her nose and replied, "Anything."

She raised her head slightly and said, "I would like for you to take Ihzell and Audrell and leave the castle for a while."

His brow lowered and he asked, "Why?"

Shahly took a deep breath and answered, "Someone is coming, and I would rather you were not here when he arrives."

The Prince raised his chin and asked, "Who is coming that I should flee my castle?"

She looked down, then back to him and answered, "I will not tell you now. Please, just go. And take Ocnarr as well. Will you do this for me? Please?"

He hesitantly nodded. "I suppose I can. You will not tell me why?"

She shook her head. "No, not yet, Love. I can't yet. Just go."

"I have to get you out of the castle first," he insisted.

She shook her head. "I cannot go yet, Arden. There is something I must do first."

"What?" he questioned.

"The other unicorn," she replied softly. "I have to save him."

Arden nodded. "I see. What is he to you?"

Shahly took a deep breath, unsure of how he would take her answer and fearful of hurting him, but she finally said, "He is my stallion." Instantly, she felt the pain of hearing this stab into him.

He looked away from her and softly said, "I see." After a moment, he smiled slightly and laughed under his breath. "You know. I almost wish I was in his place."

She playfully butted him with her nose. "Just go, you scamp!"

He smiled and stroked her neck. "Will I ever see you again?"

"I am sure of it, Arden," she confirmed, then nudged him again. "Go on, now. There is not much time."

The Prince patted her neck and admitted, "I still love you, you know."

"And I you. That is why you must go."

He nodded, smiling, then informed, "First things first."

"Now what?" she asked almost impatiently.

Arden raised his chin and insistently replied, "I am going to get you out of here. Follow me." He turned and strode toward the exit.

Shahly followed, hoping this would not get him into trouble.

He kicked the door open and ordered the guards, "One of you report to the stables and tell them to get my horse saddled and ready. You. Go and find Ocnarr and bring him here."

Shahly saw them both leave, then cautiously stepped out the door and looked around, finally looking to Arden.

He smiled at her. "It really is good to be Prince."

They walked side by side away from the stable.

Something tugged at Shahly's memory and she raised her head and asked, "Aren't there usually four guards at that door?"

"Usually," Arden confirmed. "There were only two when I arrived."

They stopped and looked at each other.

"Arden," Shahly started. "You don't suppose…"

They looked ahead as four guards wheeled around the corner of the second stable, then behind them as four more armed with crossbows came from the stable behind.

Arden and Shahly looked back to each other.

The Prince finished for Shahly, "That Bexton anticipated me doing this?"

"Your highness," one of the guards armed with a crossbow informed, "we have orders to take this unicorn with us or kill it if we have problems."

Arden turned on him, his eyes like stone and his brow low.

The guard continued, "We also have orders to detain you should you try to interfere."

"I will be King some day," the Prince reminded.

"You are not King yet, Highness," the guard pointed out, "and my orders come from your mother, the Queen. Please, just let us take her so we can avoid any further complications."

Shahly met the Prince's eyes and thought to him, *Just go, Arden. Please, just leave the castle.*

He stared back at her for long seconds, then asked, "Where are you taking her?"

"The arena," the guard answered.

Perfect! Shahly declared. *Allow them to take me, Arden, please. This is just what I want them to do.*

The Prince sighed and nodded, then looked to the guard and coldly informed, "I will remember this." Then he glanced at Shahly and stormed toward the palace.

As Shahly watched him, one of the guards slipped a rope over her head and gently tightened it around her neck, saying, "Let's go, girl."

Something about his voice touched Shahly's memory, but given the circumstances she ignored that little twinge in her belly, turned easily with him and paced just behind him toward the back of the palace. She did not want to cause more problems and definitely did not want to antagonize them into killing her. The journey seemed to take forever, giving Shahly's thoughts time to drift from Arden to Vinton and back again.

She was led into a tunnel that opened in what appeared to be the palace wall. It was about a height and a half tall, round at the top and went into a part of the palace she had never entered before. It was dimly lit with infrequent lamps and the few doorways which were recessed in the walls were all closed.

Sunlight ahead betrayed an opening through which a variety of noises mixed and echoed in the tunnel, growing louder as she and the guards proceeded forward.

As they neared the end of the tunnel, a shadow fell across the light and Shahly's eyes narrowed as she recognized the mind of the black unicorn.

Bexton raised his head as Shahly and her entourage of guards reached him and stopped. "You are even more clever and resourceful than I thought you were, and much more stubborn."

Shahly just glared at him.

"My offer still stands," he informed.

"I must kill an innocent just to have my life spared?" she questioned spitefully.

He glanced aside, then offered, "I may be convinced to kill the child for you, if that is what you really want."

Love was about sacrifice, about giving. If Shahly could not give her life to save her Vinton, possibly her Arden, then she would have to give something else, something even more precious. She raised her head, staring coldly at Bexton as she agreed, "I will join you, then."

His eyes widened slightly. "Oh? Well, isn't this a pleasant little surprise."

"If," Shahly continued, "you will let Vinton and the child go. I do not need to kill an innocent to give my life to you."

He shook out his mane, then looked into her eyes and said, "I am afraid that does not conform to my plans. You will drink the child's blood and join me or you will die in the arena. Make your choice now."

Shahly's lips tightened as she said, "I have never wished death on anyone in my life, Bexton, until now."

He seemed to smile. "You are learning, young mare." He loosed a deep breath and informed, "I have changed my mind. I will allow you to die with Vinton. Seeing you two in the arena will give the crowd no end of amusement." He glanced at the guard holding Shahly, then turned and paced away.

"No longer interested in me joining you?" she spat.

He did not answer.

Shahly was led out into the oval, open area that was surrounded by stone walls with three openings distributed equally around it. At the far end were huge timber and iron gates that were easily five heights tall and nearly as wide. On each side of it were smaller gates. She did not want to imagine what might be behind them. The earth beneath her hooves grew no grass and was churned up in places, especially toward the center. The faint scent of blood lingered in the air all around.

She watched the black unicorn disappear into one of the openings in the wall, a timber door closing behind him, then she faced forward again.

Hundreds of human voices exploded into cheers as Shahly and the guards neared the center of the arena, and she looked up and around her to see them crowding around the wall, stair-stepped one behind another to form a bowl of living, fanatical beings who shared one common, grisly thought. More filed in from many entrances that opened at different intervals around the arena seating.

This felt much like her first dinner with Arden and the other maidens of the castle, when so much attention was focused on her. So different, though. These people did not want to know about unicorns. They wanted to see a unicorn die. They wanted violence and blood.

Shahly pitied them, feared them a little, and felt anger and loathing for them.

She looked ahead again, staring at the arena wall across the barren lake of dirt. She knew she would die soon, that the humans would greatly enjoy watching. Spending her last moments with Vinton allowed her some comfort. At least they would spend their final moments together. A great calmness swept over her and for the first time since this whole ordeal had begun and she finally felt at peace.

She saw a metal ring sticking up out of the ground. A rusty chain lay on the ground beside it, one end attached to the ring, the other ending in a shackle with a pin closing it.

When they reached the chain, the guard leading her stopped and handed the rope to one of the others, then turned and walked to the ring, picked up the shackle and secured it around one of Shahly's hind legs.

As he pushed the pin into place, Shahly looked back to him and snorted, just wanting him to know that she disapproved.

"Don't kick me," he warned.

His voice sounded even more familiar and Shahly gasped as he looked up at her.

Traman! She thought to him.

He winked at her, then took a hammer from one of the other guards, tapped the pin a few times, then drew back and struck hard, hitting the chain instead. He tossed the hammer back and looked up at the guards, saying, "Let's go."

They all turned and left.

Shahly watched the black haired man for a time as he walked toward one of the exits, then looked down to the shackle which held her ankle, noticing that the pin was just barely in place. If she was still human, she could easily pull it out. Unfortunately, hands were no longer among her attributes.

She looked back up at the fanatical, mobbing humans who struggled to find a place to observe what would transpire. Soon, the arena seats would be full and she would face whatever they would let loose in the arena with her.

And her death would no doubt be close behind.

She only had to wait.

CHAPTER 15

The humans seemed to take forever to get themselves organized, so Shahly spent the hour or so she waited laying on her belly in the sun and reflecting on the brief life that seemed to be behind her, especially the last four days. Never had she realized that her life could become so complicated, or that it would end so soon. Still, she had known freedom, come to appreciate it as she had also known imprisonment, and she had learned to love more deeply than she knew was even possible. Twice. She would miss this world, her family, the whole herd, and especially the two loves she had found, one a human and the other her stallion.

She looked around her, up at the humans who struggled to get themselves settled to watch her death. She looked to the huge gates ahead of her on the other side of the arena, and the two smaller gates that were on the sides of it. Something was behind them, something very frightening behind the larger of them. She had no doubts she would face what was behind there, though she could not imagine why it would need such a big door.

With a deep breath and a sigh, she looked up behind her to the Talisman tower, clearly visible over the wall of the arena and a constant reminder that she could expect no help from the black dragon of the desert, though hope was still there that he would find some way to come anyway, just as he had said he would. The elders of the herd had told her some time ago that dragons, like unicorns, were creatures of truth, that they would not lie but they would use the truth to deceive, something which sounded odd in itself.

Noise to one side caught her ears and she looked to see a gate into the arena open and two palace guards take their positions on either side of it.

Vinton paced out, his eyes blank as the crowd of humans went into frenzied cheers once again.

Seeing him sent a rush throughout Shahly and she stood, facing him, and whinnied his name.

Vinton stopped and raised his head, looking directly at her, then he galloped toward her as fast as he could.

Shahly tried to go to him, but the chain abruptly stopped her and she looked back at it, mumbling, "Forgot about that," as she tugged against it.

"Shahly!" Vinton whinnied as he neared, then slowed to a stop as he reached her.

For a long moment they just nuzzled each other, glad to have the contact they had not enjoyed for four endless days.

The stallion caressed Shahly's neck and mane with the side of his snout, whispering, "I am so glad to see you, and yet…"

"I know," she replied, nuzzling his neck. "Vinton, we cannot give up, even now. We have to live and put a stop to what they are doing."

He backed away a few steps and hopelessly looked into her eyes. "I do not see what we can do to stop them, Shahly, especially considering the circumstances. Did Bexton not tell you what they plan for us?"

"He expects us to die here," she answered. "I know it has something to do with some beast they keep here."

"Not just a beast, Shahly," Vinton informed grimly. "He has a mountain ogre here. He has Dreads and a huge forest cat. We will face one or all of them."

Shahly raised her head, her heart suddenly slamming away within her. She knew that the Dreads and the mountain cat they could handle in the forest, but not here in the open. The ogre, especially the huge mountain ogre Vinton spoke of, unicorns had no defense against but to trick their minds and hide. Again, that would be impossible in the open.

She looked away and sighed, then turned her eyes back to Vinton and straightly said, "You have to find a way out of here. I am chained and cannot follow. You must warn the herd."

"No, Shahly!" he insisted. "Not without you!"

"You sent *me* away!" she barked. "It is my turn to save you, and your turn to warn the herd."

"Shahly…."

"Vinton, you have to. Bexton has told the Queen that the herd will gather at the Spagnah River soon. They will be waiting for the unicorns there. One of us has got to get to the herd and warn them to go somewhere else. I cannot. It is up to you, my stallion."

Vinton turned his head and looked to the huge timber gates at the end of the arena. His eyes were as stones as he stared at the gates for long seconds, then he said, "Bexton made me a cruel offer, but I do not trust him."

Shahly leaned her head and asked, "Offer? To join him?"

"To escape," he said softly, "without you. He will have one of the ways out of here left open. He said all I have to do is run away, leave you here to face the beast alone." He lowered his head, venting a deep breath.

"Go!" Shahly insisted. "Vinton, the whole herd is more important than just me. You have to go and save them!"

He looked back to her and shook his head. "I could never leave you, Shahly, and I do not trust him. I think he will have some of his humans waiting within the tunnel or just outside, ready to kill me as soon as I flee."

Shahly nodded. "I have noticed that he lacks the honesty of the real unicorn he used to be."

Vinton raised his head, looking behind her.

Shahly also looked, then turned fully as two humans emerged with a small table that had a glass orb mounted on it. Two guards with crossbows followed them, their eyes locked on Shahly and Vinton.

As they drew closer, Shahly recognized the table and orb as the very items which had caught her eye in the Talisman chamber. The red scale was still suspended within the orb, not even shifting as it was carried into the arena.

Shahly turned fully as three more humans emerged, the red haired woman struggling in the grips of the two guards. Her hands were behind her, obviously bound there and she fought them at every step as they wrestled her closer to the unicorns. Shahly met Vinton's glance, then watched as the humans threw Falloah to the ground three or four paces away.

"What are they doing?" Vinton asked in a low voice.

Falloah was turned forcibly on her belly. One of the guards pulled her hands up and she screamed as her shoulders were stretched. This guard knelt on her back and looked up to the other. The second guard wrapped an arm around her calves, restraining her legs enough to wind a piece of rope tightly around her ankles. He tied it off, leaving enough to tie tightly around her wrists. She screamed again as her body was arched backward and she struggled after the guards released her.

They backed away, laughing as they watched her struggle, and one said, "You'll be killing no more of our people, wench. Just enjoy your last moments in this world."

She struggled to her side and glared up at him, hissing back, "You just enjoy your own miserable life. We'll see how long it lasts."

They laughed and walked away from her.

The table with the glass orb was taken to Shahly's other side and set down, and the two humans who had carried it retreated back toward the tunnel they had emerged from, the guards following. They did not close the door to the tunnel as they left.

Falloah struggled a moment longer, then, out of breath, stopped moving and laid her head to the ground.

Shahly tried to go to her but was stopped by the chain. She watched the red haired woman begin to struggle again and ordered, "Stop! You will hurt yourself."

Falloah did stop and looked over her shoulder, eyeing Shahly with a little confusion on her features. "You seem familiar, but I do not remember speaking with any unicorns before."

"I am Shahly. We met before in the dungeon."

The red haired woman's mouth fell open as her eyes darted to the amulet around Shahly's neck, then she looked back to Shahly's eyes and breathed, "It *is* you." She struggled to turn, having little success, then anxiously asked, "Did you do as I said? Did you get to the Talisman and summon the dragon?"

"Dragon?" Vinton asked.

Shahly looked away and admitted, "Well, not exactly. I met Ralligor in the forest, but I kind of forgot about the Talisman until I had already met him."

"Oh, joy," Falloah snarled.

Looking suspiciously down at Falloah, Vinton snorted and observed, "Something about you does not feel right."

The crowd of humans suddenly exploded into a roar of cheers.

Shahly, Vinton and Falloah looked around them, then to the huge timber gates as they opened, and Shahly's eyes widened, her mouth falling open as she watched the ogre emerge.

He was easily five times the height of a human and was covered with thin, red-brown fur. He was very stout and quite heavily muscled, but fat around what was supposed to be his waist. Short, thick legs propelled him forward as long, muscular arms swung back and fourth as he walked. He raised a hand and shielded his small eyes from the sunlight, then saw his intended victims and bared jagged yellow and brown teeth as he strode toward them.

Shahly tore her eyes from the ogre and looked to Vinton.

He looked back at her, desperately, as if he was looking for some way to protect her, then he turned to the ogre and said, "I will delay it as long as I can. See if you can find a way to free your leg and get out of here."

"But—" she protested, watching him run toward an enemy he had no hope to defeat.

"He is very brave," Falloah observed.

"What can we do?" Shahly asked desperately. "We cannot just let him charge to his death."

"I would be glad to help in some way," the red haired woman offered, "but I'm afraid my hands are tied. And my legs."

Shahly watched Vinton charge right at the ogre, then dodge around him, bounding away each time the ogre tried to strike. She knew this would tire him and that he would make a mistake sooner or later that would cost him his life. Her lips tightened as she pondered what to do, then she turned and looked down to the red haired woman, ordering, "See if you can move closer to me."

Falloah began to struggle toward Shahly, arching her body as much as she could to slither closer, and she strained to ask, "What are you thinking?"

"We can free each other," Shahly replied. She glanced at her stallion and urged, "Hurry!"

"I can't go any faster!" Falloah spat. "This isn't as easy as it looks."

Shahly looked back down to her and admitted, "It does not look easy at all."

At last, Falloah was close enough for Shahly to nibble at the ropes that bound her, which she did as carefully and quickly as she could. A few good bites later the ropes holding Falloah's wrists to her ankles loosened and then broke, and Falloah was finally able to straighten out her body.

When Shahly went after the rope binding her ankles, Falloah barked, "No! Free my hands first."

Shahly met her eyes, looked back to her gallant stallion who bounded nimbly around the frustrated ogre, then lowered her head to Falloah's wrists, nibbling carefully.

While her wrists were being freed, the red haired woman looked to the glass orb and said, "We have to get that scale out of there."

Shahly glanced back at it, then went back to the task of chewing the rope through and suggested, "I could kick it, or knock it over so it breaks."

"No, that wouldn't be wise," Falloah informed. "There are dangerous magics in there that will seek out and kill whoever releases them. We have to figure out a way to break the glass without any direct involvement in doing so."

The ogre roared angrily.

Shahly met Falloah's glance, then they both looked to the duel which raged some thirty paces away.

"The ogre!" they said together.

A few nibbles more and Falloah pulled her hands free of the rope, then rolled over and sat up, working frantically with the rope around her ankles. When they were free she stood and turned to face the battle at hand, striding toward the ogre and unicorn.

"Wait!" Shahly shouted. "It is my turn."

The red haired woman stopped and looked back to her, shaking her head. "I would need the tools they use to free the pin."

"No!" Shahly corrected. "It is not fastened all the way."

Falloah looked down to the pin and hesitantly approached, kneeling down to Shahly's leg. She examined the shackle for a moment, then reached to it and tugged on the pin that held it together.

Shahly watched intently, not realizing that it was still stubbornly in place.

Clearly frustrated, the red haired woman vented a hard breath as she tugged and twisted at the pin, mumbling, "This is hopeless."

"Please keep trying," Shahly urged, looking back to the dueling stallion and ogre.

Though Vinton fought gallantly, bounding about and occasionally ramming his horn into the ogre's leg, he was clearly beginning to tire and his attacks were doing no more than annoying his mountainous opponent. At least, however, the ogre was kept at bay while Shahly and Falloah worked to free each other.

"Yes!" Falloah shouted as the pin finally pulled free.

Shahly looked back to her, seeing the red haired woman gazing down at her prize with a big smile on her lips.

Falloah looked up to Shahly and stood, then looked to the ogre and bared her teeth as she said, "Let's go and give your stallion some rest."

Together, they charged the ogre, Falloah pausing to pick up a few stones to throw at him.

While the ogre's back was turned and his eyes down on the stallion, Shahly lowered her head and rammed her horn into the back of his calf, channeling all of her essence into her attack. Seconds later, she shook her aching head and realized she was lying on her belly. Hitting that ogre's leg had been like hitting solid rock. She looked up and gasped as she noticed him turning fully on her and she struggled to her hooves, barely moving in time as the ogre's fist slammed onto the ground where she had been laying. She looked back as she retreated, horrified to see him still in pursuit of her.

A stone struck his head, then another, then the shackle pin.

Falloah stood to one side of the ogre, waving her arms as she shouted, "Over here, half-wit!"

He stopped and turned his head, growling as he saw the defiant human.

Shahly veered sharply and stopped, her eyes locked on the glass orb containing the red scale. She leaned her head, wondering if that scale was what was keeping the dragon away, then looked back to the ogre as he turned on her retreating stallion. Her eyes narrowed as her mind whirled in thoughts not unlike those she had concocted as a filly. She approached the glass orb and positioned herself carefully between it and the ogre, then turned and reared up, whinnying as loudly as she could.

As she had hoped, the ogre turned and looked right at her.

Shahly lowered her head and snorted, her eyes locked on the ogre's as she thought, *Come and get me!*

The ogre bared his teeth and strode toward her.

Attentively, Vinton charged the ogre, lowering his head to ram his leg still again.

Shahly raised her head and shouted, "Vinton, no!"

He stopped, looking very confused as he stared at her.

Shahly looked back up at the ogre as he quickly drew nearer, swallowed her fear back and reared up again, whinnying to antagonize him further.

Growling, the ogre raised a hand and brought it down toward her.

Shahly waited until the ogre's hand was nearly upon her, then she leaped toward him and veered sharply to one side, sprinting away from him. She looked back as the ogre's hand slammed onto the glass orb, crushing it and the table it was on, then she stopped and turned toward him as she saw a brilliant violet light explode from under his hand.

The ogre roared again as white and violet lightning lanced forth from the shattered orb, slamming into his head and chest. He retreated and tried to shield himself from an unseen enemy that was fierce and relentless.

Falloah screamed.

Shahly looked to see her cover her face with her hands as an emerald light enveloped her.

The red haired woman seemed to be changing within the light that grew brighter and expanded from her in every direction. The light finally grew too bright to look directly at and Shahly turned away from it, looking back at the ogre as the attack of spells on him grew weak and finally disappeared.

He shook his head and looked back down to where the orb had been, appearing to be more annoyed than hurt.

Shahly swallowed hard and backed away as his eyes found her again. From what Falloah had told her, the spells should have at least injured him, but he wasn't even scratched. She looked toward Falloah, her eyes locking on what she saw.

Falloah was gone. A scarlet dragon with ocher breast and belly stood in her place. Her mind and thoughts were still very much the same, though Shahly felt astonishment from her. Falloah looked to her wings, extending them to reveal the same fiery ocher webbing between the fingers of her wings. Horns curved gracefully back from her head, starting dark orange and fading to black as they reached the tips. Her head and features were rounded and supple, very feminine. Even the dorsal scale ridges which ran from between her horns all the way down her back and to the end of her tail were rounded. Three human's heights tall, her body was very sleek with smooth lines that looked as if she was meant to fly from the beginning. Everything about her seemed feminine for a dragon, even her lean muscle tone.

The crowd of humans went silent, then ripples of panic seemed to begin.

Her beautiful amber eyes widened as she turned them up to the ogre, her dorsal scale ridges growing a little more erect.

The ogre!

Shahly looked up to him, then bounded aside as his hand came at her again. Dirt and rocks pelted her as the ogre's hand hit the ground and she shook her head as she sprinted away from him.

Falloah roared, her voice still unmistakable.

Shahly stopped and turned, seeing the ogre turning on the scarlet dragon.

Falloah backed away a step, then bared her teeth and growled at him, half spreading her wings as she glared up at him and seemed ready to attack.

He charged and swung at her.

She ducked and leaped up at him, swinging back at his head and striking it as hard as she could, then backed away, shaking her hand as she looked a little fearfully up at him.

The ogre growled and reached toward her.

Vinton rammed his horn into the back of the ogre's leg.

The ogre growled and looked down at him.

Falloah took the opportunity to catch him off guard and swung at the ogre's head again, her claws glancing off much as they had done before.

He slowly turned back on her, growling.

She backed away, her eyes locked on him, then she leaped aside as he struck at her. Wheeling around, she slammed her muscular tail into his abdomen.

Even that seemed to have little effect.

The ogre turned and charged as she spun back to face him.

She stroked her wings and leaped aside, kicking him hard in the chest, then the head as she retreated from him.

Again it had little effect and he merely lurched back from the blow.

Falloah landed some distance away and turned on the ogre as he charged her again, this time meeting the swing of his arm with her teeth.

The bite was useless as it failed to penetrate his tough hide and only gave him time to get his other hand on her arm.

She roared and snapped at his face as he tightened his grip on her.

His other arm wrapped around her and he squeezed hard to crush the life from her.

Falloah struggled savagely, screeching with all of the air she had left and biting at the ogre's seemingly impenetrable skin, all to no avail.

Shahly snorted, lowered her head and charged, slamming her horn into his leg with more controlled force this time.

Bellowing angrily, the ogre threw the nearly unconscious dragon from him and turned on Shahly.

Falloah landed some distance away in a cloud of dust. She appeared to be limp and labored to breathe, not moving otherwise.

The crowd of humans roared into cheers.

Her ears laid back against her head, Shahly backed away as the ogre strode toward her relentlessly, swinging his other hand, missing, swinging again.

His barrage had Shahly moving fast back and forth, and too late did she discover she was very near the gates the ogre had emerged from and quickly running out of maneuvering room. She turned fully and planted her hooves, preparing to dodge when he swung at her again.

He roared and raised a leg, turning as Vinton bounded away from him.

The stallion stopped and turned back on the ogre, glaring up at him as he shouted, "Why don't you come at someone a little bigger?"

The ogre grunted and advanced, raising a fist and quickening his pace as Vinton backed away from him.

Shahly saw Falloah stir and raise her head.

So did the ogre.

As he turned on the dragon, Shahly charged the ogre and rammed his leg again, hitting him even harder. This left her a little stunned as she turned to retreat when the ogre struck at her. Part of his blow caught her haunch, knocking her off balance, and before she realized what had happened, she rolled to a dusty stop on her side.

After an unknown time she forced her wits back to her and struggled back up, only to find the ogre's hand closing around her neck. She whinnied in terror, fighting with all of her strength to free herself as the ogre tightly grasped her. His grip was painful and choked her as he began to lift her from the ground.

Vinton whinnied and seconds later the ogre flinched and roared, dropping Shahly.

She hit the ground with one hind leg first, trying to break her fall, but horrible pain stabbed into her hock and she collapsed fully to her side, whinnying loudly. With her eyes closed tightly, she rolled to her belly and waited for the shock of her injury to subside, then struggled just to breathe against the pain.

Shahly bayed, her teeth clenched, then she turned and looked to the ogre, seeing him pursue her stallion once again. She tried to stand and go help, but the pain in her leg was too great to support her. Helplessly, she watched her tired stallion dodge away from the advancing ogre, laboring to breathe. She knew he needed rest or he would succumb to fatigue and make a mistake that the ogre could exploit. Unwilling to allow this to happen, she raised her head and whinnied loudly.

The ogre turned.

As she saw him come at her, Shahly tried again to stand, but still could not and just watched helplessly as he approached.

Falloah stood and looked to her, half opening her wings.

Shahly realized that the battle was hopeless, even with three of them against the ogre. She met the scarlet dragon's eyes and whinnied, "Go! Get out of here!"

Falloah opened her wings, looked to the ogre, then back to Shahly.

"Please," Shahly begged. "Fly away from here! Please go!" She turned her eyes up to the ogre as he reached her and watched helplessly as he loomed over her.

Falloah landed hard on his back, one arm under his, the other over his shoulder and her jaws slamming hard around the base of his thick neck. She gripped him with all of her strength, kicking at his back and ripping at his tough hide with her hind claws.

The ogre bellowed and spun to get at her, but she held firm, wrenching her head back and forth to drive her teeth into him. He did not appear to be able to get at her and was staggering away as he tried in vain to work her loose.

Vinton ran to Shahly and stopped near her, gently touching her nose with his as he asked, "Are you hurt?"

"My leg," she answered as bravely as she could.

The stallion glanced back at the dueling ogre and dragon, then approached Shahly's leg and lowered his horn to it.

As Shahly watched, a red light swirled around his horn and sprayed like a mist from the tip, enveloping her leg in a warm, soothing glow. The pain subsided and she felt strength return to her leg.

A moment later the stallion raised his head and took a deep breath, then looked down to Shahly and asked, "How do you feel now?"

She struggled to her hooves and flexed her formerly injured leg a few times, then nuzzled him and offered, "Thank you, Vinton."

"I had to rush your healing," he informed, "so your leg may still be a little tender for a while."

The humans surrounding them cheered wildly.

Shahly and Vinton looked back to the battle at hand.

Roaring, the ogre swung his arms wildly, turning and turning to get at the dragon who ripped at his flesh and clung stubbornly to him. His dark blood stained her jaws slightly and darkened the fur around his neck.

Vinton snorted and said, "She cannot hold on forever."

Shahly sighed and shook her head. "I am hoping she does not have to."

The ogre suddenly stopped and spun the other direction.

Falloah lost her grip and was thrown off, her teeth ripping out of his neck as she clawed at him to find something to hold on to. She stroked her wings for balance and somehow landed on her feet, stumbled, and looked up, too late to avoid the ogre's fist which slammed solidly into her breast.

Shahly gasped as the dragon hit the ground some distance from the ogre and rolled to her side.

"Wait here!" Vinton ordered, charging the ogre.

The ogre roared angrily as Vinton rammed his leg and bounded away. With huge strides, he turned toward the retreating unicorn, giving Falloah just enough time to stand and charge.

The scarlet dragon rammed her horns into the small of his back, then staggered backward, raising a hand to her head.

Slowly, the ogre turned and advanced on the stunned dragon as she retreated unsteadily.

He swung and barely missed.

She wheeled around and slammed her tail solidly into his leg.

He lurched slightly, then swung at her again.

Still looking disoriented, Falloah dodged, lost her footing and fell, scrambling away from the pursuing ogre on all fours as she looked fearfully back at him.

Whinnying loudly, Shahly sprinted toward them, veering a little to one side to distract him.

Vinton rammed his calf still again.

The ogre grunted and glared down at him, then turned back on Falloah.

The black dragon's talons slammed into the ogre's chest with enough force to knock him to his back in a cloud of dust. So swift was his approach that Shahly did not even notice him coming, and apparently neither had the crowd of humans who were suddenly very quiet.

His wings were half spread as he stood between the stunned ogre and the scarlet dragoness, glaring down at an enemy that was felled for the first time that day. The dragon turned his head and looked to Shahly, then turned fully and offered his hand to Falloah.

She grasped his hand with both of hers and he easily pulled her to her feet, then growled something to her and turned back on the ogre, who was just staggering back to his feet with a hand held over his chest. The black dragon matched the ogre's height, but not his girth and clearly not his weight.

Falloah turned and strode toward Shahly, then turned back to the black dragon and protested, "But, Ralligor—"

He looked at her impatiently and roared, "Just do as I say and leave the ogre fighting to the professionals." As he finished, the ogre's fist slammed into his chest and knocked him to the ground.

The scarlet dragoness shook her head and approached Shahly, beckoning to the stallion as she neared.

Shahly's eyes were fixed on the black dragon as he rolled to all fours and faced the ogre with bared teeth and a growl.

The ogre bellowed and raised his fists.

Ralligor spun around and slammed his tail into the ogre's abdomen.

The ogre doubled over and staggered backward.

Roaring, the black dragon sprang forward and slammed his horns into the ogre's face, then brought his fist up into the ogre's chest, stroked his wings and jumped into the air, slamming his feet solidly into the ogre's chest.

As the ogre fell again, Shahly heard Falloah call her name and she blinked and looked up to her.

Vinton galloped to them and came to a dusty stop, looking back as the ogre and black dragon engaged again.

"Ralligor wants us out of here," Falloah shouted to them over the renewed cheers of the humans.

"We cannot just leave him here like this," Shahly protested.

"He can take care of himself," Falloah insisted. "We must find a way to get you two to safety."

Vinton looked up to her and raised his chin. "Why so concerned with the well-being of unicorns, dragon?"

Shahly butted him with her nose and scolded, "Does it matter? We need to do as he said and get out of here."

Vinton sighed and glanced away. "I suppose so. Bexton said he would leave one of the ways out of this place open for me to leave at my choosing, but I don't trust him."

"On this we agree," Falloah admitted, then her eyes darted to the Talisman tower, her jaws parting slightly as she breathed, "Oh, no."

Shahly looked and saw a bright violet glow emanating from within the top level of the tower. She could feel the unicorn essence within and the terrible power that seemed to hum along the very air around her. The power she felt was uncomfortable, almost painful to her as it was made up of very strong emotions, terror mostly, but she knew the unicorn essence would cause the dragons no end of harm. She looked to Falloah and shouted, "Go! Fly away from here!"

Already appearing disoriented, the scarlet dragoness looked down to her and argued, "I cannot just leave you two here."

Vinton snorted and snapped, "It will not matter if that thing gets you killed as well. Someone has to survive!"

"But, Ralligor," Falloah whimpered, looking to the fighting black dragon. "I cannot leave him again."

Shahly turned fully to the black dragon, who was locked up in a test of strength with the ogre, and thought to him, *Ralligor, the Talisman is awake!*

Without even looking at her, he thought back, *I know, I know. Just give me a moment.*

The black dragon thrust his arms up, breaking the grip the ogre had on him, then swept his wings and kicked the ogre hard in the chest, backing away as he did.

The ogre stumbled backward, then bared his teeth and charged.

Ralligor's throat and neck swelled and his jaws gaped as he belched fire at his enemy's face.

The flames scorched the ogre's face, making him shield his small eyes.

The dragon rammed his horns into the ogre's belly, then he opened his wings and swept himself into the air, spun around and slammed his tail into the ogre's head.

Tremors shook the ground as the ogre fell again.

Ralligor looked to Falloah, to Shahly, then turned to the Talisman tower, his eyes glowing red, then emerald.

A faint green light pierced the violet light which emanated from the tower windows. The green quickly grew in intensity until it completely swallowed the violet, then the top of the tower exploded in flames and fleeing streaks of light.

Shahly flinched and soon noticed panic among the humans who were watching the spectacle. Quickly, she realized that the power she felt from the Talisman was gone. A little wide eyed, she looked to the dragon.

He met her eyes, then motioned with his head for her to leave before turning back on the ogre, who staggered back to his feet to continue the battle.

"Let's pick an exit," Vinton advised.

Shahly looked to the open doors of the tunnel she had been brought through and raised her head, declaring, "That one!" then she galloped toward it.

She reached the tunnel quickly and stopped, peering inside as she heard Vinton and Falloah stop behind her.

Falloah lowered her head and sniffed, then withdrew and shook her head, reporting, "Human scent is still very strong in there."

Shahly nodded and confirmed, "That is because there were humans in there."

Falloah growled, "There may still be humans in there."

Ralligor's roar drew their attention.

The black dragon landed hard thirty paces away and rolled about another ten before coming to a dusty stop.

The ogre raised his arms and roared.

Falloah stepped toward the black dragon and cried, "Ralligor!"

Slowly, the black dragon raised his head and looked back at the ogre, then to Falloah.

"Leave the ogre fighting to the professionals?" she asked sharply.

Ralligor staggered to his feet and turned on the ogre as he advanced, saying, "I'm just toying with him while you make your escape."

Shahly watched him charge the ogre again, then looked up to Falloah.

The dragoness shook her head and said, "Agarxus makes it look so easy." Her eyes narrowed as she looked to the tunnel. "Wait a moment." She crouched and stuck her snout into the tunnel, roaring loudly.

Vinton and Shahly jumped back.

Falloah withdrew her snout and stood, looking down at the unicorns as she said, "That should scare off any humans who lingered behind in there. I will fly over the wall and make certain the way is clear." She opened her wings and swept herself into the air."

Shahly looked to Vinton.

He met her eyes, raising his head as he informed, "I will go through first to be sure there are no humans waiting for us. If all is clear then I will come back for you."

Shahly nuzzled him, softly saying, "Be careful."

He nuzzled her back, then turned and stalked into the tunnel.

Still very concerned for him, Shahly watched for long seconds after, then a cheer surging from the crowd of humans and the ogre bellowing loudly caught her attention and she turned to see the combatants still locked in battle, and her eyes widened as she watched the dragon hoist the ogre into the air by the throat and leg and slam him on his back onto the ground. Clearly, this dragon was far stronger than she had even begun to imagine.

The ogre, however, seemed undaunted and rolled to his feet, facing the dragon again.

Movement at a tunnel opening behind the dragon caught Shahly's eye and she looked to see two guards emerge and take up their positions on either side of the doorway, then her eyes widened and she drew a hard breath as she saw the black unicorn pace from the tunnel, his eyes locked on the black dragon.

She turned her eyes back to Ralligor and noticed the ogre backing away, the black dragon pursuing. Dark unicorn essence swirled around the ogre as if Bexton was communicating with him, controlling him!

An amethyst light lanced from the black unicorn's horn, striking the dragon's shoulder.

Ralligor roared and lurched forward, reaching for his struck shoulder.

Almost immediately, the ogre brought his fist down hard on the base of the dragon's neck, sending him to his knees.

Still stunned from the attacks, Ralligor held himself up with one hand, trying to get back to his feet, but the ogre struck again and he nearly collapsed completely. As he reared up on his knees and tried to defend himself, the amethyst light struck him again and he roared and went back down.

Shahly snorted and spat, "That isn't fair!" then she lowered her head and charged the black unicorn, running at him with all of her speed. Shahly was upon him as he lowered his head to strike the dragon again and she rammed her shoulder into his head as she galloped by, then turned hard and ran at him again.

He staggered at first, then turned on her and reared up, lashing at her with his steel-shod hooves.

Shahly dodged away and turned at him again.

Bexton came down and faced her, lowering his horn as he glared at her and snorted.

Shahly looked to the combatants behind him.

The ogre appeared dazed and backed away.

Ralligor looked back, meeting her eyes, then belched fire in her direction.

She ducked as it went over her head and looked behind her as it struck the tunnel Bexton had emerged from. The explosion that followed collapsed part of the tunnel and consumed the guards. She looked back to the dragon just as he turned and blasted the ogre with fire, striking his chest and face repeatedly to give himself time to stand.

The black unicorn also looked, then snorted and turned narrow eyes on Shahly, growling, "Do you intend to fight me yourself?"

"I will do what I have to," Shahly spat back. The crowd of humans, the fighting dragon and ogre, even her own sore muscles seemed to disappear from her attention as she faced off with the larger unicorn before her. Her emotions were a whirlwind of fear, anger and anxiousness.

The black unicorn nodded and slowly paced toward her. "Very well, Shahly. Since I am certain you had something to do with the destruction of my talisman I will use your spiral to complete the second." He lowered his head and charged her.

She leapt aside and ran behind him.

Bexton turned, thrusting his horn.

Far nimbler than the black unicorn, Shahly easily bounded away from him, then wheeled around and brought her horn against his as he thrust it at her again. A shock lanced throughout her entire body and she whinnied and backed away, shying away from the emerald and violet light that burst from the horns as they met.

"You still do not understand, do you?" the black unicorn asked harshly as he advanced.

J.R. KNOLL

"Why you send the humans to kill your own people?" Shahly snapped, still retreating from him. "No, I do not! And I do not want to!"

"It's about the Talismans," the black unicorn hissed deeply, "and it's about power. Power to rule the land as it needs to be ruled, to rid the land of our enemies, the dragons once and for all. It is about power over life and death, the weak and the strong! *I* am the strong, now, and the weak shall be ruled as I see fit."

Shahly shook her head and reminded," But you are unicorn!"

"I am much more than unicorn now," he insisted.

"No!" she cried, stopping her retreat. "Unicorns do not crave this power you speak of and we do not want to dictate life and death."

He stopped advancing, and stared at her blankly.

Shahly took a step toward him, pleading, "Bexton, please try to remember that you are unicorn. You cannot continue this."

His eyes narrowed and he corrected, "Weak little fool! Of course I can!" He reared up and kicked Shahly on the side of the head before she could turn away.

She whinnied and stumbled away, her eyes closed as she shook her head to clear her wits. Looking back at him as she retreated, she saw him in pursuit and thrusting his spiral at her, which she met with her own barely in time. Emerald and amethyst light flashed and that horrid shock ran through her again, and before she realized what was happening she hit the ground on her side hard enough to knock the breath from her.

By the time she recovered her senses the black unicorn stood over her, glaring down at her with death in his eyes and his spiral trained on her.

Shahly drew a quick breath and shrank away from his unraveled, pewter colored horn as it drew closer.

"You should have joined me when you had the chance," Bexton sneered. "You could have known power as I do. Now, you can join the other short sighted fools who did not listen—in my Talisman!" He reared up and brought his horn down hard at her.

She whinnied and kicked desperately to struggle away.

A brilliant red light flashed as another spiral hooked under the black unicorn's, stopping it just before it reached her.

Bexton was thrown brutally to one side and he stumbled to keep his footing. He looked up and shied away from the large, shiny bronze hoof that slammed into the side of his head and he staggered back still more, then shook his head and set himself, standing his ground as he glared at his new foe.

265

Like something from a dream, Vinton stood over Shahly, surrounded by a golden glow of sunlight as he glared back at the black unicorn and slowly raised his head, saying, "You are good against a young mare. How are you against an opponent of your own size?"

Bexton's eyes narrowed. "Vinton. I see you were foolish enough to return as well."

As Vinton advanced, Shahly struggled to her hooves and backed away.

"I came to stop you," Vinton informed coldly.

Bexton circled, his eyes locked on his foe's as he taunted, "Revenge?"

"Call it what you will, Bexton."

The black unicorn stopped and raised his head, offering, "I give you one last chance to join me, Vinton, to know real power."

"Freedom is power!" Vinton countered. "That is something you have long since denied yourself."

Bexton nodded and said, "I see. So I have to kill you as well?"

Vinton's eyes narrowed and he lowered his head, training his horn on the black unicorn as he growled, "Try."

Bexton charged, thrusting his horn. Vinton knocked it away with his own in a flash of ruby and amethyst light. The spirals were wielded as swords as the two stallions engaged in a duel to the death. Black manes and tails flailed as they wheeled around each other, charging and dodging. Occasionally, one would rear up and kick, one would bite, and they rammed at each other with their shoulders.

Shahly had never seen such violence among unicorns and watched fearfully as the two fought each other, looking almost like wolves or rutting deer.

A thrust sent Bexton's horn deep into Vinton's shoulder and the bay unicorn whinnied and retreated, limping badly.

Bexton pursued, glaring at his enemy with wild eyes as he said, "You know pain, Vinton. Now you will know death!"

"You just don't remember, do you?" Vinton asked, still limping backward.

Bexton stopped his advance and raised his head. "Remember what? Prancing mindlessly around the forest? Avoiding humans and predators?" He bared his teeth and stomped toward Vinton as he shouted, "I am powerful now! They avoid me!"

Vinton held his ground, grunted a laugh and shook his head, saying, "You still do not understand. Tasting that blood five seasons ago did not make you powerful, it made you evil. Nothing more."

"Good and evil are illusions of the weak!" the black unicorn whickered. He seemed to be growing upset, not at Vinton's defiance of him, but at something much deeper within him. He huffed and growled, "You could not possibly know what it was like. I was caged and tormented with promises of an easy existence. I was denied my freedom. I was dying! It was either free myself or perish, attack or die!"

"So you tried to kill him?" the bay unicorn questioned.

"No!" Bexton whinnied. "It was an accident!"

"And the second time?" Vinton pressed, glaring at the black unicorn. "Even after you rejoined the herd? Was *that* an accident?"

Wide eyed, Bexton looked away from him.

"You killed, Bexton, not to defend yourself, but because you liked it!"

Shahly could feel in the black unicorn's mind that he remembered something, something terrible, something *he* had done. His mind was racing about aimlessly, drowning in a lake of confusion.

Then the confusion was gone, and evil ruled him again.

Bexton snorted and looked back to his foe, coldly saying, "Perhaps so. Perhaps I still do." He raised his head. "Die, my old friend." He charged forward and reared up, lashing at Vinton with his steel-shod hooves.

Baying loudly, Vinton lunged forward and slammed his shoulder into the black unicorn's chest, driving him backward and to the ground on his side.

Bexton was back to his senses quickly and kicked to find ground under his hooves and stand to finish the battle.

Vinton wheeled around and kicked hard with his hind legs.

Bexton's head was snapped around with brutal force as Vinton's hooves found their mark and he fell limply to the ground, his dark, half-open eyes staring blankly ahead.

Vinton swung back around, ready for his foe to rise and come at him again.

Instead, the black unicorn was still.

Shahly felt emotions pour from her stallion and she felt regret and shame from him for the first time. He was in pain, not from his wounds but from the knowledge that he had struck down one of his brethren, one of his own herd, even if it was this one. Slowly, she approached her stallion and nuzzled him, trying to ease his pain.

He turned to her and nuzzled her back, his eyes closed.

A tremor shook the ground and they looked out into the arena, seeing the battered and bleeding ogre lying on his back as a shroud of dust settled all around him. The black dragon, bleeding from his head, chest and one arm himself, advanced on his unmoving enemy with several heavy steps. He glared down at the ogre, then turned to the unicorns and roared, "Get yourselves out of here!"

Shahly butted Vinton with her nose, then turned and galloped toward the tunnel they knew should be clear of humans, glancing back at her stallion to be sure he was following.

They reached the tunnel and Shahly sped into it, kicking her stride as long as she could to be out of there. When she emerged, she abruptly stopped to find the scarlet dragoness seated before her, staring down at her almost anxiously.

Falloah glanced at Vinton as he emerged, then looked back to Shahly and asked, "What took so long?"

"Bexton," she answered. "He came into the arena and attacked Ralligor."

Falloah's eyes widened and she drew her head back.

"He's been dealt with," Vinton added coldly. "He will not bother the dragons again." He lowered his head and looked to the ground. "Or kill unicorns."

"I am glad to hear that," Falloah said. "Where is Ralligor now?"

"He is too big to follow us through the tunnel," Shahly replied.

Falloah's eyes darted to her.

The black dragon landed hard behind the scarlet, startling her, and she spun around and growled at him. He seemed to smile at her as he asked, "How does freedom feel?"

"I'll let you know when my heart slows!" she spat.

"Humans are coming!" Vinton shouted, looking to one side with his head held up and his ears back.

Shahly looked and saw a small army of armored humans approaching, each armed with sword, axe or halberd. Each of them held a shield, no doubt ready to ward off fire. They looked menacing, but Shahly sensed a wall of fear advancing before them.

Ralligor shook his head, then raised a hand to the Castle's defensive wall, fifty or so paces away, and loosed a bright burst of emerald light from his palm which blasted a rather sizeable hole in the base of it, then he looked down to the unicorns and said, "The rest of the way should be clear, but stay on your guard." He motioned toward the advancing troops and assured, "I will deal with them." He looked to the scarlet dragoness and ordered, "Follow them and make certain they are not followed. I will join you shortly."

"Don't be long, *Unisponsus,*" she said softly, then swept her wings and lifted herself into the air.

As Ralligor bared his teeth and strode toward the humans, who began their retreat as soon as he came at them, Shahly butted Vinton with her nose and whinnied, "Come on!" then she turned and bolted to the hole in the wall.

She burst through it and stopped, wheeling around.

Vinton was not far behind, but was still limping from his wounded shoulder, though he was clearly exhilarated to be free once again and stopped a pace or so from her.

Shahly approached and tenderly licked his wound to clean it, then closed her eyes to calm herself as she channeled her essence through her horn. She looked to his wound and lowered her head, aiming her horn at his shoulder, and loosed her essence.

Healing him took a while.

Finally, she backed away and asked, "How does it feel now?"

He looked to his shoulder, raising his leg several times, then he turned back to her and said, "Race you."

Before she could accept, he turned and bolted along the wall, toward the road that would take them away from the castle.

Shahly watched him for a moment, a little surprised, then she whinnied and sprang into a full gallop, pursuing the stallion she had wanted since she was a filly.

The traumas of the day dissolved away and recent memories seemed unable to keep up with them.

CHAPTER 16

Only a league away from the castle, Shahly's weary body cried out for rest, and with no crisis or perils to make her push herself on, she slowed to a trot, then a walk down the road that led her and her stallion back to the Southlands and the forest she missed so.

Vinton also looked as if he needed rest and slowed to meet her pace, walking abreast of her for some time in silence.

All this time apart. So much to say, yet neither could speak.

Lost in thoughts and memories, and still trying to realize she was finally going home, Shahly was barely aware of her own aching body and just stared blankly ahead as she paced at Vinton's side, feeling half asleep.

"You are very quiet," the stallion observed.

Shahly flinched and looked to him, then forward again as she confessed, "Just thinking."

"What about?" he asked gently.

"The last few days," she answered blankly. A short time later she shook her head and wondered aloud, "I wonder if what Bexton said is true?"

"What is that?"

Shahly looked to Vinton, meeting his eyes as she replied, "He said some part of being human would always be with me, that it would someday eat a hole in what I am as a unicorn."

Vinton seemed to smile and nuzzled her, assuring, "I do not think it will hurt you, Shahly. Unicorn you are and unicorn you will always be. That time you spent as a human will always be with you, the memories and feelings, but only that. Being human is something no other unicorn has experienced to my knowledge."

Shahly turned her eyes forward again. Vinton's words already had her feeling better. And he was right. How many other unicorns could say that they had been human? It made her feel a little special.

A short time later, Vinton bumped her with his shoulder and said, "Tell me what it was like to be human."

She glanced at him, then away, answering, "Wondrous, strange...." She trailed off, her voice becoming little more than a whisper as she fully remembered her feelings for the Prince, then she lowered her head and finished softly, "Painful."

He nuzzled her and urged, "Tell me."

Shahly glanced at him, then turned her eyes down and confessed, "I am ashamed."

"I don't understand," Vinton pressed.

With a deep breath, Shahly finally admitted, "I fell in love with a human. I did not mean to, it just happened. The dragon warned me, but I forgot. Before I realized, I was so tangled in my life as a human that I almost did not get you out in time." A tear spilled and she drew a broken breath and continued, "Another human did not like me or the attention that Arden was giving me. She sent someone to get me, but they got my friend Audrell instead. She almost died because of me and I hurt Arden because I was so selfish."

"Selfish?" the stallion questioned. "I would not say that, Shahly. You are too giving, if a little naïve. It is never a crime to love."

"Even one who is not my chosen mate?" she asked dryly.

Vinton nuzzled her and assured, "Shahly you ventured to the castle to save me and faced perils I cannot begin to even imagine. You placed yourself in jeopardy just to win my freedom. Being deceived by your own heart cannot be something that I can—"

"Vinton, I truly love him!" she cried, then sighed and looked away from her stallion. "I miss him and I still think of him."

"So you care for him and you love him," Vinton said softly. "That is your nature, Shahly, and I wouldn't have you change that for all the world." He drew a breath and released it through his nose. "Everyone else in the herd would have had the sense to just leave me there and not put themselves at risk." He shot a glance at her. "I'm glad to see you are still the adventurous scamp you have always been, and I feel I have no truer friend in the world."

She turned her eyes to the road before her and smiled a weary little smile, softly saying, "Thank you, Vinton."

Another silence passed between them, broken only by singing birds, the wind in the trees and the clopping of cloven hooves on the dirt and gravel road beneath them. Her thoughts whirled on the day and everything they had endured. They were together and free at last, and yet she felt that nothing had changed. In her heart, she knew she wanted to spend her life with him, but perhaps just rejoining the herd as only friends would do as well. She finally resigned herself to that, but struggled not to let it break her heart.

He bumped her with his shoulder again and asked, "If I try to tell you what I need to again, will you run away like before?"

She groaned and shook her head. "I don't want to run anymore for a while. I'm still a little sore."

"I am feeling a bit stiff and sore, myself," he confessed.

Glancing at him, she asked, "You too?" She also wanted to put off his *talk* as long as she could.

Vinton whickered a laugh and nodded. "Yes, me too. Shahly, I really need to tell you something, and it will not be easy."

"I know," she confessed. "Vinton, I will always cherish your friendship as well. And I know you will make this mare in the herd you speak of very happy. Any mare would be so lucky to have you at her side and I can't see how she could be anything but happy with you as her stallion."

"You really think so?" he asked.

She nodded, not wanting to answer otherwise. When she glanced at him, he was smiling slightly.

"You know," he started, "I only have half a heart in me now."

Shahly puzzled, then raised her head and asked, "Huh?"

"It was whole, but now it is only half." He looked to her and something on his face, in his eyes changed. "Two hearts are two hearts until they become one, until they join two people forever. I want you at my side, Shahly. I want to be your stallion and I want you to be my mare."

Her hooves planted solidly onto the road and did not move another step as her eyes fell open wide. She watched the stallion she loved stop a few paces beyond her and look back. When his eyes met hers, they were not the eyes of an older unicorn who had taught her, or one who just cherished her friendship. She finally saw how he loved her and felt it from him. The vision she saw of him blurred and she blinked and looked away from him, letting the tears roll from her eyes. She had saved the stallion she loved, and now he felt he had to pay a debt to her. Closing her eyes as more tears formed streams from them, she softly said, "Vinton, you don't have to. You owe me nothing."

He turned fully and approached her, touching his spiral to hers. "It isn't like that."

"But it is," she insisted. Backing away, she looked into the forest and shook her head. "I only want you to choose me if it is what your heart truly wants, not because..."

He snorted. "Shahly, if you try to run this time I swear I will jump on top of you and pin you to the ground! Do you know how long it took me to muster the courage to ask you the first time?"

Her eyes snapped to him and her ears perked. "The first time?"

Vinton's eyes narrowed. "The first time, when you ran away and wanted me to chase you. I'm not doing that again."

She took a few steps back, her gaze locked on his. "You mean... Oh, Vinton!" She bolted to him, weeping as she pressed her neck to his and laid her chin onto his back. "Vinton, yes! Yes! I'll be your mare! You've made me the happiest unicorn in the whole world!" New tears streamed from her eyes as she felt him nuzzle her.

"You aren't the happiest unicorn, Shahly," he corrected. "I am."

As the wind picked up, she backed away enough to look up into his eyes, and he bent his head down enough to touch his nose to hers.

"I love you, Vinton," she whispered.

"I love you, too, Shahly," he replied in a whisper. "Just don't run away from me again."

"I won't," she assured. Shahly looked behind him as the wind brought her a familiar scent, and she raised her nose and tested the air.

Vinton looked behind him and did the same, then he snorted and growled, "Humans."

"Arden," Shahly breathed.

The stallion glanced at her. "What?"

"Arden," she repeated, then sniffed the air again. "Ihzell. Audrell. He kept his promise." She leapt forward, her heart racing as she shouted, "Let's go and see them!"

"Shahly!" Vinton protested as he fell behind.

The scent and sound of the river was ahead and Shahly knew right where to find them, running hard toward the bridge that she and Audrell had visited before.

There, in the distance, She saw several humans gathered by the water with their backs to her.

She closed half of the distance, then slowed and folded her essence around herself, concealing her presence from them. She wanted to surprise Arden and Audrell, and especially Ihzell. Four guards were with them, including Ocnarr. Shahly's instincts warned her to fear them, but experience had taught her better. Among the guards was the younger one who had guarded her door and escorted her from the dungeon. She was glad to see him, too.

She stopped a few paces behind them and just watched for a time.

Audrell wanted to be closer to the Prince, but he kept his distance, his hands folded behind him as he watched the water. He was sad, missing something from inside of him, it seemed. Shahly knew it was her that he missed and he would allow no one to touch his heart so long as his forest blossom was still there. Ihzell tried to comfort him, but he pulled away from even her.

Shahly glanced back at Vinton, who watched from the trees about thirty paces away, then she carefully, silently approached, and when she was close enough to the Prince, she butted him hard in the back with her nose.

As he stumbled toward the water, the young guard and Ihzell took his arms to keep him from falling in.

"Careful," Ocnarr warned. "That water is freezing."

Arden jerked his arms free and wheeled around, his eyes widening as he saw Shahly.

"The water is *very* cold," she informed.

"Shahly!" he cried, rushing to her.

As he wrapped his arms around her neck, she nuzzled him and asked, "Are you happy to see me?"

"Shahly?" Ihzell asked, bewilderment in her voice.

Shahly whickered a laugh and looked to her. "I tried to tell you."

Arden looked to the steward and shook his head, confessing, "We seem to have a lot of explaining to do."

Audrell slowly approached, cautiously reaching for Shahly's mane. Although she had known about Shahly's true form for some time, she still looked awed at the sight of a unicorn right in front of her and was clearly reluctant to actually touch her.

Shahly turned fully to her and assured, "I don't bite." When Audrell was still hesitant to approach further, Shahly took the final steps and nuzzled her shoulder.

Barely able to breathe, Audrell slowly slipped her hands around Shahly's neck, gently stroking her mane, then tightly embraced her and whispered, "Thank you. Thank you for showing me who you really are."

"Are we still friends?" Shahly asked.

Audrell laughed, and she wept.

Soon, all of the humans stroked and petted her. Shahly felt loved by each of them and tried to divide her attention equally, but she found herself favoring Arden.

"How can we mindlessly kill such beauty as this?" Ocnarr asked.

"We cannot," Arden assured, his eyes on Shahly's. "I am not yet King, but I will do everything in my power to ensure the safety of your kind. I promise."

Shahly nuzzled him and assured, "I trust you, Arden."

Ihzell sniffed and wiped her eyes, shaking her head as she sobbed, "I so enjoyed making those dresses for you."

"And I thank you for every one," Shahly replied, then looked to Audrell and added, "But there is someone who you will enjoy making them for just as much, someone who would make a fine princess." She glanced at Audrell.

Audrell turned her eyes down and shook her head, softly informing, "I don't think I am quite worthy."

The Prince slipped an arm around her shoulders and said, "You just let *me* decide that."

Audrell smiled and looked to him, then to Shahly and gasped as she saw something behind her.

Ihzell also looked and declared, "My goodness!"

Shahly looked behind her, seeing that Vinton had approached to about two paces away, staring at her with protective eyes.

"Jealous?" she asked teasingly.

He laid his ears back and snorted.

Arden stroked Shahly's neck and guessed, "This must be Vinton."

Shahly nodded and confirmed, "Yes, this is my stallion."

That familiar, powerful presence swept down the road and enveloped them and Vinton abruptly swung around, looking up.

The black dragon dropped from the sky and slammed onto the road about forty paces away, casually folding his wings as he strode toward Shahly and her group of humans. He was walking somewhat stiffly and with a slight limp, no doubt from sore and battered muscles.

Arden, Ihzell and Audrell backed away while the four guards drew their weapons and rushed forward, holding their ground between the dragon and Vinton.

"That would be Ralligor," Shahly introduced.

The black dragon stopped only five or so paces from the guards, his eyes narrowing as he stared down at them for a few horrifying seconds before he roared, "Move!"

The guards darted aside as the dragon strode forward again.

Ralligor stopped and looked down at Vinton, then to Shahly and boomed, "Our business here is complete?"

Shahly approached Vinton and nuzzled him, confirming, "Yes, I think so."

The black dragon growled and looked to the Prince, coldly informing, "You may return to your castle. I left it standing this time but I make no promises about the next. You will leave the unicorns alone and build no more talismans that will harm dragons."

Nervously, Arden nodded, clearly both awed and terrified at the sight of the dragon before him.

"He has already promised all of that," Shahly snapped.

The dragon growled, "Now he has incentive to keep that promise."

Slowly, Arden approached Shahly and stroked her mane, softly saying, "I suppose we should be going now."

"Just remember," Shahly reminded, "we are not going to say good-bye."

He smiled. "You really think we will see each other again some day?"

She nuzzled him, assuring, "If I have anything to say about it we will."

"You will always be in my heart, Forest Blossom," he whispered.

"And you in mine," Shahly confessed.

Slowly, Shahly's human friends approached her to say their farewells, then they went to their frightened horses near the trees, and rode cautiously past the dragon, back toward the castle.

Audrell looked back once more.

Shahly reared up and whinnied, just for her.

Smiling, Audrell blew her a kiss, then turned forward again and took Prince Arden's side.

"As it should be," Shahly whispered as she watched them ride away. She felt so happy for them, and yet was near tears as she already missed them.

Once they were out of sight, Ralligor shook his head and looked back down to Shahly, grumbling, "Humans as your friends. What will the other unicorns think?"

"That she has a loving, open heart," Vinton answered straightly.

Falloah landed some distance behind Ralligor and approached, looking down at Shahly as she said, "Thank you for coming back for me. I was afraid I would be in that dungeon forever."

"And thank you for your help," Shahly replied.

Vinton added, "Thank you both." He looked up at Ralligor and finished, "And you too, I suppose."

The black dragon rolled his eyes and growled, "You two just stay away from that castle from now on and avoid any humans you see. They clearly cannot be trusted."

Shahly looked up at him and said, "Humans are not all evil, Ralligor. I think they are just misunderstood."

He nodded. "Perhaps so, little unicorn, but you should not take the chance. Just stay away from them."

"And the white haired human you keep in your company?" Shahly asked teasingly.

Ralligor raised a brow and growled, "Go home."

Shahly smiled at the black dragon, looking up at him very tenderly as she said, "Take care of yourself, Ralligor."

He nodded, then looked away and shook his head, growling in an amused tone, "This is surely one for the legends."

Shahly leaned her head and asked, "What is?"

He looked back to her and replied, "An alliance of dragons and unicorns, and friendship with it. Who'd have figured?" He huffed a laugh, then opened his wings and swept himself into the air, the scarlet dragoness following.

Vinton watched them, then looked to Shahly and grimly asked, "Friendship?"

She whinnied a laugh, then butted him with her nose, saying, "Let's go home, Love."

They galloped across the bridge and down the road on the other side, and as the sun ascended high over the trees, they disappeared into the forest.

And so their lives and adventures would truly begin.

9313238R00161

Made in the USA
San Bernardino, CA
12 March 2014